ACCLAIM FOR *Richard Ford's*

THE SPORTSWRITER

"With its small gallery of sharply drawn characters, its deep vision of the way we live, its forceful and often soaring, sometimes downright moving way of speech, and its reverberating, redemptive plot, Ford's novel overcomes an excess of virtues . . . with a deftness and intensity that we find in few books."

—*Los Angeles Herald Examiner*

"A book of pitiless truth-telling, at once cruel and full of comfort . . . as clear and cold as early-morning light over the water. And it is suffused with love for small, fleeting mysteries of life."

—*New York* magazine

"Without intruding on the very real momentum of his many characters, Ford lifts his story into the realm of fable."

—*Village Voice*

"As humane a novelist as America can offer." —*Kansas City Star*

"A compelling novel about a survivor, shell-shocked by life, who just happens to be a sportswriter the way Willy Loman just happens to be a salesman. . . . Ford is writing about modern uncommitted man, lashing himself to the railing of mundane daily life, trying to get through the storm." —*The New York Times*

"An appreciation of the mystery of things as they are." —*Time*

"A first-class storyteller . . . one of America's best writers."

—United Press International

Richard Ford

THE SPORTSWRITER

The author of six novels and two collections of stories, Richard Ford has received the Pulitzer Prize, the PEN/Faulkner Award, and the PEN/Malamud Award for short fiction. His work has been translated into sixteen languages. He lives in Maine and New Orleans.

THE
SPORTSWRITER

Richard Ford

Vintage Contemporaries

Vintage Books

A Division of Random House, Inc.

New York

Kristina

Second Vintage Edition, June 1995

Portions of this book were previously published in *Esquire*.

Library of Congress Cataloging-in-Publication Data
Ford, Richard, 1944–
The sportswriter.
(Vintage contemporaries)
"A Vintage original"—Tp verso.
I. Title.
PS3556.0713S6 1986 813'.54 85-40675
ISBN 0-679-76210-8

Manufactured in the United States of America
D 9 8 7

THE
SPORTSWRITER

I

My name is Frank Bascombe. I am a sportswriter.

For the past fourteen years I have lived here at 19 Hoving Road, Haddam, New Jersey, in a large Tudor house bought when a book of short stories I wrote sold to a movie producer for a lot of money, and seemed to set my wife and me and our three children—two of whom were not even born yet—up for a good life.

Just exactly what that good life was—the one I expected—I cannot tell you now exactly, though I wouldn't say it has not come to pass, only that much has come in between. I am no longer married to X, for instance. The child we had when everything was starting has died, though there are two others, as I mentioned, who are alive and wonderful children.

I wrote half of a short novel soon after we moved here from New York and then put it in the drawer, where it has been ever since, and from which I don't expect to retrieve it unless something I cannot now imagine happens.

Twelve years ago, when I was twenty-six, and in the blind way of things then, I was offered a job as a sportswriter by the editor of a glossy New York sports magazine you have all heard of, because of a free-lance assignment I had written in a particular way he liked. And to my surprise and everyone else's I quit writing my novel and accepted.

And since then I have worked at nothing but that job, with the exception of vacations, and one three-month period after my son died when I considered a new life and took a job as an instructor in a small private school in western Massachusetts where I ended up not liking things, and couldn't wait to leave and get back here to New Jersey and writing sports.

My life over these twelve years has not been and isn't now a bad one at all. In most ways it's been great. And although the older I get the more things scare me, and the more apparent it is to me that bad things can and do happen to you, very little really worries me or keeps me up at night. I still believe in the possibilities of passion and romance. And I would not change much, if anything at all. I might not choose to get divorced. And my son, Ralph Bascombe, would not die. But that's about it for these matters.

Why, you might ask, would a man give up a promising literary career—there were some good notices—to become a sportswriter?

It's a good question. For now let me say only this: if sportswriting teaches you anything, and there is much truth to it as well as plenty of lies, it is that for your life to be worth anything you must sooner or later face the possibility of terrible, searing regret. Though you must also manage to avoid it or your life will be ruined.

I believe I have done these two things. Faced down regret. Avoided ruin. And I am still here to tell about it.

I have climbed over the metal fence to the cemetery directly behind my house. It is five o'clock on Good Friday morning, April 20. All other houses in the neighborhood are shadowed, and I am waiting for my ex-wife. Today is my son Ralph's birthday. He would be thirteen and starting manhood. We have met here these last two years, early, before the day is started, to pay our respects to him. Before that we would simply come over together as man and wife.

A spectral fog is lifting off the cemetery grass, and high up in the low atmosphere I hear the wings of geese pinging. A police car has murmured in through the gate, stopped, cut its lights and placed me under surveillance. I saw a match flare briefly inside the car, saw the policeman's face looking at a clipboard.

At the far end of the "new part" a small deer gazes at me where I wait. Now and then its yellow tapetums blink out of the dark toward the old part, where the trees are larger, and where three signers of the Declaration of Independence are buried in sight of my son's grave.

My next-door neighbors, the Deffeyes, are playing tennis, calling their scores in hushed-polite early-morning voices. "Sorry." "Thanks." "Forty-love." Pock. Pock. Pock. "*Ad* to you, dear." "Yes, thank you." "Yours." Pock, pock. I hear their harsh, thrashing nose breaths, their feet scraping. They are into their eighties and no longer need sleep, and so are up at all hours. They have installed glowless barium-sulphur lights that don't shine in my yard and keep me awake. And we have stayed good neighbors if not close friends. I have nothing much in common with them now, and am invited to few of their or anyone else's cocktail parties. People in town are still friendly in a distant way, and I consider them fine people, conservative, decent.

It is not, I have come to understand, easy to have a divorced man as your neighbor. Chaos lurks in him—the viable social contract called into question by the smoky aspect of sex. Most people feel they have to make a choice and it is always easier to choose the wife, which is what my neighbors and friends have mostly done. And though we chitter-chatter across the driveways and hedges and over the tops of each other's cars in the parking lots of grocery stores, remarking on the condition of each other's soffits and down-drains and the likelihood of early winter, sometimes make tentative plans to get together, I hardly ever see them, and I take it in my stride.

Good Friday today is a special day for me, apart from the other specialness. When I woke in the dark this morning, my heart pounding like a tom-tom, it seemed to me as though a change were on its way, as if this dreaminess tinged with expectation, which I have felt for some time now, were lifting off of me into the cool tenebrous dawn.

Today I'm leaving town for Detroit to begin a profile of a famous ex-football player who lives in the city of Walled Lake, Michigan, and is confined to a wheelchair since a waterskiing accident, but who has become an inspiration to his former teammates by demonstrating courage and determination, going back to college, finishing his degree in communications arts, marrying his black physiotherapist and finally becoming honorary chaplain for his old team. "Make a contribution" will be my angle. It is the kind of story I enjoy and find easy to write.

Anticipation rises higher, however, because I'm taking my new girlfriend Vicki Arcenault with me. She has recently moved up to New Jersey from Dallas, but I am already pretty certain I'm in love with her (I haven't mentioned anything about it for fear of making her wary). Two months ago, when I sliced up my thumb sharpening a lawnmower blade in my garage, it was Nurse Arcenault who stitched me up in the ER at Doctors Hospital, and things have gone on from there. She did her training at Baylor in Waco, and came up here when her marriage gave out. Her family, in fact, lives down in Barnegat Pines, not far away, in a subdivision close to the ocean, and I am scheduled to be exhibit A at Easter dinner—a vouchsafe to them that she has made a successful transition to the northeast, found a safe and good-hearted man, and left bad times including her dagger-head husband Everett far behind. Her father, Wade, is a toll-taker at Exit 9 on the Turnpike, and I cannot expect he will like the difference in our ages. Vicki is thirty. I am thirty-eight. He himself is only in his fifties. But I am in hopes of winning him over and eager as can be under the circumstances. Vicki is a sweet, saucy little black-hair with a delicate width of cheekbone, a broad Texas accent and a matter-of-factness with her raptures that can make a man like me cry out in the night for longing.

You should never think that leaving a marriage sets you loose for cheery womanizing and some exotic life you'd never quite grasped before. Far from true. No one can do that for long. The Divorced Men's Club I belong to here in town has proven that to me if nothing else—we don't talk much about women when we are together and feel relieved just to be men alone. What leaving a marriage released me—and most of us—to, was celibacy and more fidelity than I had ever endured before, though with no one convenient to be faithful to or celibate for. Just a long empty moment. Though everyone should live alone at some time in a life. Not like when you're a kid, summers, or in a single dorm room in some crappy school. But when you're grown up. *Then* be alone. It can be all right. You can end up more within yourself, as the best athletes are, which is worth it. (A basketball player who goes for his patented outside jumper becomes nothing more than the simple wish personified that the ball go in the hole.) In any case, doing the brave thing isn't easy and isn't supposed to be. I do my work and do it well and remain expectant of the best without knowing in the least what it will be. And the bonus is that a little bundle like Nurse Arcenault seems sent straight from heaven.

For several months now I have not taken a trip, and the magazine has found plenty for me to do in New York. It was stated in court by X's sleaze-ball lawyer, Alan, that my travel was the cause of our trouble, especially after Ralph died. And though that isn't technically true—it was a legal reason X and I invented together—it is true that I have always loved the travel that accompanies my job. Vicki has only seen two landscapes in her entire life: the flat, featureless gloom-prairies around Dallas, and New Jersey—a strange unworldliness these days. But I will soon show her the midwest, where old normalcy floats heavy on the humid air, and where I happen to have gone to college.

It is true that much of my sportswriter's work is exactly what you would think: flying in airplanes, arriving and departing airports, checking into and out of downtown hotels, waiting hours in corridors and locker rooms, renting cars, confronting unfriendly bellmen. Late night drinks in unfamiliar bars, up always before dawn, as I am this morning, trying to get a perspective on things. But there is also an assurance to it that I don't suppose I could live happily without. Very early you come to the realization that nothing will ever take you away 'from yourself. But in these literal and anonymous cities of the nation, your Milwaukees, your St. Louises, your Seattles, your Detroits, even your New Jerseys, something hopeful and unexpected can take place. A woman I met at the college where I briefly taught, once told me I had too many choices, that I was not driven enough by dire necessity. But that is just an illusion and her mistake. Choices are what we all need. And when I walk out into the bricky warp of these American cities, that is exactly what I feel. Choices aplenty. Things I don't know anything about but might like are here, possibly waiting for me. Even if they aren't. The exhilaration of a new arrival. Good light in a restaurant that especially pleases you. A cab driver with an interesting life history to tell. The casual, lilting voice of a woman you don't know, but that you are allowed to listen to in a bar you've never been in, at a time when you would otherwise have been alone. These things are waiting for you. And what could be better? More mysterious? More worth anticipating? Nothing. Not a thing.

The barium-sulphur lights die out over the Deffeyes' tennis court. Delia Deffeyes' patient and troubleless voice, still hushed, begins assuring her husband Caspar that he played well, while they walk toward their dark house in their pressed whites.

The sky has become a milky eye and though it is spring and nearly Easter, the morning has a strangely winter cast to it, as though a high fog is blotting its morning stars. There is no moon at all.

The policeman has finally seen enough and idles out the cemetery gate onto the silent streets. I hear a paper slap on a sidewalk. Far off, I hear the commuter train up to New York making its belling stop at our station—always a consoling sound.

X's brown Citation stops at the blinking red light at Constitution Street, across from the new library, then inches along the cemetery fence on Plum Road, her lights on high beam. The deer has vanished. I walk over to meet her.

X is an old-fashioned, solidly Michigan girl from Birmingham, whom I met in Ann Arbor. Her father, Henry, was a Soapy Williams best-of-his-generation liberal who still owns a plant that stamps out rubber gaskets for a giant machine that stamps out car fenders, though he is now a Republican and rich as a Pharaoh. Her mother, Irma, lives in Mission Viejo, and the two of them are divorced, though her mother still writes me regularly and believes X and I will eventually reconcile, which seems as possible as anything else.

X could choose to move back to Michigan if she wanted to, buy a condominium or a ranch-style home or move out onto the estate her father owns. We discussed it at the divorce, and I did not object. But she has too much pride and independence to move home now.

In addition, she is firmly behind the idea of family and wants Paul and Clarissa to be near me, and I'm happy to think she has made a successful adjustment of her new life. Sometimes we do not really become adults until we suffer a good whacking loss, and our lives in a sense catch up with us and wash over us like a wave and everything goes.

Since our divorce she has bought a house in a less expensive but improving section of Haddam called The Presidents by the locals, and has taken a job as teaching pro at Cranbury Hills C.C. She co-captained the Lady Wolverines in college and has lately begun entering some of the local pro-ams, now that her short game has sharpened up, and even placed high in a couple last summer. I believe all her life she has had a yen to try something like this, and being divorced has given her the chance.

What was our life like? I almost don't remember now. Though I remember *it*, the space of time it occupied. And I remember it fondly.

I suppose our life was the generic one, as the poet said. X was a housewife and had babies, read books, played golf and had friends, while I wrote about sports and went here and there collecting my stories, coming home to write them up, mooning around the house for days in old clothes, taking the train to New York and back now and then. X seemed to take the best possible attitude to my being a sportswriter. She thought it was fine, or at least she said she did and seemed happy. She thought she had married a young Sherwood Anderson with movie possibilities, but it didn't bother her that it didn't turn out that way, and certainly never bothered me. I was happy as a swallow. We went on vacations with our three children. To Cape Cod (which Ralph called Cape God), to Searsport, Maine, to Yellowstone, to the Civil War battlefields at Antietam and Bull Run. We paid bills, shopped, went to movies, bought cars and cameras and insurance, cooked out, went to cocktail parties, visited schools, and romanced each other in the sweet, cagey way of adults. I looked out my window, stood in my yard sunsets with a sense of solace and achievement, cleaned my rain gutters, eyed my shingles, put up storms, fertilized regularly, computed my equity, spoke to my neighbors in an interested voice—the normal applauseless life of us all.

Though toward the end of our marriage I became lost in some dreaminess. Sometimes I would wake up in the morning and open my eyes to X lying beside me breathing, and not recognize her! Not even know what town I was in, or how old I was, or what life it was, so dense was I in my particular dreaminess. I would lie there and try as best I could to extend not knowing, feel that pleasant soaring-out-of-azimuth-and-attitude sensation I grew to like as long as it would last, while twenty possibilities for who, where, what went by. Until suddenly I would get it right and feel a sense of— what? Loss, I think you would say, though loss of what I don't know. My son had died, but I'm unwilling to say that was the cause, or that anything is ever the sole cause of anything else. I know that you can dream your way through an otherwise fine life, and never wake up, which is what I almost did. I believe I have survived that now and nearly put dreaminess behind me, though there is a resolute sadness between X and me that our marriage is over, a sadness that does not feel sad. It is the way you feel at a high school reunion when you hear an old song you used to like played late at night, only you are all alone.

X appears out of the agate cemetery light, loose-gaited and sleepy, wearing deck shoes, baggy corduroys and an old London Fog I gave her years ago. Her hair has been cut short in a new-style way I like. She is a tall girl, big and brown-haired and pretty, who looks younger than she is, which is only thirty-seven. When we re-met fifteen years ago in New York, at a dreary book signing, she was modeling at a Fifth Avenue clothing store, and sometimes even now she has a tendency to slouch and walk about long-strided in a loose-limbed, toes-out way, though when she takes a square stance up over a golf ball, she can smack it a mile. In some ways she has become as much of a genuine athlete as anyone I know. Needless to say, I have the greatest admiration for her, and love her in every way but the strictest

one. Sometimes I see her on the street in town or in her car without
expecting to and without her knowing it, and I am struck by wonder:
what can she want from life now? How could I have ever loved her
and let her go.

"It's chilly, still," she says, in a small, firm voice when she is close
enough to be heard, her hands stuffed down deep inside her raincoat.
It is a voice I love. In many ways it was her voice I loved first, the
sharpened midwestern vowels, the succinct glaciated syntax: Binton
Herbor, himburg, Gren Repids. It is a voice that knows the mini-
mum of what will suffice, and banks on it. In general I have always
liked hearing women talk more than men.

I wonder, in fact, what my own voice will sound like. Will it be
a convincing, truth-telling voice? Or a pseudo-sincere, phony, ex-
husband one that will stir up trouble? I have a voice that is really
mine, a frank, vaguely rural voice more or less like a used car salesman: a no-frills voice that hopes to uncover simple truth by a straight-
on application of the facts. I used to practice it when I was in college.
"Well, okay, look at it this way," I'd say right out loud. "All right,
all right." "Yeah, but look here." As much as any, this constitutes
my sportswriter voice, though I have stopped practicing by now.

X leans herself against the curved marble monument of a man
named Craig—at a safe distance from me—and presses her lips
inward. Up to this moment I have not noticed the cold. But now
that she said it, I feel it in my bones and wish I'd worn a sweater.

These pre-dawn meetings were my idea, and in the abstract they
seem like a good way for two people like us to share a remaining
intimacy. In practice they are as uncomfortable as a hanging, and
it's conceivable we will just forgo it next year, though we felt the
same way last year. It is simply that I don't know how to mourn
and neither does X. Neither of us has the vocabulary or temperament
for it, and so we are more prone to pass the time chatting, which
isn't always wise.

"Did Paul mention our rendezvous last night?" I say. Paul, my
son, is ten. Last night I had an unexpected meeting with him standing
in the dark street in front of his house, when his mother was inside

and knew nothing of it, and I was lurking about outside. We had a talk about Ralph, and where he was and about how it might be possible to reach him—all of which caused me to go away feeling better. X and I agree in principle that I shouldn't sneak my visits, but this was not that way.

"He told me Daddy was sitting in the car in the dark watching the house like the police." She stares at me curiously.

"It was just an odd day. It ended up fine, though." It was in fact much more than an odd day.

"You could've come in. You're always welcome."

I smile a winning smile at her. "Another time I will." (Sometimes we do strange things and say they're accidents and coincidences, though I want her to believe it *was* a coincidence.)

"I just wondered if something was wrong," X says.

"No. I love him very much."

"Good," X says and sighs.

I have spoken in a voice that pleases me, a voice that is really mine.

X brings a sandwich bag out of her pocket, removes a hard-boiled egg and begins to peel it into the bag. We actually have little to say. We talk on the phone at least twice a week, mostly about the children, who visit me after school while X is still out on the teaching tee. Occasionally I bump into her in the grocery line, or take a table next to hers at the August Inn, and we will have a brief chairback chat. We have tried to stay a modern, divided family. Our meeting here is only by way of a memorial for an old life lost.

Still it is a good time to talk. Last year, for instance, X told me that if she had her life to live over again she would probably wait to get married and try to make a go of it on the LPGA tour. Her father had offered to sponsor her, she said, back in 1966—something she had never told me before. She did not say if she would marry me when the time came. But she did say she wished I had finished my novel, that it would have probably made things better, which surprised me. (She later took that back.) She also told me, without being particularly critical, that she considered me a loner, which surprised me too. She said that it was a mistake to have made as few superficial friends as I have done in my life, and to have concentrated only on the few things I have concentrated on—her, for one. My children, for another. Sportswriting and being an ordinary citizen. This did not leave me well enough armored for the unexpected, was her opinion. She said this was because I didn't know my parents very well, had gone to a military school, and grown up in the south, which was full of betrayers and secret-keepers and untrustworthy people, which I agree is true, though I never knew any of them. All that originated, she said, with the outcome of the Civil War. It was much better to have grown up, she said, as she did, in a place with no apparent character, where there is nothing ambiguous around to confuse you or complicate things, where the only thing anybody ever thought seriously about was the weather.

"Do you think you laugh enough these days?" She finishes peeling her egg and puts the sack down deep in her coat pocket. She knows about Vicki, and I've had one or two other girlfriends since our divorce that I'm sure the children have told her about. But I do not think she thinks they have turned my basic situation around much. And maybe she's right. In any case I am happy to have this apparently intimate, truth-telling conversation, something I do not have very often, and that a marriage can really be good for.

"You bet I do," I say. "I think I'm doing all right, if that's what you mean."

"I suppose it is," X says, looking at her boiled egg as if it posed a small but intriguing problem. "I'm not really worried about you." She raises her eyes at me in an appraising way. It's possible my talk with Paul last night has made her think I've gone off my bearings or started drinking.

"I watch Johnny. He's good for a laugh," I say. "I think he gets funnier as I get older. But thanks for asking." All this makes me feel stupid. I smile at her.

X takes a tiny mouse bite out of her white egg. "I apologize for prying into your life."

"It's fine."

X breathes out audibly and speaks softly. "I woke up this morning in the dark, and I suddenly got this idea in my head about Ralph laughing. It made me cry, in fact. But I thought to myself that you have to strive to live your life to the ultimate. Ralph lived his whole life in nine years, and I remember him laughing. I just wanted to be sure you did. You have a lot longer to live."

"My birthday's in two weeks."

"Do you think you'll get married again?" X says with extreme formality, looking up at me. And for a moment what I smell in the dense morning air is a swimming pool! Somewhere nearby. The cool, aqueous suburban chlorine bouquet that reminds me of the summer coming, and all the other better summers of memory. It is a token of the suburbs I love, that from time to time a swimming pool or a barbecue or a leaf fire you'll never ever see will drift provocatively to your nose.

"I guess I don't know," I say. Though in truth I would love to be able to say *Couldn't happen, not on a bet, not this boy.* Except what I do say is nearer to the truth. And just as quick, the silky-summery smell is gone, and the smell of dirt and stolid monuments has won back its proper place. In the quavery gray dawn a window lights up beyond the fence on the third floor of my house. Bosobolo, my African boarder, is awake. His day is beginning and I see his dark shape pass the window. Across the cemetery in the other direction I see yellow lights in the caretaker's cottage, beside which sits the green John Deere backhoe used for dredging graves. The bells of St. Leo the Great begin to chime a Good Friday prayer call. "Christ Died Today, Christ Died Today" (though I believe it is actually "Stabat Mater Dolorosa").

"I think I'll get married again," X says matter-of-factly. Who to, I wonder?

"Who to?" Not—please—one of the fat-wallet 19th-hole clubsters, the big hale 'n' hearty, green-sports-coat types who're always taking her on weekends to the Trapp Family Lodge and getaways to the Poconos, where they take in new Borscht Belt comedians and make love on waterbeds. I hope against all hope not. I know all about those guys. The children tell me. They all drive Oldsmobiles and wear tasseled shoes. And there is every good reason to go out with them, I grant you. Let them spend their money and enjoy their discretionary time. They're decent fellows, I'm sure. But they are not to be married.

"Oh, a software salesman, maybe," X says. "A realtor. Somebody I can beat at golf and bully." She smiles at me a mouth-down smirky smile of unhappiness, and bunches her shoulders to wag them. But unexpectedly she starts to cry through her smile, nodding toward me as if we both knew about it and should've expected this, and that in a way I am to blame, which in a way I am.

The last time I saw X cry was the night our house was broken into, when, in the search for what might've been stolen, she found some letters I'd been getting from a woman in Blanding, Kansas. I don't know why I kept them. They really didn't mean anything to me. I hadn't seen the woman in months and then only once. But I was in the thickest depths of my dreaminess then, and needed—or thought I did—something to anticipate away from my life, even though I had no plans for ever seeing her and was in fact intending to throw the letters away. The burglars had left Polaroid pictures of the inside of our empty house scattered about for us to find when we got back from seeing *The Thirty-Nine Steps* at the Playhouse, plus the words, "We are the stuffed men," spray-painted onto the dining room wall. Ralph had been dead two years. The children were with their grandfather at the Huron Mountain Club, and I was just back from my teaching position at Berkshire College, and was hanging around the house more or less dumb as a cashew, but otherwise in pretty good spirits. X found the letters in a drawer of my office desk while looking for a sock full of silver dollars my mother had left me, and sat on the floor and read them, then handed them to me when I came in with a list of missing cameras, radios and fishing equipment. She asked if I had anything to say, and when I didn't, she went into the bedroom and began tearing apart her hope chest with a claw hammer and a crowbar. She tore it to bits, then took it to the fireplace and burned it while I stood outside in the yard mooning at Cassiopeia and Gemini and feeling invulnerable because of dreaminess and an odd amusement I felt almost everything in my life could be subject to. It might seem that I was "within myself" then. But in fact I was light years away from everything.

In a little while X came outside, with all the lights in the house left shining and her hope chest going up the chimney in smoke—it was June—and sat in a lawn chair in another part of the dark yard from where I was standing and cried loudly. Lurking behind a large rhododendron in the dark, I spoke some hopeful and unconsoling words to her, but I don't think she heard me. My voice had gotten so soft by then as to be inaudible to anyone but myself. I looked up at the smoke of what I found out was her hope chest, full of all those precious things: menus, ticket stubs, photographs, hotel room receipts, place cards, her wedding veil, and wondered what it was, what in the world it *could've been* drifting off into the clear spiritless New Jersey nighttime. It reminded me of the smoke that announced a new Pope—*a new Pope!*—if that is believable now, under those circumstances. And in four months I was divorced. All this seems odd now, and far away, as if it had happened to someone else and I had only read about it. But that was my life then, and it is my life now, and I am in relatively good spirits about it. If there's another thing that sportswriting teaches you, it is that there are no transcendent themes in life. In all cases things are here and they're over, and that has to be enough. The other view is a lie of literature and the liberal arts, which is why I did not succeed as a teacher, and another reason I put my novel away in the drawer and have not taken it out.

"Yes, of course," X says and sniffs. She has almost stopped crying, though I have not tried to comfort her (a privilege I no longer hold). She raises her eyes up to the milky sky and sniffs again. She is still holding the nibbled egg. "When I cried in the dark, I thought about what a big nice boy Ralph Bascombe should be right now, and that I was thirty-seven no matter what. I wondered about what we should all be doing." She shakes her head and squeezes her arms tight against her stomach in a way I have not seen her do in a long time. "It's not your fault, Frank. I just thought it would be all right if you saw me cry. That's my idea of grief. Isn't that womanish?"

She is waiting for me to say a word now, to liberate us from that old misery of memory and life. It's pretty obvious she feels something is odd today, some freshening in the air to augur a permanent change in things. And I am her boy, happy to do that very thing—let my optimism win back a day or at least the morning or a moment when it all seems lost to grief. My one redeeming strength of character may be that I am good when the chips are down. With success I am worse.

"Why don't I read a poem," I say, and smile a happy old rejected suitor's smile.

"I guess I was supposed to bring it, wasn't I?" X says, wiping her eyes. "I cried instead of bringing a poem." She has become girlish in her tears.

"Well, that's okay," I say and go down into my pants pockets for the poem I have Xeroxed at the office and brought along in case X forgot. Last year I brought Housman's "To An Athlete Dying Young" and made the mistake of not reading it over beforehand. I had not read it since I was in college, but the title made me remember it as something that would be good to read. Which it wasn't. If anything, it was much too literal and dreamily so about real athletes, a subject I have strong feelings about. Ralph in fact had not been much of an athlete. I barely got past "townsman of a stiller town," before I had to stop and just sit staring at the little headstone of red marble, incised with the little words RALPH BASCOMBE.

"Housman hated women, you know," X had said into the awful silence while I sat. "That's nothing against you. I just remembered if from some class. I think he was an old pederast who would've loved Ralph and hated us. Next year I'll bring a poem if that's okay."

"Fine," I had answered miserably. It was after that that she told me about my writing a novel and being a loner, and having wanted to join the LPGA back in the sixties. I think she felt sorry for me— I'm sure of it, in fact—though I also felt sorry for myself.

"Did you bring another Housman poem?" she says now and smirks at me, then turns and throws her nibbled egg as far as she can off into the gravestones and elms of the old part, where it hits soundlessly. She throws as a catcher would, snapping it by her ear in a gainly way, on a tape-line into the shadows. I admire her positive form. To mourn the loss of one child when you have two others is a hard business. And we are not very practiced, though we treat it as a matter of personal dignity and affection so that Ralph's death and our loss will not get entrapped by time and events and ruin our lives in a secret way. In a sense, we can do no wrong here.

Out on Constitution Street an appliance repair truck has stopped at the light. Easler's Philco Repair, driven by Sid (formerly of Sid's Service, a bankrupt). He has worked on my house many times and is heading toward the village square to hav-a-cup at The Coffee Spot before plunging off into the day's kitchens and basements and sump pumps. The day is starting in earnest. A lone pedestrian—a man—walks along the sidewalk, one of the few Negroes in town, walking toward the station in a light-colored, wash-and-wear suit. The sky is still milky, but possibly it will burn off before I leave for the Motor City with Vicki.

"No Housman today," I say.

"Well," X says and smiles, and seats herself on Craig's stone to listen. "If you say so." Lights are numerous and growing dim with the daylight along the backs of houses on my street. I feel warmer.

It is a "Meditation" by Theodore Roethke, who also attended the University of Michigan, something X will be wise to, and I start it in my best, most plausible voice, as if my dead son could hear it down below:

"I have gone into the waste lonely places behind the eye. . . ."

X has already begun to shake her head before I am to the second line, and I stop and look to her to see where the trouble is.

She puches out her lower lip and sits her stone. "I don't like that poem," she says matter-of-factly.

I knew she would know it and have a strong opinion about it. She is still an opinionated Michigan girl, who thinks about things with certainty and is disappointed when the rest of the world doesn't. Such a big strapping things-in-order girl should be in every man's life. They alone are reason enough for the midwest's existence, since that's where most of them thrive. I feel tension rising off me like a fever now. It is possible that reading a poem over a little boy who never cared about poems is not a good idea.

"I thought you'd know it," I say in a congenial voice.

"I shouldn't really say I don't like it," X says coldly. "I just don't believe it, is all."

It is a poem about letting the everyday make you happy—insects, shadows, the color of a woman's hair—something else I have some strong beliefs about. "When I read it, I always think it's me talking," I say.

"I don't think those things in that poem would make anybody happy. They might not make you miserable. But that's all," X says and slips down off the stone. She smiles at me in a manner I do not like, tight-lipped and disparaging, as if she believes I'm wrong about everything and finds it amusing. "Sometimes I don't think anyone can be happy anymore." She puts her hands in her London Fog. She probably has a lesson at seven, or a follow-through seminar, and her mind is ready to be far, far away.

"I think we're all released to the rest of our lives, is my way of looking at it," I say hopefully. "Isn't that true?"

She stares at our son's grave as if he were listening and would be embarrassed to hear us. "I guess."

"Are you really getting married?" I feel my eyes open wide as if I knew the answer already. We are like brother and sister suddenly, Hansel and Gretel, planning their escape to safety.

"I don't know." She wags her shoulders a little, like a girl again, but in resignation as much as anything else. "People want to marry me. I might've reached an age, though, when I don't need men."

"Maybe you *should* get married. Maybe it would make you happy." I do not believe it for a minute, of course. I'm ready to marry her again myself, get life back on track. I miss the sweet specificity of marriage, its firm ballast and sail. X misses it too, I can tell. It's the thing we both feel the lack of. We are having to make everything up now, since nothing is ours by right.

She shakes her head. "What did you and Pauly talk about last night? I felt like it was all men's secrets and I wasn't in on it. I hated it."

"We talked about Ralph. Paul has a theory we can reach him by sending a carrier pigeon to Cape May. It was a good talk."

X smiles at the idea of Paul, who is as dreamy in his own way as I ever was. I have never thought X much liked that in him, and preferred Ralph's certainty since it was more like hers and, as such, admirable. When he was fiercely sick with Reye's, he sat up in bed in the hospital one day, in a delirium, and said, "Marriage is a damnably serious business, particularly in Boston"—something he'd read in Bartlett's, which he used to leaf through, memorizing and reciting. It took me six weeks to track the remark down to Marquand. And by then he was dead and lying right here. But X liked it, thought it proved his mind was working away well underneath the deep coma. Unfortunately it became a kind of motto for our marriage from then till the end, an unmeant malediction Ralph pronounced on us.

"I like your new hair," I say. The new way was a thatch along the back that is very becoming. We are past the end of things now, but I don't want to leave.

X fingers a strand, pulls it straight away from her head and cuts her eyes over at it. "It's dikey, don't you think?"

"No." And indeed I don't.

"Well. It'd gotten to a funny length. I had to do something. They screamed at home when they saw it." She smiles as if she's realized this moment that children become our parents, and we just become children again. "You don't feel old, do you, Frank?" She turns and stares away across the cemetery. "I don't know why I've got all these shitty questions. I feel old today. I'm sure it's because you're going to be thirty-nine."

The black man has come to the corner of Constitution Street and stands waiting as the traffic light flicks from red to green across from the new library. The appliance truck is gone, and a yellow minibus stops and lets black maids out onto the same corner. They are large women in white, tentish maid-dresses, talking and swinging big banger purses, waiting for their white ladies to come and pick them up. The man and women do not speak. "Oh, isn't that the saddest thing you ever saw," X says, staring at the women. "Something about that breaks my heart. I don't know why."

"I really don't feel a bit old," I say, happy to be able to answer a question honestly, and possibly slip in some good advice on the side. "I have to wash my hair a little more often. And sometimes I wake up and my heart's pounding to beat the band—though Fincher Barksdale says it isn't anything to worry about. I think it's a good sign. I'd say it was some kind of urgency, wouldn't you?"

X stares at the maids who are talking in a group of five, watching up the street where their rides will come from. Since our divorce she has developed the capability of complete distraction. She will be talking to you but be a thousand miles away. "You're very adaptable," she says airily.

"I am. I know you don't have a sleeping porch in your house, but you should try sleeping with all your windows open and your clothes on. When you wake up, you're ready to go. I've been doing it for a while now."

X smiles at me again with a tight-lipped smile of condescension, a smile I don't like. We are not Hansel and Gretel anymore. "Do you still see your palmist, what's-her-name?"

"Mrs. Miller. No, less often." I'm not about to admit I tried to see her last night.

"Do you feel like you're at the point of understanding everything that's happened—to us and our life?"

"Sometimes. Today I feel pretty normal about Ralph. It doesn't seem like it's going to make me crazy again."

"You know," X says, looking away. "Last night I lay in bed and thought bats were flying around my room, and when I closed my eyes I just saw a horizon line a long way off, with everything empty and flat like a long dinner table set for one. Isn't that awful?" She shakes her head. "Maybe I should lead a life more like yours."

A small resentment rises in me, though this is not the place for resentment. X's view of my life is that it is a jollier, more close to the grain business than hers, and certainly more that way than I know it to be. She'd probably like to tell me again that I should've gone ahead and written a novel instead of quitting and being a sportswriter, and that she should've done some things differently herself. But that would not be right, at least about me—there were even plenty of times when she thought so herself. Everything looks old gloomy to her now. One strain in her character that our divorce has touched is that she is possibly less resilient than she has been before in her life, and worry about getting older is proof of it. I'd cheer her up if I could, but that is one of the talents I lost a long time ago.

"I'm sorry again," she says. "I'm just feeling blue today. There's something about your going away that makes me feel like you're leaving for a new life and I'm not."

"I hope I am," I say, "though I doubt it. I hope you are." Nothing, in fact, would I like better than to have a whole new colorful world open up to me today, though I like things pretty well as they are. I will settle for a nice room at the Pontchartrain, a steak Diane and a salad bar in the rotating rooftop restaurant, seeing the Tigers under the lights. I am not hard to make happy.

"Do you ever wish you were younger?" X says moodily.

"No. I'm fairly happy this way."

"I wish it all the time," she says. "That seems stupid, I know."

I have nothing I can say to this.

"You're an optimist, Frank."

"I hope I am." I smile a good yeoman's smile at her.

"Sure, sure," she says, and turns away from me and begins making her way quickly out through the tombstones, her head up toward the white sky, her hands deep in her pockets like any midwestern girl who's run out of luck for the moment but will soon be back as good as new. I hear the bells of St. Leo the Great chime six o'clock, and for some reason I have a feeling I won't see her for a long time, that something is over and something begun, though I cannot tell you for the life of me what those somethings might be.

2

All we really want is to get to the point where the past can explain nothing about us and we can get on with life. Whose history can ever reveal very much? In my view Americans put too much emphasis on their pasts as a way of defining themselves, which can be death-dealing. I know I'm always heartsick in novels (sometimes I skip these parts altogether; sometimes I close the book and never pick it up again) when the novelist makes his clanking, obligatory trip into the Davy Jones locker of the past. Most pasts, let's face it, aren't very dramatic subjects, and should be just uninteresting enough to release you the instant you're ready (though it's true that when we get to that moment we are often scared to death, feel naked as snakes and have nothing to say).

My own history I think of as a postcard with changing scenes on one side but no particular or memorable messages on the back. You can get detached from your beginnings, as we all know, and not by any malevolent designs, just by life itself, fate, the tug of the ever-present. The stamp of our parents on us and of the past in general is, to my mind, overworked, since at some point we are whole and by ourselves upon the earth, and there is nothing that can change that for better or worse, and so we might as well think about something more promising.

I was born into an ordinary, modern existence in 1945, an only child to decent parents of no irregular point of view, no particular sense of their *place* in history's continuum, just two people afloat on the world and expectant like most others in time, without a daunting conviction about their own consequence. This seems like a fine lineage to me still.

My parents were rural Iowans who left farms near the town of Keota and moved around a lot as young marrieds, settling finally in

Biloxi, Mississippi, where my father had some work that involved plating ships with steel at the Ingalls ship-building company, for the Navy, which he'd served in during the war. The year before that they had been in Cicero, doing what I'm not really sure. The year before that in El Reno, Oklahoma, and before that near Davenport, where my father had something to do with the railroad. I'm frankly hazy about his work, though I have enough memory of him: a tall rangy blade-faced man with pale eyes—like me—but with romantically curly hair. I have tried to place him in a Davenport or a Cicero, where I've gone myself to report sports events. But the effect is strange. He was not a man—at least in my memory—for those places.

I remember my father played golf and sometimes I went with him around the flat course on hot days in the Biloxi summer. He played on the Air Force Base links which were tanned and bleached out and frequented by non-coms. This was so my mother could have a day to herself and go to the movies or get her hair fixed or stay home reading movie magazines and cheap novels. Golf seemed to me then the saddest kind of torture, and even my poor father didn't seem to have much fun at it. He was not really the golf type, but more the type to race cars, and he took it up, I believe, in a mindful way because it meant something to him, some measure of success in the world. I remember standing on a tee with him, both of us wearing shorts, looking down the long palm-lined fairway beyond which you could see a sea wall and the Gulf, and seeing him grimace toward the far-away flag as if it represented a fortress he was reluctantly about to lay seige to, and him saying to me, "Well, Franky, do you think I can hit it that far?" And my saying, "I doubt it." He was sweating and smoking a cigarette in the heat, and I have a very clear memory of him looking at me then as if in wonder. Who was I again? What was it I was planning? He seemed struck by such questions. It was not exactly a heartless look, just a look of profoundest wonder and resign.

My father died when I was fourteen, and after that my mother placed me in what she called "the naval academy," which was in fact a little military school near Gulfport called Gulf Pines (we cadets called it Lonesome Pines) and where I never once minded being. In fact, I liked the military bearing that was required there, and I think there is an upright part of my character which at least respects the appearance of rectitude if not the fact, and which school was responsible for. My situation at Lonesome Pines was somewhat more than average, since most of the cadets had come there from the broken homes of rich people or from abandonment, or because they had stolen something or burned something down and their families were able to get them off and sent there instead of reform school. Though the other students never seemed any different from me, just boys full of secrecy and not-knowing and abject longing, who thought of this time as something simply to be gotten through, so that no one made attachments. It was as if we all sensed we'd be gone someday soon in a sudden instant—often it happened in the middle of the night—and didn't want to get involved. Or else it was that none of us wanted to know anybody later on who was the way we were now.

What I remember of the place was a hot parade grounds surrounded by sparse pine trees, a flag pole with an anchor at its base, a stale shallow lake where I learned to sail, a smelly beach and boat house, hot brown stucco classroom buildings and white barracks houses that reeked with mops. There were some ex-Navy warrant officers who taught there—men unsuited for regular teaching. One Negro even taught there, a man named Bud Simmons who coached baseball. The Commandant was an old captain from World War I, named Admiral Legler.

We took our leaves in bunches, out on Highway 1 in the little Gulf Coast towns we could get to by public bus, in the air-conditioned movie and tamale houses, or hanging out in the vicinity of Keesler Air Force Base, in the hot, sandy parking lots of strip joints, all of us in our brown uniforms trying to get the real servicemen to buy us booze, and wretched because we were too young to go in ourselves and had too little money to be able to do anything but squander it.

I went home on holidays to my mother's bungalow in Biloxi, and occasionally I saw her brother Ted who lived not far away, and who came to see me and took me on trips to Mobile and Pensacola, where we did not do much talking. It may be just the fate of boys whose fathers die young never to be young—officially—ourselves; youth being just a brief dream, a prelude of no particular lasting moment before actual life begins.

My only personal athletic experience came there at Lonesome Pines. I tried to play baseball on the school team, under Bud Simmons, the Negro coach. I was relatively tall for my age—though I'm more normal now—and I had the lanky, long-loose-arm grace of a natural ball player. But I could never do it well. I could always see myself as though from outside, doing the things I was told to do. And that was enough never to do them well or fully. An inbred irony seemed to haunt me, and served no useful purpose but to make me a musing, wiseacre kid, shifty-eyed and secretive—the kind who belongs in exactly such a place as Lonesome Pines. Bud Simmons did what he could with me, including make me throw with my other arm, which I happily did, though it didn't help at all. He referred to my problem as not being able to "give it up," and I knew exactly what he meant. (Today I am amazed when I find athletes who can be full-fledged people and also "give it up" to their sport. That does not happen often, and it is a dear gift from a complex God.)

I did not see so much of my mother in those years. Nor does this seem exceptional to me. It must've happened to thousands of us B. 1945s, and to children in earlier centuries as well. It seems odder that children see their parents *so much* these days, and come to know them better than they probably ever need to. I saw my mother when she could see me. I stayed in her house when I was back from school and we acted like friends. She loved me as much as she was able to, given her altered situation. She might've liked having a closer life with me. I'm sure I would've liked it. But it's possible she was dreamy herself and in no particular mind to know exactly what to do. I'm sure she never thought my father would die, in the same way I didn't think Ralph would die, except he did. She was only thirty-four, a small dark-eyed woman with skin darker than mine, and who strikes me now as having been shocked by how far she had come from where she was born, and having been more absorbed by that than anything. Her life just distracted her the way another person would, not in a hateful or a selfish way, possibly even the way my father had, but that I knew nothing about. I think she must've been worried about going back to Iowa, and didn't want to.

Eventually she went to work in a large hotel called the Buena Vista in Mississippi City as the night cashier, and while she was there she met a man named Jake Ornstein, a jeweler from Chicago, and after a few months in which he made several trips down, she married him and moved to Skokie, Illinois, where she lived until she got cancer and died.

At almost that same time I won an NROTC scholarship through Lonesome Pines, and by pure chance enrolled at the University of Michigan. The Navy's idea was to achieve a mix, and nobody got to go where they wanted to go, though I don't even remember where I wanted to go, except it probably wasn't there.

I do remember that there were times when I visited my mother in Skokie, taking the fragrant old New York Central from Ann Arbor and spending the weekend lounging around trying to be comfortable and make conversation in that strangely suburban ranch-style house with plastic slipcovers on the furniture and twenty-five clocks on the walls, in a Jewish neighborhood and in a town where I had no attachments. Jake Ornstein was fifteen years older than my mother and was quite a nice fellow, and I got along well with him and his son Irv—better, in fact, than I ended up getting along with my mother. She mentioned she thought my college was "one of the good schools," but treated me like a nephew she didn't know very well, and who worried her, even though she liked me. (She gave me a smoking jacket and pipe when I left for school—she was already in Skokie by then so that my leaving was from there.) For my part I'm sure I stared a lot and kept a distance. I'm sure we both tried to approach one another on some new level that could've flattered us both when we saw how we'd adjusted. But her life had gotten in front of her somehow, and I became someone out of another time, a fact I don't hold against my mother and haven't felt abandoned or disaffected because of it.

What could *her* life have been like, after all? Good, bad, both by turns? A long pathway through which she hoped to be not too unhappy? She knew. But *only* she knew. And I am not prone to judge a life I don't know much about, in particular since things have turned out all right for me. The best I knew then, and still, is of my own life, which at the time my mother was married to Jake Ornstein, I was on fire to get on with. I know that she and Jake were happy, and that I loved my mother very much in whatever way I was able, knowing so little about her. When she died I was still in school. I went to the funeral, acted as a pallbearer, sat around Jake's house for a weekend afternoon with the people they both knew, tried to think of what my parents had taught me in their lives (I came up with "a sense of independence"). And that night I got back on the train and slipped out of that life for good. Jake, after-wards, moved to Phoenix, married again, and died of cancer himself. Irv and I kept in touch for a few years, but have drifted apart.

But does that seem like an odd life? Does it seem strange that I do not have a long and storied family history? Or a list of problems and hatreds to brood about—a bill of particular grievances and nostalgias that pretend to explain or trouble everything? Possibly I was born into a different time. But maybe my way is better all around, and is actually the way with most of us and the rest tell lies.

Still. Do I ever wonder what my family would think of me? Of my profession? As a divorced man, a father, a quester after women? As an adult heading for life and death?

Sometimes. Though it never stays with me long. And, indeed, *when* I think of it, I think this: that they would probably have approved of everything I've done—particularly my decision to quit writing and get on to something they would think of as more prac-tical. They would feel about it the way I do: that things sometimes happen for the best. Thinking that way has given me a chance for an interesting if not particularly simple adulthood.

*B*y 9:30 I have nearly finished the few odds-and-ends details remaining before picking up Vicki and heading for the airport. Usually this would include a cup of coffee with Bosobolo, my boarder from the seminary in town, a custom I enjoy, but not today. We have had some good give-and-takes on such subjects as whether the bliss of the redeemed is heightened by the sufferings of the damned— something he feels Catholic about, but I don't. He is forty-two and from the country of Gabon, and a stern-faced apologist for limitless faith. I usually argue for works, but without any illusions about where it'll get me.

Why take a boarder? To ward off awful loneliness. Why else? The consolation in the disinterested footfalls of another human in an otherwise empty house, especially a six-foot-five-inch Negro from Africa living in your attic, can be considerable. This morning, though, he is away early on his own business and I see him from the window larruping up Hoving Road like a Bible salesman, heading for school— white shirt, black trousers and truck-tread sandals. He has told me that he is a prince in his tribe—the Nwambes—but I have never known an African who wasn't. Like me, he has a wife and two children. We're both Presbyterians, though I am not a good one.

My other duties require the usual phone calls from my desk: first to the magazine, for business with Rhonda Matuzak, my editor, who has dug into the rumors that all is not roses on the Detroit team, which could be a problem. The general feeling at the editors' meeting is I should do the story and take what I get. Sports thrives on this kind of turmoil and patented misinformation, though I am not much interested in it.

Rhonda is divorced and lives alone with two cats in a large dark-walled, high-ceilinged floor-thru in the West Eighties, and is always trying to get me to meet her at Victor's for dinner, or to haul off to some evening's activity after work. Though except for one painful night after my divorce I've always managed just to have a drink at Grand Central, put her in a cab, then hurry off to Penn Station and home.

Rhonda is a tall raw-boned, ash-blond girl in her late thirties with an old-fashioned, chorus-line figure, but with a face like a racehorse and a loud voice I don't like. (Illusion would be well-nigh impossible even with the lights off.) For a time after my divorce everything began to seem profoundly ironic to me. I found myself thinking of other peoples' worries as sources of amusement and private derision which I thought about at night to make myself feel better. Rhonda helped me out of all that by continuing to invite me to dinner and leaving notes on my desk which said "all loss is relative, Jack," "nobody ever died of a broken heart," and "only the young die good." On the one night I agreed to have dinner with her—at Mallory's on West 70th Street—we ended up in her apartment sitting in facing Bauhaus chairs, with me unhappily coming down with a case of the dreads so thick they seemed to whistle out the heating ducts and swarm the room like a dark mistral. I needed to take a walk in the street for air, I said, and she was considerate enough to believe I was still having trouble getting adjusted to being single again, and not that I was for some reason scared out of my wits to be alone with her. She walked me downstairs and out into the dark and windy canyons of West End Avenue, where we stood at the curb and talked about her favorite subject, American furniture history, and after a while I thanked her, clambered into a cab like a refugee and beat it down to 33rd Street and my safe train to New Jersey.

What I didn't tell Rhonda and what is still true, is that I cannot stand being alone in New York after dark. Gotham takes on a flashing nighttime character I just can't bear. The lights of bars demoralize me, the showy glow of taxi cabs whiz-banging down Fifth Avenue or careening out of the Park Avenue tunnel make me somehow heartsick and turmoiled and endangered. I feel adrift and badly so when the editors and the agents stroll out of their midtown offices in their silly garb, headed for assignations, idiot softball games or cocktails on the cuff. I can't bear all the complications, and long for something that is façades-only and non-literate—the cozy pseudo-colonial Square here in conventional Haddam; the nicotine clouds of New Jersey as seen from a high office building like mine at dusk; the poignancy of a nighttime train ride back down the long line home. It was bad enough that one night to have Rhonda "walk me" down West End three blocks to a good cross street, but it was worse afterwards to ride in that bouncing, clanging cab clear to the station and then to dart—my feet feeling frozen—in and down the escalator from Seventh before the whole city reached out and clutched me like the pale hand of a dead limo driver.

"Why stay out there like a hermit, Bascombe?" Rhonda is louder than usual on the phone this morning. As an equalizer she refers to men by our last names, as if we were all in the Army. I could never yearn for anyone who called me Bascombe.

"A lot of people are where they belong, Rhonda. I'm one of them."

"You're talented, God knows." She taps something hard near the phone with a pencil eraser. "I've read those short stories, you know. They're very, very good."

"Thanks for saying so."

"Did you ever think about writing another book?"

"No."

"You should. You should move up here. At least stay in sometime. You'd see."

"What would I see?"

"You'd see it's not so bad."

"I'd rather have something wonderful, not just *not so bad*, Rhonda. I've pretty much got it right here."

"In New Jersey."

"I like it here."

"New Jersey's the back of an old radio, Frank. You should smell the roses."

"I have roses in my yard. I'll talk to you when I get back, Rhonda."

"Great," Rhonda says loudly and blows smoke into the receiver. "Do you want to make any trades before the deadline?" There is an office baseball league that Rhonda is running and I'm in on it this year. It's a good way to ride out a season.

"No. I'm sitting pat."

"All right. Try to get some insider stuff on the NFL draft. Okay? They're putting together the Pigskin Preview Sunday night. You can call it in."

"Thanks, Rhonda. I'll do my best."

"Frank? What're you searching for?"

"Nothing," I say. I hang up before she has a chance to think of something else.

I make my other calls snappy—one is to an athletic shoe designer in Denver for a "Sports Chek" round-up box I'm pulling together on foot injuries, and which other people in the office have worked on. He tells me there are twenty-six bones in the foot, and only two people in eight will ever know their correct shoe size. Of those two, one will still suffer permanent foot injury before he or she is sixty-two—due to product defect. Women, I learn, are 38 percent more susceptible than men, although men have a higher percentage of painful injuries due to body weight, stress and other athletic-related activities. Men complain less, however, and consequently amount to a hidden statistic.

Another call is to a Carmelite nun in Fayetteville, West Virginia, who is trying to run in the Boston Marathon. Once a polio victim, she is facing an uphill credentials fight in her quest to compete, and I'm glad to put a plug in for her in our "Achievers" column.

I make a follow-up call to the public relations people at the Detroit Football Club to see if they have someone they'd like to speak on behalf of the organization about Herb Wallagher, the ex-lineman, but no one is around.

Finally a call to Herb himself in Walled Lake, to let him know I'm on my way. The research department has already done a work-up on Herb, and I have a thick pile of his press clips, photographs, as well as transcribed interviews with his parents in Beaver Falls, his college coach at Allegheny, his surgeon, and the girl who was driving the ski boat when Herb was injured and whose life, I've learned, has been changed forever. On the phone Herb is a friendly, ruminative fellow with a Beaver Falls way of swallowing his consonants—*wunt* for wouldn't, *shunt* for shouldn't. I've got before-and-after pictures of him in his playing days and today, and in them he does not look like the same person. Then he looks like a grinning tractor-trailer in a plastic helmet. Now he wears black horn-rims, and having lost weight and hair, looks like an overworked insurance agent. Linemen often tend to be more within themselves than most athletes, particularly once they've left the game, and Herb tells me he has decided to go to law school next fall, and that his wife Clarice has signed on for the whole trip. He tells me he doesn't see why anybody *shunt* get all the education they can get, and that you're never too old to learn, and I agree wholeheartedly, though I detect in Herb's voice a nervy formality I can't quite make out, as if something was bothering him but he didn't want to make a fuss about it now. It could easily be the team troubles I've been hearing about. But more than likely this is just the way with all wheelchair victims: after you lift weights, eat a good breakfast, use the toilet, read the paper and bathe, what's left for the day but news broadcasts, reticence and turning inward? A good sense of decorum can make life bearable when otherwise you might be tempted to blow your brains out.

"Listen, I'll sure be glad to see you, Frank." We have never laid eyes on each other and have talked on the phone only once, but I feel like I know him already.

"It'll be good to see you, Herb."

"You miss a lot of things now, you know," Herb says. "Television's great. But it's not enough."

"We'll have a good talk, Herb."

"We'll have a time, won't we? I know we will."

"I'll say we will. See you tomorrow."

"You take care, Frank. Safe trip and all that."

"Thanks, Herb."

"Think metric, Frank. Hah." Herb hangs up.

Whatever's left to tell of my past can be dispensed with in a New York minute. At Michigan I studied the liberal arts in the College of Literature, Science and the Arts (along with ROTC). I took all the courses I was supposed to, including Latin, spent some time at the *Daily* writing florid little oversensitive movie reviews, and the rest with my feet up in the Sigma Chi house, where one crisp autumn day in 1965, I met X, who was the term party date of a brother of mine named Laddy Nozar, from Benton Harbor, and who—X—impressed me as ungainly and too earnest and not a girl I would ever care to go out with. She was very athletic-looking, with what seemed like too large breasts, and had a way of standing with her arms crossed and one leg in front of the other and slightly turned out that let you know she was probably sizing you up for fun. She seemed like a rich girl, and I didn't like rich Michigan girls, I didn't think. Consequently I never saw her again until that dismal book signing in New York in 1969, not long before I married her.

Shortly after our first meeting—but not because of it—I quit school and joined the Marines. This was in the middle stages of the war, and it seemed the right thing to do—with my military bearing—and the NROTC didn't mind. In fact, I joined with Laddy Nozar and two other boys, at the old post office on Main Street in Ann Arbor and had to cross an embarrassing protest line to do it. Laddy Nozar went to Vietnam and got killed at Con Thien with the Third Marines. The two others finished their tours and now run an ad agency in Aurora, Illinois. As it happened, I contracted a pancreatic syndrome which the doctors thought was Hodgkin's disease but which turned out to be benign, and after two months in Camp Lejeune I was discharged without killing anyone or being killed, but designated a veteran anyway and given benefits.

This event happened when I was twenty-one years old, and I report it only because it was the first time I remember feeling dreamy in my life, though then what I felt was not so pleasant and I think I would've said I felt sullen more than anything. I used to lie in bed in the Navy hospital in South Carolina and think about nothing but dying, which for a while I felt interested in. I'd think about it the way you'd think of a strategy in a ball game, deciding one way then deciding another, seeing myself dead then alive then dead again, as if considerations and options were involved. Then I'd realize I didn't have any choices and that it wasn't going to be that way, and I felt nostalgic for a while, but then got sullen as hell so that the doctors ended up giving me antidepressants to stop my thinking about it altogether, which I did. (This happens to a lot of people who get sick at a young age, and, in fact, can ruin your life.)

What it did for me, though, was let me go back to college, since I had only missed a semester, and, by 1967, entertain the idea I'd been entertaining since reading the seafaring diaries of Joshua Slocum at Lonesome Pines—to write a novel. Mine was to be about a bemused young southerner who joins the Navy but gets discharged with a mysterious disease, goes to New Orleans and loses himself into a hazy world of sex and drugs and rumored gun-running and a futile attempt to reconcile a vertiginous present with the guilty memories of not dying alongside his Navy comrades, all of which is climaxed in a violent tryst with a Methodist minister's wife who seduces him in an abandoned slave-quarters, though other times too, after which his life is shattered and he disappears permanently into the Texas oil fields. It was all told in a series of flashbacks.

This novel was called *Night Wing*, the title of a sentimental nautical painting that hung above the sweetheart couch in the Sigma Chi chapter room (I used a quotation from Marvell up front). In the middle of my senior year I wrapped it up and sent it off to a publisher in New York who wrote back in six months to say it "showed promise," and could he see "other things." The manuscript got lost in the mail back and I never saw it again, and naturally I hadn't kept a copy. Though I can remember the opening lines as clearly as if I had written them this morning. They described the night the narrator of the story was conceived. "It was 1944, and it was April. Dogwoods bloomed in Memphis. The Japanese had not given in and the war plowed on. His father came home from work tired and had a drink, not thinking of the white-coated men with code names, imagining at that moment an atomic bomb. . . . "

After graduation I bought a car and drove straight out to Manhattan Beach, California, where I rented a room and for four weeks walked in the sand, stared at the women and the oil derricks, but could not see much there that was worth writing about—which I'd decided was what I was going to do. I was getting disability money from the Navy by then, which was supposedly going to pay a tuition, and I managed to have the checks cashed by a woman I met who worked in the bursar's office of Los Angeles City College, and who sent them to me where I went, to the village of San Miguel Tehuantepec in Mexico, to write stories like a real writer.

Inside six months of arriving, all in a rush, I wrote twelve stories— one of which was a reduced form of *Night Wing*. Without sending one to a magazine, I shipped the whole book to the publisher I'd been in touch with the year before, who wrote back inside of four weeks to say that his company might publish the book with a number of changes I was only too happy to make, and sent back immediately. He encouraged me to keep writing, which I did, though without much enthusiasm. I had written all I was going to write, if the truth had been known, and there is nothing wrong with that. If more writers knew that, the world would be saved a lot of bad books, and more people—men and women alike—could go on to happier, more productive lives.

The rest is of even less interest. My book, *Blue Autumn*, was officially accepted while I was on the road driving up from San Miguel Tehuantepec. (They wired me a check for $700.) I stopped off that evening and took in a Little League game under the lights in the town of Grants, New Mexico, and drank a bottle of Cold Duck sitting alone in the stands to toast myself and my fortunes. Almost the next day a movie producer offered to buy the book for a good price, and by the time I got to New York—which my editor suggested was a good place to live—I was rich, at least for those times. It was 1968.

Right away I rented a railroad apartment on Perry Street in Greenwich Village and tried to set up some kind of writer's life, a life I actually liked. My book was published in the spring; I gave readings at some small local colleges, interviews on the radio, went out with a lot of girls, acquired a literary agent I still get Christmas cards from. I had my picture in *Newsweek*, stayed up late almost every night drinking and carousing with the new friends I was making, wrote very little (though I stayed at my desk a lot), met X at the book signing on Spring Street and took an advance from my publisher to write a novel I claimed to have an idea for, but had no interest in at all, nor any idea in the world what I could write about.

In the fall of 1969, X and I began to spend a great deal of time together. I took my first trip to the Huron Mountain Club and to the cushy golf clubs her father had memberships in. I found out she was not ungainly or too earnest at all, but was actually a wonderful, unusual, challenging girl (she was still modeling and making plenty of money). We got married in February of 1970, and I began doing some magazine assignments to deflect the agony of writing my novel, which was entitled *Tangier*, and took place in Tangier—where I had never been, but assumed was like Mexico. The first line of *Tangier* was, "Autumn came later that year to the rif of the Low Atlas, and Carson was having an embarrassing time staying publicly sober." It was about a Marine who had deserted the war and wandered across the edges of continents in search of his sense of history, and was told in the first person and also mostly in flashbacks. It sits in my drawer in a closet under a lot of old life-insurance forms and catalogs to this very moment.

In the spring, my book was still in some book stores because a New York reviewer had said, "Mr. Bascombe is a writer who could turn out to be interesting." The movie producer decided he could "see a movie" in my stories, and paid me the rest of the money he owed me (though one was never made). I began churning out more work on *Tangier*, which everybody including me thought I should write. Ralph began to be on the way. X and I were having a fine time going to ball games at Yankee Stadium, driving to Montauk, taking in movies and plays. And suddenly one morning I woke up, stood at the window from which I could see a slice of the Hudson, and recognized that I had to get out of New York immediately.

When I think about it now, I'm not sure why we didn't just move into a larger apartment. If you were to ask X she would tell you it wasn't her idea. Yet something in me just suddenly longed for it. I felt at the time that going into things with a sense of certainty and confidence was everything. And that morning I woke up with the feeling my passport to New York had been invalidated and I had insurmountable wisdom as to the ways of the world; a feeling that we had to get out of town pronto so that my work could flourish in a place where I knew no one and no one knew me and I could perfect my important writer's anonymity.

Faced with this, X put in a vote for Lime Rock, Connecticut, up the Housatonic, where we had taken drives. But I couldn't have been more fearful of that indecisive Judas country. Its minor mountains and sad Shetland-sweater, Volvo-wagon enclaves spoke to me only of despair and deceit, sarcasm and overweening informalities—no real place for a real writer; only for second-rate editors and agents of textbook writers, was my judgment.

For lack of a better idea I cast my vote for New Jersey: a plain, unprepossessing and unexpectant landscape, I thought, and correctly. And for Haddam with its hilly and shady seminary niceness (I'd seen an ad in the *Times*, making it sound like an undiscovered Woodstock, Vermont), where I could invest my movie money in a sound house (I wasn't wrong), and where there was a mix of people (there was), and where a fellow might sit down with good hope and do a serious piece of work himself (I wasn't right there, but couldn't have known it).

X did not think it was worth a hard stand about Connecticut, and in the fall of 1970 we bought the house I now live alone in. X had quit her job to get ready for Ralph. I moved with renewed enthusiasm up to an "office" on the third floor—the part I now rent to Mr. Bosobolo—and set about trying to invent some more serious writing habits and a good attitude toward my novel, which I'd let drift over the summer. In a few months we fell in with a younger group of people (some of whom were writers and editors), began attending rounds of cocktail parties, took walks along the nearby

Delaware, went to literary events in Gotham, attended plays in Bucks County, took drives in the country, stayed home evenings to read, were looked upon as a couple who were a little exceptional (I was just twenty-five), and generally felt fine about our lives and the choices we had made. I gave a talk entitled "The Making of a Writer" at the library and to the Rotarians in a neighboring town; wrote a piece in a local magazine about "Why I Live Where I Live," in which I talked about the need to find a place to work that is in most ways "neutral." I worked on an original screenplay for the producer who'd bought my book, and wrote several large magazine pieces—one about a famous center fielder from the old Sally League, who later became a petroleum baron and spent some time in prison for bank fraud, had several wives, but as a parolee went back to his arid West Texas home of Pumpville and built a therapeutic swimming pool for brain-damaged children and even brought Mexicans up for treatment. A year somehow managed to go by. Then I simply stopped writing.

I didn't exactly know I'd stopped writing. For a good while I'd gone to my office every day at eight, come downstairs at lunch and lounged around the house reading research books about Morocco, "doping out a few structural problems," making graphs and plot-flow outlines and character histories. But the fact was, I was washed up. Sometimes I would go upstairs, sit down, and not have any idea of what I was there for, or what it was I meant to write about, and had simply forgotten everything. My mind would wander to sailing on Lake Superior (something I had never done), and after that I would go back downstairs and take a nap. And as if I needed proof I was washed up, when the managing editor at the magazine I now work for called me and asked if I had any interest in going to work writing sports full-time—his magazine, he said, had a nose for good writing of the type he'd seen in my article about the Texas millionaire-convict-Samaritan—I was more than interested. He said he'd seen something complex yet hard-nosed in that piece of writing, in particular the way I didn't try to make the old center fielder either a villain or a hero to the world, and he had a suspicion I might have just the right temperament and eye for detail to do their kind of work, though he said I might just as well think the entire call was a joke. I took the train up the very next morning and had a long talk with the man who had called me, a fat, blue-eyed Chicagoan named Art Fox, and his young assistants, in the old oak-chaired offices the magazine then occupied on Madison and 45th. Art Fox told me that if you're a man in this country you probably already know enough to be a good sportswriter. More than anything, he said, what you needed was a willingness to watch something very similar over and over again, then be able to write about it in two days' time, plus an appreciation of the fact that you're always writing about people who wanted to be doing what they're doing or they wouldn't be doing it, which was the only urgency sportswriting could summon, but also the key to overcoming the irrelevancy of sports itself. After lunch, he took me out into the big room full of old-fashioned cubicles which still had typewriters and wooden desks, and introduced me around. I shook everyone's hand and heard them out about what was on their minds (no one mentioned anything about my book of stories), and at three o'clock I went home in brimming spirits. That night I took X out to a high-priced dinner with champagne at the Golden Pheasant, hauled her off on a romantic moonlight walk up the towpath in a direction we'd never gone, told her all about what I had in mind, what I thought we could practically hope to get from this kind of commitment (I thought plenty), and she simply said she thought it all sounded just fine. I remember that moment, in fact, as one of the happiest of my life.

The rest is history, as they say, until my son Ralph got Reye's syndrome some years later and died, and I launched off into the dreaminess his death may or may not have even caused but didn't help, and my life with X broke apart after seeing *The Thirty-Nine Steps* one night, causing her to send her hope chest chuffing up the chimney stack.

Though as I began by saying, I'm not sure what any of this proves. We all have histories of one kind or another. Some of us have careers that do fine or that do lousy. Something got us to where we are, and nobody's history could've brought another Tom, Dick or Harry to the same place. And to me that fact limits the final usefulness of these stories. To the extent that it's incompletely understood or undisclosed, or just plain fabricated, I suppose it's true that history can make mystery. And I am always vitally interested in life's mysteries, which are never in too great a supply, and which I should say are something very different from the dreaminess I just mentioned. Dreaminess is, among other things, a state of suspended recognition, and a response to too much useless and complicated factuality. Its symptoms can be a long-term interest in the weather, or a sustained soaring feeling, or a bout of the stares that you sometimes can not even know about except in retrospect, when the time may seem fogged. When you are young and you suffer it, it is not so bad and in some ways it's normal and even pleasurable.

But when you get to my age, dreaminess is *not* so pleasurable, at least as a steady diet, and one should avoid it if you're lucky enough to know it exists, which many people aren't. For a time—this was a period after Ralph died—I had no idea about it myself, and in fact thought I was onto something big—changing my life, moorings loosed, women, travel, marching to a different drummer. Though I was wrong.

Which leaves a question which might in fact be interesting.

Why did I quit writing? Forgetting for the moment that I quit writing to become a sportswriter, which is more like being a businessman, or an old-fashioned traveling salesman with a line of novelty household items, than being a genuine writer, since in so many ways words are just our currency, our medium of exchange with our readers, and there is very little that is ever genuinely creative to it at all—even if you're not much more than a fly-swat reporter, as I'm not. Real writing, after all, is something much more complicated and enigmatic than anything usually having to do with sports, though that's not to say a word against sportswriting, which I'd rather do than anything.

Was it just that things did not come easily enough? Or that I couldn't translate my personal recognitions into the ambiguous stuff of complex literature? Or that I had nothing to write about, no more discoveries up my sleeve or the pizzaz to write the more extensive work?

And my answer is: there are those reasons and at least twenty better ones. (Some people only have one book in them. There are worse things.)

One thing certain is that I had somehow lost my sense of anticipation at age twenty-five. Anticipation is the sweet pain to know whatever's next—a must for any real writer. And I had no more interest in what I might write next—the next sentence, the next day—than I cared what a rock weighed on Mars. Nor did I think that writing a novel could make me interested again.

Though I minded like all get out the loss of anticipation. And the glossy sports magazine promised me that there would always be something to look forward to, every two weeks. They'd see to it. And it wouldn't be something too hard to handle in words (my first "beat" was swimming, and some of the older writers put me through a pretty vigorous crash apprenticeship, which always happens). I had no special store of sports knowledge, but that wasn't needed. I was as comfortable as an old towel in a locker room, had plenty of opinions and had always admired athletes anyway. The good-spirited, manly presence of naked whites and Negroes has always made me feel well-located, and I was never out of place asking a few easy-to-answer questions and being somewhat less imposing than everybody around.

Plus, I'd be paid. Well paid—and there'd be travel. I would regularly see "Frank Bascombe" in print above a piece of workmanlike journalism many people would read and possibly enjoy. Occasionally I'd get to be some fellow's guest on a call-in show (a hook-up in my own living room) and answer questions from fans in St. Louis or Omaha, where one of my articles had stirred up a bees' nest of controversy. "This is Eddie from Laclede, Mr. Bascombe, whaddaya think's wrong with the whole concept of competition on the college level these days? I think it stinks, Mr. Bascombe, if you want to know what I think." "Well, Eddie, that's a pretty good question. . . ." Beyond all that I could look forward to the occasional company of good-natured men who, at least on a superficial level, shared my opinions—something you don't often have in the real writer's business.

What I determined to do was write well everything they told me to write—mixed pairs body-building, sky-diving, the luge, Nebraska 8-man football—I could've written three different stories for every assignment. I thought of things in the middle of the night, jumped out of bed, practically ran down to the study and wrote them. Raw material I had up to then—ruminations, fragments of memory, impulses I might've tried to struggle into a short story suddenly seemed like life I already understood clearly and could write about: fighting the battle with age; discovering how to think of the future in realistic terms.

It must happen to thousands of people that a late calling is missed, with everything afterwards done halfway—a sense of accomplishment stillborn. But for me it was the reverse. Without knowing I had a natural calling I had hit on a perfect one: to sit in the empty stands of a Florida ball park and hear the sounds of glove leather and chatter; talk to coaches and equipment managers in the gusty autumn winds of Wyoming; stand in the grass of a try-out camp in a mid-size Illinois grain town and watch footballs sail through the air; to bone up on the relevant stats, then go home or back to the office, sit down at my desk and write about it.

What could be better, I thought, and still think? How more easily assuage the life-long ache to anticipate than to write sports—an ache only zen masters and coma victims can live happily without?

I have talked this very subject over with Bert Brisker, who was also once a sportswriter for the magazine, but who has since become a book reviewer for one of the slick weeklies, and he has a remarkably similar set of experiences. Bert is as big as a den bear but gentle as they come now that he's stopped drinking. He is the closest acquaintance I still have in town from the old cocktail-dinner party days, and we are always trying to arrange for me to have dinner at their house, though on the one occasion I did, Bert got jittery as a quail halfway through the evening (this was about at the point it became clear we had nothing to talk about), and ended up downing several vodkas and threatening to throw me through the wall. Consequently we see each other only on the train to Gotham, something that happens once a week. It is, I think, the essence of a modern friendship.

Bert was once a poet and has two or three delicate, spindly-thin books I occasionally see in used bookstore racks. For years, he had a wild-man's reputation for getting drunk at public readings and telling audiences of nuns and clubwomen to go straight to hell, then falling off stages into deep trance-like sleeps and getting into fistfights in the homes of professors who had invited him there and thought he was an artist. Eventually, of course, he ended up in a rehab hospital in Minnesota and, later, running a poetry program in a small New Hampshire college—very like the one I taught at—and eventually getting fired for shacking up with most of his female students, several of whom he moved right into the house with his wife. It is not an unusual story, though that was all years ago. He came to sportswriting precisely as I did, and now lives nearby on a farm in the hills outside of Haddam with his second wife, Penny, and their two daughters, and raises sheepdogs in addition to writing about books. Bert's specialty, when he was a sportswriter, was ice hockey, and I will commend him by saying he was very good at making an uninteresting game played by Canadians seem sometimes more than uninteresting. Many of our writers are former college teachers or once-aspiring writers who simply couldn't take it, or rougher-cut graduates of Ivy League schools who didn't want to be stockbrokers or divorce lawyers. The day of the old bulldog reporter up from the Des Moines *Register* or the Fargo *Dakotan*—your Al Bucks and your Granny Rices—are long gone, though that wasn't as true when I started twelve years ago.

Bert and I have talked about this subject on our train rides through the New Jersey beltland—why he quit writing, why I did. And we've agreed, to an extent, that we both got gloomy in an attempt to be serious, and that we didn't understand the vital necessity of the play of light and dark in literature. I thought my stories were good at the time (even today I think I might like them). They seemed to have a feeling for the human dilemma and they *did* seem hard-nosed and old-eyed about things. It was also true, though, that there were a good many descriptions of the weather and the moon, and that most of them were set in places like remote hunting camps on Canadian Lakes, or in the suburbs, or Arizona or Vermont, places I had never been, and many of them ended with men staring out snowy windows in New England boarding schools or with somebody driving fast down a dark dirt road, or banging his hand into a wall or telling someone else he could never *really* love his wife, and bringing on hard emptinesses. They also seemed to depend on silence a lot. I seemed, I felt later, to have been stuck in bad stereotypes. All my men were too serious, too brooding and humorless, characters at loggerheads with imponderable dilemmas, and much less interesting than my female characters, who were always of secondary importance but free-spirited and sharp-witted.

For Bert, being serious meant he ended up writing poems about stones and savaged birds' nests, and empty houses where imaginary brothers he believed were himself had died grisly ritual deaths, until finally, in fact, he could no longer write a line, and substituted getting drunk as a donkey, shacking up with his students and convincing them how important poetry was by boinking the daylights out of them in its name. He has described this to me as a failure to remain "intellectually pliant."

But we were both stuck like kids who had reached the end of what they know they know. I did not, in fact, know how people felt about *most* things—and didn't know what else to do or where to look. And needless to say that is the very place where the great writers—your Tolstoys and your George Eliots—soar off to become great. But because I didn't soar off to become great—and neither did Bert—I have to conclude we suffered a failure of imagination right there in the most obvious way. We lost our authority, if that is a clear way of putting it.

What I did, as I began writing *Tangier*, which I hoped would have some autobiographical parts set in a military school, was become more and more grave—over my literary voice, my sentences and their construction (they became like some heavy metallic embroidery no one including me would want to read), and my themes, which became darker and darker. My characters generally embodied the attitude that life is always going to be a damn nasty and probably baffling business, but somebody has to go on slogging through it. This, of course, can eventually lead to terrible cynicism, since I knew life wasn't like that at all—but was a lot more interesting—only I couldn't write about it that way. Though before that could happen, I lost heart in stringing such things together, became distracted, and quit. Bert assures me his own lines took on the same glum, damask quality. "Waking each day / at the end / of a long cave / soil is jammed / in my nostrils / I bite through / soil and roots / and bones and / dream of a separate existence" were some he quoted me from memory one day right on the train. He quit writing not long after he wrote them and went chasing after his students for relief.

It is no coincidence that I got married just as my literary career and my talents for it were succumbing to gross seriousness. I was crying out, you might say, for the play of light and dark, and there is no play of light and dark quite like marriage and private life. I was seeing that same long and empty horizon that X says she sees now, the table set for one, and I needed to turn from literature back to life, where I could get somewhere. It is no loss to mankind when one writer decides to call it a day. When a tree falls in the forest, who cares but the monkeys?

3

By a quarter to ten I have surrendered to the day and am in my Malibu and down Hoving Road, headed for the Great Woods Road and the Pheasant Run & Meadow condos where Vicki lives—really nearer to Hightstown than to Haddam proper.

Something brief should be said, I think, about Haddam, where I've lived these fourteen years and could live forever.

It is not a hard town to understand. Picture in your mind a small Connecticut village, say Redding Ridge or Easton, or one of the nicer fieldstone-wall suburbs back of the Merritt Parkway, and Haddam is like these, more so than a typical town in the Garden State.

Settled in 1795 by a wool merchant from Long Island named Wallace Haddam, the town is a largely wooded community of twelve thousand souls set in the low and rolly hills of the New Jersey central section, east of the Delaware. It is on the train line midway between New York and Philadelphia, and for that reason it's not so easy to say what we're a suburb of—commuters go both ways. Though as a result, a small-town, out-of-the-mainstream feeling exists here, as engrossed as any in New Hampshire, but retaining the best of what New Jersey offers: assurance that mystery is never longed for, nor meaningful mystery shunned. This is the reason a town like New Orleans defeats itself. It longs for a mystery it doesn't have and never will, if it ever did. New Orleans should take my advice and take after Haddam, where it is not at all hard for a literalist to contemplate the world.

It is not a churchy town, though there are enough around because of the tiny Theological Institute that's here (a bequest from Wallace Haddam). They have their own brick and copper Scottish Reform Assembly with a choir and organ that raises the roof three days a week. But it is a village with its business in the world.

There is a small, white-painted, colonial Square in the center of town facing north, but no real main street. Most people who live here work elsewhere, often at one of the corporate think-tanks out in the countryside. Otherwise they are seminarians or rich retirees or faculty of De Tocqueville Academy out Highway 160. There are a few high-priced shops behind mullioned windows—men's stores and franchised women's undergarments salons are in ascendance. Book stores are down. Aggressive, sometimes bad-tempered divorcées (some of them seminarians' ex-wives) own most of the shops, and they have given the Square a fussy, homespun air that reminds you of life pictured in catalogs (a view I rather like). It is not a town that seems very busy.

The Post Office holds high ground, since we're a town of mailers and home shoppers. It's no chore to get a walk-in haircut, or if you're out alone at night—which I often was after my divorce—it isn't hard to get a drink bought for you up at the August Inn by some old plaid-pantser watching the ball game, happy to hear a kind word about Ike instead of heading home to his wife. Sometimes for the price of a few daiquiris and some ardent chitchat, it's even possible to coax a languid insurance broker's secretary to drive with you out to a roadhouse up the Delaware, and to take in the warm evening of springtime. Such nights often don't turn out badly, and in the first few months, I spent several in that way without regrets.

There is a small, monied New England émigré contingent, mostly commuters down to Philadelphia with summer houses on the Cape and on Lake Winnepesaukee. And also a smaller southern crowd—mostly Carolinians attached to the seminary—with their own winter places on Beaufort Island and Monteagle. I never fitted exactly into either bunch (even when X and I first got here), but am part of the other, largest group who're happy to be residents year-round, and who act as if we were onto something fundamental that's not a matter of money, I don't think, but of a certain awareness: living in a place is one thing we all went to college to learn how to do properly, and now that we're adults and the time has arrived, we're holding on.

Republicans run the local show, which is not as bad as it might seem. Either they're tall, white-haired, razor-jawed old galoots from Yale with moist blue eyes and aromatic OSS backgrounds; or else retired chamber of commerce boosters, little guys raised in town, with their own circle of local friends, and a conservator's clear view about property values and private enterprise know-how. A handful of narrow-eyed Italians run the police—descendants of the immigrants who were brought over in the twenties to build the seminary library, and who settled The Presidents, where X lives. Between them, the Republicans and Italians, the rule that *location is everything* gets taken seriously, and things run as quietly as anyone could want—which makes you wonder why that combination doesn't run the country better. (I am lucky to be here with my pre-1975 dollars.)

On the down side, taxes are sky high. The sewage system could use a bond issue, particularly in X's neighborhood. But there are hardly any crimes against persons. There are doctors aplenty and a fair hospital. And because of the southerly winds, the climate's as balmy as Baltimore's.

Editors, publishers, *Time* and *Newsweek* writers, CIA agents, entertainment lawyers, business analysts, plus the presidents of a number of great corporations that mold opinion, all live along these curving roads or out in the country in big secluded houses, and take the train to Gotham or Philadelphia. Even the servant classes, who are mostly Negroes, seem fulfilled in their summery, keyboard-awning side streets down Wallace Hill behind the hospital, where they own their own homes.

All in all it is not an interesting town to live in. But that's the way we like it.

Because of that, the movie theater is never noisy after the previews and the thanks-for-not-smoking notices. The weekly paper has mostly realty ads, and small interest in big news. The seminary and boarding school students are rarely in evidence and seem satisfied to stay put behind their iron gates. Both liquor stores, the Gulf station and the book stores are happy to extend credit. The Coffee Spot, where I sometimes ride up early on Ralph's old Schwinn, opens at five A.M. with free coffee. The three banks don't bounce your checks (an officer calls). Black boys and white boys—Ralph was one—play on the same sports teams, study together nights for the SATs and attend the small brick school. And if you lose your wallet, as I have, on some elm-shaded street of historical reproductions—my Tudor is kitty-cornered from a big Second Empire owned by a former Justice of the New Jersey Supreme Court—you can count on getting a call by dinner just before someone's teenage son brings it over with all the credit cards untouched and no mention of a reward.

You could complain that such a town doesn't fit with the way the world works now. That the real world's a worse and devious and complicated place to lead a life in, and I should get out in it with the Rhonda Matuzaks of life.

Though in the two years since my divorce I've sometimes walked out in these winding, bowery streets after dark on some ruminative errand or other and looked in at these same houses, windows lit with bronzy cheer, dark cars hove to the curbs, the sound of laughing and glasses tinking and spirited chatter floating out, and thought to myself: what good rooms these are. What complete life is here, audible—the Justice's is the one I'm thinking of. And though I myself wasn't part of it and wouldn't much like it if I were, I was stirred to think all of us were living steadfast and accountable lives.

Who can say? Perhaps the Justice himself might have his own dark hours on the streets. Maybe some poor man's life has hung in the balance down in sad Yardville, and the lights in my house—I usually leave them blazing—have given the Justice solace, moved him to think that we all deserve another chance. I may only be inside working over some batting-average charts, or reading *Ring* or poring through a catalog in the breakfast nook, hopeful of nothing more than a good dream. But it is for just such uses that suburban streets are ideal, and the only way neighbors here can be neighborly.

Certainly it's true that since there is so much in the world now, it's harder to judge what is and isn't essential, all the way down to where you should live. That's another reason I quit real writing and got a real job in the reliable business of sports. I didn't know with certainty what to say about the large world, and didn't care to risk speculating. And I still don't. That we all look at it from someplace, and in some hopeful-useful way, is about all I found I could say— my best, most honest effort. And that isn't enough for literature, though it didn't bother me much. Nowadays, I'm willing to say yes to as much as I can: yes to my town, my neighborhood, my neighbor, yes to his car, her lawn and hedge and rain gutters. Let things be the best they can be. Give us all a good night's sleep until it's over.

Hoving Road this morning is as sun-dappled and vernal as any privet lane in England. Across town the bells of St. Leo the Great chime a brisk call to worship, which explains why no Italian gardeners are working on any neighbors' lawns, clearing out under the forsythias and cutting back the fire thorns. Some of the houses have sunny Easter-lily decorations on their doors, whereas some still abide by the old Episcopal practice of Christmas wreaths up till Easter morning. There is a nice ecumenical feel of holiday to every street.

The Square this morning is filled up with Easter buyers, and to avoid tie-ups I take the "back door" down Wallace Hill through the little one-ways behind the hospital Emergency entrance and the train station. And soon I am out onto the Great Woods Road, which leads to U.S. 1 and across the main train line into the suave and caressing literalness of the New Jersey coastal shelf. It is the very route I took yesterday afternoon when I drove to Brielle. And whereas then my spirits were tentative—I still had this morning's duties ahead—today they are rising and soaring.

Six miles out, Route 33 is astream with cars, though a remnant fog from early morning has clung to the roadway as it sways and swerves toward Asbury Park. A light rain draws in a soughing curtain of apple greens from the south and across the accompanying landscape, softening the edges of empty out-of-season vegetable stands, farmettes, putt-putts and cheerless Ditch Witch dealers. Though I am not displeased by New Jersey. Far from it. Vice implies virtue to me, even in landscape, and virtue value. An American would be crazy to reject such a place, since it is the most diverting and readable of landscapes, and the language is always American.

'An Attractive Retirement Waits Just Ahead'

Better to come to earth in New Jersey than not to come at all. Or worse, to come to your senses in some spectral place like Colorado or California, or to remain up in the dubious airs searching for some right place that never existed and never will. Stop searching. Face the earth where you can. Literally speaking, it's all you have to go on. Indeed, in its homeliest precincts and turn-outs, the state feels as unpretentious as Cape Cod once might've, and its bustling suburban-with-good-neighbor-industry mix of life makes it the quintessence of the town-and-country spirit. Illusion will never be your adversary here.

An attractive retirement is Pheasant Run & Meadow. I make the turn up the winding asphalt access that passes beneath a great water tower of sleek space-age blue, then divides toward one end or the other of a wide, unused cornfield. Far ahead—a mile, easy—billowing green basswoods stand poised against a platinum sky and behind them the long, girdered "Y" stanchions of a high-voltage line, orange balls strung to its wires to warn away low-flying planes.

Pheasant Run to the left is a theme-organized housing development where all the streets are culs-de-sac with "Hedgerow Place" and "The Thistles" painted onto fake Andrew Wyeth barnboard signs. All the plantings are young, but fancy cars already sit in the drive-ways. Vicki and I drove through once like tourists, admiring the farm-shingled and old-brick homesteads with price tags bigger than I paid for my three-story in town fourteen years ago. Vicki's father and stepmother live in the same sort of place down in Barnegat Pines, and I have a feeling she would like nothing better than for herself and some prospective hubby to move right in.

Pheasant Meadow sits at the other lower end of the stubble field— a boxy, unscenic complex of low brown-shake buildings overlooking a shallow man-made mud pond, a yellow bulldozer, and some other apartments already half-built. In the ideal plan of things, these are for the younger people just starting in the world and on the way up—secretaries, car salesmen, nurses, who will someday live to buy the complete houses over in Pheasant Run on resale. Starter people, I call them.

Vicki's aqua Dart sits out front in slot 31, still with black and white Texas plates, and shining with polish. The last hiss of rain squall thrums off north into the Brunswicks as I pull in beside her, and the air is thick with a silvery, chemical smell. But before I can get out, and to my surprise, I see Vicki in the front seat of her car, nearly hidden by its big head rest. I roll down the passenger window and she sits peeking out at me from the driver's seat, her black hair orchestrated Loretta Lynn style, two thick swags taken toward the back of her head and ears, then straight down in sausage curls to her shoulders.

Across in the new units two hardhats sit grinning on unfinished Level Two. It's clear they've been having a good time over something before I got here.

"I figured you probably wouldn't show up," Vicki says out her open window, as tentative as a school girl. "I was sitting up there waiting on the phone to ring for you to give me the bad news, and so I just came down here and listened to some tapes I like to hear when I'm sad." She smiles out at me, a sweet-natured, chancy smile. "You're not going to be hot at me are you?"

"If you don't get over here in about two seconds I am," I say.

"I knew it," she says, running her window up quick and grabbing her bag, bouncing out of her Dart and into my life in a twinkling. "I told myself, I said, self, if you go out there he'll come, and sure enough."

All fears are put instantly to rest, leaving the two hardhats shaking their heads. I wouldn't mind, as I back out, blinking my lights and wishing them just half the fun I'm expecting. But they'd probably get the wrong idea. As we back up, though, I give them a grin and we wheel out of Pheasant Meadow down the access road toward Route 33 and the NJTP, Vicki cleaving to me, squeezing my arm and sighing like a new cheerleader.

"Why'd you think I wouldn't show up?" I say, as we weave

through rain-drenched Hightstown, and I am thinking how glad I am to own a car with an old-fashioned bench seat.

"Oh it's just old silly-milly. Seemed like too good a thing to happen, I guess." Vicki is wearing black slacks that fit her tight but not too, a white, frilly-dressy blouse-and-scarf combination, a blue Ultrasuede jacket straight from Dallas and shoes with clear plastic heels. These are her dressy travel clothes, along with her nylon Le Sac weekender tossed in the back and her little black clutch where she keeps her diaphragm. She is a girl for every modern occasion, and I find I can be interested in the smallest particulars of her life. She stares out as the upright Federalist buildings of Hightstown slide past. "Plus. I had a patient kick out on me last night just right when I was talking to him, asking him questions about how he felt and everything. I wasn't even s'posed to be workin, but a gal got sick. He was this colored man. And he *was* C-liver terminal, already way into uremia when he admitted, which is not *that* bad cause it usually starts 'em dreamin about their pasts and off their current problem." (A tiny sigh of relief as to her whereabouts last night. I had called and found no one there, and my worst fears were loosed.) "Only you don't really get that used to death, which is why I came down to ER from ONC. We're supposed to be used to it and all, but I'm just not. I'd lot rather see a guy busted up and bleeding than some guy dying inside. I guess that was why I started worrying. I knew you went to the cemetery this morning."

"That all went fine, though," I say, and in most ways it did.

Vicki takes a Merit Light out of her little purse and lights up. She is not the kind of girl who smokes, but likes to smoke when she's nervous. I reach a hand across her plump thighs and pull her closer to me, leg-side to leg-side. She lowers her window a crack and blows smoke that way. "When's your birthday, anyway?"

"Next week."

"Okay, that's what you're supposed to say. Now when is it really?"

"That's the truth. I'm going to be thirty-nine." I snake a glance down to see if there's adverse reaction to this news. We have not discussed my age in the eight weeks I've known her. I assume she thinks I'm younger.

"You are not. Liar."

"I'm afraid it's true," I say, and try to smile.

"Well, maybe I'll make you a present of an eight-track, and tape you all my favorites. How'd you like that?" There is no more reaction to this news about my age. There are women I know who care about men's ages, and women who don't. X didn't, and I have always counted that as a sign of good sense. Though where Vicki is concerned—her possible reasons for not caring are probably related to a bad first marriage and a wish to hook up with someone at least kind—it is another in a burgeoning number of happy surprises. Maybe we'll get married in Detroit, fly back and move out to Pheasant Run, and live happily like the rest of our fellow Americans. What would be wrong with that?

"I'd like that fine," I say.

"You weren't mad at me for bein out in the car like a tart?"

"You're too pretty to be mad at."

"That's about what them dimwits thought, too."

We approach the Turnpike, take our ticket and start north, above the flat, featureless bedrenched Jersey flatlands—a landscape perfect for easy golf courses, valve plants and flea markets.

The reason Vicki is worried that I would be mad at not getting to come to her door is because she knows I love the tribal ritual of picking her up for our dates, even if I'm hoping to spend the night. Usually I am formal and bring a gift, something I quit doing long ago when X and I went on outings. Though it's true that X and I lived together, and such things are easy to forget. But with Vicki, I usually bring something down from New York, where she has only been once and claims she can't abide. For her part, she is always *almost* ready and pretends I hurry her, runs to the bedroom with straight pins in her mouth, or holding her hair up in back, needing to stitch a hem or iron a pleat. We are throwbacks in this, straight out of an earlier era, but I like this nervous and over-produced manner of things between us. We seem to know what each other wants without really knowing each other, which was a dilemma between X and me at the end. We didn't seem to be tending the same ways. Though it may simply be that at my age I'm satisfied with less and with things less complicated.

Whatever the reason, I'm always happy when I am invited to spend the night or just an hour waiting in the pristine and nursey neatness of Vicki's little 1-BR condo, on which her dad holds the note, and which the two of them furnished in a one-day whirlwind trip to the Miracle Furniture Mile in Paramus.

Vicki made all her own choices: pastel poof-drapes, sunburst mirror, bright area rugs with abstract designs, loveseat with a horse-and-buggy print, a maple mini-dining room suite, a China-black enamel coffee table, all brown appliances and a whopper Sony. All Wade Arcenault had to do was write a big check and set his little girl's life back on track after the bad events with husband Everett.

Each time I'm inside, all is precisely as it was the time before, as if riveted in place and clean as newsprint: a fresh *Nurse* magazine, a soap opera archive and *TV Guide* shingling the piecrust table. A shiny saxophone on its stand unused since high school band days. The guest bathroom spotless. Dishes washed and put away. Everything reliable as the newly-wed suite in the Holiday Inn.

My own house represents other aims, with its comfortable, over-stuffed entities, full magazine racks, faded orientals, creaky sills and the general residue of mid-life eclecticism—artifacts of a prior life and goals (many unmet), yet evidence that does not announce a life's real quality any more eloquently than a new Barca Lounger or a Kitchen Magician, no matter what you've heard. In fact, I have become a committed no-muss, no-fuss fellow. And the idea appeals to me of starting life over in such a new and genial place with an instant infusion of colorful, fresh and impersonal furnishings. I might've done the same if it hadn't been for Paul and Clarissa, and if I hadn't believed I wasn't so much starting a new life as raising the ante on an old one. And if I hadn't felt our house was still a sound investment. All of which has worked out well, and most nights I drift off to sleep (wherever I am—a St. Louis, an Atlanta, a Milwaukee or even a Pheasant Meadow) convinced I have come away, as they say, with the best of both worlds—the very thing we all crave.

Vicki has dowsed her cigarette and begun pinching at her sausage curls in the visor mirror. "Doesn't it seem strange to you we'd be takin a trip together?" She squinches up her nose, first at her own face then at mine, as if she didn't expect to hear a word she could believe.

"This is what grownups do—go on trips together, stay in hotels, have wonderful times."

"Rilly?"

"Really."

"Well. I guess." She takes a bobby pin out of her blouse cuff and puts it in her mouth. "It just never seemed like anything I'd be doin. Everett and me went to Galveston sometimes. I been to Mexico, but just to cross over." She removes the pin and buries it deep in her black hair. "What *are* you, anyway, by the way?"

"I'm a sportswriter."

"Yes, I know that. I read things you wrote." (This is news to me! What things?) "I mean, are you Libra or the Twins. You said your birthday wasn't but less than a month from now. I want to figure you out."

"I'm the Taurus."

"What does that one mean?" She watches me keenly now out the side of her eye while she finishes with her hair.

"I'm pretty intelligent. I'm not cynical, but I'm intuitive about people, and that might make me seem cynical." All this comes straight from Mrs. Miller, my palmist. It is part of her service to give information like this if I ask her for it, in addition to speculating on the future. I try to see her at least every two weeks. "I'm also pretty generous."

"I'll admit that, at least you been that with me. I wonder if that stuff'll make your dreams come true. I don't know much about it. I guess I could learn more."

"What dreams of yours have come true?"

She folds her arms under her breasts like a high school girlfriend and stares straight ahead for miles. It is possible to think of her as being sixteen and chaste instead of thirty and divorced; as never having witnessed a single bad or unhappy thing, despite the fact she attends death and mayhem nearly every day. "Well, look," she says, staring up the Turnpike. "Did you know I always wanted to go to Detroit?" She pronounces Detroit so as to rhyme with knee-joint.

"No."

"Well then all right. I did though. I almost fell over when you asked me." She puts her chin down as though deep in serious thought and makes a little clucking sound with her tongue. "If you'd asked me to go to Washington, D.C., or Chicago, Illinois, or Timbuktu, I probably would've said no. But when I was a little girl my Daddy used to always say, 'De-troit makes, the world takes.' And that was just such a puzzle to me I figured I *had* to see it. It seemed so unusual, you know, to me. And romantic. He'd gone up there to work after the Korean War, and when he came back he had a picture postcard of a great big tire stood up on its tread. And that's what I wanted to see, but I never got to. I got married instead on the way to no place special. Then I met you."

She smiles up at me sweetly and puts her hand inside my thigh in a way she hasn't quite done before, and I have to keep from swerving and causing a big pile-up. We are just now passing Exit 9, New Brunswick, and I take a secret look over along the line of glass booths, only two of which are lighted OPEN and have cars pulling through. Indistinct, gray figures lean out and lean back, give directions, make change, point toward surface roads for weary travelers. What could be more fortuitous or enticing than to pass the toll booth where the toll-taker's only daughter is with you and creeping up on your big-boy with tender, skillful fingers?

"Do you like my name?" She keeps her hand close up on my leg, her built-on fingernails doing a little audible skip-dance.

"I think it's great."

"Is that right?" She squinches her nose again. "I never liked it,

but thanks. I don't mind Arcenault. I like that. But Vicki sounds
like a name you'd see on a bracelet at Walgreen's." She glances at
me, then back toward the wide estuary and wetlands of the Raritan,
stretching like wheat to the tip of Staten Island and the Amboys.
"Looks like someplace the world died out there, doesn't it?"

"I like it out there," I say. "Sometimes you can imagine you're in
Egypt. Sometimes you can even see the World Trade Center."

She gives my leg a friendly pinch and turns me loose to sit up
straight. "Egypt, huh? You probably *would* like that. You're in from
the nut department, too. Tell me what that little boy of yours died
of?"

"Reye's."

She shakes her head as though mystified. "Boy-shoot. What'd you
do when he died?"

This is a question I'm not interested in exploring, though I know
she wouldn't ask if she weren't concerned about me and felt some
good could come out of it. She is as much a literalist in these matters
as I am, and much more savvy about men than I am about women.

"We were both sitting beside his bed. It was early in the morning.
Before light. We may have been asleep, really. But a nurse came in
and said, 'I'm sorry, Mr. Bascombe, Ralph has expired.' We both
just sat there a few minutes, stunned, though we knew it was going
to happen. And then she cried a while and I did, too. And then I
went home and cooked up some bacon and toast, and ended up
watching television. I had a tape of great NBA championships, and
I watched that until it got light."

"Death'll make you nutty, won't it?" Vicki rests her head on the
seat back, pulls her feet up, and hugs her shiny black knees. Far
ahead I see a plane—a great jet—floating earthward where I know
Newark airport to be; it is a promising sign. "You know what *we*
did when my Mama died?" She glances up, as if to see if I'm still
here.

"No."

"We all went out and ate Polynesian. It wasn't a big surprise or
anything, either. She had everything you can have and I was working

right in Texas Shriners and knew everything from talking to the doctors, which I don't think is really that good. Everett and Daddy, Cade and me, though, went out to the Garland Mall in the middle of the hot afternoon and ate poo-poo pork. We just wanted to eat. I think you want to eat when someone dies. Then we just went and spent money. I bought a gold add-a-bead necklace I didn't need. Daddy bought a three-piece suit at Dillards' and a new wristwatch. Cade bought something. And Everett bought a new-used red Corvette he probably still owns, I guess. He *did* have it." She extends her lower lip over the other one and focuses down beetle-browed on the visible memory of Everett's Corvette, which stands out now more than death. Her nature is to put her faith in objects more than essences. And in most ways that makes her the perfect companion.

Her story, however, has left me with an unexpected gloominess. Some aspects of hidden-life-revealed have a certain bedrock factuality I don't like. I'd be a braver soldier if the story had someone discovering they had Lou Gehrig's disease or a brain tumor on the eve of his last track meet, and deciding to run anyway. But in this I am unprotected from the emotions—vivid ones—of true death, and I suddenly feel, whipping along the girdered Turnpike, exactly as I did that morning I described: bereaved and in jeopardy of greater bereavement sweeping me up.

Women have always *lightened* my burdens, picked up my faltering spirits and exhilarated me with the old anything-goes feeling, though anything doesn't go, of course, and never did.

Only this time the solace-spirit has been sucked out of the car by a vagrant boxcar wind, leaving my stomach twitching and my mouth grimmed as though the worst were happening. I have slipped for a moment out onto that plane where women can't help in the age-old ways (this, of course, is something X said this morning and I passed off). Not that I've lost the old yen, just that the old yen seems suddenly defeatable by facts, the kind you can't sidestep—the essence of a small empty moment.

Vicki eyes me in little threatening glances, her brows arched. "What's the matter, did a bug bite you?"

If we were as far north as the Vince Lombardi Rest Area, I'd pull in and spend a half-hour admiring Vince's memorabilia—the bronze bust, the picture of the Five Blocks of Granite, the famous gabardine overcoat. We have plenty of time today. But Vince's Area is all the way past Giant's Stadium, and we are here down among the flaming refineries, without a haven.

"Would you just give me a big hug," I say. "You're a wonderful girl."

And instantly she throws an armlock around me with a neck-crunching ferocity. "Oh, oh, oh," she sighs into my ear, and as easy as that (I was not wrong) rapture rises in me. "Does it make you happy to have me here?" She is patting my cheek softly and staring straight at it.

"We're going to have us some fun, you better believe what I say."

"Oh, boy blue," she murmurs, "boy, boy blue." She kisses my ear until my legs tingle, and I want to squeeze my eyes shut and give up control. This is enough to bring us back up to ground level, and send us to the airport with all my old hopes ascendant.

I am easily rescued, it's true.

*A*t this moment it may be of interest to say a word about athletes, whom I have always admired without feeling the need to be one or to take them at all seriously, and yet who seem to me as literal and within themselves as the ancient Greeks (though with their enterprises always hopeful).

Athletes, by and large, are people who are happy to let their actions speak for them, happy to be what they do. As a result, when you talk to an athlete, as I do all the time in locker rooms, in hotel coffee shops and hallways, standing beside expensive automobiles— even if he's paying no attention to you at all, which is very often the case—he's never likely to feel the least bit divided, or alienated, or one ounce of existential dread. He may be thinking about a case of beer, or a barbecue, or some man-made lake in Oklahoma he wishes he was waterskiing on, or some girl or a new Chevy shortbed, or a discothèque he owns as a tax shelter, or just simply himself. But you can bet he isn't worried one bit about you and what *you're* thinking. His is a rare selfishness that means he isn't looking around the sides of his emotions to wonder about alternatives for what he's saying or thinking about. In fact, athletes at the height of their powers make literalness into a mystery all its own simply by becoming absorbed in what they're doing.

Years of athletic training teach this; the necessity of relinquishing doubt and ambiguity and self-inquiry in favor of a pleasant, self-championing one-dimensionality which has instant rewards in sports. You can even ruin everything with athletes simply by speaking to them in your own everyday voice, a voice possibly full of contingency and speculation. It will scare them to death by demonstrating that the world—where they often don't do too well and sometimes fall into depressions and financial imbroglios and worse once their careers are over—is complexer than what their training has prepared them for. As a result, they much \prefer their own voices and questions or the jabber of their teammates (even if it's in Spanish). And if you are a sportswriter you have to tailor yourself to their voices and answers: "How are you going to beat this team, Stu?" Truth, of course, can still be the result—"We're just going out and play our kind of game, Frank, since that's what's got us this far"—but it will be *their* simpler truth, not your complex one—unless, of course, you agree with them,which I often do. (Athletes, of course, are not *always* the dummies they're sometimes portrayed as being, and will often talk intelligently about whatever interests them until your ears turn to cement.)

An athlete, for example, would never let a story like the one Vicki just told me get to him, even though the same feelings might strike him in the heart. He is trained not to let it bother him too much or, if it bothers him more than he can stand, to go outside and hit five hundred balls off the practice tee or run till he drops, or bash himself head-on into a piece of complicated machinery. I admire that quality more than almost any other I can think of. He knows what makes him happy, what makes him mad, and what to do about each. In this way he is a true adult. (Though for that, it's all but impossible for him to be your friend.)

For the last year I was married to X, I was always able to "see around the sides" of whatever I was feeling. If I was mad or ecstatic, I always realized I could just as easily feel or act another way if I wanted to—somber or resentful, ironic or generous—even though I might've been convinced that the way I was acting probably represented the way I *really* felt even if I hadn't seen the other ways open. This can be an appealing way to live your life, since you can convince yourself you're really just a tolerant generalist and kind toward other views.

I even had, in fact, a number of different voices, a voice that wanted to be persuasive, to promote good effects, to express love and be sincere, and make other people happy—even if what I was saying was a total lie and as distant from the truth as Athens is from Nome. It was a voice that totally lacked commitment, though it may well be this is as close as you can ever come to yourself, your own voice, especially with someone you love: mutual agreement with no significant irony.

This is what people mean when they say that so-and-so is "distanced from his feelings." Only it's my belief that when you reach adulthood that distance has to close until you no longer see those choices, but simply do what you do and feel what you feel—marriage you may have to relinquish, of course. "Seeing around" is exactly what I did in my stories (though I didn't know it), and in the novel I abandoned, and one reason why I had to quit. I could always think of other ways I might be feeling about what I was writing, or other voices I might be speaking in. In fact, I could usually think of quite a number of things I might be doing at any moment! And what real writing requires, of course, is that you merge into the *oneness of the writer's vision*—something I could never quite get the hang of, though I tried like hell and eventually sunk myself. X was always clear as spring water about how she felt and why she did everything. She was completely reliable and resistant to nuance and doubt, which made her a wonderful person for a fellow like me to be married to, though I'm not certain she's so sure about things now.

Though about athletes, I want to say just one more thing: you can learn too much about them, even learn to dislike them, just as you can with anybody. When you look very closely, the more everybody seems just alike—unsurprising and factual. And for that reason I sometimes tell less than I know, and for my money the boys in my racket make a mistake with in-depth interviews.

I'd just as soon pull a good heartstring. Write about the skinny Negro kid from Bradenton, Florida, who can't read, suffered rickets and had scrapes with the law, yet who later accepts a basketball scholarship to a major midwestern university, becomes a star, learns to read and eventually majors in psychology, marries a white girl and later starts a consulting firm in Akron. That is a good story. Maybe the white girl would be of eastern European extraction. Her parents would oppose, but get won over.

If all this makes it seem that being a sportswriter is at best a superficial business, that's because it is. And it is not for that reason a bad profession at all. Nor am I, I will admit, altogether imperfectly suited for it.

A t Terminal A we become two veteran travelers. I stand in line at United while Vicki goes to powder her nose and buy flight insurance. As it turns out, she is as much a denizen of airports as I am. When everything turned bad with old dagger-head Everett, she informed me on the escalator, she used to drive out to the new airport in Dallas, watch planes leave, and pretend she was on all of them. "If you stayed in that airport for one year," she said, beaming like a carhop as we headed up the glittering ticket concourse full of passengers and loved ones looking for partners, "you'd see everybody in the world. And you'd sure see Charley Pride a hundred times at least."

Vicki also believes flight insurance to be the world's best bargain, and who am I to say no, though I advise her not to make me her beneficiary.

"Well, I guess *not*," she says, with a vaguely disgusted look. "I always make the R.C. Church my heir in everything."

"That's fine then," I say, though she and I have never discussed religion.

"I just went to Catholics when I married Everett, in case you're wondering," she says, and looks at me oddly. "They do a lot for the hospitals. And the Pope's a good old guy I think. I wadn't but a dirty Methodist before, like everybody else in Texas except the Baptists."

"That's great," I say and give her arm a squeeze.

"Freedom to choose," she says, then skitters away toward the insurance machines.

By wide degrees now I am better. Public places always work this curative on me, and if anything I suffer the opposite of agoraphobia. I enjoy the freely shared air of the public. It is, in a way, my element. Even the yellow-aired Greyhound terminals and murky subway stations make me feel a well-being, that a place has been provided for me and my fellow man together. When I was married to X, I hated the grinding summer weeks we'd spend first at the Huron Mountain Club, and, later, at Sumac Hills down in Birmingham, where her father was a founding member. I hated that still air of privilege and the hushed, nervous noises of midwestern exclusivity. I thought it was bad for the children and kept stealing off with Ralph to the Detroit Zoo and the Belle Isle Botanical Garden, and once all the way out to the Arboretum in Ann Arbor. X's had been an entire life of privilege—clubs and reserved tables and private boxes at the ball game—though I think all that means nothing if you have a sound enough character to weather it, which she has.

Across from me studying the departures board I spy a face I recognize but hope to get away without acknowledging. It is the long face of Fincher Barksdale. Fincher is holding his white United ticket folder and has a big TWA golf bag over his shoulder. Fincher

is my internist, and I have visited him, as I said, to inquire about
my pounding heart, and have heard from him that it is likely a
matter of my age, and that many men approaching forty suffer from
symptoms inexplicable to medical science, and that in a while they
just go away by themselves.

Fincher is one of those lanky, hairy-handed, hip-thrown, vaguely
womanish southerners who usually become bored lawyers or doctors, and whom I don't like, though X and I were friendly with him
and his wife, Dusty, when we first came to Haddam and I had a
small celebrity with my picture in *Newsweek*. He is a Vanderbilt
grad, and older than I am by at least three years though he looks
younger. He took his medicine and a solid internist's residency at
Hopkins, and though I do not like him one bit, I am happy to have
him be my doctor. I try to look away in a hurry, out the big window
toward the spiritless skyline of Newark, but I'm sure Fincher has
already seen me and is waiting to be sure I've seen him and absolutely
don't want to talk to him before he pipes up.

"Now look out here. Where're we slippin off to, brother Frank."
It is Fincher's booming southern baritone, and without even looking
I know he is stifling a white, toothy smile, tongue deep in his cheek,
and having a wide look around to see who else might be listening
in. He extends me his soft hand without actually noticing me. We
are not old fraternity brothers. He was a Phi Delt, though he once
suggested we might have a distant aunt in common, some Bascombe
connection of his from Memphis. But I squelched it.

"Business, Fincher," I say nonchalantly, shaking his long, bony
hand, hoping Vicki doesn't come back anytime soon. Fincher is a
veteran lecher and would take pleasure in making me squirm on
account of my traveling companion. One of the bad things about
public places is that you sometimes see people you would pay money
not to see.

Fincher is wearing green jackass pants with little crossed ensigns
in red, a blue Augusta National pullover and black-tasseled spectator
shoes. He looks like a fool, and is undoubtedly flying off on a golfing

package somewhere—Kiawah Island, where he shares a condo, or San Diego, where he goes for doctors' conventions six or eight times a year.

"What about you, Fincher?" I say, without the slightest interest.

"Just a hop down to Memphis, Frank, down to Memphis for the holiday." Fincher rocks back on his heels and jingles change in his pockets. He makes no mention of his wife. "Since we lost Daddy, Frank, I go down more, of course. Mother's doing real fine, I'm happy to say. Her friends have closed ranks around her." Fincher is the kind of southerner who will only address you through a web of deep and antic southernness, and who assumes everybody in earshot knows all about his parents and history and wants to hear an update on them at every opportunity. He looks young, but still manages to act sixty-five.

"Glad to hear it, Fincher." I take a peek down past Delta and Allegheny to see if Vicki's coming this way. If Fincher and the two of us are flying the same flight, I'll change airlines.

"Frank, I've got a little business venture I want to tell you about. I started to get into it in the office the other day, but things went right on and got ahead of me. It's something you absolutely ought to consider. We're past the venture capital stages, but you can still get in on the second floor."

"We're due out of here in a minute, Fincher. Maybe next week."

"Now who're we here with, Frank?" A definite mistake there. I have set Fincher nosing all around again like a bird dog.

"With a friend, Fincher."

"I see. Now this is one minute to tell, Frank. Just while we're standing here. See now, some boys and I are starting up a mink ranch right down in south Memphis, Frank. It's always been my dream, for some damn reason." Fincher smiles at me in stupid self-amazement. He is picturing his stupid farm at this moment, I can tell, his tiny lizard's eyes dull with lusterless blue absorption. They are without question the peepers of a fool.

"It'd get hot for the minks, wouldn't it?"

"Oh well, you *have* to air-condition, Frank. Definitely. No way around that mountain. The start-up's sky high, too." Fincher is nodding like a banker, his blond and grayed head a pleasant puzzle of fresh financial wranglings. He crams both hands in his pockets and gives whatever's down there another stern jingle. Though just for the moment I am struck by Fincher's hair, the thinning top of which sinks into view as he glances ritually at his spectators. His hair is barbered into the dopey-blond Tab Hunter brushcut circa 1959, crisp as a saltine and with just a soupçon of odorless colloid to hold it in place. He is the perfect southerner-in-exile, a slew-footed mainstreet change jingler in awful clothes—a breed known only *outside* the south. At Vandy he was the tallish, bookish Memphian meant for a wider world—brushcut, droopy suntans, white bucks, campaign belt and a baggy long-sleeved Oxford shirt, hands stuffed in his pockets, arrogantly bored yet supremely satisfied and accustomed to the view from his eyrie. (Essentially the very way he is now.) At Hopkins he met and married a girl from Goucher who couldn't stand the South and craved the suburbs as if they were the Athens of Pericles, and Fincher has been free ever since to jingle his change and philander around the links with the other southern renegades of whom, as I've said, there is a handsome cadre. When the awful day of reckoning comes to Fincher, I want to be somewhere far away in a boat, I know that.

"Frank," Fincher says, having gone on talking about mink farms while I rode up over the clouds, "now don't you think it'd be a high-water mark for the New South? You care about all those things, don't you?"

"Not much," I say, and the truth is not at all.

"Well now, Frank, everybody thought old Tom Edison was crazy, didn't they?" Fincher pulls his ticket folder out of his back pocket and whacks it across his palm and smirks.

"I'm pretty sure everybody thought Edison was smart, Fincher."

"Okay. You know what I mean, son."

"It's forward thinking, Fincher, I'll give it that much."

And Fincher suddenly assumes an unexpected dazed look as if that was the signal he has been waiting for. And for a moment we stand in silence among hundreds of milling passengers, just the way we might stand together at the window up in the Petroleum Club in Memphis, brainstorming and conniving over next year's tail-gate party at the Commodore–Ole Miss game. Somehow or other Fincher has managed to set himself at ease, despite my reservations with his mink farm, and I actually admire him for it.

"You know, Frank. I've probably never said this to you." Fincher nods his head like a sage old trial judge. "But I admire the hell out of what you do and how you lead your life. There's a lot of us would like to do that, but lack the nerve and the dedication."

"What I do's pretty easy, Fincher. You'd probably be as good at it as I am. You ought to give it a try." I squeeze my toes inside my shoes.

"Now you'd need to tie me up in chains and beat me with a stick to get me to write, Frank. I get the ants nowadays just writing a scrip." Fincher's mouth mulls down in a mock-grimace. He secretly knows he could do it as well as I can and most likely better, but feels the need to pay me some kind of unfelt compliment. "There's a whole lot of us would like to mouse off with a little nurse, too," Fincher says with a big wink.

I turn and look off down the crowded concourse and see Vicki skittering back with her insurance papers, walking with difficulty on her plastic high heels. She looks like a secretary on an urgent trip to the copy machine, elbows thrown out for balance, her feet seemingly made of wood. Fincher *has* seen her and recognized her from the hospital halls, and I am caught.

Fincher has suddenly adopted the old dirty-leg innuendo he perfected in the Phi Delt house down at Vanderbilt, and means to reduce me to fun or force a briny confidence. A sinister uneasiness surrounds us both. He is more untrustworthy than I thought, and I am as on my guard as any man who has something worth defending—though wretched ever to have let him hold me in a conversation. Fincher is threatening to pull the plug on all anticipation, and I'll be damned if I'll let him do it.

"Why don't you mind your own business, Fincher," I say, and

look him dead in the eyes. I could punch him in the nose, bloody
up his jackass pants, and send him home to Memphis in stitches.

"Now-now-now." Fincher raises his chin and saunters back a half
step onto his heels, glancing up over my shoulder toward Vicki.
"We're white men, here, Frank."

"I'm not married anymore," I say fiercely. "Anything I do is all
right."

"Yes indeed." Fincher flashes his big-tooth smile, but it is for
Vicki, not me. I am defeated and cannot help wondering if Fincher
hasn't been on this very track before me.

"Well, look what you see when you aren't properly armed," Vicki
says, fastening a good grip on my arm, and giving Fincher a nasty
little smile to let me know she's got his number. I love her more
than I can say.

Fincher mumbles something like "mighty small world," but he
has become half-hearted at best. "I got the in-surance," Vicki says
and flutters the papers up to me, ignoring Fincher completely. "You
might see a name you know if you look. I changed religions, too."
Her sweet face is gone plain with seriousness. It is a face I did not
even want to see two moments before, but that I welcome now as
a friend of my heart. I unfold the thick onionskin sheaf from Mutual
of Omaha, and see Vicki's name here as Victory Wanda Arcenault—
and mine partway down as beneficiary. The sum is $150,000.

"What about the Pope?" I say.

"He's still a good ole bird. But I'll never *see* him." She blinks her
eyes up at me as if a light had burst into view around my ears. "I'll
see *you*, though."

I would like to hug her till she squeaked, but not in Fincher's
presence. It would give him something to think about, and I want
to give him nothing. At the moment he is standing with his mouth
formed into a small, perfect *o*. "Thanks," I say.

"I liked the idea of you spending all that money and thinking
about me. It'd make me happy then wherever I was. You could buy
a Corvette—only you'd probably want a Cadillac."

"I just want you," I say. "Anyway we'll be together if it crashes."

She rolls her eyes up at the high crystal-lighted airport ceiling. "That's true, isn't it?" She takes the policy back and kneels down to put it in her Le Sac bag.

"I 'spec I'll just steal on off," Fincher says, eyes flashy-darty since something has taken place here outside his ken. He has bent himself slightly at the waist and is on the verge of embarrassment, an emotion he has not felt, in all likelihood, for twenty years.

The concourse has begun welling up around us with people wearing paper tags on their breasts that say "Get-Away." They appear from nowhere and begin flowing in the direction of gates 36–51. The air suddenly smells sweet and peanutty. A plane has been held up for late-arrivers, and a feeling of relief circles us like a spring breeze.

"It's good to see you, Fincher," I say. Fincher, of course, is no more a lecher than the rest of us, and I am relieved to let him and his grave Ichabod's features slip away.

"Uh-huh, you bet," Vicki says and glances at Fincher with distaste, a look he seems to accept with gratitude.

"I guess they're lettin us on a little early." Fincher flashes a smile.

"You have a good trip," I say.

"Yep, yep," Fincher says and hoists his clubs onto his bony shoulder.

"Don't do it in the lake," Vicki says. But Fincher is already out of her range, and I watch him pick up his step with the other expectants, in from Buffalo, his clubs hitched high up, happy to be in with a new crowd, ready for some good earnest talk and arm-squeezing on their way south.

"You and Fincher have a falling out?" I say this in a chummy voice.

"I 'magine we did." Vicki is kneeling, elbow-deep in her weekender bag, digging for something at the bottom. We are next up to have our tickets validated. "He's some kinda joker. A real sneak-up-behind-you guy if you know what that means. A bad potato. We all watch out for him."

"Did he sneak up behind you?"

"No sir." She looks up at me in surpirse. "Nasty mind. I keep an eye on who's back of me."

"What do you think I think?"

"It's on your face like eggs."

"I'm just jealous," I say. "Can't you tell?"

"I wouldn't know." She finds a tiny perfume phial from her bag, uncaps it and takes it to her neck and arms while she kneels on the airport floor. She smiles up at me in a spicy way I know she knows I like. "You ain't got nothin to worry about, lemme tell you, Mister. You're numero uno and there's no number two."

"Tell me about Fincher, then."

"One-a-these days. You won't be surprised, though, I'll tell you that."

"You'd be surprised what surprises me."

"And what *don't* surprise me. Ever." She stands to take my hand in the ticket line. Her hand's moist, and the air smells of Chanel No. 5.

"You win."

"Right. I'm a winner all the way," she says airily. And if I could make the moment last—lost in the anticipation of a safe trip, a fatal crash, a howling success, a grinding bitter failure—I would, and never leave this airport, never gain on or rejoin myself, and never know what's to come, the way you always have to know, though it's only the same, the same you waiting.

4

On the plane we are in the midwest from the first moment we take
our seats. The entire tourist cabin of our 727 virtually vibrates with
its grave ying-yangy appeal. Hefty stewardesses with smiles that
say "Hey, I could love you once we're down and safe" stow away
our carry-ons. Vicki folds her weekender strap inside and hands it
up. "Gaish, now is that ever neat," says a big blond one named Sue
and puts her hands on her hips in horsey admiration. "I wanta show
Barb that. We've got the pits with our luggage. Where're you guys
headed?" Sue's smile shows a big canine that is vaguely tan-colored,
but she is full of welcome and good spirits. Her father was in the
Air Force and she has a lot of athletic younger brothers, I would
stake my life on it. She's seen plenty.

"De-troit," Vicki announces proudly, taking a secret peek at me.

Sue cocks her blond head to the side with pride. "You gyz'll love
Detroit."

"Well, I'm really lookin forward to it," Vicki says with a grin.

"Greet, reelly greet," Sue says and sways off to start the coffee
around. All about me, almost immediately, people begin to converse
in the soft nasalish voices and mildish sentiments familiar from my
college days. Everyone seems to be a native Detroiter heading home
for the holidays, and no one coming west just to visit but us. Someone
nearby claims to have stayed up and watched an entire telethon and
missed two days of work. Someone else headed up to "the thumb"
on a fishing trip but had motor trouble and ended up marooned in
Bad Axe for a weekend. Someone had started Wayne State and
pledged Sigma Nu but by last Christmas was back to work at his
dad's sheet metal business. It might be said, of course, that the
interiors of all up-to-date conveyances of travel put one in mind of
the midwest. The snug-fitted overhead bins, the comfy pastel re-

cliners, disappearing tray-tables and smorgasbord air of anything-you-want-within-sensible-limits. All products of midwestern ingenuity, as surely as a waltz is Viennese.

In a little while Barb and Sue circulate back and conduct a serious Q&A with Vicki about her weekender bag, which neither of them has seen the exact likes of, they say, and Vicki is only too happy to discuss. Barb is a squat little strawberry blondie with too much powder makeup and slightly heavy hands. She is interested in something called "price points" and "mean value mark-up," and whether or not an identical bag couldn't be bought at Hudson's boutique in a mall near her own condo in Royal Oak; it turns out she studied retailing in college. Vicki says hers came from Joske's, but that's all she knows, and the girls talk about Dallas for a while (Barb and Sue have both been based there at different times) and Vicki says she likes a store called Spivey's and a rib place in Cockrell Hill called Atomic Ribs. They all three like each other a lot. Then all at once we're in the air rising out over the cloud-shaded Watchungs and a bright blue-green industrial river, toward Pennsylvania, making for Lake Erie, and the girls slide off to other duties. Vicki picks up the arm rest and shoves close to me on our three-across seats, her shiny, encased thigh as hard as a saucepan, her breath drowsy with excitement. We are well above the morning's storminess now.

"What're you thinking about, old Mr. Man?" She has attached her pair of pink earphones around her neck.

"About what a sweet thigh you've got and how much I'd like to pull it my way."

"Well you surely can. Won't nobody see you but Suzie and little Barbara, and they don't care long as no clothes come off. That wasn't what you were thinking anyway. I know about you, old tricky."

"I was thinking about Candid Camera. The talking mailbox. I think that's about the funniest thing I've ever seen in my life."

"I like 'em, too. Ole Allen Funk. I thought I saw him one day in the hospital. I'd heard he lived someplace around. But then it wasn't. A lot of people look alike now, you know it? But that still isn't it. I'll just let you run on."

"You're a smart girl."

"I got a good memory, which you need to nurse. But I'm not really smart. I wouldn't have married Everett if I had been." She fattens her cheeks and smiles at me. "Are you not gonna tell me what you're sitting there worrying?" She takes a good two-armed hold on my arm and squeezes it. She is a girl who likes squeezing. "Or am I gon have to squeeze you till you talk." She is strong, which I think would also be a requirement for a nurse, though I am sure she doesn't really care what's on my mind.

In truth, of course, I have nothing to answer. Undoubtedly I was thinking something, but most things I find myself thinking seem to fly right out of my mind and I can't remember them at all. It is a trait of character which made being a writer hard and often downright tedious. I either had to sit down and write out whatever I happened to be thinking about at any time of the day or night I happened to think it, or else just forget it all, which is what happened at the end of the time I was working on my novel. Finally I became happy to forget everything and let it all lapse. Real writers have to be more attentive, of course, and attentive was what I wasn't much interested in being.

I do not think, in any event, it's a good idea to want to know what people are thinking (that would disqualify you as a writer right there, since what else is literature but somebody telling us what somebody else is thinking). For my money there are at least a hundred good reasons not to want to know such things. People never tell the truth anyway. And most people's minds, like mine, never contain much worth reporting, in which case they just make something up that's patently ridiculous instead of saying the truth—namely, I was thinking nothing. The other side, of course, is that you will run the risk of being told the *very* truth of what someone is thinking, which can turn out to be something you don't want to hear, or that makes you mad, and ought to be kept private anyway. I remember when I was a boy in Mississippi, maybe fifteen years old—just before I left for Lonesome Pines—a friend of mine got killed in a hunting accident. The very night after, Charlieboy Neblett and I (he was one of my few friends in Biloxi) sat out in Charlieboy's car drinking beer and complaining about our having thought, then forgiving each other for thinking, that we were glad Teddy Twiford got killed. If Teddy's mother had come by just then and asked us what we were thinking, she would've been flabbergasted to find out what lousy friends of Teddy's we were. Though in fact we weren't lousy friends at all. Things just come into your mind on their own and aren't your fault. So I learned this all those years ago—that you don't need to be held responsible for what you think, and that by and large you don't have any business knowing what other people think. Full disclosure never does anybody any favors, and in any event there are few enough people in the world who are sufficiently within themselves to make such disclosure pretty unreliable right from the start. All added to the fact that this constitutes intrusion where you least need to be intruded upon, and where telling can actually do harm to everyone involved.

I remember, in fact, the Lebanese woman I knew at Berkshire College saying to me, after I told her how much I loved her: "I'll always tell you the truth, unless of course I'm lying to you." Which at first I didn't think was a very good idea; though stewing over it after a while I realized that it was actually a piece of great luck. I was being promised truth *and* mystery—not an easy combination. There would be important things I would and wouldn't know, and I could count on it, could look forward to it, muse on it, worry about it if I was idiot enough, which I wasn't, and all I had to do was agree, and be forever freed.

She was a literary deconstructionist and had a mind trained for that kind of distinction. And she managed to make a policy out of a fact of life: how much of someone you can actually get to know about. Very little. Though I don't think in the three vertiginous months we spent together she ever lied to me. There was never a reason to! I saw to that by never asking a question whose answer wasn't already obvious. X and I might in fact have made a better go of it if she could've tried that strategy out on me by not asking me to explain anything that night I stood out in the rhododendrons marveling at Gemini and Cassiopeia, while her hope chest was fast going up the chimney. She might've understood my predicament for what it was—an expression of love and inevitability, instead of just love's failure. Though I will not complain about it. She is fine now, I think, in most ways. And if she is not as certain about things as she once was, that is not a tragedy, and I think she will be better as time goes on.

By the time the copilot pokes his head through the tourist class curtain and gives us all the high sign, Vicki has drifted off to sleep, her head on a tiny pillow, her mouth slightly ajar. I intended to show her Lake Erie, which we're now passing high above, green and shimmering, with gray Ontario out ahead. She is tired from too much anticipation, and I want her full of energy for our whirlwind trip. She can see the lake on the flight home, and be a slug-a-bed on Sunday night when we return from her parents.

An odd thing happened to me last night, and I would like to say something about it because it touches on the whole business of full disclosure, and because it has stayed on my mind ever since. It is, of course, what I wasn't prepared to tell Vicki.

For the past two years I have been a member of a small group in town which we got together and called—with admirable literalness—the Divorced Men's Club. There are five of us in all, though the constituency has changed once or twice, since one fellow got married again and moved away from Haddam to Philadelphia, and another died of cancer. In both instances someone has come along at just the right time to fill in the space, and we have all been happy to have five since that number seems to strike a balance. There have been several times when I have nearly quit the club, if you can call it a club, since I don't think of myself as a classic joiner and don't feel, at least anymore, that I need the club's support. In fact, almost all of it bores the crap out of me, and ever since I began to concentrate on becoming more within myself I've felt like I was over the shoals and headed back to the mainstream of my own lived life. But there have been good reasons to stay. I did not want to be the first to leave as a matter of choice. That seemed niggardly to me—gloating that

I had "come through," whereas maybe the others hadn't, even though no one has ever admitted that we do anything to support one another. To start with, none of us is that kind of confessional, soulful type. We are all educated. One fellow is a banker. One works in a local think tank. One is a seminarian, and the last guy is a stocks analyst. Ours is much more a jocular towel-popping raffish-rogueishness than anything too serious. What we mostly do is head down to the August, puff cigars, talk in booming businessmen's voices and yuk it up once a month. Or else we pile into Carter Knott's old van and head down to a ball game in Philadelphia or go fishing over at the shore, where we get a special party deal at Ben Mouzakis' Paramount Show Boat Dock.

Though there's another reason I don't leave the club. And that is that *none* of the five of us is the type to be in a club for divorced men—none of us in fact even seems to belong in a place like Haddam—given our particular circumstances. And yet we are there each time, as full of dread and timidness as conscripts to a firing squad, doing what we can to be as chatty and polite as Rotarians—ending nights, wherever we are, talking about life and sports and business, hunched over our solemn knees, some holding red-ended cigarettes as the boat heads into the lighted dock, or before last call at the Press Box Bar on Walnut Street, all doing our best for each other and for non-confessional personal expression. Actually we hardly know each other and sometimes can barely keep the ball moving before a drink arrives. Likewise there have been times when I couldn't wait to get away and promised myself never to come back. But given our characters, I believe this is the most in friendship any of us can hope for. (X is dead right about me in this regard.) In any case the suburbs are not a place where friendships flourish. And even though I cannot say we like each other, I definitely can say that we don't *dislike* each other, which may be exactly the quiddity of all friendships that have not begun with fellows you knew before your own life became known to you—which is the case with me, and, I suppose, for the others, though I truly don't know them well enough to say.

We met—the original five—because we'd all signed up for the

"Back in Action" courses at Haddam High School, courses designed expressly for people like us, who didn't feel comfortable in service clubs. I was enrolled in "Twentieth-Century American Presidents and Their Foreign Policies." A couple of the other fellows were in "Water-Color Foundations" or "Straight-Talking" and we used to stand round the coffee urn on our breaks keeping our eyes diverted from the poor, sad, skinny divorced women who wanted to go home with us and start crying at 4 A.M. One thing led to another, and by the time our courses were half over we'd started going over to the August, jawing about fishing trips to Alaska and baseball trades, singling out one another's idiosyncracies, and assigning funny names for each other like "ole Knot-head" for Carter Knott, the banker; "ole Basset Hound" for Frank Bascombe; "ole Jay-Jay" for Jay Pilcher— who, inside of a year, died alone in his house with a brain tumor he never even knew about. Perfect Babbitts, really, all of us, even though to some extent we understood that.

In a way, I suppose you could say all of us were and are lost, and know it, and we simply try to settle into our lost-ness as comfortably and with as much good manners and little curiosity as we can. And perhaps the only reason we have not quit is that we can't think of a compelling reason to. When we do think of a good reason we'll all no doubt quit in an instant. And I may be getting close.

But that is not so much the point as a way of getting around to it.

Yesterday was the day of our spring fishing excursion for flukes and weakfish, out of Brielle. Knot-head Knott made all the arrangements, and while Ben Mouzakis does not give us one of his boats all to ourselves for the money we pay, he usually just books one other party of congenial fellows for the afternoon and takes us out at cost since he knows we'll talk it up in Haddam and come back ourselves next year, and because I honestly think he enjoys our company. We are all good fellows for an afternoon.

I had left Haddam in the glum spirits I've fallen into each year on the day before Ralph's birthday. It had rained early just the way it did today, but by the time I had come round the traffic rotary in

Neptune and turned toward the south Shore Points, the rain had swept up into the Amboys leaving me drenched in the supra-real seashore sunshine and traffic hum of Shark River, as indistinguishable from my fellow Jerseyites as a druggist from Sea Girt.

It is of course an anonymity I desire. And New Jersey has plenty to spare. A passing glance down off the bridge-lock at Avon and along the day-trip docks where the plastic pennants flutter and shore breezes dance always assures me that any one of these burly Bermuda-shorts fellows waiting impatiently with their burly wives for the *Sea Fox* to weigh its anchor or the *Jersey Lady* to cast off, could just as well be me, heading out after monkfish off Mantoloking or Deauville. Such random identifications always strike me as good practice. Better to think that you're like your fellow man than to think—like some professors I knew at Berkshire College—that no man could be you or take your place, which is crazy and leads straight to melancholy for a life that never existed, and to ridicule.

Anyone could be anyone else in most ways. Face the facts.

Though possibly because of my skittishness, yesterday the Bermuda-shorts guys on the docks didn't seem altogether hopeful from my distance. They seemed to be wandering off bandy-legged from their spouses down the dock planks, arms folded, faces querulous in the mealy sunshine, their natural Jersey pessimism working up a fear that the day might go wrong—in fact *couldn't* go right. Someone would charge them too much for an unwanted and insignificant service; the wife would get seasick and force the boat in early; there'd be no fish and the day would end with a sad chowder at a rueful chowder house a stone's throw from home. In other words, all's ahead to be regretted; better to start now. I could've yelled right out to them: Cheer up! Chances are better than you think! Things could pan out. You could have a whale of a time, so climb aboard. Though I didn't have quite the spirits for it.

But as it happened, I would not have been more right. Ben Mouzakis had chartered half the boat to a family of Greeks—the Spanelises—from his own home village near Parga on the Ionian, and the divorced men were all on best behavior, acting like good-will ambassadors on a fortunate posting, assisting the women with their stubby rods, baiting hooks with brown chub and untangling back-lashed reels. The Greek men had their own way of fixing on bait so that it was harder to pick clean, and a good deal of time was spent learning this procedure. Ben Mouzakis eventually broke out some retsina, and by six o'clock fishing was over, the few fluke caught off the "secret reef" were packed in ice, the radio was beamed into a Greek station in New Brunswick, and everyone—the divorced men and the Spanelises, two men, three pretty women and two chil-dren—were sitting inside the long gallery cabin, elbows on knees, nodding and cupping glasses of wine and talking solemnly with the best good-neighborly tolerance about the value of the drachma, Mel-ina Mercouri and the trip to Yosemite the Spanelises were plan-ning for June if their money held out.

I was contented with the way the day had turned out. Sometimes an awful sense of loss comes over me when I am with these men, as profound as a tropical low. Though it has been worse in the past than yesterday. Something about them—earnest, all good-hearted fellows—seems as dreamy to me as it's possible to be, dreamier than I am by far. And dreamy people often do not mix well, no matter what you might believe. Dreamy people actually have little to offer one another, tend in fact to neutralize each other's dreaminess into bleary nugatude. Misery does not want company—happiness does. Which is why I have learned to stay clear of other sportswriters when I'm not working—avoid them like piranhas—since sports-writers are often the dreamiest people of all. It is another reason I will not stay in Gotham after dark. More than one drink with the boys from the office at Wally's, a popular Third Avenue watering hole, and the dreads come right down out of the fake tin ceiling and the Tiffany hanging lamps like cyanide. My knee starts to hop under the table, and in three minutes I'm emptied of all conviction and struck dumb as a shoe and want nothing but to sit and stare away at the pictures on the wall, or at how the moldings fit the ceiling or how the mirrors in the back bar reflect a different room from the one I'm in, and fantasize about how much I'm going to enjoy my trip home. A group of sportswriters together can narrow your view far beyond pessimism, since the worst of them tend to be cynics looking only for false drama in the germs of human defeat.

Beyond that, what is it that makes me back off from even the best like-minded small talk when there is no chance of the willies nor the least taint of cynicism, and when in principle at least I like the whole idea of comradeship (otherwise why would I go fishing with the Divorced Men)? Simply, that I hate for things to get finally pinned down, for possibilities to be narrowed by the shabby impingement of facts—even the simple fact of comradeship. I am always hoping for a great surprise to open in what has always been a possible place for it—comradeship among professionals; friendship among peers; passion and romance. Only when the facts are made clear, I can't bear it, and run away as fast as I can—to Vicki, or to sitting up all night in the breakfast nook gazing at catalogs or to writing a good sports story or to some woman in a far-off city whom I know I'll never see again. It's exactly like when you were young and dreaming of your family's vacation; only when the trip was over, you were left faced with the empty husks of your dreams and the fear that that's what life will mostly be—the husks of your dreams lying around you. I suppose I will always fear that whatever *this* is, is *it*.

Even so, I have been happy enough on the Divorced Men's fishing trips. My habit is not to rent a rod and reel but to walk around and exchange a wry word with the men who are fishing like demons, go get their beers, sit in the passengers' cabin and watch television, or go up top and stand beside Ben and watch the sonar on the pilot's deck, where he finds the fish like clouds of white metal on the dark green baize. Ben never remembers my name, though after a while he recognizes me as someone named John, and we have diverse conversations about the economy or Russian fishing vessels or base- ball, which Ben is a fanatic for, and which serves as a good man- to-man connection.

On yesterday's excursion I finished the day doing what I like best, standing at the iron rail near the bow of the *Mantoloking Belle* staring off at the jeweled shore lights of New Jersey, brightening as dark fell, and feeling full of wonder and illusion—like a Columbus or a pilgrim seeing the continent of his dreams take shape in the dusk for the first time. My plans for the evening were to be at Vicki's by eight, to surprise her with an intimate German dinner at Truegel's Red Palace on the river at Lambertville—celebrating two months of love—then have her home early. Altogether it was not a bad bunch of prospects.

Down the railing from me, staring as I was into the sequined gloom, was Walter Luckett, pensive as a judge and quite possibly cold in the spring night, from the way he was hunched over his elbows.

Walter is the newest member of the Divorced Men. He took Rocko Ferguson's place when Rocko got remarried and moved down to Philadelphia, and came in as an old acquaintance of Carter Knott's from Harvard Business School. Walter is from Coshocton, Ohio, attended Grinnell, and pronounces Ohio as if it both begins and ends in a U. He is a special-industries analyst for Dexter & Warburton in New York and looks like it, with tortoise-shell glasses and short, slicked hair. Occasionally I spy him on the train platform going to work, but we rarely speak. In fact I know almost nothing else about him. Carter Knott told me Walter's wife, Yolanda, left him and ran off to Bimini with a water ski instructor; that it'd been a big shock, but he seemed to be "handling things better now." That could happen to any of us, of course, and the Divorced Men seemed like just the thing for him.

Occasionally, I've slipped out to the Weirkeeper's Tavern after eleven—I do this sometimes to see the sports final on the big screen—and there was Walter, a little drunk and talkative. Once he yelled out, "Hey Frank! Where're all the women?" after which I couldn't wait to get out.

Another time I was in The Coffee Spot at dinnertime when Walter came in. He sat down in the booth across from me, and we talked about the Jaycees and what a bunch of phonies he thought they all were, and about the quality of silk underwear you can get out of most catalogs. Some, he said, were made in Korea, but the best ones came right from China; it was one of his industries. And then we just sat for a long time—a hundred years, it felt like—while our eyes tried to find a place to rest, until they finally settled on each other. And then we sat and stared at each other for four, maybe five horrible, horrible minutes, then Walter just got up and walked out without ordering anything or saying another word. Since then he has never mentioned that terrible moment, and I have frankly tried to duck him and on two occasions know that he walked in the door at the August, saw me and walked out again—something I respect him for. All together, I think I like Walter Luckett. He does not really belong in a divorced men's club any more than I do, but he is willing to try it on for size, not because he thinks he'll eventually like it, or that this is the thing he's always missed, but because it's in some ways the last thing in the world he can imagine doing, and probably feels he should do it for that reason alone. We should all know what's at the end of our ropes and how it feels to be there.

"Do you happen to know what I like about standing here at the rail and looking out at the coast, Frank?" Walter said softly, after I had declined to speak a word.

"What's that, Walter?" I was surprised he had even noticed me. Walter had caught one weakfish all afternoon, the biggest one caught, and after that he had quit fishing and curled up with a book on one of the bench seats.

"I like seeing things from an angle you don't live them. You know what I mean?"

"Sure," I said.

"I'm out there embedded in life every day. Then I come just a mile off shore, and it's dark, and suddenly it's all different. Better. Right?" Walter looks around at me. He is not a large man, and tonight he is wearing white walking shorts, a baggy blue tennis shirt and deck shoes, which makes him seem even smaller.

"It seems better. Probably that's why we come out here."

"Right," Walter said, and stared for a time out at the darkly dazzling coast, the sound of water slapping the side of the boat. Far up I could see the glow of the Asbury Park ferris wheel, and due north the ice-box glow of Gotham. It was consoling to see those lights and know that lives were there, and mine was here. And for the moment I was glad to have come along, and considered the Divorced Men all pretty darn solid fellows. Most of them, in fact, were inside the main cabin yakking with the Spanelises, having the time of their lives. "It's not the way I always see it though, Frank," Walter said soberly, clasping his hands over the rail and leaning on his forearms.

"How do you usually see it, Walter?"

"Okay. It's funny. When I was a kid in eastern Ohio, our whole family used to take these long trips. Fairly long, anyway. From Coshocton, in the east part of the state, all the way to Timewell, Illinois, which is in the west part of that state. All of it just flatland, you know. One county same with another one. And I used to ride in the car while my sister played hubcaps or lucky-lives-license or whatever, concentrating on remembering certain things—a house or maybe a silo or a swell of land, or just a bunch of pigs, something I'd be able to remember on the way back. So it would be the same to me, all part of the same experience, I guess. Probably everybody does that. I *still* do. Don't you do it?" As Walter looked at me again, his glasses caught a glint of shore light and twinkled at me.

"I guess I'm your opposite here, Walter," I said. "The highway never seems the same coming and going to me. I even think about meeting myself in the cars I pass. I actually forget it all pretty much right away, though I tend to forget a lot of things."

"That's a better way to be," Walter said.

"To me, it makes the world more interesting."

"I guess I'm having to learn that, Frank," Walter said and shook his head.

"Is something bothering you, Walter," I said—and shouldn't have, since I broke the rules of the Divorced Men's Club, which is that we're none of us much interested in that kind of self-expression.

"No," Walter said moodily. "Nothing's bothering me." And he stood for a while staring out at the jet coast of Jersey—the boxy beach house lights linking us to whatever hopeful life was proceeding there. "Let me just ask you something, Frank," Walter said.

"All right."

"Who do you have to confide in?" Walter did not look at me when he said this, though I somehow felt his smooth soft face was both sad and hopeful at the same moment.

"I guess I don't, to tell the truth," I said. "I mean I don't have anyone."

"Did you not even confide in your wife?"

"No," I said. "We talked about things plenty of times. That's for sure. Maybe we don't mean the same thing by confiding. I'm not particularly a private person."

"Good. That's good," Walter said. I could tell he was puzzled but also satisfied by my answer, and what's more I had given him the best answer I could. "Frank, I'll see you later," Walter said unexpectedly and gave me a pat on the arm, and walked off down the deck into the dark where one of the Spanelis men was still fishing, though it was black on the water and the tart spring air was chilling enough that I went inside and watched a couple of innings of a Yankees game on the boat's TV.

Once we got in, though, and all said our goodbyes, and the divorced men had given the few weakfish and fluke they'd caught to the Spanelis kids, I was walking across the gravel lot to my car, ready to head straight for Vicki's and steal her away to Lambertville, and here was Walter Luckett scuffing his deck shoes alongside my car and looking, in the dark, strangely like a man who wanted to borrow some money.

"What-say now, Wally," I said cheerfully, and went about putting the key in the door lock. I had an hour to get there, and I was for getting going. Vicki goes to bed early even when she doesn't have to work the next day. She is damned serious about her nursing career, and likes being bright and cheerful, since she believes many of her patients have no one who understands their predicament. The result is I don't drop in after eight, no matter what.

"This is a helluva life, isn't it, Frank?" Walter said and leaned against my back fender, arms folded, staring off as if in amusement as the other divorced men and the Spanelises were barging out of the lot up toward Route 35, their lights brightly swaying. They were honking horns and yelling, and the Spanelis kids were squealing.

"It sure is, Walter." I opened my door and stopped to look at him in the dark. He stuffed his hands in his pockets and bunched his shoulders. He had on a pale sweater draped in the old lank, country club style. "I think it's a pretty good life, though."

"You couldn't really plan it, could you?"

"You certainly couldn't."

"There's so much you can't foresee, yet it's all laid out and clear."

"You look cold, Walter."

"Let me buy you a drink, Frank."

"Can't tonight. Got things to do." I smiled at him conspiratorially.

"Just a bone warmer. We can sneak right over into the Manasquan." Across the lot was the Manasquan Bar, a barny old hip-roofed fisherman's roadhouse with a red BAR sign on top. Ben Mouzakis had invested in it with his wife's brother, Evangelis, as he told me once when we talked about tax shelters up on deck. "What d'ya say?" Walter said and started off. "Let's drink one, Frank."

I did not want to have a nightcap with Walter Luckett. I wanted to go speeding back toward Vicki and drowsy Lambertville while the last flickers of sunlight clung in the western sky. The memory of those awful centuries spent in The Coffee Spot rose up in my thoughts suddenly, and I almost jumped in the car and rammed out of the lot like a desperado. But I didn't. I stood and looked at Walter, who by now had walked halfway across the empty lot in his walking shorts and sweater, and had turned toward me and assumed a posture I can only describe as heartbreaking. And I could not say no. Walter and I had something in common—something insignificant, but something that his heartbreaking posture made undeniable. Walter and I were both men, Vicki or no Vicki, Lambertville or no Lambertville.

"Only one," I said into the parking lot darkness. "I've got a date."

"You'll make it," Walter said, lost now in the bleary seaside low-lights of Brielle. "I'll see to that myself."

In the Manasquan Walter ordered a scotch and I ordered a gin, and for a while we sat in complete uncomfortable silence and stared at the old pictures behind the bar that showed record stripers caught off the dock. I thought I could detect Ben Mouzakis in several—a chesty young roughneck of the Fifties, a big immigrant's crazy grin, no shirt, muscles bristling, standing beside some other taller men in khakis and two hundred dead fish strung along a rafter board.

The Manasquan is a dark, pine-board, tar-smelling pile of sticks inside and in truth it is one of my favorite places for small departures. Any other time I wouldn't have minded being there one bit. It has a long teak bar with a quasi-nautical motif, and no one makes the first attempt to be friendly, though drinks are poured honestly and at a reasonable price for a touristy seaside area. Sometimes, arriving too early for our excursion, I have walked over, taken a seat at the bar and bought a good greasy hamburger and felt right at home reading a newspaper or watching TV alongside the few watchcap fishermen who huddle and mutter at the end of the bar, and the woman or two who float around speaking brashly to strangers. It is a place where you'd be happy to consider yourself a regular, though when all is said and done you have nothing at all in common with anyone there except some speechless tenor of spirit only you know a damn thing about.

"Frank, were you ever an athlete?" Walter said forthrightly after our long and studious staring.

"Just an athletic supporter, Walter," I said and gave him a grin to set him at his ease. He obviously had something on his mind; and the sooner he got it out, the sooner I could be blazing a trail west.

Walter smiled back at me ironically, gave his nose a disapproving pinch, pushed up at his glasses. Walter, I realized, was actually a handsome man, and it made me like him. It isn't easy for handsome people to be themselves, or even try to be. And I had a feeling

Walter was trying to be himself for the moment, and I liked him for that reason, though I wished he'd get on with it.

"You were out at Michigan, is that right," Walter asked.

"Right."

"That's Ann Arbor, not East Lansing."

"Right."

"I know that's different." Walter nodded thoughtfully and sniffed again. "You couldn't be an athlete there, I comprehend that. That's like a factory."

"It wasn't that bad."

"I was an athlete out at Grinnell. Anybody could be one. It wasn't a big thing, although I'm sure it's gotten bigger now. I never go back anymore."

"I don't go back to Ann Arbor, either. What'd you do?"

"Wrestled. One forty-five. We wrestled against Carleton and Macalester and those places. I wasn't very good."

"Those are good schools, though."

"They *are* good schools," Walter said. "Though you don't hear much about them. I guess everybody wants to talk about sports, right?" Walter looked at me seriously.

"Sometimes," I said. "But I don't mind it. Other people know a lot more about sports than I do, to tell you the truth. It's a pretty innocent part of people, and talking has the effect of bringing us all together on a good level." I don't know why I started talking to Walter in this Grantland Rice after-dinner speech way, except that he seemed to want that and it was truthfully the only thing I could think of. (It's also true that I believe every word of it, and it's a lot better than talking about some pretentious book that only one person's read.)

Walter moved the ice around in his drink using his finger. "What would you say's the worst part about your job, Frank? I hate traveling myself, and I have to do it. I bet that's it, right?"

"I don't mind it," I said. "There're things about it I'm not sure I could live without anymore. In particular, now that I'm home alone."

"Okay, sure." Walter drank down his scotch in one gulp and

signaled for another in one continuous finger-wiggle gesture. "So it's not the travel. Okay, that's good."

"I think the hardest part about my job, Walter, since you asked, is that people expect me to make things better when I come. If I come to interview them or write about them or just call them up on the phone, they want to be enriched. I'm not talking about money. It's just part of the natural illusion of my profession. The fact is, we can sometimes not make things worse, or we can make things worse. But we can't usually make things better for individuals. Sometimes we can for groups. But then not always."

"Interesting." Walter Luckett nodded as though it was anything but interesting. "What do you mean, worse?"

"I mean sometimes things can seem worse just by not being better. I don't know if I ever thought about it before," I said. "But I think it's right."

"People don't have any right to think you can make life better for them," Walter said soberly. "But it's what they want, all right. I agree."

"I don't know about rights," I said. "It'd be nice if we could. I think I once thought I could."

"Not me," Walter said. "One lousy marriage proved that."

"It's a disappointment. I don't mean marriage is a disappointment. Just ending it."

"I guess." Walter looked down at the fishermen at the dim-lit end of the bar, where they were huddling over some playing cards with fat Evangelis. One of the men laughed out loud, then another man put the cards in his coat pocket and smirked, and the talk got quiet. I would've given anything for a peek at those cards and to have had a good laugh with the fishermen instead of being land-locked with Walter. "Your marriage wasn't disappointing to you, then?" Walter said in a way I found vaguely insulting. Walter had just the tips of his slender fingers touching the glass of scotch, and then he looked at me accusingly.

"No. It was really a wonderful marriage. What I remember of it."

"My wife's in Bimini," Walter said. "My ex-wife, I need to say now. She went down there with a man named Eddie Pitcock, a man I've never seen and know nothing about except his name, which I know from a private detective I hired. I could find out a lot more. But who cares? Eddie Pitcock's his name. Isn't that a name for the guy who runs away with your wife?"

"It's just a name, Walter."

Walter pinched his nose again and sniffed.

"Right. You're right about that. That isn't what I want to talk about anyway, Frank."

"Let talk about sports, then."

Walter stared intently at the fish pictures behind the bar and breathed forcefully through his nose. "I feel pretty self-important hauling you over here like this, Frank. I'm sorry. I'm not usually self-important. I don't want this to be the story of my life." Walter had completely ignored my offer of a good sports conversation, which seemed to mean something more serious was on the way, something I was going to be sorry about. "It isn't a very amusing life. I'm sure of that."

"I understand," I said. "Maybe you just wanted to have a drink and sit in a bar with someone you knew but didn't have to confide in. That makes plenty of sense. I've done that."

"Frank, I went in a bar in New York two nights ago, and I let a man pick me up. Then I went to a hotel with him—the Americana, as a matter of fact—and slept with him." Walter stared furiously out into the fishing pictures. He stared so hard that I knew he would like nothing in the world better than to be one of those happy, proud khaki-clad fishermen displaying his fat stripers to the sun on a happy July day, say, in 1956, when we would have been, Walter and me, eleven years old—assuming we are the same age. I would've been doubly happy at the moment to be there myself.

"Is that what you wanted to tell me, Walter?"

"Yes." Walter Luckett said this as if stunned, looking deadly serious.

"Well," I said. "It doesn't matter to me."

"I know that," Walter said, his chin vaguely moving up and down in a kind of secret nod to himself. "I knew that ahead of time. Or I thought I did."

"Well, that's fine, then," I said. "Isn't it?"

"I *feel* pretty bad, Frank," Walter said. "I don't feel dirty or ashamed. It's not a scandal. I probably ought to feel stupid, but I don't even feel that way. I just feel bad. It's like it's loosed a bad feeling in me."

"Do you think you want to do it again, Walter?"

"I doubt it. I hope not, anyway," Walter said. "He was a nice guy, I'll just say that. He wasn't one of these leather bullies or what have you. And neither am I. He's got a wife and kids up in north Jersey. Passaic County. I'll probably never see him again. And I'll never do that again, I hope. Though I could, I guess. I certainly don't think anyone would care if I did. You know?" Walter drank down his scotch and quickly cut his eyes to me. I wondered if we were talking loud enough for the fishermen to hear us. They would probably have something to say about Walter's experience if we wanted to include them.

"Why do you think you told me, Walter?"

"I think I wanted to tell you, Frank, because I knew you wouldn't care. I felt like I knew the kind of guy you are. And if you did care, I could feel better because I'd know I was better than you. I have some real admiration for you, Frank. I got your book out of the library when I joined the group, though I admit I haven't read it. But I felt like you were a guy who didn't hold opinions."

"I've got a lot of opinions," I said. "But I tend to keep them to myself, usually."

"I know that. But not about something like this. Am I right?"

"It doesn't matter to me. If I have an opinion about it, I'll only know about it later."

"I'd be happy if you wouldn't tell me about it then, frankly, if you do. I don't think it would do me any good. I don't really think of this as a confession, Frank, because I don't really want a response from you. And I know you don't like confessions."

"No, I don't," I said. "I think most things are better if you just let them be lonely facts."

"I agree," Walter said confidently.

"You did tell me, though, Walter."

"Frank, I needed a context. I think that's what friends are for." Walter jiggled ice in his glass in a summary fashion, like a conventioneer.

"I don't know," I said.

"Women are better at this kind of thing, I think," Walter said.

"I never thought about it."

"I think women, Frank, sleep together all the time and don't really bother with it. I believe Yolanda did. They understand friendship better in the long run."

"Do you think you and this fellow, whatever his name is, are friends?"

"Probably not, Frank. No. But you and I are. I can say that I don't have a better friend in the world than you are right now."

"Well that's good, Walter. Do you feel better?"

Walter thumped the space between his brown eyes with his middle finger and let go a deep breath. "No. No. No, I don't. I didn't even think I would, to tell you the truth. I don't think I told you to feel better. Like I said, I didn't want anything back. I just didn't want it to be my secret. I don't like secrets."

"So, how do you feel?"

"About what?" Walter stared at me strangely.

"About sleeping with this man. What else have we been talking about?" I darted a look down the long bar. One of the fishermen was sitting staring at us, apart from the others who were watching a TV above the cash register, watching the Yankees game. The fisherman looked drunk, and I suspected he wasn't really listening to what we were saying, though that was no sign he couldn't hear it by accident. "Or about telling me. I don't know," I said almost in a whisper. "Either one."

"Have you ever been poor, Frank?" Walter glanced at the fisherman, then back at me.

"No. Not really."

"Me, too. Or me either. I haven't been. But that's exactly how I feel now. Like I'm impoverished, just suddenly. Not that I want anything. Not that I even can lose anything. I just feel bad, though I'm probably not going to kill myself."

"Do you think that's what being poor's like? Feeling bad?"

"Maybe," Walter said. "It's my version anyway. Maybe you've got a better one."

"No. Not really. That's fine."

"Maybe we all need to be poor, Frank. Just once. Just to earn the right to live."

"Maybe so, Walter. I hope not. I wouldn't like it much."

"But don't you feel sometimes, Frank, like you're living way up on the top of life, and not really living all of it, all the way down deep?"

"No. I never felt that way, Walter. I just always felt like I was living all the life I could."

"Well, then you're lucky," Walter Luckett said bluntly. He tapped his glass on the bar. Evangelis looked around, but Walter waved him off. He let a couple of ice cubes wiggle around in his mouth a moment. "You've got a date, don't you pal?" He tried to smile around the ice cubes and looked stupid.

"I did, anyway."

"Oh, you'll be fine," Walter said. He laid a crisp five-dollar bill out on the bar. He probably had plenty of such bills in his pocket. He adjusted his sweater around his shoulders. "Let's take a walk, Frank."

We walked out of the bar, past the fishermen and Evangelis, standing under the TV looking up at the color screen and the game. The fishermen who'd been staring at us still sat staring at the space where we'd been. "Come back, fellas," Evangelis said, smiling, though we were already out the door.

Awash down the boat channel and the dark Manasquan River, the night air was fresher than I could've imagined it, a cool, after-rain airishness, an evening to soothe away human troubles. Over the water, halyards were belling on the metal masts in the dark, a lonely elegiac sound. Lighted condos rose above the far river bank.

"Tell me something, would you." Walter took a deep breath and let it out. Two young black men holding their own gear and plastic bait-buckets were loitering on the gangplank of the *Mantoloking Belle,* ready for an all-night adventure. Ben Mouzakis stood in his pilot's house staring down at them from the dark.

"If I can." I said.

Walter seemed to be feeling better in spite of himself. "Why'd you quit writing?"

"Oh that's a long story, Walter." I crammed my hands in my pockets and weasled away a step or two toward my car.

"I guess so, I guess so. Sure. They're all long stories, aren't they?"

"I'll tell you sometime, since we're friends, Walter. But not right now."

"Frank, I'd like that. I really would. Sit down over a drink and hear it all out. We've all got our stories, don't we?"

"Mine's a pretty simple one."

"Well, good. I like 'em simple."

"Take care, Walter. You'll feel better tomorrow."

"You take care, Frank."

Walter started toward his car at the far end of the gravel lot, though when he was twenty yards from me he started running for some reason, and ran until I couldn't see him anymore, only his white shorts and his thin legs fading in the night.

Central Jersey dozed in a sweet spring somnolence. DJ's as far south as Tom's River crooned along the seaboard that it was after eight. Nighttime streets were clearing from Bangor to Cape Canaveral, and I was out of luck with Vicki, though I tried to make good time.

At Freehold I stopped for the hell of it and called her apartment where no one answered; she unplugged the phone after bedtime. I called the nurses' private hospital number—a number I'm not supposed to know, reserved for loved ones in case of emergency; the regular hospital number with the last digit changed to zero. A woman answered in a startled voice and said her records showed Miss Arcenault wasn't scheduled. Was it an emergency? No. Thanks, I said.

For some reason I called my house. The answering machine clicked on with my voice, cheerier than I could bear to hear myself. I beeped for a message and there was X's managerial-professional voice saying she would meet me the next morning. I hung up before she was finished.

Once, when our basset hound, Mr. Toby, was killed by a car that didn't bother to stop—right on Hoving Road—X, in tears, said she wished that time could just be snatched back. Precious seconds and deeds retrieved for a better try at things. And I thought, while I dug the grave behind the forsythias along the cemetery fence, that it was like a woman to grieve over a simple fact in that hopeless-extravagant way. Maturity, as I conceived it, was recognizing what was bad or peculiar in life, admitting it has to stay that way, and going ahead with the best of things. Only that's exactly what I craved now! A precious hour returned to me; a part of Walter's sad disclosures held over till a later date—hardly the best of things.

What's friendship's realest measure?

I'll tell you. The amount of precious time you'll squander on someone else's calamities and fuck-ups.

And as a consequence, zipping along the Jersey darkside past practical Hightstown, feeling ornery as a bunkhouse cook, the baddies suddenly swarmed my car like a charnel mist so dense that not even opening the window would rout them.

Nothing in the world is as hopeful as knowing a woman you like is somewhere thinking about only you. Conversely, there is no badness anywhere as acute as the badness of no woman out in the world thinking about you. Or worse. That one has quit because of some bone-headedness on your part. It is like looking out an airplane window and finding the earth has disappeared. No loneliness can compete with that. And New Jersey, muted and adaptable, is the perfect landscape for that very loneliness, its other pleasures notwithstanding. Michigan comes close, with its long, sad vistas, its desolate sunsets over squatty frame houses, second-growth forests, flat interstates and dog-eared towns like Dowagiac and Munising. But *only* close. New Jersey's is the purest loneliness of all.

By disclosing an intimacy he absolutely didn't have to disclose (he didn't want advice, after all), Walter Luckett was guilty of both spoiling my superb anticipation and illuminating a set of facts-of-life I'd have been happy never to know about.

There are things in this world—plenty of them—we don't need to know the facts about. The noisome fact of two men's snuggle-buggle in some Seventh Avenue drummer's hotel has *no* mystery to it—the way, say, an electric guitar or "the twist" or an old Studebaker have no mystery either. Only facts. Walter and Mr. Whoever could live together twenty years, sell antiques, change to real estate, adopt a Korean child, change their wills, buy a summer house on Vinalhaven, fall out of love a dozen times and back again, go back to women more than once and finally find love together as senior citizens. And still not have it.

By now it seemed more than possible that Vicki had gotten bored and hied off with some oncologist from upstairs, in his dream machine Jag, and at that moment was whirling into the sunset, a thermos of mai tais on the console and Englebert Humperdinck groaning on the eight-track.

What, then, was left for me to do but make the best of things.

I drove to Route 1, then south to Mrs. Miller's little brick ranchette on a long, grassy lot between an Exxon and a Rusty Jones, where a chiropractor once kept a practice. Several older, low-slung bomber cars were in the driveway, and the lights were lit behind drawn curtains, but her *Reader-Adviser* sign was dark. I was too late here, too, though the curtained lights certainly spoke of some secret, possibly exotic goings on inside; enough to excite my curiosity, and in fact enough to excite the curiosity of anyone driving south through the night toward Philadelphia with only glum prospects to consider.

Mrs. Miller and I have done business two years now, since just before X and I got divorced, and I've become a well-known face to all the aunts and uncles and cousins who lounge around inside in the tiny, overfurnished rooms, talking in secret, low voices and drinking coffee at all hours of the day and night. They were probably, I guessed, doing exactly that and no more now, and in fact if I had walked in I'd have been as welcome as a cousin to have an after-hours consultation, inquire about my prospects for the rest of the week. But I preferred to respect her privacy, since, like a writer, her place of business is also her home.

There is nothing complicated about how I began seeing Mrs. Miller. I was driving down Route 1 heading for the hardware store with Clary and Paul in the back seat—we were intent on buying a bicycle pump—and I simply saw her open-palm *Reader-Adviser* sign and pulled in. Probably I had passed it two hundred times over the years, and never noticed. I don't remember feeling out of sorts, though it's not always possible to remember. But I believe when it comes time to see a reader-adviser you know it, if, that is, you aren't at full-scale war with your best instincts.

For a moment I paused at the end of the driveway. I cut my lights and sat a moment watching the windows, since Mrs. Miller, her house, her business, her relatives, her life, posed altogether a small but genuine source of pleasure and wonder. It was as much for that reason that I went to see her once a week, and so found it satisfying enough last night just to be there.

Mrs. Miller's advice, indeed, is almost always just the standard reader-adviser advice and frequently completely wrong: "I see you are coming into much money soon" (not true). "I see a long life" (not likely, though I wouldn't argue). "You are a good man at heart" (uncertain). And she gives me the same or similar advice almost every week, with provisory adjustments that have to do mostly with the weather: "Things will brighten for you" (on rainy days). "Your future is not completely clear" (on cloudy days). There are even days she doesn't recognize me and gives me a puzzled look when I enter. Though she giggles like a schoolgirl when we're finished and says "See you next time" (never using my name), and occasionally dispenses with giving me one of her cards, which has typed at the bottom, below the raised crystal ball emblem: A PLACE TO BRING

YOUR FRIENDS AND FEEL NO EMBARRASSMENT—I AM NOT A GYPSY.
I am certainly not embarrassed to go there, you can bet on that.
Since for five dollars she will lead you into a dimly lit back bedroom
of her sturdy suburban house, where there is plastic-brocade drapery
over the window. (I wondered, first time through, if a little Levantine
cousin or sister wouldn't be waiting there. But no.) There the light
is greenish-amber, and a tiny radio plays softly sinuous Greek-sound-
ing flute music. There is an actual clouded crystal ball on the card
table (she has never used this) and several stacks of oversized tarot
cards. Once we're in place she will hold my hand, trace its tender
lines, wrinkle her brows as if my palm revealed hard matters, look
puzzled or relieved and finally say hopeful, thoughtful things that
no other strangers would ever think to say to me.

She is *the stranger who takes your life seriously*, the personage we all
go into each day in hopes of meeting, the friend to the great mass
of us not at odds with much; not disabled from anything; not "sick"
in the strictest sense.

She herself is a handsome, dusky-skinned woman in her thirties
or forties, a bit overweight and vaguely condescending, but completely agreeable down deep—so much so that at the end of our
conferences she will almost always entertain a question or two as a
bonus. I write these questions on scraps of paper during the week,
though I almost always lose them and end up asking simple, factual-
essential questions like: "Will Paul and Clarissa be safe from harm
this week?" (a continued source of concern for anyone, especially
me). Her answers, in turn, tend always to the bright side concerning
my happiness, though toward the precautionary concerning my children: "No harm will come to them if you are a good father." (I have
told her about Ralph long ago.) Once, in a panic for a good question,
I asked if the Tigers could possibly finish tied for the American
League East, in which case a one-game, winner-take-all tie-breaker
with Baltimore would've been the decider. And this made her angry.
Betting advice, she said, was more expensive than five dollars, and
then charged me ten without giving me an answer.

I have learned over time that when her answers to my questions have been wrong, the best thing to think is that somehow it's my fault things didn't turn out.

But where else can you get, on demand, hopeful, inspiring projections for the real future? Where else, on a windy day in January, can you drive out beset by blue devils and in five minutes be semi-reliably assured by a relative stranger that you are who you think you are, and that things aren't going to turn out so crappy after all?

Would a Doctor Freud be so obliging, I've wondered? Would he be any more likely to know anything, and tell you? I doubt it. In fact, in the bad days after my divorce I met a girl in St. Louis who had by then—she was in her mid-twenties and a buxom looker—spent thousands of dollars and hours consulting the most highly respected psychiatrist in that shadowy bricktop town, until one day she bounced into the office, full of high spirits. "Oh, Dr. Fasnacht," she proclaimed, "I woke up this morning and realized I'm cured! I'm ready to stop my visits and go out into the world on my own as a full-fledged citizen. You've cured me. You've made me so happy!" To which the old swindler replied: "Why, this is disastrous news. Your wish to end your therapy is the most distressing evidence of your terrible need to continue. You are much more ill than I ever thought. Now lie down."

Mrs. Miller would never give anyone such mopish opinions. Her strategy would be to give a much more promising than usual reading for that day, shake your hand, (possibly) forgo the five dollars as a lucky sign and say with eyebrows raised, "Come back when things puzzle you." Her philosophy is: *A good day's a good day. We get few enough of them in a lifetime. Go and enjoy it.*

And that is only the literal part of Mrs. Miller's—what can I call it best? Her service? Treatment? Poor words for mystery. Since for me, mystery is the crucial part, and in fact the *only* thing I find to have value at this stage in my life—midway around the track.

Mystery is the attractive condition a thing (an object, an action, a person) possesses which you know a little about but don't know about completely. It is the twiney promise of unknown things (effects, interworkings, suspicions) which you must be wise enough to explore not too deeply, for fear you will dead-end in nothing but facts.

A typical mystery would be traveling to Cleveland, a town you have never liked, meeting a beautiful girl, going for a lobster dinner during which you talk about an island off of Maine where you have both been with former lovers and had terrific times, and which talking about now revivifies so much you run upstairs and woggle the bejesus out of each other. Next morning all is well. You fly off to another city, forget about the girl. But you also feel differently about Cleveland for the rest of your life, but can't exactly remember why.

Mrs. Miller, when I come to her for a five-dollar consultation, does not disclose the world to me, nor my future in it. She merely encourages and assures me about it, admits me briefly to the mystery that surrounds her own life, which then sends me home with high hopes, aswarm with curiosities and wonder on the very lowest level: Who is this Mrs. Miller if she is not a Gypsy? A Jew? A Moroccan? Is "Miller" her real name? Who are those other people inside— relatives? Husbands? Are they citizens of this state? What enterprise are they up to? Are guns for sale? Passports? Foreign currency? On a slightly higher level: How do *I* seem? (Who has not wanted to ask his doctor that?) Though I am fierce to find out not one fleck more than is incidental to my visitis, since finding out more would only make me the loser, submerge me in dull facts, and require me to seek some other mystery or do without.

As I expected would happen, simply proximity to the glow through her warm curtains—like the antique light of another century—plucked my spirits up like a hitchhiker who catches a ride when all hope was lost. More seemed suddenly possible, and near, whereas before nothing did. Though as I glanced back nostalgically at Mrs. Miller's squared ranchette, I sensed the front door had opened an inch. Someone there was watching me, wondering who I was, what I'd been up to. A love car? The police? A drunk sleeping it off? I was not even sure the door had opened, so that this was as much a riddle to me as I was to whomever I took to be there. A shared riddle, if he/she existed, a perfect give and take in the spirit of a marriage. And I slid off quickly into the south-bound traffic as renewed as a baby born to middle life.

I took the first jug-handle turn and zipped back up the Great Woods Road through the dark apple orchards, sod farms, beefalo barns, the playing fields of De Tocqueville Academy and the modern world-headquarters lawns, all of which keep Haddam sheltered from the dazzling hubcap emporia, dairy barns and swank Radio Shack hurdy-gurdy down Route 1 toward the sullen city of brotherly love. I was not ready for bed now. Far from it. Factuality and loneliness had been put in their places, and an anticipation awakened. The day, changed to a spring evening, held promise only an adventure would unearth.

I idled down Seminary Street, abstracted and empty in the lemony vapor of suburban eventide. (It could always be a sad town.) The two stoplights at either end were flashing yellow, and on the south side of the square only Officer Carnevale waited in his murmuring cruiser, lost in police-radio funk, ready to catch speeders and fleeing ten-speed thieves. Even the seminary was silent—Gothic solemnity and canary lights from the quarreled windows aglimmer through the elms and buttonwoods. Sermonizing midterms were soon, and everybody'd buckled down. Only Carnevale's exhaust said a towny soul was breathing inside a hundred miles, where above the trees the gladlights of New York City paled the sky.

Nine o'clock on the Thursday before Easter far down the suburban train line. A town, almost any town, would seem to have secrets all its own. Though if you believed that you'd be wrong. Haddam in fact is as straightforward and plumb-literal as a fire hydrant, which more than anything else makes it the pleasant place it is.

None of us could stand it if every place were a grizzled Chicago or a bilgy Los Angeles—towns, like Gotham, of genuine woven intricacy. We all need our simple, unambiguous, even factitious townscapes like mine. Places without challenge or double-ranked complexity. Give me a little Anyplace, a grinning, toe-tapping Terre

Haute or wide-eyed Bismarck, with stable property values, regular garbage pick-up, good drainage, ample parking, located not far from a major airport, and I'll beat the birds up singing every morning.

I slowed to take a peek at the marquee of the First Presbyterian, at the edge of the seminary grounds. I occasionally pop in on a given Sunday just to see what they're up to and lift my spirits with a hymn. X and I attended when we first moved here, but she eventually lost interest, and I began working Sundays. Years ago, when I was a senior and in need of an antidote to the puddling, laughless, guilty ironies of midwar Ann Arbor, I began attending a liberal and nondogmatic Westminster group on Maynard Street. The preacher, who referred to himself as a "moderator," was a tall, acned, open-collared scarecrow who aimed his mumbled sermons toward world starvation, the UN and SEATO, and who seemed embarrassed when it came time to stand up and pray and always kept his darting eyes open. A skinny little anorexic wife was his assistant—they were both from Muskegon—and our congregation consisted mostly of elderly professors' widows, a few confused and homely coeds and a homosexual or two just coming to grips with things.

I lasted five weeks, then put my Bible away and started staying up Saturday nights at the fraternity and getting good and drunk. Christianity, like everything else in the Ann Arbor of those times, was too factual and problem-solving-oriented. The spirit was made flesh too matter-of-factly. Small-scale rapture and ecstasy (what I'd come for) were out of the question given the mess the world was in. Consequently I loathed going.

But the First Presbyterians of Haddam offer a good, safe-and-sound approach to things. Their ardent hope is to bring you down to earth by causing your spirit to lift—a kind of complex spiritual orienteering. The regulars all have no doubts about what they're there for; they're there to be saved or give a damned good impression of it, and nobody's pulling the wool over anybody else's eyes.

What I could read off the marquee, however, seemed strange business, though it will probably turn out to be as ordinary as toast—

a trick to lure the once-a-year guys into thinking church has changed.

"The Race To The Tomb"

The preacher will have some witty, eyebrow-arching joke to start off: "Now this fella, Jesus, he was really some heckuva peculiar kind of guy, wouldn't you say so?" And we all would. Then straight away we'd get to the hard-nosed corroborating of the resurrection and suggesting how such a fate might be ours.

I slipped on by, gave Officer Carnevale the lucky thumbs-up, which he managed moodily to return, then drove straight over to The Presidents—up Tyler, down Pierce and winding a sinewy way to Cleveland Street, before stopping under a giant tupelo across from 116, X's little white clapboard colonial. Her Citation sat in the narrow drive, an unknown blue car parked at the curb.

Quick as a ferret I left my car, crossed the street, crouched and laid my hand on the hood of the unknown blue car—a Thunderbird—then stole back to mine before anyone on Cleveland Street could see. As I had hoped, the Bird was as cold as a murderer's heart, and I was relieved to believe it belonged to a neighbor, or to some relative visiting the Armentis next door. Though it could've been a suitor I knew nothing about—one of the fat-belly credit card boys from the country club, a thought which changed relief back to doubt.

My plan had been to pay an innocent visit. I hadn't seen Paul and Clarissa in four days, a long interval in the normal course of our lives. The two of them usually waltz by after school, eat a sandwich, sit and chat together, rummage around their former rooms the way they used to, play Yahtzee or Clue, read books, all while I try by fervent misdirection to prove a continuity in their little lives with my presence. Periodically I quit the work I'm doing and clump upstairs to tease and flirt with them, answer their questions, challenge them and try to woo them back to me in some plain and forthright way, a strategy they're wise to but don't mind because they love me, know I love them, and have no choice, really. We are, all four of us in this, a solid and divided family, doing our level bests to see our duty clearly.

Last night I hoped to stay for a drink, see the kids to bed, yak with X for half an hour, then end up, possibly, spending the night on the couch, something I hadn't done in some time (not, in fact, since I met Vicki) but felt a fierce urge to do suddenly.

Still if I'd gone hat-in-hand up to the door, on a mission of somber fatherhood, I couldn't be sure I wouldn't have interrupted an *intime*—the kids away on overnights at the Armentis, the lights turned up to facilitate the best atmosphere of grownup-bittersweet-excitement-since-so-much-has-gone-before, for the benefit of neighbors interested in seeing a proud woman make the best of a fractured life. I would've been thunderstruck to intercept some well-dressed corporate-level type with love in his eyes, athwart the precise couch I hoped to curl up on. X would've been in her rights to say I'd torpedoed her attempts at getting her feet on the ground, and the fellow would've been in his rights to run me out or punch me. And we'd have both ended up having to leave (the two men always have to trudge off into the night alone, though occasionally they become friends if they meet up later in a bar).

My whole scenario, in short, had lost its glow, and I was left in the dark understory, facing the blue intruder car with nothing to do more than breathe the plush air and endorse X's neighborhood. The Presidents, with their precise fifty-foot frontages, their mature mulberries and straight sidewalks, are actually an excellent location for a young, divorced lady with children, steady means and an independent bent, to dig her heels in. Up and down the street are other young free-thinking people on the way someplace in the world, sharp-eyed, idealistic folks who spotted a good investment and acted fast, and now have some value to sit on. The immigrant Italians who built them (some chosen right out of Sears catalogs) now prefer Delray Beach and Fort Myers and citizens' groups more their own age, and have left their neighborhoods to the young, though hardly ever their own young, who prefer the likes of Pheasant Run and Kendall Park. The banks have proved compassionate with mortgage points and variable rates, and as a result the young liberals—most of them prospering stockbrokers, corporate speech writers, and public defenders—have revived a proud, close-knit neighborhood and property-value ethic where everybody looks after everybody else's kids and grinds their own espresso. Bright new façades and paint jobs. New footings dug. A reshingled weather stoop. Smart art-deco numerals and a pane of discreetly stained glass done at home. All of it promisingly modern.

X, I think, is happy here. My children are close to their school, their friends and me. It is not the same as Hoving Road where we all once hung our hats, but things change in ways none of us can expect, no matter how damn much we know or how smart and good-intentioned each of us is or thinks he is. Who'd know that Ralph would die? Who'd know that certainty would grow rare as diamonds? Who'd know our home would be broken into and everything suddenly break apart? Did Walter Luckett know he'd meet Mr. Wrong two nights ago and alter his life again after his wife already had? No, you bet not. None of our lives is really ordinary; nothing humdrum in our delights or our disasters. Everything is as problematic as geometry when it's affairs of the heart in question. A life can simply change the way a day changes—sunny to rain, like the song says. But it can also change again.

The clock at St. Leo the Great sounded ten, and something began happening at 116 Cleveland.

The yellow stoop light flashed on. Someone inside spoke in a tone of patient instruction, and the front door opened. My son, Paul, stepped out.

Paul in tennis shorts, and a Minnesota Twins shirt I brought him from a trip I took. He is ten, small and not overly clever yet, a serious, distractable boy with a good heart, and all the sweet qualities of second sons: patience, curiosity, some useful inventiveness, sentimentality, a building vocabulary, even though he is not much of a reader. I have tried to think that things will turn out well for him, though when we powwow up in his room, a place he keeps furnished with Sierra Club posters of eagles and large Audubon mergansers and grebes, he always seems to display a moody enthrallment, as if there is some sovereign event in his life he senses is important but cannot for some reason remember. Naturally I am very proud of him, and his sister, too. They both carry on like soldiers.

Paul had brought outside with him one of the birds from his dovecote. A mottled rock dove, a handsome winger. He toted it manfully to the curb, using the two-handed professional bird handler's way he's taught himself. I surveilled him like a spy, slumped behind the steering wheel, the shadow of the big tupelo making me not especially noticeable, though Paul was too intent on his own business to see me.

At the curb he took the pigeon in one small hand, slipped the hood and neatly pocketed it. The bird cocked its head peckishly at his new surroundings. The sight, though, of Paul's familiar, serious face calmed it.

Paul studied the pigeon for a time, grappling it once again in both hands, and via the still darkness I could hear his boy's voice talking. He was coaching the bird in some language he had practiced. "Remember this house." "Fly this special route." "Be careful of this hazard or that obstacle." "Think of all we've worked on." "Remember who your friends are"—all of it good advice. When he'd finished, he held the bird to his nose and sniffed behind its beaky head. I saw him close his eyes, and then it was up, pitched, the bird's large bright wings seizing the night instantly, up and gone and out of sight like a thought, its wings white and then quickly small as it cleared the closure of trees—gone.

Paul looked up a moment, watching it. Then, as if he'd forgotten all about any loosed bird, he turned and stared at me across the street, slouched like Officer Carnevale in my cruiser car. He had seen me probably for quite some time, but had gone on with his business like a big boy who knows he's watched and doesn't care for it, but understands those are the rules.

Paul walked across the street in his little boy's ungainly gait but with a gainly smile, a smile he'd give, I know, to a total stranger.

"Hi Dad," he said through the window.

"Hi, Paul."

"So what's up?" He still smiled at me like an innocent boy.

"Just sort of sitting here now."

"Is it all right?"

"It's great. Whose car's that out front there?"

Paul looked back behind him at the Thunderbird. "The Litzes."
(Neighbor, lawyer, no problem.) "Are you coming inside?"

"I just wanted to check up on you folks. Just being a patrol car."

"Clary's asleep. Mom's watching news," Paul said, adopting his
mother's way of dropping definite articles, a midwest mannerism.
They went to market. She has flu. We bought tickets.

"Who was that you gave his freedom to?"

"Ole Vassar." Paul looked up the street. Paul names his birds
after hillbilly tunesters—Ernest, Chet, Loretta, Bobby, Jerry Lee—
and had adopted his father's partiality for *ole* as a term of pure
endearment. I could've hauled him through the window and hugged
him till we both cried out, so much did I love him at that moment.
"I didn't give him his freedom right off, though."

"Old Vassar has a mission first, then?"

"Yes sir," Paul said and looked down at the pavement. It was
clear I was burdening his privacy, of which he has plenty. But I
knew he felt he had to talk about Vassar now.

"What's Vassar's mission?" I asked bravely.

"To see Ralph."

"Ralph. What's he going to see Ralph for?"

Paul sighed a small boy's put-on sigh, transformed back from a
big boy. "To see if he's all right. And tell him about us."

"You mean it's a report."

"Yeah. I guess." Head still down at the pavement.

"On all of us?"

"Yeah."

"And how did it come out?"

"Good." Paul avoided my eyes in another direction.

"My part okay, too?"

"Your part wasn't too long. But it was good."

"That's all right. Just so I made it in. When's Ole Vassar reporting back?"

"He isn't. I told him he could live in Cape May."

"Why is that?"

"Because Ralph's dead. I think."

I had taken him and his sister to Cape May only last fall, and I was interested now that he supposed the dead lived there. "It's a one-way mission, then."

"Right."

Paul stared fiercely at the door of my car and not at me, and I could sense he was confused by all this talk of dead people. Kids are most at home with sincerity and the living (who could blame them?), unlike adults, who sometimes do not have an unironical bone in their bodies, even for things that are precisely in front of them and can threaten their existence. Paul's and mine, though, has always been a friendship founded on sincerity's rock.

"What do you know tonight to tickle me?" I said. Paul is a secret cataloger of corny jokes and can make anyone laugh out loud, even at a joke they've heard before, though he often chooses to withhold. I myself envy his memory.

For this question, though, he had to consider. He wagged his head backwards in pretend-thought, and stared into the tree boughs as if all the good jokes were up there. (What did I say about things always changing and surprising us? Who would've thought a drive down a dark street could produce a conversation with my own son! One in which I find out he's in contact with his dead brother—a promising psychological indicator, though a bit unnerving—plus get to hear a joke as well.)

"Ummm, all right," Paul said. He was all Johnny now. By the way he stuffed his hands in his pockets and averted his mouth I could tell he thought it was a pretty funny one.

"Ready?" I said. With anyone else this would spoil the joke. But with Paul it is protocol.

"Ready," he said. "Who speaks Irish and lives in your back yard?"

"I don't know." I give in straight away.

"Paddy O'Furniture." Paul could not hold back his laughter a second and neither could I. We both held our sides—he in the street, I in my car. We laughed like monkeys loud and long until tears rose in his eyes and mine, and I knew if we did not rein ourselves in, his mother would be out wondering (silently) about my "judgment." Ethnics, though, are among our favorite joke topics.

"That's a prize-winner," I said, wiping a tear from my eye.

"I have another one, too. A better one," he said, grinning and trying not to grin at the same time.

"I have to drive home now, sonny," I said. "You'll have to remember it for me."

"Aren't you coming inside?" Paul's little eyes met mine. "You can sleep on the couch."

"Not tonight," I said, joy bounding in my heart for this sweet Uncle Milty. I would've accepted his invitation if I could, taken him up and tickled his ribs and put him in his bed. "Rain Czech." (One of our oldest standbys.)

"Can I tell Mom?" He had sprung past the strange confusion of my not coming inside, and on to the next most important issue: disclosure, the reporting of what had happened. In this he is not at all like his father, but he may come to it in time.

"Say I was driving by, and saw you and we stopped and had a conversation like old-timers."

"Even though it isn't true?"

"Even though it isn't true."

Paul looked at me curiously. It was not the lie I had instructed him to tell—which he might or might not tell, depending on his own ethical considerations—but something else that had occurred to him.

"How long do you think it'll take Ole Vassar to find Ralph?" he said very seriously.

"He's probably almost there now."

Paul's face went somber as a churchman's. "I wouldn't like it to take forever," he said. "That'd be too long."

"Goodnight, son," I said, suddenly full of anticipation of quite another kind. I started my motor.

"Goodnight, Dad." He broke a smile for me. "Happy dreams."

"You have happy dreams your own self."

He walked back across Cleveland Street to his mother's house, while I eased away into darkness toward home.

5

The air in Detroit Metro is bright crackling factory air. New cars revolve glitteringly down every concourse. Paul Anka sings tonight at Cobo Hall, a flashing billboard tells us. All the hotels are palaces, all the residents our best friends. Even Negroes look different here—healthy, smiling, prosperous, expensive-suited, going places with briefcases.

Our fellow passengers are all meeting people, it turns out, and are not resident Michiganders at all, though they all have come from here originally, and their relatives are their mirror-image: the women ash-blond, hippy, smiling; the men blow-dried and silent-mouthed, secretive, wearing modern versions of old-time car coats and Tyroleans, earnest beefsteak handshakes extended. This is a car coat place, a place of wintry snuggle-up, a place I'm glad to have landed. If you seek a beautiful peninsula, look around you.

Barb and Sue walk us down the concourse. They have bags-on-wheels, snazzy red blazers and shoulder purses, and they are both in jolly moods. They are looking forward to "fun weekends," they say, and Sue gives Vicki a big lascivious wink. Barb says that Sue is married to a "major hunk" from Lake Orion who owns a bump shop, and that she may quit flying soon to get the oven warmed up. She and Ron, her own husband, she says, "are still 'dining out.' "

"Don't let this old gal fool ya," Sue sings out with a big grin. "She's a party doll. The things I could tell you would fill a book. Some of the trips we go on. Whoa." Sue rolls her eyes and snaps her blond head famously.

"Just don't pay any attention to all that," Barb says. "Just enjoy yourselves, you two, and hev a seef trip home."

"We surely will," Vicki boasts, smiling her newcomer's smile. "And you have a nice night, too, okay?"

"No stopping us," Sue calls back, and off the two go toward the crew check-in, gabbing like college girls with the handsomest boys on campus waiting at the curb in big convertibles and the house-mother already hoodwinked.

"Weren't they just nice?" Vicki says, looking sentimentally de-tached in the midst of the mile-long Detroit bustle. She has grown momentarily pensive, though I suspect this is also from too much anticipation, and she will be herself in a jiffy. She is a great antic-ipator, as much as I am and maybe more. "I didn't realize those gals were that nice and all."

"They sure were," I say, thinking of all the cheerleaders Sue and Barb are the spitting image of. Put a bulky letter-sweater on either of them, a flippy pleated skirt and bobby sox, and my heart would swell for them. "They were wonderful."

"How wonderful?" Vicki says, giving me a suspicious frown.

"About one half as wonderful as you." I grab her close to me high up under her tender arm. We are awash in shuffling Detroiters, a rock in a stream.

"Lilacs are pretty, too, but they make an ugly bush," Vicki says, her eyes knowledgeable and small. "You've got the wander-eye, mister. No wonder your wife signed them papers on you."

"That's in the past, though," I say. "I'm all yours, if you want me. We could get married right now."

"I had one forever already that didn't last," Vicki says, meanly. "You're talking like a nut now. I just came here to see the sights, so let's go see 'em." She beetles her brows as if something had briefly confused her, then the shiny smile breaks through once again and she reclaims the moment. I am, of course, talking like a nut, though I'd marry her in a flash, in the airport nondenominational chaplain's office, with a United skycap as my best man, Barb and Sue as cosmetologically perfect bridesmaids. "Let's get the bags, what d'ya say, boy?" she says, perky now, and on the move. "I want to get a look at that big tire 'fore they tear the sucker down." She arches her brows at me and there's a secret fragrant promise embedded, a sex code known only to nurses. How can I say no? "You sure have got a case of the dismal stares, all of a suddenly," she says, ten yards away now. "Let's get going."

Anything can happen in another city. I had forgotten that, though it takes a real country girl to bring it home. Then I'm away, catching up, smiling, trundling on eager feet toward the baggage carrousels.

*D*etroit, city of lost industrial dreams, floats out around us like a mirage of some sane and glaciated life. Skies are gray as a tarn, the winds up and gusting. Flying papers and cellophane skirmish over the Ford Expressway and whap the sides of our suburban Flxible like flak as we lug our way toward Center City. Flat, dormered houses and new, brick-mansard condos run side by side in the complicated urban-industrial mix. And, as always, there is the expectation of new "weather" around the corner. Batten down the hatches. A useful pessimism abounds here and awaits.

I have read that with enough time American civilization will make the midwest of any place, New York included. And from here that seems not at all bad. Here is a great place to be in love; to get a land-grant education; to own a mortgage; to see a game under the lights as the old dusky daylight falls to blue-black, a backdrop of stars and stony buildings, while friendly Negroes and Polacks roll their pants legs up, sit side by side, feeling the cool Canadian breeze off the lake. So much that is explicable in American life is made in Detroit.

And I could be a perfect native if I wasn't settled in New Jersey. I could move here, join the Michigan alums and buy a new car every year right at the factory door. Nothing would suit me better in middle life than to set up in a little cedar-shake builder's-design in Royal Oak or Dearborn and have a try at another Michigan girl (or possibly even the same one, since we would have all that ready-made to build on). My magazine could install me as the midwest office. It might even spark me to try my hand at something more adventurous—a guiding service to the northern lakes, for example. A change to pleasant surroundings is always a tonic for creativity.

•   •   •

"It's just like it's still winter here." Vicki's nose is to the bus's tinted window. We have passed the big tire miles back. She peered at it silently as we drifted by, a tourist seeing a lesser pyramid. "Well," she said as a big fenced-in Ford plant, flat and wide as Nebraska, hauled next into view, "I got that all behind me."

"If you don't like the weather, wait ten minutes. That's an expression we used to say in college."

She fattens her cheeks as Walter Reuther Boulevard flashes by, then the Fisher Building and the lumpish Olympia rises in the furred, gray distance. "They say that in Texas all the time. They prob'ly say it everywhere." She looks back at the cityscape. "You know what my daddy says about De-troit?"

"He must not've liked it very much."

"When I told him I was coming out today with you, he just said, 'If De-troit was ever a state, it'd be New Jersey.' " She smiles at me cunningly.

"Detroit doesn't have the diversity, though I really like both places."

"He likes New Jersey, but he didn't like this place." We swerve into the long concrete trench of the Lodge freeway, headed to midtown. "He hasn't ever liked a place much, which I always thought was kind of a shame. This place doesn't look so bad, though. Lots of colored, but that's all right with me. They gotta live, too." She nods seriously to herself, then takes my hand and squeezes it as we enter a vapor-lit freeway tunnel which takes us to the riverfront and the Pontchartrain.

"This was the first city I ever knew. We used to come into town when I was in college and go to burlesque shows and smoke cigars. It seemed like the first American city to me."

"That's the way Dallas is to me. I'm not upset to be gone from it, though. Not a little teensy." She purses her lips hard and turns loose of my hand. "My life's lots better now, I'll tell you that."

"Where *would* you rather be?" I ask as the milky light of Jefferson Avenue dawns into our dark bus and passengers begin to murmur and clutch belongings up and down the aisle. Someone asks the driver about another stop farther along the hotel loop. We are all of us itchy to be there.

Vicki looks at me solemnly, as if the gravity of this city had entered her, making all lightheartedness seem sham. She is a girl who knows how to be serious. I had hoped, of course, she'd say there's no place she'd rather than with m-e me. But I cannot mold *all* her wishes to my model for them, fulfill her every dream as I do my own. Yet she is as unguarded to this Detroit chill as I am, and secretly it makes me proud of her.

"Didn't you say you went to college around here somewhere?" She's thinking of something hard for her to come to, a glimmering of a thought.

"About forty miles away."

"Well, what was that like?"

"It was a nice town with trees all around. A nice park for spring afternoons, decent profs."

"Do you miss it? I bet you do. I bet it was the best time in your life and you wish you had it back. Tell the truth."

"No ma'am," I say. And it's true. "I wouldn't change from right this moment."

"Ahhh," Vicki says skeptically, then turns toward me in her seat, suddenly intense. "Do you swear to it?"

"I swear to it."

She fastens her lips together again and smacks them, her eyes cast to the side for thinking power. "Well, it idn't true with me. This is to answer where would I rather be."

"Oh."

Our Flxible comes hiss to a lumbering stop in front of our hotel. Doors up front fold open. Passengers move into the aisle. Behind Vicki out the tinted glass I see Jefferson Avenue, gray cars moiling by and beyond it Cobo, where Paul Anka is singing tonight. And far away across the river, the skyline of Windsor—glum, low, retrograde, benumbed reflection of the U.S. (The very first thing I did after Ralph was buried was buy a Harley-Davidson motorcycle and take off driving west. I got as far as Buffalo, halfway across the

Peace Bridge, then lost my heart and turned back. Something in Canada had taken the breath of spirit out of me, and I promised never to go back, though of course I have.)

"When I think about where would I rather be," Vicki says dreamily, "what I think about is my first day of nursing school out in Waco. All of us were lined up in the girls' dorm lobby, clear from the reception desk out to the Coke machine between the double doors. Fifty girls. And across from where I was standing was this bulletin board behind a little glass window. And I could see myself in it. And written on that bulletin board in white letters on black was 'We're glad you're here' with an exclamation. And I remember thinking to myself, 'You're here to help people and you're the prettiest one, and you're going to have a wonderful life.' I remember that *so* clearly, you know? A very wonderful life." She shakes her head. "I always think of that." We are last to leave the bus now, and other passengers are ready to depart. The driver is folding closed the baggage doors, our two sit on the damp and crowded sidewalk. "I don't mean to be ole gloomy-doomy."

"You're not a bit of gloomy-doomy," I say. "I don't think that for a minute."

"And I don't want you to think I'm not glad to be here with you, because I am. It's the happiest day of my life in a long time, 'cause I just love all of this so much. This big ole town. I just love it so much. I didn't need to answer that right now, that's all. It's one of my failings. I always answer questions I don't need to. I'd do better just going along."

"It's me that shouldn't ask it. But you're going to let me make you happy, aren't you?" I smile hopefully at her. What business do I have wanting to know any of this? I'm my own worst enemy.

"I'm happy. God, I'm *real* happy." And she throws her arms around me and cries a tiny tear on my cheek (a tear, I want to believe, of happiness), just as the driver cranes his neck in and waves us out. "I'd marry you," she whispers. "I didn't mean to make fun of you asking me. I'll marry you any time."

"We'll try to fit it into our agenda, then," I say and touch her moist soft cheek as she smiles through another fugitive tear.

And then we are up and out and down and into the dashing wet wind of Detroit, and the squabbly street where our suitcases sit in a sop of old melted snow like cast-off smudges. A lone policeman stands watching, ready to chart their destination from this moment on. Vicki squeezes my arm, her cheek on my shoulder, as I heft the two cases. Her plaid canvas is airy; mine, full of sportswriter paraphernalia, is a brick.

And I feel exactly what at this debarking moment?

At least a hundred things at once, all competing to take the moment and make it their own, reduce undramatic life to a gritty, knowable kernel.

This, of course, is a minor but pernicious lie of literature, that at times like these, after significant or disappointing divulgences, at arrivals or departures of obvious importance, when touchdowns are scored, knock-outs recorded, loved ones buried, orgasms notched, that at such times we are any of us altogether *in* an emotion, that we are within ourselves and not able to detect other emotions we might also be feeling, or be about to feel, or prefer to feel. If it's literature's job to tell the truth about these moments, it usually fails, in my opinion, and it's the writer's fault for falling into such conventions. (I tried to explain all of this to my students at Berkshire College, using Joyce's epiphanies as a good example of falsehood. But none of them understood the first thing I was talking about, and I began to feel that if they didn't already know most of what I wanted to tell them, they were doomed anyway—a pretty good reason to get out of the teaching business.)

What I feel, in truth, as I swing these two suitcases off the wet concrete and our blue bus sighs and rumbles from the curbside toward its other routed hotels, and bellboys lurk behind thick glass intent on selling us assistance, is, in a word: a *disturbance*. As though I were relinquishing something venerable but in need of relinquishing. I feel a quickening in my pulse. I feel a strong sense of lurking evil (the modern experience of pleasure coupled with the certainty that it will end). I feel a conviction that I have no ethics at all and little consistency. I sense the possibility of terrible regret in the brash air. I feel the need suddenly to confide (though not in Vicki or anyone else I know). I feel as literal as I've ever felt—stranded, uncomplicated as an immigrant. All these I feel at once. And I feel the urge—which I suppress—to cry, the way a man would, for these same reasons, and more.

That is the truth of what I feel and think. To expect anything less or different is idiotic. Bad sportswriters are always wanting to know such things, though they never want to know the truth, never have a place for that in their stories. Athletes probably think and feel the fewest things of anyone at important times—their training sees to that—though even they can be counted on to have more than one thing in their mind at a time.

"I'll carry my own bag," Vicki says, pressed against me like my shadow, sniffing away a final tear of arrival happiness. "It's light as a feather duster."

"You're not going to do anything from now on out but have fun," I say, both bags up and moving. "You just let me see a smile."

And she smiles a smile as big as Texas. "Look, I ain't p.g., you know," she says as the pneumatic hotel doors glide away. "I always carry what's mine."

It is four-thirty by the time we get to our room, a tidy rectangle of pretentious midwestern pseudo-luxury—a prearranged fruit basket, a bottle of domestic champagne, blue bachelor buttons in a Chinese vase, red-flocked whorehouse wall décor and a big bed. There is an eleventh-story fisheye view upriver toward the gaunt Ren-Cen and gray pseudopodial Belle Isle in the middle distance—the shimmer-lights of suburbs reaching north and west out of sight.

Vicki takes a supervisory look in all spaces—closets, shower, bureau drawers—makes ooo's and oh's over what's here free of charge by way of toiletries and toweling, then establishes herself in an armchair at the window, pops the champagne and begins to take everything in. It is exactly as I'd hoped: pleased to respectful silence by the splendor of things—a vote that I have done things the way they were meant to be.

I take the opportunity for some necessary phoning.

First, a "touch base" call to Herb to firm up tomorrow's plans. He is in laughing good spirits and invites us to have dinner with him and Clarice at a steak place in Novi, but I plead fatigue and prior commitments, and Herb says that's great. He has become decidedly upbeat and shaken his glumness of the morning. (He is on pretty serious mood stabilizers, is my guess. Who wouldn't be?) We hang up, but in two minutes Herb calls back to check whether he's given me right directions for the special shortcut once we leave I-96. Since his injury, he says, he's suffered mild dyslexia and gets numbers turned around half the time with some pretty hilarious results. "I do the same thing, Herb," I say, "only I call it normal." But Herb hangs up without saying anything.

Next I call Henry Dykstra, X's father, out in Birmingham. I have made it my policy to keep in touch with him since the divorce. And though things were strained and extremely formal between us while X's and my affairs were in the lawyers' hands, we have settled back since then into an even better, more frank relationship than we ever had. Henry believes it was Ralph's death pure and simple that caused our marriage to go kaput, and feels a good measure of sympathy for me—something I don't mind having, even if my own beliefs about these matters are a good deal more complex. I have also stayed an intermediary message-carrier between Henry and his wife, Irma, out in Mission Viejo, since she writes to me regularly, and I have let him know that I can be trusted to keep a confidence and to relay timely information which is often something surprisingly intimate and personal. "The old plow still works," he once asked me to tell her, and I did, though she never answered that I know of. Families are very hard to break apart forever. I know that.

Henry is a robust seventy-one and, like me, has not remarried, though he often makes veiled but conspicuous references to women's names without explanation. My personal belief—seconded by X—

is that he's as happy as a ram living on his estate by himself and would've had it that way from the day X was born if he could've negotiated Irma. He is an industrialist of the old school, who worked his way up in the Thirties and has never really understood the concept of an intimate life, which I contend is not his fault, though X thinks otherwise and sometimes claims to dislike him.

"We're going broke, Franky," Henry says, in a bad temper. "The whole damn country has its pants around its ankles to the unions. And we elected the S.O.B.s who're doing it to us. Isn't that something? Republicans? I wouldn't give you a goddamned nickel for the first one they ever made. I stand somewhere to the right of Attila the Hun, I guess is what that means."

"I'm not much up on it, Henry. It sounds tricky to me."

"Tricky! It isn't tricky. If I wanted to steal and lay off everybody at my plant I could live for a hundred years, exactly the way I live now. Never leave the house. Never leave the chair! I came up a Reuther man, you know that, Frank. Life-long. It's these gangsters in Washington. All of them. They're all goddamn criminals, want to run me in the ground. Retire me out of the gasket business. What's going on at home, anyway? You still divorced?"

"Things're great, Henry. Today's Ralph's birthday."

"Is that so?" Henry does not like to talk about this, I know, but for me it is a day of some importance, and I don't mind mentioning it.

"I think he would've made a fine adult, Henry. I'm sure of that."

For a moment then there is stupefied emptiness in our connection while we think over lost chances.

"Why don't you come out here and we'll get drunk," Henry says abruptly. "I'll have Lula fix duck en brochette. I killed the sons-of-bitches myself. We can call up some whores. I've got their private phone numbers right here. Don't think I don't call them, either."

"That'd be great, Henry. But I'm not alone."

"Got a shady lady with you yourself?" Henry guffaws.

"No, a nice girl."

"Where're you staying?"

"Downtown. I have to go back tomorrow. I'm on business today."

"Okay, okay. Tell me why you think our golfing friend left you, Frank? Tell the truth. I can't get it off my mind today, for some damn reason."

"I think she wanted her life put back in her own hands, Henry. There's not much else to it."

"She always thought I ruined her life for men. It's a hell of a thing to hear. I never ruined anybody's life. And neither did you."

"I don't really think she thinks that now."

"She *told* me she did last week! As late as that. I'm glad I'm old. It's enough life. You're here, then you're not."

"I wasn't always such a great guy, Henry. I tried hard but sometimes you can just fool yourself about yourself."

"Forget all that," Henry says. "God forgave Noah. You can forgive yourself. Who's your shady lady?"

"You'd like her. Her name's Vicki." Vicki swings her smiling head around and holds up a glass of champagne to toast me.

"Bring her out here, I'll meet her. What a name. Vicki."

"Another visit, Henry. We're on a short schedule this time." Vicki goes back to watching the night fall.

"I don't blame you," Henry says brashly. "You know, Frank, sometimes the fact of living with somebody makes living with them impossible. Irma and I were just like that. I sent her to California one January, and that was twenty years ago. She's a lot happier. So you stay down there with Vicki whatever."

"It's hard to know another person. I admit that."

"You're better off assuming anybody'll do anything, anytime, than that they won't. That way you're safe. Even my own daughter."

"I wish I could come out there and get drunk with you, Henry, that's the truth. I'm glad we're pals. Irma told me to tell you she'd seen a real good performance of *The Fantasticks* in Mission Viejo. And it made her think of you."

"Irma did?" Henry says. "What's the fantastics?"

"It's a play."

"Well, that's good then, isn't it?"

"Any messages to go back? I'll probably write her next week. She sent me a birthday card. I could add something."

"I never really knew Irma, Frank. Isn't that something?"

"You were pretty busy making a living, though, Henry."

"She could've had boyfriends and I wouldn't have even noticed. I hope she did. *I* certainly did. All I wanted."

"I wouldn't worry about that. Irma's happy. She's seventy years old."

"In July."

"What about a message. Anything you want to say?"

"Tell her I have bladder cancer."

"Is that true?"

"I *will* have, if I don't have something else first. Who cares anyway?"

"I care. You have to think of something else, or I'll think of something for you."

"How's Paul and how's Clarissa?"

"They're fine. We're taking a car trip around Lake Erie this summer. And we'll be stopping to see you. They're already talking about it."

"We'll go up to the U.P."

"There might not be time for that." (I hope not.) "They just want to see you. They love you very much."

"That's great, though I don't know how they could. What do you think about the Maize and Blue, Franky?"

"A powerhouse, is my guess, Henry. All the seniors are back, and the big Swede from Pellston's in there again. I hear pretty awesome stories. It's an impressive show out there." This is the only ritual part of our conversations. I always check with the college football boys, particularly our new managing editor, a little neurasthenic, chain-smoking Bostonian named Eddie Frieder, so I can pass along some insider's information to Henry, who never went to college, but is a fierce Wolverine fan nonetheless. It is the only use he can think to make of my profession, and I'm not at all sure he doesn't concoct an interest just to please me, though I don't much like football per se. (People have some big misunderstandings about sportswriters.) "You're going to see some fancy alignments in the defensive backfield this fall, that's all I'll say, Henry."

"All they need now is to fire that meathead who runs the whole show. He's a loser, if you ask me. I don't care how many games he wins."

"The players all seem to like him, from what I hear."

"What the hell do they know? Look. The means don't always justify the end to me, Frank. That's what's wrong with this country. You ought to write about that. The abasement of life's intrinsic qualities. That's a story."

"You're probably right, Henry."

"I feel hot about this whole issue, Frank. Sports is just a paradigm of life, right? Otherwise who'd care a goddamn thing about it?"

"I know people can see it that way." (I try to avoid that idea, myself.) "But it's pretty reductive. Life doesn't need a metaphor in my opinion."

"Whatever that means. Just get rid of that guy, Frank. He's a Nazi." Henry says this word to rhyme with snazzy in the old-fashioned way. "His popularity's his biggest threat." In fact, the coach in question is quite a good coach and will probably end up in the Hall of Fame in Canton, Ohio. He and Henry are almost exactly alike as human beings.

"I'll pass a word along, Henry. Why don't you write a letter to *The Readers Speak.*"

"I don't have time. You do it. I trust you that far."

Light is falling outside the Pontchartrain now. Vicki sits in the shadows, her back to me, hugging her knees and staring out toward the Seagram's sign upriver half a mile, red and gold in the twilight, while little Canuck houses light up like fireflies on a dark and faraway lake beach where I have been. I could want nothing more than to hug her now, feel her strong Texas back, and fall into a nestle we'd break off only when the room service waiter tapped at our door. But I can't be sure she hasn't lulled to sleep in the sheer relief of expectations met—one of life's true blessings. In a hundred ways we could not be more alike, Vicki and I, and I miss her badly, though she is only twelve feet away and I could touch her shoulder in the dark with hardly a move (this is one of the prime evils of being an anticipator).

"Frank, we don't amount to much. I don't know why we go to the trouble of having opinions," Henry says.

"It puts off the empty moment. That's what I think."

"What the hell's that? I don't know what that is."

"Then you must've been pretty skillful all your life, Henry. That's great, though. It's what I strive for."

"How old will you be next birthday? You said you had a birthday." For some reason Henry is gruff about this subject.

"Thirty-nine, next week."

"Thirty-nine's young. Thirty-nine's nothing. You're a remarkable man, Frank."

"I don't think I'm that remarkable, Henry."

"Well no, you're not. But I advise you, though, to think you are. I'd be nowhere if I didn't think I was perfect."

"I'll think of it as a birthday present, Henry. Advice for my later years."

"I'll send you out a leather wallet. Fill it up."

"I've got some ideas that'll do just as good as a fat wallet."

"Is this this Vicki trick you're talking about?"

"Right."

"I agree wholeheartedly. Everybody ought to have a Vicki in his life. Two'd even be better. Just don't marry her, Frank. In my experience these Vickis aren't for marrying. They're sporting only."

"I've got to be going now, Henry." Our conversations often tend this way, toward his being a nice old uncle and then, as if by policy, making me want to tell him to go to hell.

"Okay. You're mad at me now, I know it. But I don't give a goddamn if you are. I know what I think."

"Fill your wallet up with that then, Henry, if you get my meaning."

"I get it. I'm not an idiot like you are."

"I thought you said I was pretty remarkable."

"You are. You're a pretty remarkable moron. And I love you like a son."

"This is the point to hang up now, Henry. Thanks. I'm glad to hear that."

"Marry my daughter again if you want to. You have my permission."

"Good night, Henry. I feel the same way." But like Herb Wallagher, Henry has already hung up on me, and never hears my parting words, which I sing off into the empty phone lines like a wilderness cry.

Vicki has indeed gone to sleep in her chair, a cold stream of auto lights below, pouring up Jefferson toward the Grosse Pointes: Park, Farms, Shores, Woods, communities tidy and entrenched in midwestern surety.

I am hungry as an animal now, though when I rouse her with a hand on her soft shoulder, ready for a crab soufflé or a lobsteak, amenable to à la carte up on the revolving roof, she wakes with a different menu in mind—one a fellow would need to be ready for the old folks' home to pass up. (She has drunk all the champagne, and is ready for some fun.)

She reaches and pulls me onto her chair so I'm across her lap and can smell the soft olive scent of her sleepy breath. Beyond the window glass in the starless drifting Detroit night an ore barge with red and green running lights aglow hangs on the current toward Lake Erie and the blast furnaces of Cleveland.

"Oh, you sweet old sweet man," Vicki says to me, and wiggles herself comfortable. She gives me a moist soft kiss on the mouth, and hums down in her chest. "I read someplace that if the Taurus tells you he loves you, you're s'posed to believe it. Is that so?"

"You're a wonderful girl."

"Hmmmm. But . . . " She smiles and hums.

I have a good handful of her excellent breast now, and what a wonderful bunch she is, a treasure trove for a man interested in romance. "Doesn't that make you happy?"

"Oh, that does. You know that. You're the only one for me." She is no part a dreamer, I know it, but a literalist from the word go, happy to let the world please her in the small ways it can (true of fewer and fewer people, women especially). Though it is probably not an easy thing to be here with me, in a strange glassy hotel in a cold and sinister town, strange as man to a mandrill, and to believe you are in love.

"Oh, my my my," she whispers.

"Tell me what'll make you happiest. That's what I'm here for, and that's the truth" (or most of it).

"Well, don't let's sit on this ole chair all night and let that big ole granddaddy bed go to waste. I'm a firecracker just thinking about you. I didn't think you'd *ever* get off that phone."

"I'm off now."

"You better look out then."

And then the cold room folds around us, and we become lost in simple nighttime love gloom, boats rafted together through a blear passage of small perils. A fair, tender Texas girl in a dark séance. Nothing could be better, more cordial than that. Nothing. Take this from a man who knows.

*B*efore my marriage ended but after Ralph died, in that wandering two-year period when I bought a Harley-Davidson, drove to Buffalo, taught at a college, suffered that dreaminess I have only lately begun to come out from under, and began to lose my close moorings with X without even noticing the slippage, I must've slept with eighteen different women—a number I don't consider high, or especially scandalous or surprising under the circumstances. X, I'm sure, knew it, and in retrospect I can see that she did her best to accommodate it, tried to make me feel not so miserable by not asking questions, not demanding a strict accounting of my days when I would be off working in some sports mecca—a Denver or a St. Louis—expecting, I feel sure, that one day or other I would wake up out of it, as she thought she already had (but probably at this moment would be willing to doubt, wherever she might be—safe I hope).

None of this would've been so terrible, I believe, if I hadn't reached a point with the women I was "seeing," at which I was trying to simulate complete immersion—something anyone who travels for a living knows is a bad idea. But when times got bad, I would, for example, find myself after a game alone in the pressbox of some concrete and steel American sports palace. Often as not there would be a girl reporter finishing up her late running story (my eyes were sharpened for just such stragglers), and we would end up having a few martinis in some atmospheric-panoramic bar, then driving out in my renter to some little suburban foot-lit lanai apartment with rattan carpets, where a daughter waited—a little Mandy or Gretchen—and no hubby, and where before I knew it the baby would be asleep, the music turned low, wine poured, and the reporter and I would be plopped in bed together. And bango! All at once I was longing with all my worth to be a part of that life, longing to enter completely into that little existence of hers as a full (if brief) participant, share her secret illusions, hopes. "I love you," I've heard myself say more than once to a Becky, Sharon, Susie or Marge I hadn't known longer than *four hours and fifteen minutes!* And being absolutely certain I did; and, to prove it, loosing a barrage of pryings, human-interest questions—demands, in other words, to know as many of the whys and whos and whats of her life as I could. All of it the better to get *into* her life, lose that terrible distance that separated us, for a few drifting hours close the door, simulate intimacy, interest, anticipation, then resolve them all in a night's squiggly romance and closure. "Why did you go to Penn State when you could've gone to Bryn Mawr?" *I see.* "What year did your ex-husband actually get out of the service?" *Hmmm.* "Why did your sister get along better with your parents than you did?" *Makes sense.* (As if knowing anything could make any difference.)

This, of course, was the world's worst, most craven cynicism. Not the invigorating little roll in the hay part, which shouldn't bother anyone, but the demand for full-disclosure when I had nothing to disclose in return and could take no responsible interest in anything except the hope (laughable) that we could "stay friends," and how early I could slip out the next morning and be about my business or head for home. It was also the worst kind of sentimentalizing—feeling sorry for someone in her lonely life (which is what I almost always felt, though I wouldn't have admitted it), turning that into pathos, pathos into interest, and finally turning that into sex. It's exactly what the worst sportswriters do when they push their noses into the face of someone who has just had his head beaten in and ask, "What were you thinking of, Mario, between the time your head began to look like a savage tomato and the moment they counted you out?"

What I was doing, though I didn't figure it out until long after I'd spent three months at Berkshire College—living with Selma Jassim, who wasn't interested in disclosure—was trying to be within myself by being as nearly as possible *within* somebody else. It is not a new approach to romance. And it doesn't work. In fact, it leads to a terrible dreaminess and the worst kind of abstraction and unreachableness.

How I expected to be within some little Elaine, Barb, Sue or Sharon I barely knew when I wasn't even doing it with X *in my own life* is a good question. Though the answer is clear. I couldn't.

Bert Brisker would probably say about me, that at that time I wasn't "intellectually pliant" enough, since what I was after was illusion complete and on a short-term, closed-end basis. And what I should've been happy with was the plain, elementary rapture a woman—any woman I happened to like—could confer, no questions asked, after which I could've gone home and let life please me in the ways I'd always let it. Though it's a rare man who can find real wonder in the familiar, once luck's running against him—which it was.

By the time I came back from teaching three months, which was near the end of this two years, I'd actually quit the whole business with women. But X had been home with Paul and Clary, and had not been communicating, and had begun reading *The New Republic*, *The National Review* and *China Today*, something she'd never done before, and seemed remote. I fell immediately into a kind of dreamy monogamy that did nothing but make X feel like a fool—she said so eventually—for putting up with me until her own uncertainty got aroused. I was around the house every day, but not around to do any good for anybody, just reading catalogs, lying charitably to avoid full disclosure, smiling at my children, feeling odd, visiting Mrs. Miller weekly, musing ironically about the number of different answers I could give to almost any question I was asked, watching sports and Johnny on television, wearing putter pants and plaid shirts I'd bought from L.L. Bean, going up to New York once a week and being a moderately good but committed sportswriter—all the while X's face became indistinct, and my voice grew softer and softer until it was barely audible, even to me. Her belief—at least her way of putting things since then—was that I'd grown "untrustworthy," which is not surprising, since I probably was, if what she wanted was to be made happy by my making life as certain as could be, which I could've sooner flown than do then. And when I couldn't do that, she just began to suspect the worst about everything, for which I don't blame her either, though I could tell that wasn't a good idea. I contend that I felt pretty trustworthy then, in spite of everything—if she could've simply trusted just that I loved her, which I did. (Married life requires shared mystery even when all the facts are known.) I'd have come around before too long, I'm sure of that, and I'd have certainly been happy to have things stay the way they were while hoping for improvements. If you lose all hope, you can always find it again.

Only our house got broken into, hateful Polaroids scattered around, the letters from the woman in Kansas found, and X seemed suddenly to think we were too far gone, farther gone than we knew, and life just seemed unascendant and to break between us, not savagely or even tragically, just ineluctably, as the real writers say.

A lot happens to you in your life and comes to bear midway: your parents can die (mine, though, died years before), your marriage can change and even depart, a child can succumb, your profession can start to seem hollow. You can lose all hope. Any one thing would be enough to send you into a spin. And correspondingly it is hard to say what *causes* what, since in one important sense *everything* causes everything else.

So with all this true, how can I say I "love" Vicki Arcenault? How can I trust my instincts all over again?

A good question, but one I haven't avoided asking myself, for fear of causing more chaos in everybody's life.

And the answer like most other reliable answers is in parts.

I have relinquished a great deal. I've stopped worrying about being completely *within* someone else since you can't be anyway—a pleasant unquestioning mystery has been the result. I've also become less sober-sided and "writerly serious," and worry less about the complexities of things, looking at life in more simple and literal ways. I have also stopped looking around what I feel to something else I might be feeling. With all those eighteen women, I was so bound up creating and resolving a complicated illusion of life that I lost track of what I was up to—that I ought to be having a whale of a good time and forget about everything else.

When you are fully in your emotions, when they are simple and appealing enough to be in, and the distance is closed between what you feel and what you might *also* feel, then your instincts can be trusted. It is the difference between a man who quits his job to become a fishing guide on Lake Big Trout, and who one day as he is paddling his canoe into the dock at dusk, stops paddling to admire the sunset and realizes how much he wants to be a fishing guide on Lake Big Trout; and another man who has made the same decision, stopped paddling at the same time, felt how glad he was, but also thought he could probably be a guide on Windigo Lake if he decided to, and might also get a better deal on canoes.

Another way of describing this is that it's the difference between being a literalist and a factualist. A literalist is a man who will enjoy an afternoon watching people while stranded in an airport in Chicago, while a factualist can't stop wondering why his plane was late out of Salt Lake, and gauging whether they'll still serve dinner or just a snack.

And finally, when I say to Vicki Arcenault, "I love you," I'm not saying anything but the obvious. Who cares if I don't love her forever? Or she me? Nothing persists. I love her now, and I'm not deluding myself or her. What else does truth have to hold?

A t twelve-forty-five I am awake. Vicki sleeps beside me, breathing lightly with a soft clicking in her throat. In the room there is the dense dimensionless feeling of going to sleep in the dark though waking up still in the dark and wondering about the hours till dawn: how many will there be still? Will I suffer some unexpected despair? How am I likely to pass the time? I am usually—as I've said—such a first-rate sleeper that I'm not bothered by these questions. Though I'm certain part of my trouble is the ordinary thrill of being here, with this woman, free to do anything I please—that familiar old *school's out* we all look and hope for. Tonight would be a good time to take a solo walk in the dark city streets, turn my collar up, get some things thought out. But I have nothing to think out.

I turn on the television with the sound off, something I often do when I'm on the road alone, while I browse a player roster or sharpen up some notes. I love the television in other cities, the assurance of looking up from my chair in some strange room to see a familiar newscaster talking in his familiar Nebraska accents, clad in a familiarly unappealing suit before a featureless civic backdrop (I can never remember the actual news); or to see an anonymous but completely engrossing athletic event acted out in a characterless domed arena, under the same lemony light, to the tune of the same faint zizzing, many miles from anywhere my face would be known. These comprise a comfort I would not like to do without.

On television the station reruns a pro basketball game I am only too happy to watch. Detroit plays Seattle. (Reruns, incidentally, are where you learn a game inside and out. They're far superior to the actual game in the actual place it's played, where things are usually pretty boring and you often forget altogether about what you're there for and find yourself getting interested in other things.)

I go get Vicki's Le Sac bag, open it up and take out one of her Merits, and light it. I have not smoked a cigarette in at least twenty years. Not since I was a freshman in college and attended a fraternity smoker where older boys gave me Chesterfields and I stood against a wall, hands in pockets, and tried to look like the boy everyone would want to ask to join: the silent, slender southern boy with eyes older than his years, something already jaded and over-experienced about him. Just the one we need.

While I'm at it, I push down through the bag. Here is a rosary (predictable). The United inflight magazine (swiped). A card of extra pearlescent buttons (useful). Car keys to the Dart on a big brass ring with a V insignia. An open tube of Velamints. Two movie ticket stubs from a theater where Vicki and I saw part of an old Charlton Heston movie (until I fell asleep). The flight-insurance policy. A paperback copy of a novel, *Love's Last Journey*, by someone named Simone La Noire. And a fat, brown leather wallet with a tooled western-motif of a big horse head on shiny grain.

In it—right up front—is a picture of a man I've never seen before, a swank-looking greaseball character, wearing an open-collared white shirt and a white big-knit shepherd's roll cardigan. The fellow has thick, black eyebrows, a complicated but strict system of dark hair waves, narrow eyeslits and a knifey smile set in the pouting, mocking angle of swarthy self-congratulation. Around his pencil-neck is a gold cross on a chain. It is Everett.

The carpet king from the other Big D is a leering, hip-sprung lounge lizard in a fourth-rate Vegas motel; the kind of fellow who wears his cigarettes under his shirt sleeve, possesses long, skinny arms and steely fingers, and as a policy drinks huge amounts of cheap beer at all hours of the day and night. I would recognize him anywhere. Lonesome Pines was full of such types, from the best possible homes, and all capable of the sorriest depravities. I couldn't be more disappointed to find his picture here. Nor more perplexed. It's possible that he is a superior, good-natured yokel and were we ever to meet (which we won't), we'd cement a sensible common ground from which to express earnestly our different opinions about the world. (Sports, in fact, is the perfect *lingua franca* for such crabwise advances between successive boyfriends and husbands who might otherwise fall into vicious fistfights.)

But in truth I couldn't give a damn about Everett's selling points. And I am of a mind to flush his picture down the commode then stand my ground when the first complaint is offered.

I take a deep, annoyed drag on my cigarette and attempt a difficult French Inhale I once saw practiced in college. But the smoke gets started backwards in my throat and not up my nose, and suddenly I'm seized by a terrifying airlessness and have to suppress a horrible gagging. I make a swift stagger into the bathroom and close the door to keep from waking Vicki with a loud grunt-cough that purples my face.

In the bathroom mirror I resemble a wretched sex-offender— cigarette dangling in my fingers, blue-piped pajamas rumpled, my face gaunt from gasping, the stern light pinching my eyes narrow as Everett's. I am not a pretty sight, and I'm not a bit happy to see myself here. I should have gone out in the streets alone and figured out something to figure out. Certain situations dictate to you how they should be used to advantage. And you should always follow the conventional wisdom in those cases—in fact, in all cases. Always go up on deck to watch the sun come up. Always take a late-night swim after your hosts are in bed. Always take a hike in the woods near your friends' cabin and try to find a new route to the waterfall or an old barn to explore. If nothing else you save yourself giving in to a more personal curiosity and the trouble that always seems to cause. I have gone poking around after full disclosure before my disavowal of it is barely out of my mouth—a disappointing testimony to self-delusion, even more disappointing than finding dagger-head Everett's picture in Vicki's pocketbook where, after all, it had every right to be and I had none.

When I exit the bathroom Vicki is seated at the dressing table, smoking one of her own Merits, elbow on the chair back, the TV off, looking sultry and alien as a dancehall girl. She is wearing a black crepe de Chine "push up" nightgown and matching toeless mules. I don't like the spiky looks of this (though it's conceivable I might've liked it earlier in the evening) since it looks like something Everett would like, might even have bought himself as a final, fragrant memento. I would not stand for it one minute if I was calling the shots, which I'm not.

"I didn't mean to wake you up," I say balefully and slink to the end of the big granddaddy bed, two feet from her sovereign knees, where I take a seat. Evil has begun to lurk the room, ready to grip with its cold literal claws. My heart begins pounding the way it was when I woke up this morning, and I feel as if my voice may become inaudible.

I am caught. Though I would save the moment, save us from anger and regret and even more disclosure, the enemy of intimacy. I wish I could blurt out a new truth; that I suffer from a secret brain tumor and sometimes do inexplicable things I afterwards can't discuss; or that I'm writing a piece on pro basketball and need to see the end of the Seattle game where Seattle throws up a zone and everything comes down to one shot the way it always does. The saved moment is the true art of love.

Staring, though, at Vicki's sculptured, vaguely padded knees, I now am clearly lost and feel the ultimate slipping away again, bereavement threatening like thunder to roll in and take its place.

"So what is it you were lookin for in my bag?" she says. Hers is a frown of focused disdain. I am the least favorite student caught looking for the gradebook in the teacher's desk. She is the friendly substitute there for one day only (though we all wish she were the regular one) but who knows a sneak when she sees him.

"I wasn't looking for anything, really. I wasn't looking." I *was* looking, of course. And this is the wrong lie, though a lie is absolutely what's needed. My first tiny skirmish with the facts goes into the debit column. My voice falls ten full decibels. This has happened before.

"I don't keep secrets," she says now in a flat voice. "I suppose you do though."

"Sometimes I do." I lose nothing admitting that.

"And you lie about things, too."

"Only if it's completely necessary. Otherwise never." (It is better than confiding.)

"And like lovin me, too, I guess?"

A sweet girl's heart only speaks truths. Evil suddenly takes an unexpected rebuke. "You're wrong there," I say, and nothing could be truer.

"Humph," she says. Her brow gathers over small prosecutorial eyes. "And I'm s'pose to believe that now, right? With you rammaging around my things and smokin cigarettes and me dreaming away?"

"You don't have to believe it for it to be true." I put my elbows on my knees, honest-injun style.

"I hate a snake," she says, looking coldly around at the ashtray beside her as if a dead snake were coiled right there. "I just swear I do. I stay way clear of 'em. Cause I seen plenty. Right? They're not hard to recognize, either." She cuts her eyes away at the door to the hall and sniffs a little mirthless laugh. "That was just a lie on me, wadn't it?"

"The only way you'll find that out, I guess, is just to stay put." Out in the chilly streets I hear a police siren wail down the wide, dark avenue and drawl off into the traffic. Some poor soul is having it worse than I am.

"So what about getting married?" she says archly.

"That, too."

She smirks her mouth into a look of disillusionment and shakes her head. She stubs out her cigarette carefully in the ashtray. She has seen this all before. Motel rooms. Two A.M. Strange sights. The sounds of strange cities and sirens. Lying boys out for the fun and a short trip home. Empty moments. The least of us has seen a hundred. It is no wonder mystery and its frail muted beauties have such a son-of-a-bitching hard time of it. They're way outnumbered and ill-equipped in the best of times.

"Well-o-well," she says and shrugs, hands down between her knees in a fated way.

But still, something has been won back, some aspirant tragedy averted. I am not even sure what it is, since evil still floods the room up to the cornices. The Lebanese woman I knew at Berkshire College would never have let this happen, no matter what I had done to provoke it, since she was steeled for such things by a life of Muslim disinterest. X wouldn't either, though for other, even better reasons (she expected more). Vicki is hopeful, but not of much, and so is never far from disappointment.

Still, the worst reconciliation with a woman is better than the best one you work out with yourself.

"There's nothing in this bag worth stealin, or even finding out about," Vicki says wearily, everting her lips at her weekender as if it were a wreckage that has washed ashore after years of not being missed. "Money," she says languidly, "I keep hid in a special place. That's one secret I keep. You won't get that."

I want to hug her knees, though this is clearly hands-to-yourself time. The slightest wrong move will see me on the phone locating another room on another floor, possibly in the Sheraton, four cold and lonely blocks away, and no coat to keep out the slick Canadian damp.

Vicki peers over at the glass desktop, at her wallet open alongside her cigarettes. The snapshot of brain-dead Everett leers upwards (it may in fact be hard to tell my somber, earnest face from his).

"I really believe there's only six people in the world," she says in a softened voice, staring down at Everett's mug. "I'd been thinking you might be one. An important one. But I think you had too many girlfriends already. Maybe you're somebody else's one."

"You might be wrong. I could still make the line-up."

She looks at me distrustfully. "Eyes are important to me, okay? They're windows to your soul. And your eyes . . . I used to think I could see your soul back in there. But now. . . ." She shakes her head in doubt.

"What do you see?" I don't want to hear the answer. It is a question I would never even ask Mrs. Miller, and one she'd never take it upon herself to speculate about. We do not, after all, deal in truths, only potentialities. Too much truth can be worse than death, and last longer.

"I don't know," Vicki says, in a thin wispy way, which means I had better not pursue it or she'll decide. "What're you so interested in my stepbrother for?" She looks at me oddly.

"I don't know your stepbrother," I say.

She picks up the wallet and holds the snapshot up so I am looking directly into the swarthy smart-aleck's face. "Him," she says. "This poor old thing, here."

So much of life can't be foreseen. A hundred private explanations and exculpations come rushing up into my throat, and I have to swallow hard to hold them back. Though, of course, there is nothing to say. Like all needless excuses, the unraveling is not worth the time. However, I feel a swirling dreaminess, an old familiar bemusement, suddenly rise into my appreciation of everything around me. Irony is returned. I have a feeling that if I tried to speak now, my mouth would move, but no sound would occur. And it would scare us both to death. Why, in God's name, isn't it possible to let ignorance stay ignorance?

"That poor boy's already dead and gone to heaven," Vicki says. She turns the picture toward her and looks at it appraisingly. "He got killed at Fort Sill, Oklahoma. A Army truck hit him. He's my Daddy's wife's son. Was. Bernard Twill. Beany Twill." She pops the wallet closed and puts it on the table. "I didn't even really know him. Lynette just gave me his picture for my wallet when he died. I don't know how come I kept it." She looks at me in a sweet way. "I'm not stayin mad. It's just an old purse with nothin in it. Women're strange on their purses."

"I'm going to get back in bed," I say in a voice that is hardly a whisper.

"Long as you're happy, to hell with the rest. That's a good motto, isn't it?"

"Sure. It's great," I say, crawling into the big cold bed. "I'm sorry about all this."

She smiles and sits looking at me as I pull the sheet up around my chin and begin to think that it is not a hard life to imagine, not at all, mine and Vicki Arcenault's. In fact, I would like it as well as it's possible to like any life: a life of small flourishes and clean napkins. A life where sex plays an ever-important nightly role—better than with any of the eighteen or so women I knew before and "loved." A life appreciative of history and its generations. A life of possible fidelity, of going fishing with some best friend, of having a little Sheila or a little Matthew of our own, of buying a fifth-wheel travel trailer—a cruising brute—and from its tiny portholes seeing the country. Paul and Clarissa could come along and join our gang. I could sell my house and move not to Pheasant Run but to an old Quakerstone in Bucks County. Possibly when our work is done, a tour in the Peace Corps or Vista—of "doing something with our lives." I wouldn't need to sleep in my clothes or wake up on the floor. I could forget about being *in* my emotions and not be bothered by such things.

In short, a natural extension of almost all my current attitudes taken out beyond what I now know.

And what's wrong with that? Isn't it what we all want? To look out toward the horizon and see a bright, softened future awaiting us? An attractive retirement?

Vicki turns on the television and takes up a rapt stare at its flicking luminance. It's ice skating at 2 A.M. (basketball's a memory). Austria, by the looks of it. Cinzano and Rolex decorate the boards. Tai and Randy are skating under steely control. He is Mr. Elegance—flying camels, double Salchows, perfect splits and lofts. She is all in the world a man could want, vulnerable yet fiery, lithe as a swan, in this their once-in-a-lifetime, everything-right for a flawless 10. Together they perform a perfect double axel, two soaring triple toe loops, a spinning Lutz jump, then come to rest with Tai in a death spiral on the white ice, Randy her goodly knight. And the Austrians cannot control it one more second. These two are as good as the Protopopovs, and they're Americans. Who cares if they missed the Olympics? Who cares if rumors are true that they despise each other? Who cares if Tai is not so beautiful up close (who is, *ever*)? She is still exotic as a Berber with regal thighs and thunderous breasts. And what's important is they have given it their everything, as they always do, and every Austrian wishes he could be an American for just one minute and can't resist feeling right with the world.

"Oh, don't you just love them two?" Vicki says, sitting cross-legged on her chair, smoking a cigarette and peering into the brightly lit screen as though staring into a colorful dream-life.

"It's pretty wonderful," I say.

"Sometimes I want to be her *so* much," she says, blowing smoke out the corner of her mouth. "Really. Ole Randy. . . ."

I turn and close my eyes and try to sleep as the applause goes on, and outside in the cold Detroit streets more sirens follow the first one into the night. And for a moment I find it is really quite easy and agreeable not to know what's next, as if the sirens were going out into this night for no one but me.

6

Snow. By the time I leave my bed, a blanket of the gently falling white stuff has covered the concrete river banks from Cobo to the Ren-Cen, the river sliding by brackish and coffee-colored under a quilted Michigan sky. So much for a game under the lights. Spring has suddenly disappeared and winter stepped in. I am certain by tomorrow the same weather will have reached New Jersey (we are a day behind the midwest in weather matters), though by then, here will have thawed and grown mild again. If you don't like the weather, wait ten minutes.

Vicki is still deep asleep in her black crepe de Chine, and though I would like to wake her and have a good heart-to-heart, last night feels otherwordly, and optimism about "us two" is what's in need of emphasizing. A talk can always wait till later.

I shower and dress in a hurry, pockets loaded with note pads and a small recorder, and head off to breakfast and my trip to Walled Lake. I leave a note on the bed table saying I'll be back by noon, and she should watch a movie on HBO and have a big breakfast sent up.

The Pontchartrain lobby has a nice languorous-sensuous Saturday feel despite the new snow, which the bellhops all agree is "freakish" and can't last past noon, though a number of guests are lining up to check out for the airport. The black newsstand girl sells me a *Free Press* with a big smile and a yawn. "I'm bout shoulda stayed in bed," she laughs in a put-on accent. On the rack there is an issue of my magazine with a story I wrote about the surge in synchronized swimming in Mexico—all the digging work was done by staff. I'm tempted to make some mention of it just in passing, but I wander off to breakfast instead.

In the La Mediterranée Room I order two poached, dry toast and juice, and ask the waiter to hurry, while I check on the early leaders in the AL East—who's been sent down, who's up for a cup of coffee. The *Free Press* sports section has always been my favorite. Photographs galore. A crisp wide-eyed layout with big, readable coldtype print and a hometown writing style anyone could feel at home with. There is a place for literature, but a bigger one for sentences that are meant to be read, not mused over: "Former Brother Rice standout, Phil Staransky, who picked up a couple timely hits in Wednesday's twi-nighter, on the way to going three-for-four, already has plenty of experts around Michigan and Trumbull betting he'll see more time at third before the club starts its first swing west. Pitching Coach Eddie Gonzalez says there's no doubt the Hamtramck native 'figures in the big club's plans, especially,' Gonzalez notes, 'since the young man left off trying to pull everything and began swinging with his head.' " When I was in college I had a pledge bring it right to my bed every morning, and was even a mail subscriber when we first moved to Haddam. From time to time I think of quitting the magazine and coming back out to do a column. Though I'm sure it's too late for that now. (The local sports boys never take kindly to the national magazine writers because we make more money. And in fact, I've been given haywire information from a few old beat writers, which, if I'd used it, would've made me look stupid in print.)

It has the feeling of an odd morning, despite the friendly anonymity of the hotel. A distinct buzzing has begun in the pit of my stomach, a feeling that is not unpleasant but insistent. Several people I saw in the lobby have reminded me of other people I know, an indicator that something exceptional's afoot. A man in the checkout line reminded me of—of all people—Walter Luckett. Even the black shop girl put me in mind of Peggy Connover, the woman I used to write in Kansas and whose letters caused X to leave me. Peggy, in fact, was Swedish and would laugh to think she looked a bit Negroid. Like all signs, these can be good or bad, and I choose to infer from them that life, anyone's life, is not as disconnected and random as it might feel, and that down deep we're all reaching out for a decent rewarding contact every chance we get.

Last night, after Vicki went to sleep, I experienced the strangest dream, a dream I've never had before and one I would rather not have again. I am not much of a dreamer to begin with, and almost never remember them past the moment just before my eyes open. When I do, I can usually ascribe everything to something I've eaten in the afternoon, or to a book I'd been reading. And for the most part there's never much that's familiar in them anyway.

But in this dream I was confronted by someone I knew—a man— but had forgotten—though not completely, because there were flashes of recollection I couldn't quite organize into a firm picture-memory. This man mentions to me—so obliquely that now I can't even re- member what he said—something shameful about me, clearly shameful, and it scares me that he might know more and that I've forgotten it, but shouldn't have. The effect of all this was to shock me roundly, though not to wake me up. When I did wake up at eight, I remembered the entire dream clear as a bell, though I could not fill in names or faces or the shame I might've incurred.

Besides not being a good collector of my dreams, I am not much a believer in them either or their supposed significance. Everyone I've ever talked to about dreams—and Mrs. Miller, I'm happy to say, feels exactly as I do, and will not listen to anyone's dreams— everyone always interprets their dreams to mean something un- pleasant, some lurid intention or ungenerous, guilty desire crammed back into the subconscious cave where its only chance is to cause trouble at a later time.

Whereas what *I* am a proponent of is forgetting. Forgetting dreams, grievances, old flaws in character—mine and others'. To me there is no hope unless we can forget what's said and gone before, and forgive it.

Which is exactly why this particular dream is bothersome. It is *about* forgetting, and yet there seems to be a distinct thread of un- forgiving in it, which is the source of the shock I felt even deep in sleep, in an old town where I feel as comfortable as a Cossack in Kiev, and where I want nothing more than that the present be happy and for the future—as it always does—to look after itself. I would prefer to think of all signs as good signs, or else to pay no attention to them at all. There are enough bad signs all around (read the *New York Times*) not to pick out any particular one for attention. In the case of my dream, I can't even think of what I ought to be anxious about, since I am eager—even ascendant. And if it is that I'm anxious in the old mossy existential sense, it will have to stay news to me.

It is, of course, an irony of ironies that X should've left me because of Peggy Connover's letters, since Peggy and I had never committed the least indiscretion.

She was a woman I met on a plane from Kansas City to Minneapolis, and whom in the space of an afternoon, a dinner, and an evening, I came to know as much about as you could know in that length of time. She was thirty-two and not at all an appealing woman. She was plump with large, white teeth and a perfectly pie-shaped face. She was leaving her family with four children, back in the town of Blanding, Kansas, where her husband sold insulation, to go live with her sister in northern Minnesota and become a poet. She was a good-natured woman, with a nice dimpled smile, and on the plane she began to tell me about her life—how she had gone to Antioch, studied history, played field hockey, marched in peace marches, written poems. She told me about her parents who were Swedish immigrants —a fact that had always embarrassed her; that she dreamed sometimes of huge trucks going over cliffs and woke up terrified; about writing poems that she showed to her husband, Van, then hearing him laugh at them, though he later told her he was proud of her. She told me she had been a sexpot in college, and had married Van, who was from Miami of Ohio, because she loved him, but that they weren't on the same level educationally, which hadn't mattered then, but did now, which was why she felt she was leaving him.

When we got off the plane she asked me, standing in the concourse, where I was staying, and when I told her the Ramada, she said she could just as easily stay there and that maybe we could have dinner together because she liked talking to me. And since I had nothing else to do, I said okay.

In the next five hours we had a buffet dinner, then after that went down to my room to drink a bottle of German wine she had bought for her sister, and she talked some more, with me just adding a word here and there. She told me about her break with Lutheranism, about her philosophy of child-rearing, about her theories of Abstract Expressionism, the global village, and a Great Books course she'd built up to teach somewhere if the chance ever came along.

At eleven-fifteen, she stopped talking, looked down at her pudgy hands and smiled. "Frank," she said, "I just want to tell you that I've been thinking about sleeping with you this whole time. But I don't really think I should." She shook her head. "I know we're supposed to do what our senses dictate, and I'm very attracted to you, but I just don't think it would be right, do you?"

Her face looked troubled by this, but when she looked at me a big hopeful smile came on her lips. And what I felt for her then was a great and comprehending nostalgia, because for some reason I thought I knew just exactly how she felt, alone and at the world's mercy, the same way I'd felt when I'd been in the Marines, suffering from an unknown disease with no one but unfriendly nurses and doctors to check on me, and I had had to think about dying when I didn't want to. And what it made me feel about Peggy Connover was that I wanted to make love to her—more, in fact, than I'd wanted to do that in a long time. It's possible, let me tell you, to become suddenly attracted to a woman you don't really find attractive; a woman you'd never want to take to dinner, or pick up at a cocktail party, or look twice at in an elevator, only just suddenly it happens, which was the case with Peggy.

Though what I said was, "No, Peggy, I don't think it would be right. I think it'd cause a lot of trouble." I don't know why I said this or said it in this way, since it wasn't what *my* senses were dictating.

Peggy's face lit up with pleasure, and also, I think, surprise. (This is always the most vulnerable time in such encounters. At the very moment you absolve yourself of any intention to do wrong, you often roll right into each other's arms. Though we didn't.) What happened was that Peggy came over to the bed where I was sitting, sat beside me, took my hand and squeezed it, gave me a big damp kiss on the cheek and sat smiling at me as if I were a man like no other. She told me how lucky she felt to meet me and not some "other type," since she was vulnerable that night, she said, and probably "fair game." We talked for a while about how she was probably going to feel in the morning after having drunk all that wine, and that we would probably want a lot of coffee. Then she said that if it was all right she'd like to find something I'd written and read it and write me about it. And I said I'd like that. Then as if by some secret signal she came around the bed, pulled back the covers, climbed in beside me and went immediately to snoring sleep. I slept beside her the rest of the night fully clothed, on top of the covers, and never touched her once. And in the morning I left before she woke up, to go interview a football coach, and never saw her again.

After about a month, a fat letter—the first of several from Peggy Connover—arrived at the house, full of talk about her kids, humorous remarks about her welfare, her weight, her ailments, about Van, whom she'd decided to go back to live with, what plans she was making for their life; but also about stories of mine she'd read in the magazine and had comments on (she liked some but not every one), all of it in the same chatty voice as when we'd talked, closing each time with "Well, Frank, hope to see you again real soon. Love, Peg." All of which I was happy to hear about, and even answer a time or two, since it pleased me that, as we had never been more than friends, we could still be, with everything hunky-dory. And it pleased me that somewhere out in the remote world someone was thinking of me for no bad reason at all, and even wishing me well.

These, of course, were the letters X found in the drawer of my desk when she was looking for the sack of silver dollars she feared might've been stolen. And it was these letters that in some way made our life seem to break apart for her, and made continuing somehow seem impossible (I found it likewise impossible to explain anything then, since much else was wrong already). X believed, I think, when she read Peggy Connover's letters, that if these chatty, normal over-the-fence-sounding sentiments were hidden there in my drawer (they weren't hidden, of course), in all probability more letters full of similar good sense and breezy humor were going out (she was right). And that there was none of that around the house for her. And she began to think, then, that love was simply a transferable commodity for me—which may even be true—and she didn't like that. And what she suddenly concluded was that she didn't want to, or have to, be married to someone like me a second longer—which is exactly how it happened.

*O*utside, it is no longer snowing, but the streets impress me as too icy to risk a rental car. Our time in town feels already much too short, and in bad weather even the idea of the botanical garden begins to sink into the unlikely zone—though for Vicki, my guess is, it will make no difference.

I'm sorry, however, to miss a renter. There is nothing quite like the first moments inside a big, strapping fleet-clean LTD or Montego—mileage checked, tank full, seat adjusted, the heavy door closed tight, the stirring "new" smell in your nostrils—the confidence that here is a car better even than the one you own (and even better than that, since you have only to ask for another one if this one craps out). To me, there is no feeling of freedom-within-sensible-limits quite like that. New today. New tomorrow. Eternal renewal on a manageable scale.

I walk down to the snowy cab queue at Larned Street, but as I reach the icy corner I am stopped short and for a moment by a sound. On the chill Saturday morning airs, a faint *hsss* murmurs up the city streets from the sewers and alleyways, as if a cold wind was thrashing ditch grass somewhere nearby and, out here near the river, on the edge of things, I was in danger. Of what I have no idea. Though what I know, of course, is that I am running a tricky race now with my spirits, trusting my enthusiasm will outstrip the perils of usual, midwestern literalness which can gang up against you quick and do you in like a doomed prisoner.

My cab driver is a giant Negro named Lorenzo Smallwood, who reminds me of the actor Sydney Greenstreet, and who drives with both arms straight out in front of him. On the dashboard he has an assortment of small framed pictures of babies, two pairs of baby shoes and a mat of white fringe, though he is not much for talking, and we get quickly out into the snowy traffic, weaving around dingy warehouse blocks and old hotels to Grand River, then head for the northwest suburbs. It is faster today, Mr. Smallwood says with humming uninterest, to stay on the "real streets," and avoid "the Lodge," where it's already wall-to-wall assholes heading for their cabins up north.

Strathmore, Brightmoor, Redford, Livonia, another Miracle Mile. We speed through the little connected burgs and townlets beyond the interior city, along white-frame dormered-Cape streets, into solider red-brick Jewish sections until we emerge onto a wide boulevard with shopping malls and thick clusters of traffic lights, the houses newer and settled in squared-off tracts. Outside everyone is "dressed for it," a point of traditional pride among Michiganders. A freak spring snowstorm means nothing. Everyone still has "snows" on his Plymouth, and a winter face of workmanlike weather how-to. Michigan is a place where every man is handy with a jumper cable, a metal lathe and a snow blower. The mechanical nuts-and-bolts of anything is never a problem here. It's what's reliable and appealing in such an otherwise gray and unprepossessing panorama.

Far out crowded Grand River I am struck by what seems like thousands of restaurants, and by how dedicated the population is to going out to eat. As much as cars, meals are what's on people's minds. Though there is a small and heart-swelling glory to these places—chop houses, hofbraus, rathskellers, rib joints, cafés of all good quality. Part of life's essence is here. And on a brooding spring eve, a fast foray out to any one of them can be just enough to make any out-of-the-way loneliness bearable another nighttime through.

In most ways, I can promise you, Michigan knows exactly what it's doing. It knows the enemy and the odds.

Mr. Smallwood pulls into a white enamel drive-in called The Squatter, and asks if I want a sinker. I am full to the gills from breakfast, but while he is inside I step out and give a call back to the Pontchartrain. I have briefly won back some enthusiasm for the day—the buzzing in my stomach having subsided—and I want to share it all with Vicki, since there is no telling what new world and circumstances she has waked to, given the night's shenanigans and the strange, whitened landscape confronting her in the daylight.

"I was just layin here watching the television," she says in a bright voice. "Just like you said for me to do in your cute note. I already ordered up a Virgin Mary and a honey pull-apart. There's nothing on TV yet, though. A movie's next, supposedly."

"I'm sorry about last night," I say softly, my voice taking a sudden decibel dive, so that I can barely make it out myself in the traffic noise on Grand River.

"What happened last night, lessee?" I can hear the TV and the sound of ice cubes in her Virgin Mary tinking against the glass. It is a reassuring sound, and I wish I could be there to snuggle up under the warm covers with her and wait for the movie.

"I wasn't at my best, but I'll do better," I say almost soundlessly. I smell warm hash browns, a waffle, an order of French toast humming out of The Squatter's exhaust fan, and I am suddenly starving.

"This hotel's a good place to spend your money," she says, ignoring me completely.

"Well then, go spend some."

"I'm watching something real cerebral right now," she says, distracted. "It's about how the government takes back fifteen tons of old money every week. Mostly just ones. That's the work-horse bill. A hundred-dollar bill lasts for years, though it dudn't in my pocket, I'll tell you that. They *are* trying to figure out how to make shingles out of them. But right now all they can make is note pads."

"Are you having a swell time?"

"So far." She laughs a happy girlish laugh. I see Mr. Smallwood come rolling out the front of The Squatter, a small white paper bag in one huge hand and a sinker half in his mouth. The snow has already begun to melt to slush in the curb gutters.

"I love you, okay," I say, and suddenly feel terribly feeble. My heart pounds down on itself like an anvil, and I have that old ague-sense that my next breath will bring down a curtain of bright red over my eyes, and I will slump to the phone booth glass and cease altogether. "I love you," I hear myself murmur again.

"It's okay with me. But you're a nut, I'll tell you that." She is gay now. "A real Brazil nut. But I like you. Is that all you called up here to say?"

"You just wait'll I get back," I say, "I'll. . . ." But for some reason I do not finish the sentence.

"Do you miss your wife?" she says as gay as can be.

"Are you crazy?" It is clear she has not gotten my point.

"Oh boy. You're some kind of something," she says. I hear silverware clink against plates, the sound of the receiver getting far away from her. "Now you hurry back and let me go and watch this." Clickety-click.

Ten minutes later we are into the rolling landscape of snowy farmettes and wide cottage-bound lakes beyond the perimeter of true Detroit suburbia, the white-flight areas stretching clear to Lansing. It is here that Mr. Smallwood suggests we turn off the meter and arrange a flat rate, which, when I agree, starts him whistling and suggesting he could hang around till I'm ready to go back. He has friends, he says, in nearby Wixom, and we agree that I'll be ready to roll by noon. I remember, briefly, a boy I knew in college from Wixom, Eddy Loukinen, and I enjoy a fond wonder as to where Eddy might be—running a car dealership in his hometown, or down in Royal Oak with his own construction firm. Possibly an insulated window frame outlet in the UP—trading cars every year, checking his market shares, quitting smoking, flying to the islands, slipping around on his wife. These were the futures we all had looking at us in 1967. Good choices. We were not all radicals and wild-eyes. And most of my bunch would tell you they're glad to have a good thirty years left to see what surprises life brings. The possibility of a happy ending. It is not unique to me.

It takes two gas station stops to find Herb's. Both owners claim to know him and to work on his cars exclusively. And both give me a suspicious, bill-collector look, as if I might be looking for big Herb to do him harm or steal his fame. And in each instance Mr. Smallwood and I drive off feeling that phone calls are being made, a protective community rising to a misconstrued threat against its fallen hero. All of which makes me realize just how often I am with people I don't know and who don't know me, and who come to know me—Frank Bascombe—only as a sportswriter. It is possibly not the best way to go into the world, as I explained to Walter two nights ago; with no confidants, with no real allies except ex-allies; no lovers except a Vicki Arcenault or her ilk. Though maybe this is the best for me, given my character and past, which at most are inconclusive. I could have things much worse. At least as a stranger to almost everyone and a sportswriter to boot, I have a clean slate almost every day of my life, a chance not to be negative, to give someone unknown a pat on the back, to recognize courage and improvement, to take the battle with cynicism head-on and win.

Out front of Herb's house, I'm greeted from around the side by a loud "Hey now!" before I can even see who's talking. Mr. Smallwood stares out his closed cab window. He has heard of Herb, he's said, though he has the story of Herb's life wrong and thinks Herb is a Negro. In any case he wants to see him before he cuts out for Wixom.

Herb's house is on curvey little Glacier Way, a hundred yards from Walled Lake itself and not far from the amusement park that operates summers only. I came here long ago, when I was in college, to a dense, festering old barrely dancehall called the Walled Lake Casino. It was at the time when line dances were popular in Michigan, and my two friends and I drove over from Ann Arbor with the thought of picking up some women, though of course we knew no one for forty miles and ended up standing against the firred, scarred old walls being wry and sarcastic about everyone and drinking Cokes spiked with whiskey. Since then, Mr. Smallwood has informed me, the Casino has burned down.

Herb's house is like the other houses around it—a little white Cape showing a lot of dormered roof and with a small picture window on one side of the front door. The kind of house a tool-and-dye maker would own—a sober Fifties structure with a small yard, a two-car garage in back and a van in the drive with HERB's on its blue Michigan plates.

Herb wheels into view from around the corner of the house, making tire tracks in the melting snow. The moment he is visible, Mr. Smallwood puts his cab in gear and goes whooshing off down the street and around the corner, leaving me alone in the front yard with Herb Wallagher, stranded like a prowler.

"I thought you'd be bigger," Herb shouts with a big gap-toothed grin. He shoots a great hand out at me, and when I embrace it he nearly hauls me down to the ground.

"I thought *you'd* be smaller, Herb," I say, though this is a lie. He is much smaller than I thought. His legs have shrunk and his shoulders are bony. Only his head and arms are good-sized, giving him a gaping, storkish appearance behind his thick horn-rims. He has twice cut himself shaving and doctored it with toilet paper, and is wearing a T-shirt that says BIONIC on the front, and a pair of glen-plaid Bermudas below which a brand new pair of red tennis shoes peek out. It is hard to think of Herb as an athlete.

"I like to be outside on a day like this, Frank. It's a wonderful day, isn't it?" Herb looks all around at the sky like a caged man, making his head go loose on its stem.

"It's a great day, Herb." We both, for the moment, affect the corny accents of Kansas hay farmers, though Herb is dead wrong about the weather. It looks like it may snow again and go nasty before the morning is over.

"Every year it got to be spring, ya know, I'd start thinking about motorcycles or some kind of hot car to buy. I had four or five cars and two or three bikes." Herb sits looking away toward a spot above the coping of the house across the street, a house exactly like his except for the pale-blue roof. Beyond it several streets away Walled Lake shines through the yard gaps like metal. I am sorry to hear Herb referring to his life in the past tense. It is not an optimistic sign. "Well, Frank, how do you wanna get this over with," Herb almost shouts at me in his put-on Kansas brogue. He smiles another big fierce smile, then pops both his hands on the black, plastic armrests of his chair as though he'd like nothing better than to spring up and strangle me. "You wanna go in the house or walk to the lake or what? It's your choice."

"Let's try the lake, Herb," I say. "I used to come over here when I was in college. I'd be happy to see it again."

"Clarice!" Herb bellows, frowning up toward the little front door, squirming in his chair and muling it to face the way he wants. He is not interested in my past, though that's no crime since I am not much interested myself. "Clar-eeeece!"

The door opens behind the storm-glass and a slender, pretty black woman with extremely short hair and wearing jeans steps half out onto the step. She gives me a watery half-smile. "Clarice, this is old Frank Bascombe. He's gonna try to make a monkey outa me, but I'm going to kick his keister for him. We're going to the lake. You better bring us a coupla bathing suits, cause we might take a swim." Herb grins back at me in mockery.

"I'm keeping my distance from him, Mrs. Wallagher." I give her a friendly smile to match the frail one she has given me.

"Herb'll talk too much to swim," Clarice says, shaking her head patiently at Herb the perennial bad boy.

"Okay, okay, don't let's get her started," Herb growls, then grins. It is their little burlesque, though it's an odd thing to see in people of two different races, and so young. Herb couldn't be thirty-four yet, though he looks fifty. And Clarice has entered that long, pale, uncertain middle existence in which years behind you is not a faithful measure of life. Possibly she is thirty, but she is Herb's wife, and that fact has made everything else—race, age, hopes—fade. They are like retirees, and neither has gotten what he or she bargained for.

When I look around, Herb has wheeled himself down the walk and is already out in the street. I offer his pretty little wife a little wave which she answers with a wave, and I go off hauling up the rear after Herb.

"Okay now, Frank, what's this bunch of lies supposed be about," Herb says gruffly as we whirl along. There is one more street of lined Capes—some with campers and boat trailers out front—then a wider artery road that leads back to the expressway, and beyond that is the lake, lined with small cottages owned mostly, I'm sure, by people from the city—policemen, successful car salesmen, retired teachers. All are closed and shuttered for the winter. It is not a particularly nice place, a shabby summer community of unattractive bungalows. Not the neighborhood I'd expected for an ex-all-pro.

"I've got my mind on an update on Herb Wallagher, Herb. How he's doing, what're his plans, how life's treating him. Maybe a little inspirational business on the subject of character for people with their own worries. Maybe a touch of optimism in the soup."

"All *right*," Herb says. "Super. Super."

"I know readers would be interested in hearing about your job as spirit coach. Guys you played with taking their cue from you on going the extra half-mile. That kind of thing."

"I'm not going to be doing that anymore, Frank," Herb says grimly, pushing harder on his wheels. "I'm planning to retire."

"Why so, Herb?" (Not the best news for starters.)

"I just wasn't getting the job done down there, Frank. Too much bullshit involved."

An uneasy silence descends as we cross the road to Walled Lake. Most of the snow has melted here and only a gray crust remains on the shoulder where passersby have tossed their refuse. A hundred years ago, this country would've been wooded and the lake splendid and beautiful. A perfect place for a picnic. But now it has all been ruined by houses and cars.

Herb coasts on down the concrete boat ramp in between two boarded-up and fenced-in cottages, and wheels furiously up onto the plank dock. Across Walled Lake is the expressway, and up the lakeside beyond the cottages a roller coaster track curves above the tree line. The Casino must've been nearby, though I see no sign of it.

"It's funny," Herb says, where he can see the lake from an elevation. "When I first saw you, you had a halo around your head. A big gold halo. Do you ever notice that, Frank?" Herb whips his big head around and grins at me, then looks back at the empty lake.

"I never have, Herb." I take a seat on the pipe bannister that runs the length of the dock at the end of which two aluminum boats ride in the shallow water.

"No?" Herb says. "Well." He pauses a moment in a reverie. "I'm glad you came, Frank," he says, but does not look at me.

"I'm glad to be here, Herb."

"I get mad sometimes, Frank, you know? God *damn* it. I just get boiling." Herb suddenly whacks both his big open hands on the black armrests, and shakes his head.

"What makes you mad, Herb?" I have not taken a note yet, of course, nor have I touched my recorder, something I will need to do since I have a terrible memory. I am always too involved with things to pay strict attention. Though I feel like the interview has yet to get started. Herb and I are still getting to know each other on a personal level, and I've found you can rush an interview and come away with such a distorted sense of a person that he couldn't recognize himself in print—the first sign of a badly written story.

"Do you have theories about art, Frank?" Herb says, setting his jaw firmly in one fist. "I mean do you, uh, have any fully developed concepts of, say, how what the artist sees relates to what is finally put on the canvas?"

"I guess not," I say. "I like Winslow Homer a lot."

"All right. He's a good one. He's plenty good," Herb says, and smiles a helpless smile up at me.

"He'd paint Walled Lake here, and it'd feel and look pretty much like this, I think."

"Maybe he would." Herb looks away at the lake.

"How long did you play pro ball, Herb?"

"Eleven years," Herb says moodily. "One in Canada. One in Chicago. Then they traded me over here. And I stayed. You know I've been reading Ulysses Grant, Frank." He nods profoundly. "When Grant was dying, you know, he said, 'I think I am a verb instead of a personal pronoun. A verb signifies to be; to do; to suffer. I signify all three.' " Herb takes off his glasses and holds them in his big linesman's fingers, examining their frames. His eyes are red. "That has some truth to it, Frank. But what the hell do you think he meant by that? A verb?" Herb looks up at me with a face full of worry. "I've been worried about that for weeks."

"I couldn't begin to say, Herb. Maybe he was taking stock. Sometimes we think things are more important than they are."

"That doesn't sound good, though, does it?" Herb looks back at his glasses.

"It's hard to say."

"Your halo's gone now, Frank. You know it? You've become like the rest of the people."

"That's okay, isn't it? I don't mind." It's pretty clear to me that Herb suffers from some damned serious mood swings and in all probability has missed out on a stabilizing pill. Possibly this is his gesture of straight-talk and soul-baring, but I don't think it will make for a very good interview. Interviews always go better when athletes feel fairly certain about the world and are ready to comment on it.

"I'll just tell you what I think it means," Herb says, narrowing his weakened eyes. "I think he thought he'd just become an act. You understand that, Frank? And that act was dying."

"I see."

"And that's terrible to see things that way. Not to *be* but just to do."

"Well, that was just how Grant saw things, Herb. He had some other wrong ideas, too. Plenty of them."

"This is goddamn real life here, Frank. Get serious!" Herb's face struggles with the fiercest intensity, then just as promptly goes blank.

"I was just reading the other day that Americans always feel like the real life is somewhere else. Down the road, around the bend. But this is it right here." Herb cracks his palms on his armrests again. "You know what I'm getting at Frank?"

"I think so, Herb. I'm trying."

"God damn it!" Herb breathes a savage sigh. "You haven't even taken any notes yet."

"I keep it up here, Herb," I say and give my head a poke.

Herb stares up at me darkly. "You know what it's like to lose the use of your legs, Frank?"

"No I don't, Herb. I guess that's pretty obvious."

"Have you ever had someone close to you die?"

"Yes." I could actually see myself getting angry at Herb before this is over.

"Okay," Herb says. "Your legs go silent, Frank. I can't hear mine anymore." Herb smiles a wild smile at me meant to indicate there might be a hell of a lot more I don't know about the world. People, of course, are always getting you all wrong. Because you come to interview them, they automatically think you're just using them to confirm the store of what's already known in the world. But where I'm concerned, that couldn't be wronger. It's true I have expected a different Herb Wallagher from the Herb Wallagher I've found, a stouter, chin-out, better tempered kind of guy, a guy who'd pick up the back of a compact car to help you out of a jam if he could. And what I found is someone who seems as dreamy as a barn owl. But the lesson is not new to me. You can't go into these things thinking you know what can't be known. That ought to be rule one in every journalism class and textbook; too much of life, even the life you think you should know, the life of athletes, can't be foreseen.

There is major silence now that Herb has told me what it's like not to have his legs to use. It is not an empty moment, not for me anyway, and I am not discouraged. I would still like to think there's the possibility for a story here. Maybe by going off his medicine Herb will finally come back to his senses with some unexpected and interesting ideas to bring up and end up talking a blue streak. That happens every day.

"Do you ever miss playing football, Herb?" I say, and smile hopefully.

"What?" Herb is drawn back from a muse the glassy lake has momentarily fostered. He looks at me as though he had never seen me before. I hear trucks pounding the interstate corridor to Lansing. The wind has wandered back now and a chill picks up off the black water.

"Do you ever miss athletics?"

Herb stares at me reproachfully. "You're an asshole, Frank, you know that?"

"Why do you say that?"

"You don't know me."

"That's what I'm *doing* here, Herb. I'd *like* to get to know you and write a damn good story about you. Paint you as you are. Because I think that's pretty interesting and complex in itself."

"You're just an asshole, Frank, yep, and you're not going to get any inspiration out of me. I dropped all that. I don't have to do for anybody, and that means you. Especially you, you asshole. I don't play ball anymore." Herb plucks a piece of the toilet paper off his cheek and peers at it for blood.

"I'm ready to give up on inspiration, Herb. It was just a place to start."

"Do you want to hear the dream I have over and over?" Herb rolls the paper between his fingers, then pushes himself out toward the end of the dock. I sit on the pipe bannister, looking at his back. Herb's bony shoulders are like wings, his neck thin and rucked, his head yellowish and balding. I do not know if he knows where I am or not, or even where *he* is.

"I'd be glad to hear a dream," I say.

Herb stares off toward the lake as if it contained all his hopes gone cold. "I have a dream about these three old women in a stalled car on a dark road. Two of them are taking their grandmother, who's

old, really old, back to a nursing home. Just someplace. Say New
York state, or Pennsylvania. I come along in my Jeep—I *had* a Jeep
once—and I stop and ask if I can help them. And they say yes. No
one's come by in a long time. And I can tell they're worried about
me. One woman has her money out to pay me before I even start.
And they've got this flat tire. I shine my Jeep lights on their car and
I can see this worried old grandmother, her face low in the front
seat. A chicken-wattle neck. The two other women stand with me
while I change the tire. And as I'm doing it I think about killing all
three of them. Just strangling them with my hands, then driving off
because no one would ever know who did it, since I wasn't a killer
or even known to be there. But I look around then, and I see these
deer staring at me out of the trees. These yellow eyes. And that's
it. I wake up." Herb twists his wheelchair and faces me. "How's
that for a dream? Whaddaya think, Frank? You've got a halo again,
by the way. It just came back. You look idiotic." Herb suddenly
breaks out in laughter, his whole body rumbling and his mouth wide
as a canyon. Herb, I see, is as crazy as a betsey bug, and I want
nothing in the world more than to get as far away from him as I
can. Interview or no interview. Inspiration or no inspiration. Interviewing a crazy man is a waste of anybody's time who's not crazy
himself. And I'm glad, in fact, that Herb is in his chair at the moment
since it's possible he would strangle *me* if he could.

"It's probably time we head back, Herb."

He has taken his glasses off and begun wiping them on his BIONIC
shirt. But he is really still laughing. "Sure, okay."

"I've got all I need for a good story. And it's getting pretty chilly
out here."

"You're full of shit, Frank," Herb says, smiling across the empty
boat dock. On the lake a pair of ducks flies low across the surface,
fast and slicing. They make an abrupt turn, then skin into the shiny
water and become invisible. "Oh Frank, you're really full of shit."
Herb shakes his head in complete amazement.

Herb pushes along beside me in his silver chair while we make
our way back up Glacier Way in silence. Everything has become

confused, though why, exactly, I don't know. It's possible I've had a bad effect on him. Sometimes when people realize sportswriters are just men or women they become resentful. (People often want others to be better than they are themselves.) But under these circumstances it is all but impossible to make a contribution, or to give an honest effort of any kind. It is, in fact, enough to make you want to hit the road for a pharmaceuticals house, of which New Jersey has plenty.

"We didn't talk much about football," Herb says thoughtfully. He is now as sane and reflective as an old sextant.

"I guess it didn't seem it was much on your mind, Herb."

"It really seems insignificant now, Frank. It's really a pretty crummy preparation for life, I've come to believe."

"But I'd still think it had some lessons to teach to the people who played it. Perseverance. Team work. Comradeship. That kind of thing."

"Forget all that crap, Frank. I've got the rest of my life handed to me if I can figure it out. I've got some pretty big plans. Sports is just a memory to me."

"You mean law school and all that."

Herb nods at me like an undertaker. "That's it."

"You've got a lot of courage, Herb. It takes courage to be you, I think."

"Maybe," Herb says, considering that idea. "Sometimes I'm afraid, though, Frank. I'll tell ya. Scared to death." We're just two guys jawing now. Just the way I'd hoped. Maybe a straightforward old-fashioned interview could still be worked out. I feel for my tape recorder.

"Sometimes I'm afraid, Herb. It's natural to the breed, I'd say."

"All *right*," Herb says and chuckles, nodding in forced agreement.

I see Mr. Smallwood's yellow Checker waiting out front of Herb's house as we round the curve, his visit to Wixom apparently gone awry. It has grown colder since we've been outside, and the sky has lowered. By nighttime it will be snowing to beat the band, and Vicki and I will be glad to be far from here. It is a strange turn of events, not what I would've expected, but I, on the other hand, am still not surprised.

As we pass by, a man wearing a brown car coat comes out of his house, holding a can of motor oil. His is a house in the same architectural order as Herb's, though with a room added on where the driveway once went into the back. The man stands beside his car—a new Olds with its hood up—and gives Herb a wave and a "howzitgoin."

"Primo. Numero uno," Herb calls back with a grin and waves his arm as if he's waving to a crowd. "This guy's interviewing me. I'm giving him a helluva time."

"Don't take nobody's crap," the man shouts, and bends his short trunk under the murky hood of the Olds.

"The neighbors still think I play on the team," Herb says in a hushed voice, pushing himself up Glacier Way toward his wife and home.

"How's that?"

"Well, I keep my injury pretty well a secret. Another guy plays in my place. With my number. I hope you won't write about that and ruin it."

"No way, Herb. You've got my word on that."

Herb looks up at me as we approach Mr. Smallwood's cab, and gives me a look full of wonder. "How come you do it, Frank. Tell the truth."

"How come I do what, Herb?" Though I know what's coming.

For some reason Herb seems to be having a hard time making his head be still. It's wandering all around. "You couldn't really like sports, Frank," he says. "You don't look like a guy who likes sports."

"I like some better than others." It is not that uncommon a question, really.

"But wouldn't you rather talk about something else?" Herb shakes his big head, still wondrous. "What about Winslow Homer?"

"I'd talk to you about him, Herb, Any time. Writing about something is a lot different from doing the thing itself. Does that clear anything up?" For some reason my diaphragm, or its vicinity, feels like it is quaking again.

"Pret-ty interesting, Frank." Herb nods at me with genuine admiration. "I'm not sure it explains a goddamn thing, but it's interesting. I'll give you that."

"It's pretty hard to explain your own life, Herb." I'm sure my quaking is visible, though maybe not to Herb, for whom the whole world might quake all the time. He's still having trouble keeping his head stationary. "I think I've said enough. I'm supposed to be asking you questions."

"I'm a verb, Frank. Verbs don't answer questions."

"Don't think that way, Herb." My diaphragm is crackling. Herb and I have not been together an hour, but there is a strong sense around him that he would like to strangle *someone*, and not be choosy whose neck he got his hands on. When you have spent so much of your life whamming into people and hurting them, it must be hard just to call a halt to it and sit down. It must be hard to do anything else, it seems to me, but keep on whamming. In any case, I'm always most at ease when I know the way out. There is something to be avoided here, and I intend to avoid it. "I'm going to try to write a good story, Herb," I say, inching toward the back of Smallwood's Checker.

Clarice Wallagher has stepped out onto the front stoop and stands watching us. She calls Herb's name and smiles wearily. This must happen to everyone: meetings ending in stunned silences out front; a waiting cab; Herb proclaiming himself a verb. My greatest admiration is her's. I'd hoped to have a word with her on the subject of Herb's heroism-in-life, but that has gone past us. I simply hope there is a consolation for her late on dark nights.

"Herb," Clarice says in a pretty voice that cracks on the cold Michigan wind.

"Okay!" Herb shouts heroically. "Gotta go, Frank, gotta go. You oughta write my life story. You'd make six figures." We shake hands, and once again Herb tries to jerk me to my knees. There is an odd smell on Herb now, a metallic smell that is the odor of his chair. His cheek is bleeding from where he peeled off the paper. "I wanted you to see some old game films before you left. I could put the ke-bosh on 'em, Frank. Don't let this chair fool ya."

"We'll do it next time, Herb, that's a promise."

Mr. Smallwood starts his cab with a loud whooshing and drops it into drive so that the body bucks half a foot forward.

"I don't know what happens sometimes, Frank." Herb's sad blue eyes suddenly fill with hot tears, and he shakes his big head to dash them away. It is the sadness of elusive life glimpsed and unfairly lost, and the following, lifelong contest with bitter facts. Pity, in other words, for himself, and as justly earned as a game ball. Only I do not want to feel it and won't. It is too close to regret to play fast and loose with. And the only thing worse than terrible regret is unearned terrible regret. And for that reason I will not bend to it, will, in fact, go on to the bottom with my own ship.

I take four quick steps back. "I'm glad I met you, Herb."

Herb stares at me, his face distorted by unhappiness. "Yeah sure," he says.

And I am into the boxy, musty backseat of Mr. Smallwood's Checker, and we shush off down Glacier Way without even so much as a goodbye to Clarice, leaving Herb sitting in the empty street, in his chair, waving goodbye to our tail lights, his sad face astream with helpless and literal tears.

7

Mr. Smallwood is the best possible confederate for my circumstances.

"You look like you could use a pick-me-up," he says, once we are going, and hands back a bottle half out of its flimsy paper bag. I drink down a good gulp that makes me flubber my lips—it is peppermint and sweet as cough syrup, but I'm happy to have it in me, and take a second big gulp. "You musta had you a *time*," Mr. Smallwood says as we hiss past the remnants of a long, charred building on the landward side of the lakefront road. A dismembered line of cabins stands opposite. The big building was once a Quonset hut with a barn built on behind, though snow is piled on its blackened interior timbers, one of which is a long bar. Grass has grown up. No one, apparently, has thought to find a new use for the land. My past in decomposition and trivial disarray.

"These peoples out here're cra-zy," Mr. Smallwood announces widely, steering chauffer-style with one huge hand on the plastic steering knob, the other stretched over the seat back. "Sur-burban peoples, I'm tellin you. Houses full of guns, everybody mad all the time. Oughta cool out, if you ask me. I ain't been out here in years, couldn't even figure out which street was which. I used to come out here all the time." We pull up onto the expressway back toward Big D, invisible now in mossy green clouds that tell of snow and possibly a marooning storm. "Look here now." Mr. Smallwood catches my eye in the rearview and leans backwards in his driver's seat for a speculative stretch. "How much money you got?"

"Why?"

"Well, for a hundred dollars I could make a phone call up here at a gas station and the first thing you know, somebody be done made you feel a whole lot better." Mr. Smallwood grins a big happy grin at the back seat, and I think for a moment about a hundred dollar whore, the kindness she might bring, like the pharmacy sending over an expensive prescription to get you through a rough night. A trip to the hot springs. Something wordless to patch the tissue of innocent words that holds life in its most positive attitude. Too much serious talk and self-explanation and you're a goner.

What Herb needs, of course, and can't have, is to strap on a set of pads and beat the daylights out of somebody and quit worrying about theories of art. He is a man without a sport, when a sport is exactly what he needs. With better luck we might've summoned up a vivider memory of his playing days, seen the game films. Herb could get back within himself, shake off alienation and dreary doubt, and play through pain—be the inspiration he was put on earth to be.

I tell Mr. Smallwood no thanks, and he chuckles in a mirthful-derisive way. Then for a while we wind back toward town without speaking, taking the Lodge this time since the snow is off and the traffic gone north, leaving the expressway gray and wintry.

Across from Tiger Stadium, Mr. Smallwood stops at a liquor store owned, he says, by his brother-in-law, a little Fort Knox of steel mesh and heavy bullet-proof glass. Across the avenue the big stadium hulks up white and lifeless. A message on its marquee says simply, "Sorry Folks. Have a Good One."

Mr. Smallwood ambles across and buys another pint bottle of schnapps, which I insist on paying for, and he and I treat ourselves to a warm elevation of spirits on the short trip down to the Pont-chartrain. He says he is a Tiger fan and that he believes it's time for a dynasty. He also tells me that his parents moved up from Magnolia, Arkansas, in the Forties, and that for a while he attended Wayne State before he got married and went to work at Dodge Main. He quit that last year, he says, a jump ahead of the lay-offs, and bought his taxi. And he is happy to name his own hours now and to go home every day at noon for lunch with his wife and to rest an hour before getting back onto the street for the afternoon rush. Someday he hopes to retire to Arkansas. He doesn't ask me

about myself, either too courteous or too engaged in his own interesting life of work and discretionary time. His is a nice life, a life
that would be easy to envy if you didn't have one just as good. I
calculate him to be not much older than I am.

At the hotel Mr. Smallwood leans across the seat to where he can
see me out on the windy pavement putting money back in my
wallet. For an instant I think he means to shake my hand, but that
is not on his mind at all. I have already paid him our agreed fare,
and the schnapps bottle is on the floor beside his considerable leg.
My gift to him.

"There's a good chop house down on Larned," he says in a tour
guide's voice and with a grin that makes me wonder if he isn't making
fun of me. "Steaks big as this." He holds two big chunky fingers
two full inches apart. "You can walk from here. It's safe. I take the
wife now and then. You can drink some wine, have a good time."
For some reason Mr. Smallwood has started talking like a second
generation Swede, and I understand he isn't making fun of me at
all, only trying to be a good ambassador for his city, putting on the
voice he has learned for it.

"That's great," I say, not quite hearing all this insider's dining
advice, turning an ear instead into the windy sibilance of the city
air. Snow flakes are falling now.

"Come on back when the weather's nicer," he says. "You'll like
it a whole lot better."

"When will that be?" I smile, giving him the old Michigan straight
line.

"Ten minutes maybe." He cracks a big wisecracker's grin, the
same as his hundred-dollar-whore grin. And with the slap-shut of
the yellow door, he shoots off down the street, leaving me at the
hissing curbside as solitary as a lonely end.

Though not for long.

Back in the room, the TV is on without sound. The drapery is
drawn and two trays of dishes are set outside. Vicki lies naked as a
jaybird on the rumpled bed, drinking a 7-Up and reading the in-

flight magazine. Air in the room is hot and close, changed from the sleep-soft night smell. Only the sad old familiarity from the dreamy days after Ralph died is left: lost in strangerville with a girl I don't know well enough and can't figure how to revive an interest in (or, for her sake, an interest in me that would compensate). It is a tinny, minor-key feeling, a far-flung longing for conviction among the convictionless.

"I'm sure glad to see *you*," she says, giving me a happy smile in the blinky TV light. I stand in the little dark entryway, my two feet heavy as anchors, and I can't help thinking of my life as a scene in some steamy bus station novel. *Big Sledge moved toward the girl cat-quick, trapping her where he'd wanted her, between his cheap drifter's suitcase and the pile of greasy tire chains against the back of the lube bay. Now she would see what's what. They both would.* "How'd everything work out with your old football guy?"

"Dandy." I go to the window, pull back the heavy curtain and look out. Snow is dazzling an inch from my face, falling in burly flakes onto Jefferson Avenue. The river is lost in white, as is Cobo. In the street, flashing yellow beacons signal the first snowplows. I feel I can hear their skid and clatter, but I'm sure I do not. "I don't like the looks of this weather. We might have to change our plans."

"A-Okay," she says. "I'm just happy to be here today with you. I can go to the aquarium someplace else. They must be alike." She sets her 7-Up on her bare belly and stares at it, thinking.

"I wanted this to be a nice vacation for you, though. I had a lot of plans."

"Well, keep 'em, cause I've had a plenty good time. I ordered beer-batter shrimp up here, which was a meal in itself. I put on my clothes and went downstairs and looked in the shops which're nice, though they're like Dallas's in a lot of similar ways. I think I might've seen Paul Anka, but I'm not sure. He's about half the size I thought he'd be if it was him, and I already knew he was tiny."

I sit in the chair beside the coffee table. Her uncovered beauty is unexpectedly what I need to make the transition back (the familiar

can still surprise and should). Hers is an altogether ordinary naked-
ness, a sleek curve of bust, a plump darkening thigh tapered to a
dainty ankle, a willing smile of no particular intention—all in all, a
nice bundle for a lonely fellow to call his in a strange city when
time's to kill.

On television the face of a pallid newsman is working dramatically
without sound. *Believe!* his eyes say. *This stuff is the God's truth. It's
what you want.*

"Do you believe women and men can just be friends," Vicki says.

"I guess so," I say, "once the razzle-dazzle's over. I like the razzle-
dazzle though."

"Yeah, me too." Her smile broadens and she crosses her arms
over her soft breasts. She has, I can tell, been captured by a thought,
an event she likes and wants to share. At heart she could not be
kinder and could make someone the most rewarding wife. Only for
some reason it does not seem as likely to be me as it once did. She
may have caught this very mood in the wind today and be as puzzled
by it as I am. Though she is nobody's fool.

"I called Everett on the phone," she says, and looks down at her
knees, which are bent upwards. "I used *my* charge number."

"You could've used this one."

"Well. I used mine, anyway."

"How *is* old Everett?" Of course I have never seen ole Everett
and can be as chummy as a barber with the far-off idea of him.

"He's okay. He's into Alaska now. He said people need carpets
up there. He also said he's shaved his head bald as a cue ball. I told
him I was in a big suite, looking out at a renaissance center. I didn't
say where."

"What'd he think about that."

" 'As the world turns,' is what he said, which is about standard.
He wanted to know would I send him back his stereo I got in the
divorce. Everything's sky high up there, I guess, and if you come
with all you need, you start ahead."

"Did he want you to go with him?"

"No, he did not. And I wouldn't either. You don't have to marry somebody like Everett but once in a lifetime. Twice'll kill you. He's got some ole gal with him, anyway, I'm sure."

"What did he want, then?"

"I called him, remember." She frowns at me. "He didn't want anything. Haven't you ever got the phonies in your life?"

"Only when I'm lonesome, sweetheart. I didn't think you were lonesome."

"Right," she says and looks at the silent television.

Detroit, I can see now, has not affected her exactly as I had hoped, and she has become wary. Of what? Possibly in the lobby she saw someone who reminded her too much of herself (that can happen to inexperienced travelers). Or worse. That *no* one there reminded her of anyone she ever knew. Both can be threatening to a good frame of mind and usher in a gloomy remoteness. Though calling up an old lover or husband can be the perfect antidote. They always remind you of where you've been and where you think you're going. And if you're lucky, wherever you are at the moment—in the Motor City, in a snowstorm—can seem like *the* right place on the planet. Though I'm not certain Vicki has been so lucky. She may have found an old flame burning and not know what to do about it.

"Do you feel like you wanted to be friends with Everett?" I start with the most innocent of questions and work toward the most sensitive.

"No-ho way." She reaches down and pulls the sheet up over her. She is even warier now. It may be she wants to tell me something and can't quite find the words. But if I'm to be relegated to the trash heap of friendship, I want to do a friend's one duty: let her be herself. Though I'd be happier to snuggle up under the sheets and rassle around till plane time.

"Did you hang up feeling like you wanted to be friends with *me?*" I say, and smile at her.

Vicki turns over on the big bed and faces the other wall, the white sheet clutched up under her chin and the crisp hotel percale stretched over her like a winding. I have hit the tender spot. A day and a night with me has made even Everett look good. Something else is needed, and I don't fit the bill even with champers, a demi-suite, bachelor buttons and a view of Canada. Maybe that isn't even surprising when you come down to it, since by scaling down my own pleasures I may have sold short her hopes for herself. I, however, am an expert in taking things like this lying down. For writers— even sportswriters—bad news is always easier than good, since it is, after all, more familiar.

"I don't want to be friends. Not *just*," Vicki says in a tiny, mouse voice from a mound of white covers. "I really thought I was gettin a new start with you."

"Well, what happened to make you think you weren't? Just because you caught me going through your purse?"

"Shoot. That didn't matter," she says, smally. "Live and let die, I say. You can't help yourself. Yesterday wasn't the tiptop day for you in the year."

"Then, what's the matter?" I wonder, in fact, how many times I have said that or something equal to it to a woman passing palely through my life. *What're you thinking? What's made you so quiet? You seem suddenly different. What's the matter?* Love *me* is what this means, of course. Or at least, second best: surrender. Or at the *very* least, take some time regaling me with why you won't, and maybe by the end you will.

Outside a wind makes a sharp oceanic *woo* around the corner of the hotel, then off into the cold, paltry Detroit afternoon. By five it could as easily turn to rain, by six the stars could be out and by nighttime Vicki and I could be strolling down Larned for a steak or a chop. You can never completely count on things out here. Life is counterpoised against a mean wind that could suddenly cease.

"Well," Vicki says, and turns over to face me out of a grotto of pillows and sheets. "When I went downstairs, you know, when you were gone? I just went to be a part of something. I didn't need anything. And I went in the little newsstand down there, and I picked up this paperback. *How To Take On The World*, by Doctor Barton. Because I felt like I was starting over in one way, like I said.

You and me. So I stood there at the rack and read one chapter called 'Our New-Agers.' Which was about these people who won't eat potato chips and who join these self-discovery groups, and drink mineral water and have literary discussions every day. People that think it oughta be easy to express their feelings and be how you seem. And I just started cryin, cause I realized that that was you, and I was someplace way off the beam. Back with the potato chips and people who aren't inner-looking. Here we'd come all the way out here, and all I could do was eat shrimp and watch TV and cry. And it wasn't working out. So I thought maybe we could be friends if you wanted to. I called up Everett because I knew I could bring it off with him and quit crying. I knew I was better off than him." A big handsome tear leaves her eye, goes off her nose and vanishes into the pillow. I have managed to make two different people cry inside of two hours. I am doing something wrong. Though what?

Cynicism.

I have become more cynical than old Iago, since there is no cynicism like lifelong self-love and the tunnel vision in which you yourself are all that's visible at the tunnel's end. It's embarrassing. Likewise, there's nothing guaranteed to make people feel more worthless than to think someone is trying to help them—even if you're not. A cynical "New-Ager" is exactly me, a sad introspecter and potato chip avoider with a queasy heart-to-heart mentality— though I would give the crown jewels not to be, or at least not be thought to be.

My only hope now is to deny everything—friendship, disillusionment, embarrassment, the future, the past—and make my stand for the present. If I can hold her close in this cold-hot afternoon, kiss her and hug away her worries with ardor, so that when the sun is down and the wind stops and a spring evening draws us, maybe I will love her after all, and she me, and all this will just have been the result of too little sleep in a strange town, schnapps and Herb.

"I'm not really a New-Ager," I say and take a seat on the bed shoulder, where I can touch her cheek, warm as a baby's. "I'm just an old-fashioned Joe who's been misunderstood. Let's pretend we just got here and it's late at night, and I had you in my old-fashioned arms to love."

"Oh my." She puts a tentative hand on my shoulder and gives it a friendly pat. "I bet you think I got it all wrong." She gives a stout sniff. "That I can't even make myself miserable and do it right."

"You're just no good at messin up." I put a heavy hand on her soft breast. "You just have to let good things be good if they will. Don't worry about more than you have to."

"I shouldn't read, is what it is. It always gets me in trouble." She reaches both hands around my neck and pulls hard, so hard once again a crippling pain goes down my back clear to my buttocks.

"Oh," I say, involuntarily. On TV a skier is just about to push out the timer gate onto a slope longer and higher than any I've ever seen. Snow is falling wherever he is. I wouldn't do what he's doing for a million dollars.

"Oh my," she says, for I have found her in the lemony light. "My, my, my."

"You sweet girl," I say. "Who wouldn't love you?"

Outside in the cold city the wind goes *woo* again and I can, I think, hear the tufted snow dashing against the window, sending shivers through every soul in Detroit who thinks he knows a thing or two and who is willing to bet his life on it. I leave the TV on, since even now, in its prying presence, I still find it consoling.

By five o'clock, we have taken a cab trip up Jefferson to the Belle Isle Botanical Garden, and are back in the room suffering a case of the wall-stare willies, something sportswriters know a lot about. We are like the family of a traveling salesman, come along for the adventure and diversion, but who find themselves with too much time to kill while business gets conducted; too many unfamiliar streets leading too far away; too little going on in the hotel lobby to make people-watching all that rewarding.

The Botanical Garden turned out to be cold and alien-feeling, though we trudged down aisles of ferns and succulents and passion flowers until Vicki announced a headache. The most interesting rooms all seemed to be closed—in particular a re-creation of an eighteenth-century French herb garden, which we could see through the glass door and that caught both our fancies. A sign hung in the window saying Detroit was not generous enough in its tax attitudes to support this century properly. And in less than an hour we were back out in the cold and snow of afternoon on the windy concrete steps. A muddy playing field stretched away from us toward the boat basin, with the big river invisible and low behind a crescent-line of poplar saplings. Public places can sometimes let you down no matter how promising they start out.

Delivered back outside our hotel, I offered a short walk down Larned to "a great little steak house I know about." Though when we had gone as far as Woodward, everyone we saw had become black and vaguely menacing, the taxis and police all unexplainably disappeared, and Vicki clung to me ashiver from the wintry norther that'd dropped in on us from bland Canada.

"I'm not really dressed for this, I don't think," she said beneath my arm, and smiled a daunted smile. "I'd settle for a Tuna Alladin at the coffee shop, if that's okay with you."

"I guess they've moved the steak place," I said and gazed up weekend-empty Woodward toward the Grand Circus where, when I was a college boy, Eddy Loukinen, Golfball Kirkland and I cruised the burlesque houses and the schooner bars, then drove the forty miles back to campus full of the mystique of soldiers on a last leave before shipping out to fates you wouldn't smile about. It was incongruous to me, in fact, that the year could've been 1963. Not '73 or '53. Sometimes I can even forget my own age and the year I'm living in, and think I am twenty, a kid starting new in the world—a greener, confused by life at its beginning.

"Towns aren't even towns anymore," Vicki said, sensing my distraction with this sad evolution, and giving me a hug around my middle. "Dallas wasn't *ever* one, when you get right down to it. It's just a suburb looking for a place to light."

"I remember they had a first class wine list there," I said, still gazing up Woodward toward the phantom steakhouse, past the old Sheraton and into the abandonment and dazzle of sex clubs and White Castles and *bibliothèques sensuelles* stretching to where snow made a backdrop.

"I can taste the cheddar cheese already," she said in reference to her Tuna Alladin, trying to be upbeat. "I bet they've got just as good a wine for half the price back at the hotel. You're just looking for someplace else to spend your money again." And she was right, and wheeled me around and set us off back to the Pontch, watching our toes on the snowy pavement, taking long, slew-footed strides and laughing like conventioneers turned loose on the old town.

Though by five we are room-bound here, driven in by unseasonable weather and the forbidding streets of this city. We have tried to make the most of everything that's come our way: a belly-buster lunch in the Frontenac Grill complete with a bottle of Michigan beaujolais. A long nap in a fresh bed, after which I have stood at the window and watched another ore barge down from Lake Superior ply the snowy river, headed, like the one last night, for Cleveland or Ashtabula. It's possible I should put in a call to Herb, or even to Clarice, though I don't know what I'd say and finally lack the courage. I might also call Rhonda Matuzak to report I've found out nothing usable for the Pigskin Preview. People are in the office this weekend, though it's doubtful anyone's counting on me. Mine, for the moment, is not the best sportswriter's attitude.

"I'll tell you what let's do," Vicki says suddenly. She is seated at the vanity twisting in some Navajo earrings she has bought with her money at the gift shop. They are tiny as pin-heads, lovely and blue as hyacinths.

"You just name it," I say, looking up from the *Out on the Town*, which I've read cover to cover without finding one local attraction I have the heart for—including Paul Anka, who's already left town. Even a cab ride to Tiger Stadium and a Mexican dinner seem somehow second rate.

"Let's go on out to the airport and stand-by for a flight. Nobody goes any place on Saturday. I remember from when I used to watch planes for fun, they used to let people on with tickets for other days. They're good about that."

"I thought we'd make a festive night of it," I say half-heartedly. "I was planning on Greek Town. There's still plenty to do here."

"Sometimes, you know, you just get the bug to sleep in your own bed, don't you think that's so? We're s'posed to be at Daddy's tomorrow before noon anyway. This'll make it easier."

"Aren't you going to be disappointed to miss souvlaki and baklava?"

"I don't even know where they're located so how could I miss 'em? I bet you have to drive through some snow to get there though."

"I haven't been much of a high-flier this trip. I don't really know what happened."

"Nothing did." Looking in the mirror, Vicki pulls back her dark curls to model the Navajos, pinched in behind her plump cheeks. She turns to the side to see and gives me a reassuring smile via the mirror. "I don't have to ride the merry-go-round to have fun. I take mine from who I'm with, not what I do. I've had the best time I could, just being with you, and you're a clubfoot not to know it."

"What if the airport's closed?"

"Then I'll sit and read stories to you out of movie magazines. There's worse things than spending the night in the airport. Sometimes I'd rather be there than lots of places."

"It wouldn't be that bad, would it?"

"No sir. Put yourself in one of those little TV chairs, eat dinner in a good restaurant. Get your shoes shined. It'd take you all night to hit the high spots."

"I'll call us a bellman," I say, and stand up.

"I don't know why we waited this long." She smiles at me.

"I guess I was waiting for something exciting and unusual to happen. I always hope for that. It's my weakness."

"You have to know, though, when what you're waiting for says, 'Smile, you're on candid camera.' Then you got to be ready to smile."

And I do smile, at her, as I reach for the phone to ring the bell captain. A small future brightens, and not a bad one, but an ordinary good one. And, as I dial, I feel the sky of this long day lighten about me now for the first time, and the clouds begin at last to ascend.

By ten we are in New Jersey as if by miracle of time travel, returned from the flat midwest to the diverse seaboard. Vicki has slept across Lake Erie once again after reading to me several excerpts from *Daytime Confidential*, all of which made me laugh, but which she took more seriously and seemed to want to mull over. I read a good deal of *Love's Last Journey* and found it not bad at all. There was no long flashback prologue to get past, and the writer proved pretty skillful at getting the ball rolling by page two. I woke her only when the pilot banked over what I estimated to be Red Bank, with bright Gotham (the Statue of Liberty tiny but distinct, like a Japanese doll of herself) and all of New Jersey spread out like a glittering diamond apron, the Atlantic and Pennsylvania looming dark as the Arctic.

"What's *that* thing," Vicki asked, staring and pointing below us into the distant carnival of civilized lights.

"That's the Turnpike. You can see where it meets the Garden State at Woodbridge and heads to New York."

"Hey-o," she said.

"I think it's beautiful from up here."

"You prob'ly do," she said. "No telling what you'll think's beautiful next. A junk yard I guess."

"I think you're beautiful."

"More than a junk yard. A junk yard in New Jersey?"

"Almost." I squeezed her strong little arm and held it to me.

"You said the wrong thing now." Her eyes narrowed in mock pique. "I liked you to this point. But I don't see how this can go on."

"You'll break my heart."

"It won't be the first one I broke, will it?"

"What if I'm better?"

" 'Bout too late," she said. "You should of considered all that before you were even born." She shook her head as though she meant every word of it, then settled back and closed her eyes to sleep as our silver ship perfected its descent to earth.

By eleven-fifteen I have delivered us to Pheasant Meadow. It has become a clear and intensely full-featured night, with the moon waning and tomorrow's weather giving no sign of arriving from Detroit. It's the very kind of night that used to make me disoriented and dizzy—the sort of night I stood out in the yard in, while X was inside burning her hope chest, and charted Cassiopeia and Gemini in the northern sky and felt vulnerable beside the rhododendrons. Since then, to be truthful, I have never felt all that easy with the clear night sky, as if I was seeing it from the top of a high building and afraid to look down. (I tend to prefer broken cirrus or mackerel clouds to a pure, starry vault.)

"Don't bother walkin me," Vicki says, already out the car door and with her head back inside the window. I have stopped behind her Dart. The hard-hat guys from yesterday have finished off a phony mansard across the lot, although none of the finished buildings have roofs like that. Naturally I was hoping for an invitation inside— a nightcap. But I see my hopes on that front are slim. She has become skittish now, as though someone else was waiting upstairs.

"Tomorrow's the day he rolled back the stone and raised up from the dead," she says in all seriousness, staring straight at me as if I was expected to recite a psalm. She has her Le Sac weekender looped over her shoulder and her Navajo earrings on. "I might go to early mass, just for keeping us safe, that and the in-surance. Or I might go to the drive-in Methodists in Hightstown. One's official as the other. I'm thinking twice about lapsin. I'd ask you to come, but I know you wouldn't like it."

"I'd like the music."

"Whatever floats your boat, I guess," she says. We have been together for two days now, shared another geography, slept in one bed, been quiet together and attended each other's pleasures and courtesy like married folk. Only now the end is in sight, and neither of us can find the handle to a proper parting. Flippancy and a vague churlishness is her protocol. Unwitting politeness is mine. It is not a good mix.

"I'm going to see you tomorrow, aren't I?" I am cheerful, bending to see her and seeing beyond her the big blue space-age water tank and beyond that the big Easter moon.

"You better be on time. Daddy's picky 'bout when he eats. And it takes a whole hour to get there."

"I'm looking forward to it a lot." This is not entirely true, but it is my official attitude. This part of tomorrow is actually alive with fearsome ambiguity.

"You hadn't even met him yet. Wait'll you meet my stepmother. She's a breed apart. If you like her you'll like broccoli. But Daddy's somethin. You *better* like him, only he probably won't like you. Or least that's how he'll act. His true thoughts will come to light later. Not that it matters."

"You love me, don't you?" When I lean up to be kissed, she gazes down on me with a pert, appraising face. I cannot help wondering if she's not considering Everett right now and an Alaskan adventure.

"Maybe. What if I do?"

"Then you'll give me a kiss and ask me to spend the night."

"No way on that," she says, and gives her hand a big Dinah Shore kiss and smacks me hard across the cheek with it. "That's what you got comin. Signed, sealed and delivered, ole Mister Smart." And then she is off, skittering toward the darkened apartments, across the skimpy lawn and in the lighted outside door and out of sight. And I am left alone in my Malibu, staring at the glossy moon as if it were all of mystery and anticipation, all the things we are happy to leave and happier yet to see come toward us new again.

8

A suspicious light shines in my living room. A strange car sits at the curb. On the third floor Bosobolo's desk lamp is lit, though it is after midnight. Easter undoubtedly means special preparations for him, possibly a sermon at one of the Institute's satellite churches which he services now and then to fine-tune his evangelizing techniques. He has put up a wreath on the front door, a decision we have discussed earlier that won my approval. All the houses on Hoving Road are silent and dark, odd for a Saturday night, when there is usually entertaining going on and windows brightened. In the clear sky above the buttonwoods and tulip trees, I can see only the lemony glitter of Gotham lighting the heavens fifty miles away, as though a great event was going on there—a state fair, say, or a firestorm. And I am happy to see it, happy to be this far from the action, on the leeward side of what the wider world deems important.

In my house stands Walter Luckett.

More accurately, waiting in the room I now use as a cozy study, an old side porch with French doors, overstuffed summerish furniture, brass lamps with maps for shades (bought from a catalog), bookshelves to the ceiling and a purplish Persian rug that came with the house. It is the room I normally consider *mine*, though I am not hard-nosed about it. But even Bosobolo, who has the run of everything, stays clear without having to be asked. It is the room where I finally gave up work on *Tangier*, where I do most of my sportswriting, where my typewriter sits on my desk. And when X left me, it was in this room that I slept every night until I could face going back upstairs. Most people have such comfortable, significant places if they own a home, and Walter Luckett is standing in the middle of mine with a wry self-derisive smirk that probably caused a certain kind of brainy, pock-marked girl back in Coshocton to think, "Well, now. Here's something new to the planet. . . . More's here than meets the eye," and later to put up with hell and foolishness to be his date.

Though I can't say it makes me glad to see him, since I'm tired, and as recently as twelve hours ago was in faraway Walled Lake, having a conversation with a crazy man out of which I won't get a story to write. What I want to do is put that behind me and hit the hay. Tomorrow like all tomorrows could still be a banner day.

Walter is holding a copy of a canvas luggage catalog, and, upon seeing me, has rolled it into a tight little megaphone. "Frank. Your butler let me in, or I wouldn't be here at this hour. You have my word on that."

"It's okay, Walter. He's not my butler, though, he's my roomer. What's up?"

I set down my one-suiter bought from the very catalog he is now spindling. I like this room very much, its brassy, honeyed glow, paint peeling insignificantly off its moldings, the couches and leather chairs and hatchcover table all arranged in a careless, unpretentious way that is immensely inviting. I would like nothing more than to curl up anywhere here and doze off for seven or eight unmolested hours.

Walter is wearing the same blue tennis shirt and walking shorts he wore in the Manasquan two nights ago, a pair of sockless loafers and a Barracuda jacket with a plaid lining (referred to as a *jerk's suit* in my fraternity). In all likelihood it is the same suit-of-casual-clothes Walter has worn since Grinnell days. Only behind his tortoise-shells, his eyes look vanquished, and his slick bond-salesman's hair could stand a washing. Walter looks, in other words, like private death, though I have a feeling he is here to share some of it with me.

"Frank, I haven't slept for three days," Walter blurts and takes two tentative steps forward. "Not since I talked to you over at the shore." He squeezes the Gokey catalog into the tightest tube possible.

"Let's make you a drink, Walter," I say. "And let me have that catalog before you tear it apart."

"No thanks, Frank. I'm not staying."

"How about a beer?"

"No beer." Walter sits down in a big armchair across from my chair, and leans up, forearms to knees: the posture of the confessional, something we Presbyterians know little about.

Walter is sitting under a framed map of Block Island, where X and I once sailed. I gave the map to her as a birthday present, but laid claim to it in the divorce. X complained until I said the map meant something to me, which caused her to relent instantly—and it does. It is a link to palmier times when life was simple and ungrieved. It is a museum piece of a kind, and I'm sorry to see Walter Luckett's beleaguered visage beneath it now.

"Frank, this is a helluva house. I mean, when I thought you had a colored butler with a British accent, it didn't surprise me at all." Walter looks around wide-eyed and approving. "Say about how long you've owned it." Walter smiles a big first-bike kid's grin.

"Fourteen years, Walter." I pour myself a good level of warm gin from a bottle I keep behind the children's *World Books* and drink it down with a gulp.

"Now that's old dollars. Plus location. Plus the interest rates from that era. That adds up. I have clients over here, old man Nat Farquerson for one. I live over in The Presidents now, Coolidge Street. Not a bad part of town, don't you think?"

"My wife lives on Cleveland. My former wife, I guess I should say."

"My wife's in Bimini, of course, with Eddie Pitcock. Of all things."

"I remember you said."

Walter's eyes go slitted, and he frowns up at me as if what I'd just said deserved nothing better than a damn good whipping. A silence envelops the room, and I cannot suppress an impolite yawn.

"Frank, let me get right to this. I'm sorry. Since this Americana business I've just been dead in my tracks. My whole life is just agonizing around this one goddamn event. Christ. I've done so much worse in my life, Frank. Believe me. I once screwed a thirteen-year-old girl when I was twenty and married, and bragged about it to friends. I slept like a baby. Like a baby! And there's worse than that, too. But I can't get this one out of my mind. I'm thirty-six, Frank. And everything seems very bad to me. I've quit *becoming*, is what it feels like. Only I stopped at the wrong time." A smile of wonder passes over Walter's dazed face, and he shakes his head. His is the face of a haunted war veteran with wounds. Only to my thinking it's a private matter, which no one but him should be required to care a wink about. "What're you thinking right now, Frank," Walter asks hopefully.

"I wasn't thinking anything, really." I give my own head a shake to let Walter know I'm an earnest war veteran myself, though in fact I'm lost in a kind of fog about Vicki. Wondering if she's expecting me to call and for us to make up, wondering for some reason if I'll ever see her again.

Walter leans up hard on his knees, looking more grim than earnest. "What did you think when I said what I said two nights ago? When I originally told you? Pretty idiotic, huh?"

"It didn't seem idiotic, Walter. Things happen. That's all I thought."

"I'm not putting babies in freezers, am I, Frank?"

"I didn't think so."

Walter's face sinks solemner still, in the manner of a man considering new frontiers. He would like me to ask him a good telling question, something that will then let him tell me a lot of things I don't want to know. But if I have agreed to listen, I have also agreed not to ask. This is the only badge of true friendship I'm sure of: not to be curious. Whatever Walter is up to may be as novel as teaching chickens to drive cars, but I don't want the whole lowdown. It's too late in the night. I'm ready for bed. And besides, I have no exact experience in these matters. I'm not sure what anyone—including trained experts—ought to say except, "All right now, son, let's get you on over to the state hospital and let those boys give you a shot of something that'll bring you back to the right side of things."

"What do you worry about, Frank, if you don't mind my asking?" Walter is still ghost-solemn.

"Really not that much, Walter. Sometimes at night my heart pounds. But it goes back to normal when I turn on the light."

"You're a man with rules, Frank. You don't mind, do you, if I say that? You have ethics about a lot of important things."

"I don't mind, Walter, but I don't think I have any ethics at all, really. I just do as little harm as I can. Anything else seems too hard." I smile at Walter in a bland way.

"Do you think *I've* done harm, Frank? Do you think you're better than I am?"

"I think it doesn't matter, Walter, to tell you the truth. We're all the same."

"That's evading me, Frank, because I admire codes, myself. In everything." Walter sits back, folds his arms, and looks at me appraisingly. It's possible Walter and I will end up in a fistfight before this is over. Though I would run out the door to avoid it. In fact, I feel a nice snugged wooziness rising in me from the gin. And I would be happy to take this right up to bed.

"Good, Walter." I stare fervently at Block Island, trying to find X's and my first landfall from all those years ago. Sandy Point. I scan the bookshelves behind Walter's head as if I expected to see those very words on a friendly spine.

"But let me ask you, Frank, what do you do when something worries you and you can't make it stop. You try and try and it won't." Walter's eyes become exhilarated, as if he'd just willed into being something that was furious and snapping and threatening to swirl him away.

"Well, I take a hot bath sometimes. Or a midnight walk. Or I read a catalog. Get drunk. Sometimes, I guess, I get in bed and think dirty thoughts about women. That always makes me feel better. Or I'll listen to the short-wave. Or watch Johnny Carson. I don't usually get in such a bad state, Walter." I smile to let him know I'm at least half-serious. "Maybe I should more often."

Upstairs, I hear Bosobolo walk down his hall to his bathroom, hear his door close and his toilet flush. It's a nice homey sound— as always—his last office before turning in. A long, satisfying leak. I envy him more than anyone could know.

"You know what I think, Frank?"

"What, Walter."

"You don't seem to be somebody who knows he's going to die, that's what." Walter suddenly ducks his head, like a man someone has menaced and who has barely gotten out of the way.

"I guess you're right." I smile a smile of failed tolerance. Though Walter's words deliver a cold blue impact on me—the first clump of loamy dirt thrumping off the pine box, mourners climbing back into their Buicks, doors slamming in unison. Who the hell wants to think about that now? It's one A.M. on a day of resurrection and renewal the world over. I want to talk about dying now as much as I want to play a tune out my behind.

"Maybe you just need a good laugh, Walter. I try to laugh every day. What did the brassiere say to the hat?"

"I don't know. What *did* it say, Frank?" Walter is not much amused, but then I am not much amused by Walter.

" 'You go on ahead, I'll give these two a lift.' " I stare at him. He smirks but doesn't laugh. "If you don't think that's hilarious, Walter, you should. It's really funny." In fact I have a hard time suppressing a big guffaw myself, though we're at basement-level seriousness now. No jokes.

"Maybe you think I need a hobby or something. Right?" Walter's still smirking, though not in a friendly way.

"You just need to see things from another angle, Walter. That's all. You aren't giving yourself much of a break." Maybe a hundred dollar whore would be a good new angle. Or an evening course in astronomy. I was thirty-seven before I knew that more than one star could be the North Star; it was a huge surprise and still has the aura of a genuine wonder for me.

"You know what's true, Frank?"

"What, Walter."

"What's true, Frank, is that when we get to be adults we all of a sudden become the thing viewed, not the viewer anymore. Do you know what I mean?"

"I guess so." And I *do* know what he means, and with a marksman's clarity. Divorce has plenty of these little encounter-group lessons to teach. Only I'll be goddamned if I'm going to trade epiphanies with Walter. We don't even go in for that stuff at the Divorced Men's Club. "Walter, I'm pretty beat, I've had a long day."

"And I'll tell you something else, Frank, even though you didn't ask me. I'm not going to be cynical enough to ignore that fact. I'm not going to find a hobby or be a goddamn jokemaster. Cynicism makes you feel smart, I know it, even when you aren't smart."

"Maybe so. I wasn't suggesting you take up fly-tying."

"Frank, I don't know what the hell I've gotten myself into, and there's no use acting like I'm smart. I wouldn't be in this if I was. I just feel on display in this mess, and I'm scared to death." Walter shakes his head in contrite bafflement. "I'm sorry about all this, Frank. I wanted to keep improving myself, by myself."

"It's all right, Walter. I'm not sure, though, if you *can* improve yourself much. Why don't I fix us both a drink." Unexpectedly, though, my heart suddenly goes out to Walter the self-improver, trying to go it alone. Walter is the real New-Ager, and in truth, he and I are not much different. I've made discoveries he'll make when he calms down, though the days when I could stay up all night, riled up about some *point d'honneur* or a new novel or bracing up a boon pal through some rough seas are long gone. I am too old for all that without even being very old. A next day—any new day— means too much to me. I am too much anticipator, my eye on the future of things. The best I can offer is a nightcap, and a room for the night where Walter can sleep with the light on.

"Frank, I'll have a drink. That's white of you. Then I'll get the hell out of here."

"Why don't you just bed down here tonight. You can claim the couch, or there's an extra bed in the kids' room. That'd be fine." I pour us both a glass of gin, and hand one to Walter. I've stashed away some roly-poly Baltimore Colts glasses I bought from a Balfour catalog when I was in college, in the days when Unitas and Raymond Berry were the big stars. And now seems to me the perfect time to crack them out. Sports are always a good distraction from life at its dreariest.

"This is nice of you, Franko," Walter says, looking strangely at the little rearing blue Colt, shiny and decaled into the nubbly glass from years ago. "Great glasses." He smiles up in wonderment. There is a part of me Walter absolutely cannot fathom, though he doesn't really want to fathom it. In fact he is not interested in me at all. He might even sense that I am in no way interested in him, that I'm simply performing a Samaritan's duty I would perform for anyone (preferably a woman) I didn't think was going to kill me. Still, some basic elements of my character keep breaking into his train of thought. Like my Colts glasses. At his house he has leaded Waterfords, crystals etched with salmon, and sterling goblets—unless, of course, Yolanda got it all, which I doubt since Walter is cagier than that.

"Salud," Walter says in a craven way.

"Cheers, Walter."

He puts the glass down immediately and drums his fingers on the chair arm, then stares a hole right into me.

"He's just a guy, Frank." Walter sniffs and gives his head a hard shake. "A monies analyst right on the Street with me. Two kids. Wife named Priscilla up in Newfoundland."

"What the hell are they doing way up there?"

"New Jersey, Frank. Newfoundland, New Jersey. Passaic County." A place where X and I used to drive on Sundays and eat in a turkey-with-all-the-trimmings restaurant. Perfect little bucolic America set in the New Jersey reservoir district, an hour's commute from Gotham. "I don't know what you'd want to say about either of us," Walter says.

"Nothing might be enough."

"He's an okay guy is what I'm saying. Okay?" Walter clasps his hands in his lap and gives me a semi-hurt look. "I went over to his firm to cash some certificates for a customer, and somehow we just started talking. He follows the same no-loads I do. And you know you can just talk. I was late already, and we decided to go down to the Funicular and drink till the traffic cleared. And one conversation just led to another. I mean, we talked about everything from petrochemicals in the liquid container industry to small-college football.

He's a Dickinson grad, it turns out. But the first thing I knew it was nine-thirty and we'd talked for three hours!" Walter rubs his hands over his small handsome face, right up under his glasses and into his eye sockets.

"That doesn't seem strange, Walter. You could've just shaken hands and headed on home. It's what you and I do. It's what most people do." (And ought to do!)

"Frank, I know it." He resettles his tortoise-shells using both sets of fingers. There's nothing for me to say. Walter acts like a man in a trance and waking him, I'm afraid, will only confuse things and make them go on forever. With any luck this will all end soon, and I can hop into bed. "Do you want to hear it, Frank?"

"I don't want to hear anything that'll embarrass me, Walter. Not in *any* way. I don't know you well enough."

"This isn't embarrassing. Not a bit." Walter swivels to the side and reaches for his glass, looking at me hopefully.

"It's right there." I point to the gin.

Walter goes and pours himself a drink, then slumps back in his easy chair and drinks it down. Bolting, we used to call it at Michigan. Walter just *bolted* his drink. It occurs to me, in fact, that I could *be* in Michigan at this very moment, that Vicki and I might've driven out to Ann Arbor and be eating a late supper at the Pretzel Bell. Flank steak and hot mustard with a side of red cabbage. I have made an error in my critical choices. "Do you know who Ida Simms is, Frank?" Walter looks at me judiciously, his lower lip pressed tightly above his upper. He means to imply an icy logic's being applied— the rest from here on out will deal only in the bedrock and provable facts. No gushy sentiment for this boy.

"It sounds familiar, Walter. But I don't know why."

"Her picture was in all the papers last year, Frank. An older lady with a Nineteen-forties hairdo. It looked like some kind of advertisement, which in a way it was. The woman who just disappeared? Got out of a cab at Penn Station, with two little poodles on a leash, and nobody's seen her since? The family ran the ads with her picture, asking for calls if anybody knew anything. Somebody dear to them who walked right out of the world. Boom." Walter shakes his head, both comforted and astonished by what a strange world it is. "She'd had mental problems, Frank, been in hospitals. All that came out. You'd have to figure the signs weren't too good for her if you were the family. The impulse to do away with yourself must get pretty strong in those circumstances.

Walter looks at me with his blue eyes shining significantly, and I'm forced to look up squarely at Block Island again. "You never can tell, Walter. People are gone ten years, then one day they wake up in St. Petersburg on the Sunshine Skyway, and everything's fine."

"I know it. That's true." Walter stares down at his loafers. "We talked about the whole business, Frank. Yolanda and I. She thought the picture was some kind of a fake, a massage parlor or something phony. But I couldn't. I didn't know anymore than she did. Except here was a picture of this woman, Frank, looking like somebody's mother somewhere, yours or mine, her hair all done up like the Forties, and a scared smile on her face like she knew she was in trouble, and I just was not ready to think fake. I told Yolanda she ought to believe it wasn't a fake just because it might not be. You know what I mean?"

"I guess." I saw the picture, in fact, twenty times at least. Whoever was running it had had the bright idea of putting it on the sports page of the *Times*, which I read just before the obits. I'd wondered myself if Ida Simms wasn't a unisex barber shop or an erotic catering service, and sombody'd just thought of using a picture of his mother as an ad. I finally forgot about it and got interested in the spring trades.

"Now one day," Walter says, "I was looking at the paper, and I said, 'I really wonder where this poor woman is.' And Yolanda, which was typical of her actually, said, 'There isn't any woman, Walter. It's just a come-on for some damn thing. If you don't believe me, I'll call and you can listen in on the extension.' I said I wouldn't listen in on anything because even if she was right, she ought to be wrong. I wouldn't want somebody giving up on me, would you?"

"What happened next?"

"She called, Frank. And a man answered. Yolanda said, 'Who's this?' And the man I guess said, 'This is Mr. Simms speaking. Do you have any word about my wife?' It was a special line, of course. And Yolanda said, 'No, I don't. But I'd like to know if this is on the level.' And the man said, 'Yes, on the level. My wife's been missing since February and we're crazy out of our minds worrying. We can offer a reward.' Yolanda just said, 'Sorry. I don't know anything.' And she hung up. This was about six weeks before she left with this Pitcock character." Walter's eyes grow narrow as if he can see Pitcock in the cross hairs of a high-powered rifle.

"What does that have to do with anything?"

"It's just cynical, is my point. That's all."

"I think you're way too finicky on this, Walter."

"Maybe so. Though I couldn't get it out of my mind. That poor woman wandering around God knows where—lost, maybe. Crazy. And everybody thinking her picture was an ad for something filthy, just a dirty joke. The helplessness of it got to me."

"Anything's possible, Walter." I can't suppress another yawn.

Walter suddenly presses his hands together between his bald knees, and fixes on me an odd supplicant's look. "I know anything's possible, Frank. But when I mentioned it to Warren, he said he thought it was a tragedy, the whole thing, and a shame nobody had called up with some news to put her family at ease. Even that she was dead would've been a relief."

"I doubt that."

"Okay, that's a point. We all have to die. That's not going to be any goddamn tragedy. The bad thing is a shitty, cynical, insensitive life, somebody like Yolanda calling those poor people up and making their lives miserable for an extra five minutes just because she couldn't stand not to make a joke out of dying. Something that's all around us. . . ."

"Oh, for Christ sake."

"That's okay, Frank. Never mind. I still want to tell you the rest, at least the part that won't embarrass you."

Though how could hearing about Walter's moment of magic do anything but bore me the same as watching an industrial training film, or hearing a lecture on the physics of the three-point stance. What could I hear that I couldn't figure out already if I was interested? The private parts of man are no amusement to me (only the public).

"It was like a friendship, Frank." Walter is suddenly as sorry-eyed as a pallbearer. "If you can believe that." (What is there for me to say?) "I guess I can't really explain my feelings, can I? All I know is what he said. 'Death's no tragedy,' something strange, I don't know. And then I said, 'Let's get out of here.' Just like you would with a woman you thought you were in love with. Neither of us was shocked. We just got up, walked out of the Funicular onto Bowling Green, got in a cab and headed uptown."

"How'd you choose the Americana?" I have absolutely no earthly reason to want to know that, of course. What I'd like to do is grab Walter by his Barracuda lapels and throw him out.

"His firm keeps some rooms blocked up there, Frank, for the fellas who work late. I guess that probably seems pretty ironic to you, doesn't it?"

"I don't know, Walter, you have to go somewhere, I guess."

"It sounds silly, even to me. Two Wall Street guys going at it in the Americana. You get caught in your own silliness sometimes, Frank, don't you?" He's aching to tell me the whole miserable business.

"So what's going to happen, Walter. Are you going to see Warren, or whatever his name is again?"

"Frank, who knows. I doubt it. He's pretty happy up in Newfoundland, I guess. Marriage to me is founded on the myth of perpetuity, and I think I'm wedded pretty firmly to the here and now at this point in time." Walter sniffs in a professional way, though I have no idea on earth what he could be talking about. He could as easily be reciting the Gettysburg Address in Swahili. "Warren doesn't feel that way from all I can learn. Which is fine. I don't think I'm made to be one of those guys anyway, Frank. Though I was never closer to anyone in my life. Not Yolanda. Not even my mom and dad, which is pretty scary for a farm kid from Ohio." Walter offers me a big, scared, kid-from-Ohio-grin. "I gave up all that perpetuity business, which after all is just founded on a fear of death. You know that, of course. It's the big business concept all over again. I'm not afraid of dying suddenly, Frank, and leaving everything in a mess. Are you?"

"I'm nervous about it, Walter, I'll admit that."

"Would you do what I did, Frank? Tell the truth."

"I guess I'm still stuck on the perpetuity concept. I'm pretty conventional. I don't mean to disapprove, Walter. Because I don't."

Walter cocks his head when he hears this. He has just heard some unexpected good news, and his blue, sad eyes narrow as if they saw down a long corridor where the light had gone dim as all past time. He holds me in this bespectacled gaze for a long moment, maybe a half-minute. And I know exactly what he is seeing, or trying to see, since from time to time I've assiduously tried to see the same thing— with X before she left me for good.

Himself is what Walter's trying to see! If some old-fashioned, conventional Walter Luckettness is recognizable in conventional and forgiving Frank Bascombeness, maybe things won't be so bad. Walter wants to know if he can save himself from being lost out in the sinister and uncharted waters he's somehow gotten himself into. (For all his recklessness, Walter is basically a sound senator, and not much a seeker of the unknown.)

"Frank," Walter says, cracking a big smile, wriggling back in his chair and giving his head an incongruous shake. (For the moment he has staunched badness.) "Did you ever wish somebody or something could just pick you up and move you way, way far off?"

"Plenty of times. That's why I'm in the business I'm in. I can get on a plane and that happens. That's what I was telling you about traveling the other night."

"Well, that's how I felt when I first came in here tonight, Frank— when your colored boy let me in and I was just wandering around here waiting. I didn't feel like there was any place far away enough, and I was caught in the middle of a helluva big mess, and everything was just making it worse. Do you remember how we used to feel when we were kids? Everything out of bounds, just off the map, and we weren't responsible."

"It was great, Walter, wasn't it." What I'm thinking about is the fraternity, which was great. Splendid. Whiskey, card games, girls.

"Before I got here tonight everything seemed to count against me in some crappy way."

"I'm glad you came, then, Walter."

"I am too. I *do* feel better, thanks to you. Maybe it was us swapping some ideas back and forth. I feel like some new opportunity is just about to present itself. By the way, Frank, do you ever go duck hunting?" Walter smiles a big, generous smile.

"No."

"Well, let's *go* duck hunting, then. I've got all kinds of guns. I was just looking at them yesterday, cleaning them up. You can have one. I'd like you to come back to Coshocton with me, meet my family. Maybe next fall. That Ohio River country is really something. I used to go every single day of the season when I was a kid. You know, as far as Ohio seems, it's not really that far. Just down the Penn Turnpike. I haven't been going back lately, but I'm ready to start. My folks are getting old. What about your folks, Frank, where are they now?"

"They're dead, Walter."

"Ah well, sure. We lose 'em, Frank. What plans have you got?"

"When?"

"This summer, say." Walter is veritably beaming. I wish he would go home.

"I'm going to take my kids up around Lake Erie." What business is it of his what plans I have? Everything, to him, is pertinent now.

"Real good idea."

"I've just about had it, Walter. It's been a long day."

"I was in despair when I came here, Frank. A lot of life seemed behind me. And now it doesn't. What can I do? Do you want to go out and have some eggs? There's a good place on Route 1. What d'ya say to a breakfast?" Walter is on his feet, hands in his pockets, rocking back on his heels.

"I think I'll just hit the hay, Walter. The couch is your kingdom."

Walter reaches down, picks up his Colts glass, admires it, then hands it over to me. "I think I'll get in my car and drive around. That'll settle me down."

"I'll leave the door unlocked."

"Okay," Walter says with a brash laugh. "Frank, let me give you an extra key to *my* place. You can't tell when you're going to want to disappear for a while. My place is yours."

"Aren't you going to be in it, Walter?"

"Sure, but it can't hurt. Just so you'll know you can always drop out of sight when you want to." Walter hands me the key. I have no idea why Walter would think I'd ever need to drop out of sight.

"That's nice of you." I put the key in my pocket and give Walter a good-natured smile meant to make him leave.

"Frank," Walter says. Then without my expecting it or being able to duck or run, Walter grabs my cheek and kisses me! And I am struck dumb. Though not for long. I shove him backwards and in one spasm of wretchedness shout, "Quit it, Walter, I don't want to be kissed!"

Walter blushes red as Christmas and looks dazed. "Sure, sure," he says. I know I have missed Walter's point here, but I have not missed my own point, not on your life. I would kiss a camel rather than have Walter kiss me on the cheek again. He does not get to first base with me, no matter how much he feels at home.

Walter stands blinking behind his tortoise-shells. "We lose control by degrees, don't we, Frank?"

"Go home, Walter." I'm peevish now.

"Maybe I can, Frank. Thanks to you." Walter smiles his somber war-vet's smile and walks out the door.

In a moment I hear his car start. From the window I see the headlights on the street and the car—it is an MG—buzz sadly away. Walter gives me two quick honks and disappears around the curve. I am sure he will call when he gets home; he is that kind of High-school Harry. And as I settle onto the couch as I used to in the old days when X was gone, fully clothed, a Gokey catalog for reading, I unplug my phone—a small, silent concession to the way lived life works. Don't call, my silent message says, I'll be sleeping. Dreaming sweet dreams. Don't call. Friendship is a lie of life. Don't call.

*I*n the first six months after Ralph died, while I was in the deepest depths of my worst dreaminess, I began to order as many catalogs into the house as I could. At least forty, I'm sure, came every three months. I would, finally, have to throw a box away to let the others in. X didn't seem to mind and, in fact, eventually became as interested as I was, so that quite a few of the catalogs came targeted for her. During that time—it was summer—we spent at least one evening a week couched in the sun room or sitting in the breakfast nook leafing through the colorful pages, making Magic Marker checks for the things we wanted, dogearing pages, filling out order blanks with our Bankcard numbers (most of which we never mailed) and jotting down important toll-free numbers for when we might want to call.

I had animal-call catalogs, which brought a recording of a dying baby rabbit. Dog-collar catalogs. Catalogs for canvas luggage that would stand up to Africa. Catalogs for expeditions to foreign lands with single women. Catalogs for all manner of outerwear for every possible occasion, in every climate. I had rare-book catalogs, record catalogs, exotic hand-tool catalogs, lawn-ornament catalogs from Italy, flower-seed catalogs, gun catalogs, sexual-implement catalogs, catalogs for hammocks, weathervanes, barbecue accessories, exotic animals, spurtles, slug catchers. I had all the catalogs you could have, and if I found out about another one I'd write or call up and ask for it.

X and I came to believe, for a time, that satisfying all our purchasing needs from catalogs was the very way of life that suited us and our circumstances; that we were the kind of people for whom catalog-buying was better than going out into the world and wasting time in shopping malls, or going to New York, or even going out into the shady business streets of Haddam to find what we needed. A lot of people we knew in town did the very same thing and believed that was where the best and most unusual merchandise came from. You can see the UPS truck on our street every day still, leaving off hammocks and smokers and God knows what all—packs of barbecue mitts and pirate chest mailboxes and entire gazebos.

For me, though, there was something other than the mere ease of purchase in all this, in the hours spent going through pages seeking the most virtuous screwdriver or the beer bottle cap rehabilitator obtainable nowhere else but from a PO box in Nebraska. It was that the life portrayed in these catalogs seemed irresistible. Something about my frame of mind made me love the abundance of the purely ordinary and pseudo-exotic (which always turns out ordinary if you go the distance and place your order). I loved the idea of merchandise, and I loved those ordinary good American faces pictured there, people wearing their asbestos welding aprons, holding their cane fishing rods, checking their generators with their new screwdriver lights, wearing their saddle oxfords, their same wool nighties, month after month, season after season. In me it fostered an odd assurance that some things outside my life were okay still; that the same men and women standing by the familiar brick fireplaces, or by the same comfortable canopy beds, holding these same shotguns or blow poles or boot warmers or boxes of kindling sticks could see a good day before their eyes right into perpetuity. Things were knowable, safe-and-sound. Everybody with exactly what they need or could get. A perfect illustration of how the literal can become the mildly mysterious.

More than once on a given night when X and I sat with nothing to say to each other (though we weren't angry or disaffected), it proved just the thing to enter that glimpsed but perfectly common-place life—where all that mattered was that you had that hounds-tooth sport coat by Halloween or owned the finest doormat money could buy, or that all your friends recognized "Jacques," your Brittany, from a long distance away at night, and could call him by the name stitched on his collar and save him from the log truck bearing down on him just over the rise.

We all take our solace where we can. And *there* seemed like a life—though we couldn't just send to Vermont or Wisconsin or Seattle for it, but a life just the same—that was better than dreaminess and silence in a big old house where unprovoked death had taken its sad toll.

All of which passed in time, as I got more interested in women and X did whatever she did to accommodate her loss. Months later, when I had departed home to teach at Berkshire College, I found myself alone one night in the little dance professor's house the college rented for me at the low end of the campus near the Tuwoosic River, doing what I did in those first couple of weeks to the exclusion of practically everything else—poring over a catalog. (The faculty lounge was full of them, leading me to be sure I was not alone.) In this instance I was going through the supplement of a pricey hunting outfitter based in West Ovid, New Hampshire, at the foot of the White Mountains, barely eighty miles from where I sat at that moment. Up the hillside that night, a group of students was holding a sing-along (I was meant to be in attendance), and a cool, crisp burnt-apple smell swam with the New England air and flooded my open window, making the possibility of going as remote as Neptune. I was deep in size comparisons of Swiss wicker-and-leather picnic baskets, and just flipping back toward clearance items on the black-and-white insert pages, my thoughts on a fumble-free flashlight, ankle warmers for the chilly nights ahead, a predator-pruf feeder, when suddenly what do I see on page 88 but a familiar set of eyes.

After how many years? The narrow, half-squinty, mirthful sparkle I had seen a hundred times over—though on page 88 *only* the eyes were visible behind a black silk balaclava worn by a woman modeling a pair of silk underwear from Formosa.

Off in the darkening surround, the sounds of "Scarborough Fair" drifted into the purple hills, and the smell of elm and apple wood floated lushly through my open window, but I couldn't care less.

I flipped forward and back. And suddenly here was Mindy Levinson on almost every page: with long brown hair and a tentative smile, a Swedish Angora jacket over her shoulder (not looking the least bit Jewish); farther back, standing by a red Vermont barn, wearing a Harris Tweed casual jacket and appearing proud and arrogant; just inside the cover in an Austrian hat, but seeming repentant of some untold misdeed; elsewhere toward the back, ensconced in a comfy New Hampshire kitchen, starting a fire with a brass spark-igniter made in the shape of a duck's head. And later still, coralling a bunch of munchkin kids all wearing rabbit's fur puppet hats.

When she was my first college love interest, Mindy and I used to slip off campus, into her parents' Royal Oak home and boink the daylights out of each other for days on end. It was Mindy who had traveled with me on a tour of Hemingway Country and stayed out on a beach at Walloon Lake while fireflies twinkled. She was the first girl I ever lied to a room clerk because of. Later, of course, she married a slimy land developer named Spencer Karp and settled down in the Detroit suburb of Hazel Park near her parents and had kids before I was even through with school.

But I could not have been more stupefied. Out of a disorderly and not especially welcome present came a friendly, charitable face from the past (not an experience I have that often). Here was Mindy Levinson smiling at me twenty times out of a shiny life I might've had if I'd just gone to law school, gotten bored with corporate practice, dropped it all, moved up to New Hampshire, hung out my shingle, and set up my wife in a town-and-country dress shop all her own—a pretty life, prizable and beckoning, apparently without a crumb of alienation or desperate midnight heart's pounding. A fairy-tale life for real adults.

Where, I wondered, *was* Mindy? Where was Spencer Karp? Why did she not look Jewish now? What about Detroit?

What I did was immediately pick up the phone, dial the twenty-four-hour toll-free number and talk to a sleepy-sounding older woman whom I directed to the catalog page with the kids in the puppet hats and ordered three. As I was reading off my credit card number, I happened to say that the woman in that picture looked strangely familiar, like my sister from whom I was separated by the adoption agency. Did the company use local women for their models? I asked. "Yes," came the stoical reply. Did she know who this particular woman might be? There was then a pause. "I don't know nothin about that kind of thing," the woman said suspiciously. "Is this all you want to buy?" She sighed with exasperation and lack of sleep. I admitted it was but that I had decided not to buy the puppet hats after all, after which the woman cut me off.

I sat for a while and gazed out my screenless window into the yellow-lit dale of Berkshire College, where the maples and oaks were still in summer leaf, listening to "Scarborough Fair" change to "Michael, Row the Boat Ashore," and then to "Try to Remember," trying indeed to remember as much as I could about Mindy and those long-ago days in Ann Arbor, sensing both mystery and co-incidence, and considering the small stirring caused by the two brown eyes behind the black balaclava, and the non-Jewish smile in a popcorn sweater.

A certain kind of mystery requires investigation so that a better, more complicated mystery can open up like an exotic flower. Many mysteries are not that easy to wreck and will stand some basic inquiry.

Mine entailed getting up at the crack of dawn the next day and driving the eighty miles over to West Ovid, strolling into the store whose catalog I brought with me, and asking the clerk straight out who this woman in the moleskin ratcatchers was, since she looked like a woman I had gone to college with, and who had married my best friend in the service from whom I'd been separated in a Vietnamese POW camp and did not know the fate of to this very moment.

The cash register woman—a dwarfish, ruby-faced little Hampshirewoman—was only too happy to tell me that the woman in question was Mrs. Mindy Strayhorn, wife of Dr. Pete Strayhorn, whose dental office was down in the middle of town, and that all I had to do was go down there, walk in the office and see if he was my long-lost friend. I was not the first person, she said, to recognize old friends in the catalog, but that most people, when they inquired, turned out to be mistaken.

I could not get out the door fast enough. And not to Doc Strayhorn's, needless to say. But to the phone booth in front of the Jeep dealership across the road, where I looked up Strayhorn on Raffles Road and dialed Mindy without catching a breath or blinking an eye.

"Frank Bascombe?" she said, and I would've known her playful voice in a crowded subway car. "My goodness. How in the world did you ever find us here?"

"You're in the catalog," I said.

"Oh, well sure." She laughed in an embarrassed way. "Isn't that funny. I do it for the clothes discount, but Pete thinks it isn't quite nice."

"You really look great."

"Do I?"

"Darn right. You're prettier than ever. A whole lot prettier."

"Well, I had my nose fixed after I married Spencer. He hated my old one. I'm glad you like it."

"Where *is* Spencer?"

"Oh, Spencer. I divorced him. He was a crumb, you know." (I did know.) "I've lived here ten years now, Frank. I'm married to a nice man who's a dentist. We have children with perfect teeth."

"Great. It sounds like a great life. Plus you do the modeling."

"Isn't that a riot? How are you? What's happened to you in seventeen years? A lot, I'll bet."

"Quite a bit," I said. "I don't want to talk about that, though."

"Okay."

Red and silver streamers were spinning outside down the front of the Jeep dealership's lot. Two long lines of Cherokees and Apaches sat in the brisk New England sunlight. It soon would be winter, and the mountains at this latitude were already red and yellow higher up. In a day I would have to begin teaching students I already knew

I wasn't going to like, and everything seemed to be starting on a new and perilous course. I knew, though, I wanted to see Mindy Levinson Karp Strayhorn one last time. Many, many things would've changed, but if she was who she was, I would still be me.

"Mindy?"

"What?"

"I'd sure like to see you." I felt myself grinning persuasively at the phone.

"When did you have in mind, Frank?"

"In ten minutes? I'm down the street right now. I was just passing through town."

"Ten minutes. That'll be great. It's pretty easy to find our house. Let me give you directions."

The rest of it was short but all I'd hoped for (though possibly not what you would think). I drove to her house, a rambling remodeled Moravian farmhouse with a barn, plenty of out-buildings and a pleasant pond that reflected the sky and the geese that swam on it. There was a golden dog and a housekeeper who looked at me suspiciously. Two children who might've been ten and eight, and a taller girl who might've been seventeen stood at the back end of the hall and smiled at me when their mother and I left. Mindy and I took a drive in my car with the top down toward Sunapee Lake and caught up on things. I told her about X and Ralph and my other children and my writing career and sportswriting and my plans to try teaching for a short while, all of which seemed not to interest her much, but in a pleasant way (I didn't expect anything different). She told me about Spencer Karp and about her husband and her children and how much she appreciated "just the general mental attitude" of the people up here in the "north country," and how in her mind the whole nation was changing not so much for the better as for the worse, and nobody could make her go back to Detroit now. At first she was guarded and skittish and talked like a travel agent as we skimmed along the highway, sitting over by the door as if she wasn't sure I wasn't some dark destroyer come to wreck her existence with out-of-date memories. After a while, though, when she saw how tame I really was, how enthusiastic, how all I wanted was to be near her life for a couple of hours, unquestioning and intending only to admire all from a distance and not to try and "go in" or to get her in the sack in some shabby motel on the way to Concord (exactly like I used to), then she liked me all over again and laughed and was happy the rest of the time. In fact, she eventually couldn't help giving me a kiss and a hug every little while, and putting her head on my shoulder once we were far enough from West Ovid that no one she knew would see her. She even told me she didn't intend to tell Pete about my visit, because that would make it all "the more delicious," which made me kiss her again and embarrass her.

And then I simply drove her home. She was wearing a mint-colored cotton dirndl right out of the catalog and which she raised above her excellent knees when she was sitting in the car. And she looked as pretty as her picture, which is how I remember her, and how I think of her each time I see her, season onto season, wearing one set of bright traditional clothes after another, on and on into a perfect future.

And what I felt as I drove back the long, slow road that evening toward the little town where Berkshire College sits, crossed the Connecticut and plowed my way into picture postcard Vermont, was: better. Better in all the possible ways. X and I were finally too modern for this kind of perfect, crystalized life—no matter how ours was turning out at the moment. But I had glimpsed a nearly perfect life of a kind, as literally perfect as the catalog promised it could be. And I had done it in a casual, offhand way, which was why Mindy liked me again and could kiss and hug me shamelessly. I had taken nothing away with me, had ruined nothing (though with another kiss I could've gotten her to that motel in Concord). I had had, in essence, a brief love affair not-quite. And that was quite enough for me, or for any man trying to get on a better, straighter track, trying to see the brighter side of things and put an end to his dreaminess, which I hoped was on the run by then, though I was certainly wrong.

9

A gray, silvermane mist inhabits my room. I lie on the floor of the upstairs sleeping porch, fully clothed, my head cushioned by the boards, which are cold and morning-slicked by mist. In this posture I would often wake up in the months after X left. I would go to sleep reading catalogs, out like a light on the couch as I was last night, or in my bed or in the breakfast nook—but wake up on these same cold deals, still dressed and stiff as a mummy, with no memory of moving. I do not yet know what to make of it. Back then it didn't necessarily seem a bad sign, and it doesn't now. And though a longing permeates the cool morning, it is familiar enough, and I'm happy to lie still and listen to my heart harmlessly thump. It is Easter.

What I hear are typical Sunday sounds. Someone raking spring leaves in a nearby yard, finishing a chore begun months ago; a single horn blat from the first train down—moms and dads early for services at the Institute. A fat paper slaps the pavement. A rustle of voices next door at the Deffeyes' as they putter in the early dark. I hear the squeeze-squeak of Bosobolo in his room, his radio tuned low for all-night gospel. I hear a jogger on my street heading toward town. And far away in the stillness of predawn—as far away, even, as the next sleeping town—I hear bells chiming a companionable Easter call. And I hear also: weeping. The low susurrus of a real grief being grieved somewhere in the cemetery, close by in the dark.

I go stand at the window and peer down into the early dawn, through the leafing copper beech and the tulip tree, but I can see nothing beneath the pale clouds-and-stars sky—only the low profiled shadows of white monuments and trees. No deer look up at me.

I have heard such sounds before. Early is the suburban hour for grieving—midway of a two mile run; a stop-off on the way to work or the 7-11. I have never seen a figure there, yet each one sounds the same, a woman almost always, crying tears of loneliness and remorse. (Actually, I once stood and listened, and after a while someone—a man—began to laugh and talk Chinese.)

I lie back on the bed and listen to the sounds of Easter—the optimist's holiday, the holiday with the suburbs in mind, the day for all those with sunny dispositions and a staunch belief in the middle view, a tiny, tidy holiday to remember sweetly and indistinctly as the very same day through all your life. I cannot remember a rainy Easter, or one when the sun didn't shine its heart out. Death, after all, is a mystery Christians can't get cozy with. It is too severe and unequivocal, a mistake in adding, we think. And we raise a clamor against it, call on the sun to stay cheery, preach the most rousing of sermons. "Well, now, let's us just hunker down to a *real* miracle, while we're putting two and two together." (A knowing, homiletic grin.) "Let's just let plasma physics and bubble chambers and quarks try and explain *this* one." (Grinning, nodding parishioners; sun beaming to beat the band through modern, abstract-ecumenical, permanently sunny window glass. Organ oratorio. Hearts expanding to victory.)

My only wish is that my sweet boy Ralph Bascombe could wake up from *his* sleep-out and come in the house for a good Easter tussle like we used to, then be off to once-a-year services. What a day that would be! What a boy! Many things would be different. Many things would never have changed.

X, I know, is not taking Paul and Clarissa to church, a fact which worries me—not because they will turn out godless (I couldn't care less) but because she is bringing them up to be perfect little factualists and information accumulators with no particular reverence or speculative interest for what's not known. Easter will soon seem like nothing more than a lurid folk custom, one they'll forget before they're past puberty. A myth. Naturally, there was no time for religion in the Dykstra household, where facts and figures reigned, though Irma tells me she has begun "experimenting" with Orange

County Holy Rollerism, which makes me worry that the scales might tip for my own two once they get to the end of what can be sensibly, literally disclosed—which is where extremism lurks. You can, after all, know too damn much and end up with a big thumping loss you can't replenish. (Paul's mission for his pigeon three nights ago is an encouraging, countervailing sign.)

They may already know too much about their mother and father— nothing being more factual than divorce, where so much has to be explained and worked through intelligently (though they have tried to stay equable). I've noticed this is often the time when children begin calling their parents by their first names, becoming little ironists after their parents' faults. What could be lonelier for a parent than to be criticized by his child on a first-name basis? What if they were mean children, or by knowing too much, *became* mean? The plain facts of my alone life could make them tear me apart like maenads.

I am of a generation that did not know their parents as just plain folks—as Tom and Agnes. Eddie and Wanda. Ted and Dorie—as democratically undifferentiable from their children as ballots in a box. I never once thought to call my parents by their first names, never thought of their lives—remote as they were—as being like mine, their fears the equal of my fears, their smallest desires mirrors of everyone else's. They were my parents—higher in terms absolute and unknowable. I didn't know how they financed their cars. When they made love or how they liked it. Who they had their insurance with. What their doctor told them privately (though they must've both heard bad news eventually). They simply loved me, and I them. The rest, they didn't feel the need to blab about. That there should always be something important I wouldn't know, but could wonder at, wander near, yet never be certain about was, as far as I'm concerned, their greatest gift and lesson. "You don't need to know that" was something I was told all the time. I have no idea what they had in mind by not telling me. Probably nothing. Possibly they thought I would come to truths (and facts) on my own; or maybe—and this is my real guess—they thought I'd never know and be happier for it, and that not knowing would itself be pretty significant and satisfying.

And how right they were! And how hopeful to think my own surviving children could enjoy some confident mysteries in life, and not fall prey to idiotic factualism or the indignity of endless explanation. I would protect them from it if I could. Divorce and dreary parenting have, of course, made that next to impossible, though day to day I give it my most honest effort.

To get a divorce in a town this size, I should say, is not the least bit pleasant—though it is easy, and in so many ways the town is made for it, appreciates it, and knows how to act by way of supplying "support groups" (a woman's counseling unit called X the day of our settlement and invited her to a brown bag lunch at the library). Still, it is troubling to be a litigant in the building where you have gone to pay parking fines or retrieved stolen bikes, been supposed a solid citizen by stenos and beat cops. It leaves you with a bankrupt feeling, since the law here is not made to notice you or even to be noticed, only to give you respectable, disinterested sway. From what I hear, Las Vegas divorces are much better since no one notices anything.

Ours was the most amicable of partings. We could've stayed married, of course, and waited until things got better, but that was not what happened. Alan, X's little lawyer with fragrant dreams of a rich entertainment practice—XKEs awaiting him on tarmacs, chorus girls with giant tits—huddled up with my big, slope-shouldered, bearded, ex-Peace Corps, ex-alcoholic Middlebury guy and, across a mahogany table in Alan's office, struck a bargain in an hour. In principle I surrendered everything, though X didn't want much. I kept this house in exchange for helping her buy hers with my half of the savings. I laid claim to the Block Island map and three or four other treasures. We agreed on "irreconcilable differences" as the theme for our appearance in court, then all trooped across the street together and sat chatting uncomfortably in the back until our case was called. And in less than another hour we were "done," as they

say in Michigan. X flew off with the children to a golf-and-swim
holiday on Mackinac Island, to "open some space." I drove home,
got drunk as a monkey and cried until dark.

What else could I do? The cleansing ritual of strong fluids and
hot, balming tears is all we have native to us. I looked around for
some Rupert Brooke poems or a copy of *The Prophet* but couldn't
find them. Around eight, I stretched out on the couch, put a taped
NBA slam-dunk contest on television, ate a pimento cheese sandwich, began to feel better and went to sleep watching Johnny. And
my sleep, I remember, was one of the most sound and dreamless
sleeps of my life—till eight-thirty the next day when I woke up
hungry as a lion and as trusting to the future as a blind sky-diver.

Was I not alienated? Depressed? Ashamed? In need of violent
cheering up? Schitzy? On the edge? My answer is, not much. Dreamy
as Tarzan, perhaps. Lonely. Though in a way that I got over after
while. But not chance's victim. I got myself busy after breakfast,
finishing up work on a six-pronged analysis of major-leaguers' base
stealing styles, and before I knew it I was back in the thick of things.
Which is how it's stayed. Bert Brisker told me that after his divorce
he went crazy, broke into his ex-wife's house while she was gone
on vacation, threw bricks through the TV screen, slept in her bed
and emptied cat shit in all her drawers. But that is not the way I
felt. We can make too much of our misfortunes.

Ever since I was in the Marines (I was only in six months) I've
been an early riser, and have done my best thinking then. I used to
lie nervously in my bunk, wide awake, waiting for the reveille record,
my mind thrumming, mapping out how I could do better that day,
make the Marine Corps take notice and be proud of me; make myself
less a victim of the funks and incongruities my fellow officer can-
didates were wrestling with, rise to rank quickly, and as a result
help protect the lives of my men once we got situated over in Vietnam, where I felt they'd have a lot on their minds (like getting blown
to smithereens). I had the advantage of an education, I thought, and
I'd need to be their eyes and ears over and above the level they

themselves could see and hear. I was an idiot, of course, but we're almost always wrong when we are young.

What I'd like to do as I lie here, and before the day burgeons into a glowing Easter, is put together some useful ideas about Herb, just a detail or two to act as magnets for what else will occur to me in the next days, which is the way good sportswriting gets done. You hardly ever just sit down and write it cold, staring at an empty yellow sheet expecting yourself to summon up every good idea you'll have ready at the first moment. That can be the scariest thing in the world. Instead, what you try to do is honor your random instincts, catch yourself off guard, and write a sentence or an unexpected descriptive line—the way the air smelled one day, or how the wind lifted and tricked off the lake surface in a peculiar way that might later make the story inevitable. Once those notes are on record, you put them away and let them draw up an agenda of their own that you can discover later when you're sorting through things just before the deadline, and it's time to write.

Herb, though, is no easy nut to crack, since he's obviously as alienated as Camus. It would've helped if I'd filed away one perception or recorded a quote, but I didn't know what to say or think anymore than I know now. The way the air smelled or the wind shifted or what song was playing on the radio as we drove out, don't seem to figure. Simple, declarative sentences just don't exactly flock to big Herb's aid. Everything is minor key, subjunctive and contingent. *Herb Wallagher's got his eye on the future these days* (at least until his mood stabilizer wears through). *Herb Wallagher has seen life from both sides* (and doesn't think much of either one). *It would be easy for Herb Wallagher to take a dim view of life* (if he wasn't already as crazy as a road lizard).

The cheap-drama artists of my profession would, of course, make quick work of Herb. They're specialists at nosing out failure: hinting a fighter's legs as suspect once he's over thirty and finally in his prime; reporting a hitter's wrists are stiff just when he's learned to go the opposite way and can help the team by advancing runners.

They see only the germs of defeat in victory, venality in all human endeavor.

Sportswriters are sometimes damned bad men, and create a life of lies and false tragedies. In Herb's case, they'd order up a grainy black-and-white fisheye of Herb in his wheelchair, wearing his BIONIC shirt and running shoes, looking like a caged child molester; take in enough of his crummy neighborhood to get the "flavor"; stand Clarice somewhere in the background looking haggard and lost like somebody's abandoned slave out of the dustbowl, then start things off with: "Quo Vadis Herb Wallagher?" The idea being to make us feel sorry enough for Herb, or some *idea* of Herb, to convince us we're all really like him and tragically involved, when in fact nothing of the kind is true, since Herb isn't even a very likable guy and most of us aren't in wheelchairs. (If I were paying salaries, those guys would be on the street looking for a living where they couldn't do any harm.)

Though what can I write that's better? I'm not certain. Some life does not give in to a sportswriter's point of view. It ought to be possible to take a rear-guard approach, to look for drama in the concept of retrenchment, to find the grit of the survivor in Herb—something several hundred thousand people would be glad to read with a stiff martini on a Sunday afternoon before dinner (we all have our optimal readers and times), something that draws the weave of lived life tighter. It's what's next that I have to work on. Though in the end, this is all I ask for: to participate briefly in the lives of others at a low level; to speak in a plain, truth-telling voice; to not take myself too seriously; and then to have done with it. Since after all, it is one thing to write sports, but another thing entirely to live a life.

By nine I am up, dressed in my work clothes and out in the side yard nosing around the flower beds like a porch hound. Following my speculations about Herb, I went back to sleep and woke up happy and alert—my mind empty, the sun speckling through the beech leaves and not a hint of ugly Detroit weather on the horizon. My trip to the Arcenaults, however, is still two hours off, and as is sometimes the case these days, I do not have quite enough to do. One of the down-side factors to living alone is that you sometimes get overly absorbed with how exact segments of time are consumed, and can begin to feel a pleasure with life that is hopelessly tinged with longing.

Beyond my hemlock hedge Delia Deffeyes is out in her yard in tennis whites, reading the newspaper, something I've seen her do a hundred times. She and Caspar have had their morning game, and now he has gone in for a nap. The Deffeyes and I have a policy which says that simply seeing each other in our yards is no reason to have a conversation, and normally we pass polite offhand waves and smiling nods and go about our business. Though I never mind an impromptu conversation. I am not a man who hoards his privacy, and if I am out in my yard spreading Vigaro or inspecting my crocuses, I am per se available for an encounter. Delia and I do occasionally engage in nuts and bolts publishing talk with reference to a book she's writing for the historical society on European traditions in New Jersey architecture. My experience is years old, but I maintain a kind of plain-talk, common-sense expertise about matters: "Any editor worth his or her salt ought to appreciate the hell out of the kind of attention to detail you're willing to give. You can't take that for granted, that's all I know." It *is* all I know, but Delia seems willing to take a word to the wise. She is eighty-two, born to a storied American business family in Morocco during the Protectorate, and has seen a wide world. Caspar has retired out of the diplomatic corps and came to the seminary afterward to teach ethics. Neither of them has too many years left on earth. (It is, in fact, a revelation to live in a town with a seminary, since like Caspar, seminarians are not a bit what you'd think. Most of them are not pious Bible-pounders at all, but sharp-eyed liberal Ivy League types with bony, tanned-leg second wives, and who'll stand with you toe to toe at a cocktail party, drink scotch and talk about their time-share condos in Telluride.)

Delia spies me down behind the children's jungle gym, fingering a rose bud that's ready to bloom, and wanders over to the hemlock hedge shaking her head, though apparently still reading. It is her signal and the premise of our neighborliness—all our conversations are just extensions of the last one, even though they are often on different subjects and months apart.

"Now here, Frank, look at this." Delia holds up the front page of the *Times* to show me something. Church bells have begun clamoring and gonging across town. On all streets families are off to Sunday school in spanking new Easter get-ups—cars washed and polished to look like new, all arguments suspended. "What do you think about what our government's doing to the poor people in Central America?"

"I haven't kept very close tabs on that, Delia," I say from the roses. "What's going on down there now?" I give her a sunny smile and walk over to the hedge.

Her moist blue eyes are large with effrontery. (Her hair is the precise blue color of her eyes.) "Well, they're mining all the ports down there, in, let's see," she takes a quick peek, "Nicaragua." She crushes the open paper down in front of her and blinks at me. Delia is small and brown and wrinkled as an iguana, but has plenty of strong opinions about world affairs and how they ought to work out. "Caspar's extremely discouraged about it. He thinks it'll be another Vietnam. He's in the house right now calling up all his people in Washington trying to find out what's really going on. He may still have some influence, he thinks, though I don't see how he could."

"I've been out of town a couple of days, Dee." I stand and admire Dee and Caspar's pair of pink pottery flamingos which they bought in Mexico.

"Well, I don't see why we should mine each other's ports, Frank. Do you? Honestly?" She shakes her head in private disappointment with our entire government, as though it had been one of her very favorites but suddenly become incomprehensible. For the moment, though, my mind's as empty as a jug, captured by the belling at the seminary carillon. "Come my soul, thou must be waking; now is breaking o'er the earth another day." I find I cannot bring up the name or the face of the man who is president, and instead I see, unaccountably, the actor Richard Chamberlain, wearing a burnoose and a nicely trimmed Edwardian beard.

"I guess it would depend on what the cause was. But it doesn't sound good to me." I smile across the flat-trimmed hedge. I have to work at being a full adult around Delia, since if I'm not careful our age difference—roughly forty-five years—can have the effect of making me feel like I'm ten.

"We're hypocrites, Frank, if that's our policy. You should bear in mind Disraeli's warning about the conservative governments."

"I don't remember that, I guess."

"That they're organized hypocrisy, and he wasn't wrong about that."

"I remember Thomas Wolfe wrote about making the world safe for hypocrisy. But that's not the same."

"Caspar and I think that the States should build a wall all along the Mexican frontier, as large as the Great Wall, and man it with armed men, and make it clear to those countries that we have problems of our own up here."

"That's a good idea."

"Then we could at least solve our own problem with the black man." I don't exactly know what Delia and Caspar think about Bosobolo, but I do not intend asking. For being anti-colonial, Delia has some pretty strong colonial instincts. "You writers, Frank. Always ready to set sail with any wind that blows."

"The wind can blow you interesting places, Dee." I say this with only mock seriousness, since Delia knows my heart.

"I see your wife at the grocery, and she doesn't seem very happy to me, Frank. And those two sweet babies."

"They're all fine, Dee. Maybe you caught her on a bad day. Her golf game gets her down sometimes. She really didn't get a fair start on a real career. I think she's trying to make up for lost time."

"I do too, Frank." Delia nods, her face like lean old glove leather, then folds her paper in a neat paperboy's fold that's wonderful to see. I'm ready to dawdle away back to the roses and crab apples. Delia and I are sympathetic to each other's private causes, and both realize it, and that is good enough for me. For a moment I spy Frisker, her seal-point, sleuthing around the hibiscus below Caspar's flag pole, staring up at the bird feeder where a junco's perched. Frisker has been known to prowl my roof at night and wake me up, and I've thought about getting a slingshot, but so far haven't. "Man wasn't meant to live alone, Frank," Delia says significantly, eyeing me closely all of a sudden.

"It has its plusses, Delia. I've adjusted pretty well now."

"How long has it been since you read *The Sun Also Rises*, Frank?"

"It's probably been a while now."

"You should reread it," Delia says. "There're important lessons there. That man knew something. Caspar met him in Paris once."

"He was always one of my favorites." Not true, though a lie's what's asked for. It's not surprising that Delia's view of the complex world dates from about 1925. In fact it might have been a better time back then.

"Caspar and I were married in our sixties, you know."

"I didn't realize that."

"Oh, yes. Caspar had a nice fat wife who died. I even met her once. Of course, my own poor husband died years before. Caspar and I went out of wedlock in Fez, in 1942, and kept aware of each other's whereabouts afterwards. When I heard Alma, his fat wife, had died, I called him up. I was with a niece in Maine by then, and in two months Caspar and I were married and living just below Mount Reconnaissance in Guam, which was his last posting. I certainly didn't expect what I got from life, Frank. But I didn't waste time either." She smiles fiercely, as if she can see my future and the certainty that it will not be quite as wonderful.

"It's a beautiful day, isn't it, Dee?"

"It is, yes. It's quite lovely. I believe it's Easter."

"I can't remember a prettier one."

"I can't either, Frank. Why don't you come over this week and have a scotch with Caspar. He'd love for you to come talk men's talk. I think he's pretty upset by all this mining." In the fourteen years I've lived here, I have been in the Deffeyes' house only two times (both times to fix something), and Delia means no harm by one more insincere invitation. We have reached the natural end of our neighborliness, though she's too polite to admit the inevitability of it, a quality I like in her. I gaze up from the yard into the still blue Easter morning and, to my surprise, see a balloon, large upon the currents of a gleaming atmosphere, its mooring lines adangle, a big red moon with a smiling face on its bloated bag. Two tiny stick-figure heads peer down from the basket, point arms at us, pull a chain which produces a far-off gasping.

Where did they leave earth, I wonder? The grounds of a nearby world headquarters? A rich man's mansion on the Delaware? How far can they see on a clear day? Are they safe? Do they *feel* safe?

Delia does not seem to notice, and awaits my answer to her invitation.

"I'll do that, Dee." I smile. "Tell Cap I'll stop by this week. I've got a joke to tell him."

"Any day but Tuesday." She smiles a prissy smile. This is the usual complication. "He misses men, I'm afraid."

Delia strays away now with her paper to her sunny lawn and tennis court, me to my barbecue pit and roses and day, upward-tending in most all ways, one I'll be happy to put into the file of Easters spent richly and forgotten.

Gong, go the bells in town. Gong, gong, gong, gong, gong.

Just before ten I put in a call to X, to wish the children happy Easter. It is now a holiday we "trade," and this the first one when I haven't been around. Though no one's home on Cleveland Street. X's answer message says that if I'm interested in golf lessons I should leave my name and number. In the background I hear Clary say "Later, bird brain," and break up laughing. There is an edge in X's voice now, something strange to me, an all-business, money-in-the-bank brassiness that reminds me of her father. It makes me wonder if my family is off smorging in Bucks County with one of X's software or realtor friends, some big hairy-armed guy in a green sports jacket, with everything on the company cuff.

I decide not to leave a message (though I'd like to).

For some reason I call Walter Luckett's number and let the phone ring a long time without an answer while I stare out on the paisley Easter street. Where would I be if I were Walter? In some bully bar in the West Village? Cruising the elmy streets of insular New-foundland in a devil's own fury? Hitting some backboard balls at the high school before taking in *The Robe* at Lost Bridge Mall? I'm not even certain I care to know. Some people were not made to have best friends, and I might be one. Walter might be another, though for different reasons. Acquaintanceship usually suffices for me, which was more or less the one important lesson learned from my Lebanese girfriend, Selma Jassim, at Berkshire College, since if anything, she believed mutual confidences of almost any kind were just a lot of baloney.

I decided to go teach at Berkshire College—I know now—to deflect the pain of terrible regret—the same reason I quit writing my novel, years ago, and began to write sports; the same reason most of us make our dramatic turns to the right and left about midway, and the same reason some people drive right off the course and into the ditch.

One afternoon a year after Ralph died, I was at home on one of the week-long breaks that occur at the magazine between large as-signments, and when we are supposed to rest up and re-establish a semblance of regular life. I was sitting in the breakfast nook—it was in May—reading some piled-up copies of *Life* when the phone rang. The man calling said his name was Arthur Winston and he was married to Beth Winston, who was the sister of my former literary agent, Sid Fleisher, whom I had not heard from since he had written us a condolence card. Arthur Winston said he was the chairman of the English Department at Berkshire College in Massachusetts, and he had been talking to Sid in Sid's house in Katonah, and Sid had mentioned a writer he had once represented who had written one good book of short stories, but then quit writing entirely. One thing led to another, Arthur said, and he had ended up with the book, which he claimed to have read and admired. He asked if I had been writing any other short stories since then, and for some reason I gave him an evasive answer which could've made him think I had, and that with a little coaxing I could actually be induced to write plenty more (though none of this was true). He said to me then that he was over a pretty big barrel. The usual writer at Berkshire, an older man whose name I didn't know, had suddenly gone berserk at the end of the spring semester and started vicious fist fights with several people—one of them a woman—and had begun carrying a gun under his coat, so that he had been institutionalized and would not be back in the fall. Arthur Winston said he knew it was a long shot, but that Sid Fleisher had said I was a "pretty interesting" fellow who'd lived a "pretty unusual" life since quitting writing, and he—Arthur—thought maybe a semester of teaching would be just the thing to get my work fired up again, and if I wanted to do it he would consider it a personal favor to him and would see to it I taught anything I pleased. And I simply said "Yes, that's fine," and that I would be there in the fall.

I do not exactly know what got into my thinking. I had never thought about such a thing in my life, and in one way it couldn't have been crazier. The magazine, of course, is always happy to extend leaves for what it considers widening experiences. But when I told X she just stood there in the kitchen and stared out the window at the Deffeyes' tennis court where Paul and Clary were watching Caspar play with one of his octogenarian friends—each old man wearing a crisp white sweater and hitting bright orange balls in high looping volleys—and said "What about us? We can't move to Massachusetts. I don't want to go there."

"That's fine," I said, actually for a moment seeing myself leading a graduation day exercise at some tiny Gothic-looking campus, wearing a floppy cap and crimson gown, carrying a scepter, and being the soul of everyone's admiration. "I'll commute," I said. "The three of you can come up odd weekends. We'll go stay in country inns with cider mills. We'll have a wonderful time. It'll be easy." I was suddenly eager to get up there.

"Have you lost your mind?" X turned and looked at me as if she could in fact see that I'd lost my mind. She smiled at me in an odd way then, and it seemed she knew something bad was happening but was powerless to help. (This was during the worst of the time with the other women, and she had been doing a lot of holding her peace.)

"No. I haven't lost my mind," I said, smiling guiltily. "This is something I've always wanted to do." (Which was a total lie.) "There's no time like the present if you ask me. What do you think?" I went over to give her a pat on the arm, and she just turned and went out into the yard. And that was the last time we ever talked about it. I started making arrangements with the college to provide me a house. I asked for and received my leave from the magazine (a Breadth Fellowship was what they called it). My texts were mailed down midway through the summer, and I did what I felt like was proper preparation. Then at the first of September I packed the Chevy and drove up.

What I found, of course, when I got my feet under me was that I had about as much business teaching in college as a duck has riding a bicycle, since what was true was that in spite of my very best efforts I had *nothing to teach.*

It's rare, when you think about it, that anyone ever would, given that the world is as complicated as a microchip and we all learn it slowly. I knew plenty of things, a whole lifetime's collection. But it was all just about myself, and significant only to me (love is transferable; location isn't actually everything). But I didn't care to reduce any of it to fifty minute intervals, to words and a voice ideal for any eighteen-year-old to understand. That's dangerous as a snake and runs the risk of discouraging and baffling students—whom I didn't even like—though more crucially of reducing *yourself*, your emotions, your own value system—your life—to an interesting syllabus topic. Obviously this has a lot to do with "seeing around,"

which I was in the grip of then but trying my best to get out of.
When you are not seeing around, you're likely to speak in your own
voice and tell the truth as you know it and not for public approval.
When you *are* seeing around, you're pretty damn willing to say
anything—the most sinister lie or the most clownish idiocy known
to man—if you think it might make someone happy. Teachers, I
should say, are highly susceptible to seeing around, and can practice
it to the worst possible consequence.

I could twine off sports anecdotes, Marine Corps stories, college
jokes, occasionally vet an easy Williams poem to profit, tell a joke
in Latin, wave my arms around like a poet to demonstrate enthusiasm. But that was all just to get through fifty minutes. When it
came time to teach, literature seemed wide and undifferentiable—
not at all distillable—and I did not know where to start. Mostly I
would stand at the tall windows distracted as a camel while one of
my students discussed an interesting short story he had found on
his own, and I mused out at the dying elms and the green grass and
the road to Boston, and wondered what the place might've looked
like a hundred years ago, before the new library was put up and the
student center, and before they added the biplane sculpture to the
lawn to celebrate the age of flight. Before, in other words, it all got
ruined by modernity gone haywire.

The fellows in my department, God knows, couldn't have been
a better bunch. To their way of thinking, I was a "mature writer"
trying to get back on my feet after a "promising start" followed by
a fallow period devoted to "pursuing other interests," and they were
willing to go to bat for me. To make them all feel better I claimed
to be putting together a new collection based on my experiences as
a sportswriter, but in truth any thought I had for such an enterprise
fled like thunder the minute I set foot on campus. I'd see a copy of
my book at a dozen different houses at a dozen different dinner
parties (the same library copy that made its way around ahead of
me). And though no one ever mentioned it, I was to understand
that it had been read closely and remarked on admiringly and in
private by people who mattered. One crisp October evening at the

house of a Dickens scholar, I inconspicuously removed it off the coffee table, put it in the snappy autumn fire and stood and watched it burn (with the same satisfaction X must've felt when her hope chest billowed up our chimney), then went in to dinner, ate chicken Kiev and had a good time talking in a pseudo-English accent about departmental politics and anti-Semitism in T. S. Eliot. I ended up late that night in a bar across the New York line, with Selma, who had also been a guest, arguing the virtues of the American labor movement and the checkered career of Emil Mazey with a bunch of right-to-work conservatives, and afterward sleeping in a motel.

My colleagues, I should say, were all fiercely interested in sports, especially baseball, and could carry on informative brass-tacks conversations about how statistics lie, hitting zones and who the great all-time bench managers had been—bull sessions that could last half an evening. They often knew much more than I did and wanted to talk for hours about exotic rule applications, who covers what on a double-steal, and the "personalities" of ball parks. They would often alter their own English or urban accents to a vaguely southern, "athletic" accent and then talk that way for hours, which also happened at Haddam cocktail parties. I even had some confide wistfully that they wished they'd done what I did, but had never seen where the "gap" was in a young life that let you think about such a thing as being a sportswriter. All of them, of course, had gone right out of college, raced through graduate school, and as far as possible gotten jobs, tenure, and a life set for them. If they'd had any "gaps," they didn't acknowledge them, since that might've had something to do with a failure of some kind—a bad grade, a low board score or a wishy-washy recommendation by an important professor, something that had scared the bejesus out of them and that they wanted to forget all about now.

Still, I could tell it confused them that something had happened to me that hadn't happened to them, and that here I was in their midst, and not such a bad guy after all, when their lives seemed both perfect and perfectly ordinary. They would smile at me and shake their heads, arms folded, pipes clenched tight, ties adjusted, and for some reason I didn't and still can't understand, listen to me talk! (whereas they wouldn't listen to each other for a second). I was specimen-proof that life could be different from theirs and still be life, and they marveled at it.

Writing sports was, I think, inviting to them just the way it's inviting to me, and also exotic, but because of its literalness it sometimes embarrassed and scared them and made them laugh and fold and refold their arms like Zulus.

They all seemed, however, extremely encouraging that I give another try at real writing. That was something they could understand a fellow wanting to do and then failing at nobly. They respected deeply the nobility of small failures since that was what they suspected of themselves. Though for my lights they thought too little of themselves, and didn't realize how much all of us are in the very same boat, and how much it is an imperfect boat.

I do not hold to the old belief that professors like writers because they can see us fail in a grander and sillier and therefore more unequivocal way than they have. On the contrary, they like to see someone trying, giving it all up to set a permanent mark. They may also be absolutely expecting to watch you fail, but they aren't really cynical types at all. And since I wasn't trying to set any marks (they simply *thought* I was and had some admiration for me for that reason) I probably got the best the place had to offer.

The only people whom I can say with certainty I didn't get along with were the "junior people," the sad, pencil-mouthed and wretched hopefuls. They hated the sight of me. I was, I think, too much like them—unprotected in the world—yet different in a way they found infuriating, incriminating and irrelevant. Nothing is more inciteful of disdain than somebody doing something other than what you're doing, not doing it badly but not complaining about it (though at the moment I was as much at sea as a man can be). They looked on me with real disgust and usually wouldn't even speak, as if certain human enterprise was synonymous with laughable failure, though at the same time as if something about me seemed familiar and might figure dimly in their futures if things did not work out. The gallows,

I imagine, is less scary to the condemned man than to the one not yet sentenced.

I told them without rancor or the first wish to worry them that if they didn't get tenure they might give sportswriting a serious try, as other people in that situation had. Though they never appeared to like that advice. I think they didn't appreciate the concept of interchangeability, and no one ever came by to apply for a job after they were let go.

Finally, though, what I couldn't stand was not what you might think.

I didn't mind the endless rounds of meetings, which I sat through wearing a smile and with nothing whatsoever in my mind. I didn't care a mouse's fart for "learning"—didn't even feel I understood what it meant in their language—since I couldn't begin to make my students see the world I saw. I ended up feeling an aching remorse for the boys, especially the poor athletes, and could only think of the girls in terms of what they looked like in their vivid underwear. But I was impressed with my colleagues' professionalism: that they knew where all "their books" were in the library, knew the new acquisitions by heart, never had to waste time at the card catalog. I enjoyed bumping into them down in the lower level stacks, gossiping and elbowing one another about female faculty, tenure, sharing some joke they'd heard or whatever scandal had turned up in *TLS* that week. What they did, how they conducted life, was every bit as I would've done if I was them—treated the world like an irrelevant rib-tickler, and their own comfortable lives like an elite men's club. I never once felt a sense of superiority, and would be surprised if they did. I didn't object to the fisherman's sweaters, the Wallabies, pipes, dictionary games, charades, the long dinner party palaver about "sibs" and "La Maz" and college boards and experimental treatments for autism, the frank talk about lesbianism and who was right in the Falklands (I liked Argentina). I even got used to the little, smirky, insider mailbox-talk passed between people I had just eaten dinner with the night before, but who, the next morning, would address me only in sly, crypto-ironic references from whatever we'd talked about last night: ". . . put *this* memo in *The Cantos*, right, Frank? See if Ole Ezra can translate that. Haw!" Live and let live is my motto. I'm at home with most interest groups, even in the speakers' bureau at the magazine, for whom I occasionally journey into the country to talk to citizens about the philosophy of building-from-within, or to deliver canned sports anecdotes.

To the contrary. These eternally youthful, soft-handed, lank-shouldered, blameless fellows—along with a couple of wiry lesbians—were all right with me. They could always give in to their genuine boyishness around me, which was something their wives encouraged. They could quit playing at being serious and surrender to giggly silliness most any time after a few drinks, the same as real folks.

And deep down, I think, they liked me, since that's how I treated them—like decent Joes, even the lesbians, who seemed to appreciate it. They'd have been happy to have me around longer, maybe forever, or else why would they have asked me to "stay on" when they could tell that something was wrong with me, with my life, something that made me melancholy, though all of them were careful enough never to say a word about it.

What I did hate, though, and what finally sent me at a run out of town after dark at the end of term, without saying goodbye or even turning in my grades, was that with the exception of Selma, the place was all anti-mystery types right to the core—men and women both—all expert in the arts of explaining, explicating and dissecting, and by these means promoting permanence. For me that made for the worst kind of despairs, and finally I couldn't stand their grinning, hopeful teacher faces. Teachers, let me tell you, are born deceivers of the lowest sort, since what they want from life is impossible—time-freed, existential youth forever. It commits them to terrible deceptions and departures from the truth. And literature, being lasting, is their ticket.

Everything about the place was meant to be lasting—life no less than the bricks in the library and books of literature, especially when seen through the keyhole of their incumbent themes: eternal returns, the domination of man by the machine, the continuing saga of choosing middling life over zesty death, on and on to a wormy stupor. Real mystery—the very reason to read (and certainly write) any book—was to them a thing to dismantle, distill and mine out into rubble they could tyrannize into sorry but more permanent explanations; monuments to themselves, in other words. In my view all teachers should be required to stop teaching at age thirty-two and not allowed to resume until they're sixty-five, so that they can *live* their lives, not teach them away—live lives full of ambiguity and transience and regret and wonder, be asked to explain nothing in public until very near the end when they can't do anything else.

Explaining is where we all get into trouble.

What's true, of course, is that they were doing exactly what I was doing—keeping regret at arm's length, which is wise if you understand it exactly. But they had all decided they really didn't have to regret anything ever again! Or be responsible to anything that wasn't absolutely permanent and consoling. A blameless life. Which is not wise at all, since the very best you can do is try and keep the regret you can't avoid from ruining your life until you can get a start on whatever's coming.

Consequently, when these same people are suddenly faced with a real ambiguity or a real regret, say something as simple as telling a sensitive young colleague they probably like and have had dinner with a hundred times, to go and seek employment elsewhere; or as complicated as a full-bore, rollicking infidelity right in their own homes (colleges are lousy with it)—they couldn't be more bungling, less ready, or more willing to fall to pieces because they can't explain it to themselves, or wanting to, won't; or worse yet, willing to deny the whole beeswax.

Some things can't be explained. They just are. And after a while they disappear, usually forever, or become interesting in another way. Literature's consolations are always temporary, while life is quick to begin again. It is better not even to look so hard, to leave off explaining. Nothing makes me more queasy than to spend time with people who don't know that and who can't forget, and for whom such knowledge isn't a cornerstone of life.

Partly as a result, Selma Jassim and I gave ourselves up to the frothiest kind of impermanence—reveled in it, staved off regret and the memory of loss with it. (Muslims, let me tell you, are a race of people who understand impermanence. More so even than sports-writers.)

A person with a cold eye might say what happened between Selma and me—after our romantic dinner in the starchy fireplaced Ver-mont Yankee Inn the very night I put X and the children on the bus—was simply an example of the usual shabby little intrigues visiting firemen in small New England colleges are expected to get embroiled in, since there's nothing else to do from bleary week to bleary week, and you're not really into the swing of things. And my answer is that in the grip of desperate dreaminess even the most trivial of human connections can bear a witness, and sometimes can actually improve a life that's stranded. (Beyond that, you can never successfully argue the case for your own passions.)

X had come up with the children the second weekend I was there (I'd just seen Mindy Levinson). She brought a pair of brass candle-sticks for my little house, neatened the whole place up, sat in one of my classes, went with me to faculty parties two nights in a row and seemed to have a good time. She slept late and took a long autumnish walk with me along the Tuwoosic, during which we talked about a spring driving trip with the children down to the Big Bend Country, something she had been reading about. But as we were driving out to the Bay State Tavern for the three of them to catch the bus home Sunday morning, she looked across the seat at me and said "I really don't have any idea what you're doing up here, Frank. But it really all seems pretty extremely stupid to me, and I want you to resign and come home right now with us. It's not so great being home without you."

I told her, of course, that I couldn't just leave. (Though if I had I might still be married, and I had the feeling she was dead right about my staying; that another failed writer would crawl out of the woodwork and be in my place in less than twenty-four hours, and Arthur Winston would never think of my "interesting" face again.) I felt, however, that something had brought me up there and it may have been ridiculous, but I thought I needed to see what it was— which is what I told X. Plus, I'd given my word. I told her, lamely, that I wanted her to come up every weekend, and she could even take Paul out of school and move all three of them in with me (which was, needless to say, even more ridiculous).

When I said all this, X sat in the car staring out at the waiting bus, then sighed and said sadly "I'm not coming back up here any-more at all, Frank. Something's in the air up here that makes me feel old and completely silly. So you'll just have to go it alone."

And with that she got out with Paul and Clary, and lugged their big bag onto the bus. When they climbed aboard the children both cried (X didn't), and they left me standing alone and dazed, waving at them from the Bay State parking lot.

What Selma and I did after that and for the next thirteen weeks before I went back home to New Jersey and divorce, was simply share a fitful existence. She was an acerbic cold-eyed Arab of dusky beauty, who was thirty-six at the time (exactly my age), but seemed older than I was. She had come to Berkshire College that fall from Paris only to obtain a visa (she said), so she could find a rich American "industrialist," marry him, then settle down in a rich suburb for a happy life. (She knew a pleasant, easy existence staunched almost any kind of unhappiness.)

I never visited home again until the semester was over, and X never wrote me or even called. And what Selma and I did to amuse ourselves was stay inside my little faculty cottage lolling in bed, or else drive in my Malibu wherever we could go in the time we had away from campus, talking for hours about whatever interested us— conversations I actually remember as the most engrossing of my entire life—primarily, of course, because they were stolen. We drove to Boston, up to Maine, down into Westchester, far up into Ver-mont, and as far west as Binghamton. We stayed in small motels, ate in roadhouses, stopped for drinks in bars with names like The Mohawk, The Eagle and The Adams—dark, remote, millstone places where the outside world rarely entered, and where we knew no one and were cause for no notice: a tall, long-necked Arab woman in sleek black silks, smoking French cigarettes, and an ordinary-looking Joe in a crew-neck sweater, chinos and a John Deere Tractor cap I'd affected when I got to Berkshire. We were tourists headed to and from nowhere.

We hardly ever talked about literary subjects. She was a critical theorist and as far as I could tell had only the darkest, most ironic contempt for all of literature. (As a joke, she invented a scheme for taking all the "I" pronouns out of one of F. Scott Fitzgerald's novels and gave a seminar on it that all our colleagues said was "ingenious.") What we talked about instead were small-talk things—why a particularly brilliant hillside of sugar maples changed their color at different schedules and what that might suggest of disease; why American highways ran though the places they did; what it was like to drive in London (where I have never been and she had been a student); her first husband, who was British; my only wife; an acting career she'd abandoned; how I felt about compulsory military service at various crucial stages in my life—nothing of great interest, though anything that came along and that we could chatter about without implying a future (we had no delusions about that). Yet it all served to make one day passable before we had to go back to teach, something I came to loathe. I found out a great deal about her in the course of things, though I never asked any of it, and it was always understood that I really knew nothing. There were other people in her life, I knew that, a good many of them, men and women both, people who lived in foreign countries—some possibly even in prison—others who were estranged for reasons that she simply wouldn't go into. For a period of one week I felt extremely strongly about her, entertained all kinds of impractical and romantic notions, things *I* never went into, and then I abandoned them all. I told her I loved her a hundred times, usually in chuckling, dare-devilish ways we both understood was a lot of hooey, since she laughed at the idea of almost any kind of usual affection and claimed love was an emotion she had no interest in finding out about.

She had only one, I thought, strange attachment, which was the subject of altruism and which she lectured me about at length the first morning we woke up together, when she was standing around naked in my sunny little house smoking cigarettes and staring out the window at the Tuwoosic as if it were the Irrawaddy. She said altruism drove Arabs crazy because it was always "phony" (a word she liked). She grew furious when she talked about it, threw her head from side to side and shouted and laughed, while I simply sat in bed and admired her. It was not religion or economics that fueled the flames of world hatreds, she felt; it was altruism. She told me that first morning, with a grave look, that by the time she was eighteen she'd survived two drug addictions, a "profound" involvement with terrorists in which she hinted she'd killed people; been kidnaped, raped, imprisoned, had flirtations with a number of dark *isms*, all of which had galvanized her intellect and forged unassuageably her belief that she knew why people did things—to suit themselves and no other reason—which was why she preferred to stay as remote as possible. She said she disliked the Christian members of the faculty (not the Jews), and not because of the self-satisfied squalor of their collegiate lives which she made laughing, sneering reference to (though only because they weren't rich), but because the Christians thought they were altruists and pretended to be generous and well-meaning. The only remedy for altruism, she felt, was either to be very poor or enormously rich. And she knew which of those she wanted.

What Selma thought about me I'm not exactly sure. I thought *she* was simply a knock-out, though I'm not certain she didn't think of me as pathetic, despite expressing admiration for me of the kind every American would like to inspire when traveling to far-away, more advanced cultures. I would sometimes get into sudden states of agitation during which I would clam up and get somber as a mental patient or else begin directing vicious remarks toward something I knew nothing about—often, near the end of the term, it was some colleague I'd decided had slighted me, but whom I really had nothing against and usually had never even met. Selma would humor me at that point and say she'd never met anyone like me; that I was the savvy, hard-nosed realist she had heard real Americans were (puny academics fell far below), but that I also had a thoughtful, complicatedly whole-hearted and vulnerable side which made the whole mix of my character intellectually exotic and brilliant. She said it had been a positive step to quit real writing and become a sportswriter, which she knew practically nothing about, but saw just as a way of making a living that wasn't hard. She thought my being at Berkshire College was as ridiculous as X did, and as her own presence there. Though in truth what I really think she thought of me was that we were alike, both of us displaced and distracted out of our brainpans and looking for ways to get along. "You might just as well have been a Muslim," she said more than once and raised her long sharp nose in a way I knew she meant as estimable. "You should've been a sportswriter, too," I said. (I didn't know what I meant by that, though we both laughed about it like apes.)

From a distance it could seem that Selma and I existed on the most dallying edge of cynicism. Though that would be dead wrong, since to be truly cynical (such as when I romanced all those eighteen women in all those major sports venues of this nation) you have to hoodwink yourself about your feelings. And we knew exactly what we were doing and what we were existing on. No phony love, or sentimentality, or bogus interest. No pathos. But only on anticipation, which can be as good as anything else, including love. She understood perfectly that when the object of anticipation becomes paramount, trouble begins to lurk like a panther. And since she wanted nothing from me—I was not an industrialist and had many more problems than I needed; and since I wanted nothing from her but to have her in my car or in my bed, laughing and touring the quilted New England landscape like leaf-peepers, we thrived. (I figured this out later, since we never talked about it.)

What we anticipated no one of course could ever make a whole, free-standing life out of and expect it to last very long. A nighttime drive to get dinner at a state-line roadhouse, in which you cruise through hills and autumn-smelling woods and feel almost too cold before you're home. A phone's sudden ringing on an Indian summer night when insects buzz but you have expected it. The sound of a car outside your house and a door swinging closed. The noise of what becomes a familiar deep breathing. The sound of cigarette smoke against a telephone, the tinkle-chink of ice cubes from a caressing silence. The Tuwoosic rilling in your sleep, and the slow positive feeling that all might not be entirely lost—followed by the old standard closure and sighs of intimacy. She gave in to the literal in life but almost nothing else, and for that reason mystery emanated from her like a fire alarm. And there isn't much more to life without much more complication.

There was, I should say, no one thing that happened between us, nothing that either of us said that made a difference to our lives longer than a moment. The particulars would only seem as ordinary as they were. For the two of us, ours was just a version of life briefly perfected (though in a way that showed me something) and that ended.

In any case, what more did I have to look forward to? My semester? My bunch of smiling, explaining colleagues? Life without my first son? My diminishing life at home with X? The gradual numbly-crumbly toward the end stripe? I don't know. I didn't know then. I simply found out that you couldn't know another person's life, and might as well not even try. And when it was all over (we simply went out for a drink at the Bay State and said goodbye as if we'd just met each other), I left campus after dark and headed back to New Jersey without even reporting my grades (I mailed them in), eager but apprehensive as a pilgrim, but without a flicker of loss or remorse. All bets were off from the start and no one had his or her heart broken or suffered regret, or even had their feelings hurt much. And that does not happen often in a complex world, which is worth remembering.

The day of the night of my sudden leaving, I was sitting in my office high in Old Mather Library daydreaming out the window while I should've been reading some final papers and figuring grades, when a knock came at my door. (I'd had my office changed to the remotest place possible so, I told them, I could work on my book, but actually it was so students wouldn't be tempted to drop in, and so Selma and I could have some privacy.)

At the door was the wife of one of the young associate professors, a fellow I'd barely gotten to know and who I suspected didn't much like me from the arrogant way he acted. His wife, though, was named Melody, and she and I had once had a long and friendly conversation at Arthur Winston's first-of-the-year cocktail party (which X had attended) about *The Firebird*, which I had never seen performed and knew nothing about. Afterwards she always acted like she thought I was an interesting new addition to things, and always gave me a nice smile when she saw me. She was a small mouse-haired woman with brown teary-looking eyes and, I thought, a seductive mouth that her husband probably didn't like, but I did.

At my door she seemed nervous and half-embarrassed, and seemed to want to get inside and shut us in. It was December and she was bundled up for the snow, and had on, I remember, a Peruvian cap with ear flaps that came to a peak, and some kind of woolly boots.

When I closed the door she sat down on the student's chair and immediately took out a cigarette and began smoking. I sat down and smiled at her, with my back to the window.

"Frank," she said suddenly, as if the words were simply colliding around inside her head and getting out only by accident, "I know we don't know each other very well. But I've wanted to see you again ever since we had that wonderful talk at Arthur's. That was an important talk for me. I hope you know that."

"I enjoyed it myself, Melody." (Though I didn't remember much more about it than that Melody had said she'd once hoped to be a dancer, but that her father had always been against it, and much of her life after that had been in defiance of her old man and all men. I remember thinking that she possibly thought of me as something other than a man.)

"I'm starting a dance company right in town here," Melody said.

"I've gotten local backing. I think Berkshire students will probably be in it, and the school's going to get involved. I'm taking lessons again, driving to Boston twice a week. Seth's taking care of the children. It's pretty hectic these days, but it's made a big difference. None of it will really get off the ground till next fall at the earliest, but it all started the night we talked about *The Firebird*." She smiled at me, full of pride for herself.

"That's great to hear, Melody," I said. "I have a lot of admiration for you. I know Seth's proud of you. He's mentioned it to me." (A total lie.)

"Frank, my life's really changed. With Seth particularly. I haven't moved out on him. And I'm not going to—at least not right away. But I've demanded my freedom. Freedom to do anything I want with whoever I want to do it with."

"That's good," I said. But I didn't know really if it was that good. I swiveled and looked out the window at the snowy quadrangle below, where some idiot students were building a snow fortress, then looked at the clock on the wall as if I had an appointment. I didn't.

"Frank. I don't know how to say this, but I have to say it this way, because that's the way it is. I want to have an affair. And I'd like to ask you to have it with me." She smiled a cold little smile that didn't make her plummy lips look the least bit kissable. "I know you're involved with Selma. But you can be involved with me, too, can't you?" She unbuttoned her heavy coat and let it slip behind her, and I could see she was wearing a leotard that was purple on one side and white on the other, the Berkshire College colors. "I can be appealing," she said, and pulled down one shoulder of her leotard and exposed there in my office a very handsome breast, and began to take the other shoulder, the purple one, down.

But I said, "Melody, wait a minute. This is pretty unusual."

"Everything I've done has been usual, Frank. I'm ready to get laid a lot now. Why shouldn't I?"

"That's a good idea," I said. "But you just wait right here for me. I want to do one thing. Put your coat back on." I picked up her coat off the floor where she'd dropped it, and put it around her shoulders where she sat now with both of her lovely breasts exposed, and her lips looking as full and beautiful as they probably ever would, and her purple and white leotard down to her waist. And I went out into the hall, closed the door behind me, picked up my coat off the coat rack at the bottom of the stairs and walked out into the quad, heading for my car. The students were putting the finishing touches to their snow fort and were already starting to pelt each other and yell. Classes were over. Exams were still too far away to worry. It is the best time to be on a college campus and to be leaving.

When I was halfway across the quadrangle, whom should I see but Seth Fairbanks, Melody's husband, slogging toward the gym carrying a bag full of books and a squash racquet. He was a slender, wiry man with a thin black mustache who'd gone to NYU, and taught the 18th century but also some modern novels. We had once talked about some of my favorites, and it turned out he hated everything I had ever liked and had airtight arguments for why they were laughable.

"Where to, Professor Bascombe," Seth Fairbanks said, with a derisory smile. "Heading to the library?" This was meant as some sort of joke I didn't understand. But I put a grin on my face, thinking of his wife shivering up in my office at that moment, just beyond a window that was in sight of where we were walking (if she was still there). It was five o'clock, and the day was gray and nearly dark, and we probably couldn't have been seen anyway.

"Going home to grade a set of essays, Seth," I said in a jolly voice. "I've had them writing about Robbe-Grillet." (Another lie. My students had made up their own assignments and also suggested what grade they thought they should get.) "He's a pretty smart cookie."

"I'd like to see how you phrased your questions. Drop it in my box in the morning. I might learn something. I'm teaching *The Voyeur* myself." Seth could barely suppress a laugh.

"You bet," I said. I could see my car, caked with snow, as we walked down the hill toward the lot. The old brown gymnasium was across the road, its lights burning yellow in the dusk. It was about to turn cold, and the winter would be a long one.

"I'm getting ready to teach a course in the uncanny, Frank, just for winter minisemester." I could see Seth's breath in the cold. "There're a lot of books about the weird and unusual that aren't cheap books, but real literature. I've got a little theory about it. Somebody needs to be reading those books."

"I'd like to hear about it," I said.

"I'll put a syllabus in your box. We can have lunch next week."

"That'd be great, Seth."

"It's the best of both worlds up here, Frank. I think you ought to stay on a semester. All this sportswriting can wait. You might decide you liked it up here and want to stay." Seth smiled. I knew he meant nothing of the kind. But I was going to oblige him.

"It's worth thinking about, Seth. I'll do it."

"Right." Seth raised his racquet to gesture goodbye as we reached my car, and he turned toward the gym and down the hill. I stood and looked up at the dark window of my office where Seth's wife had been, but was now in all likelihood gone home. And that seemed like the best idea to me. And I got in my car, started it up, and turned for home myself.

At ten-thirty I'm cleaned up, shaved and dressed in my Easter best—a two-piece seersucker Palm Beach I've had since college. On my way out the back, I see Bosobolo striding in through the front door. He has let Frisker slip inside and shoot down the hall past me to the kitchen.

I stop in the doorway and for a moment look him up and down in an arch, appraising way. He is a man I admire, a bony African with an austere face, almost certain the kind to have a long aboriginal penis. We believe we have the same off-beat, low-key sense of humor we've always thought as unique, and for that reason are shrewd and respectful toward each other. He likes it that I live alone with no apparent self-pity and that occasionally Vicki spends the night. I respect him for studying Hobbes as an antidote to over-spiritualizing over at the Institute.

He is dressed in his black missionary pants, white short-sleeves and sandals, but with a loudly ugly orange necktie he bought on 42nd Street the day he arrived from Gabon, and that makes him look like an old blues man. Two times lately, from my car window, I've seen him arm-in-arm with a dumpy white seminary girl half his age, the two of them strolling on the edge of the grounds. Obviously steamy romance is brewing up in her little garret or possibly even upstairs here.

What a piece of exoticism it must be! A savage old prince, old enough to be her father, whonking away on her like a frat boy.

Seeing me, Bosobolo stops under the hanging crystal lamp X inherited from her aunt, and peers at me down the hall as if I were far away. He would like, I already know, to get upstairs and turn on Brother Jimmy Waldrup from North Carolina, whom he deeply admires, though he's complained he can't understand how Brother Jimmy keeps so much in his head at once and cries so easily. He has pages of observer notes I've seen in his room. His education here is a complete one.

"How was Sunday school?" I say, unable to suppress a wry grin. Everything between us assumes the air of a complex irony.

"Yes, quite fine," he says, keeping his distance but looking serious and vaguely fussy. "You'd've enjoyed *your*self. I saw the Second Methodist Professional Advanced Men. I explained origins of the resurrection myth." He smiles a haughty smile. "The Neanderthal thought the cave bear was dead, then found out it wasn't." I can, of course, guess exactly what the professional men—group insurance sharpshooters and branch bank veeps—thought about this particular news. I'm certain they're having a few words about it now out at Howard Johnson's.

"Sounds way too anthropomorphic to me, Gus." Gus is what he's called by the Institute professors, who can't pronounce his actual first name which is full of combative consonants, though he actually seems to like being called Gus.

"Our aim is to reconcile," he says and takes a step back. "The deity enters wherever he can. In other words." His black eyes dart up the stairs and back. I would love to grill him about his little seminary squeeze, but he would be indignant. He is married with numerous children, and probably doesn't take his new arrangement jokingly. There is not enough Fincher Barksdale in me.

I shake my head in mock seriousness. "I just don't think you can make sense out of all that. Sorry." We're talking end to end in the hall, a distance in which no one can be too serious.

"Einstein believed in a God," he says quickly. "There is a clear line of logic. You should come to the discussions." He is carrying his big black gospel, though his bony fingers wrap across the front and obscure the title completely.

"I'd be afraid of using up mystery."

"We are not listening to Bach," he says. "Our faith's involved. You'd have nothing to lose." He smiles at me, proud of this reference to Bach, whom he knows I admire, and whom we both know is exhaustible.

"Do you have any doubters down at the Second Methodist?"

"Very many. I only offer what has been always available. Someday they'll all die and find out."

"That's awful strict."

Bosobolo's eyes twinkle with mirth and firmness. He is the authority here. "When I am back home, I will be more compassionate."

He raises his eyebrows and inches toward the stairs. He hasn't mentioned Walter's visit last night. He'd be amused, I'm sure, to know that Walter thought he was the butler. On the morning airishness down the middle of my house I smell his grainy sweat, a smell that goes deep in my nose and delivers a vague stinging warning: this man is no one to trifle with. Religion is not sports to him.

"How about Hobbes," I say, ready to let him go. "Do you discuss him?"

"He was a Christian, too. Temporality interested him." He is telling me in so many words, yes, he's romancing the dumpy little seminary chicken, and no, he won't repudiate it, and I should mind my own business. "You should probably come."

"I've got too much worldly business."

"Well then, today's the day for it," he says. He raises his empty hand in a wave and starts up the stairs two at a time. "God is smiling for you today," he calls from the gloomy upper story.

"Good," I say. "I'm smiling back at him." I go back to the kitchen first to find Frisker, and then to be on my way.

On the way through town I cruise up Seminary Street, which dead-ends on the Institute grounds and the small First Presbyterian, its white steeple pointing at the clouds. The Square is church-empty (though plenty of cars are parked). A man in an orange jacket, seated in a wheelchair, peers into the closed ice cream shop, and our one black policeman stands on the curb, heavy with police gear. The De Tocqueville minibus rumbles out ahead of me and disappears down Wallace Road. Both traffic lights click to green in the watery sunlight. It is a perfect time for a robbery.

I turn south toward Barnegat Pines, but after a block I make a sweeping U-turn—what Ralph used to call a "hard left"—and pull back into the empty Disabled slot at the side of the Presbyterians.

Leaving the motor on, I duck in a side door at the back. Ushers are milling, holding sheafs of special deckle-edged vanilla Easter Service bulletins. They are local businessmen, in brown suits and tie clasps, ready to whisper a "gladjerhere" as if they'd known you all your life and had your pew picked out. No seating during prayers, doxologies and Holy Communion. Slip in during hymns, announcements and, of course, collection.

This is my favorite place in church, the very farthest back door. This is where my mother used to stand with me the few times we ever went in Biloxi. I cannot sit still in a pew, and always have to leave early, disturbing people and feeling embarrassed.

The fellow who greets me has on a name tag that says "Al."

Someone has written "Big" before it in a red marker. I recognize him from the hardware store and The Coffee Spot. He is in fact a big man in his fifties, who wears big clothes and smells of Aqua Velva and cigarettes. When I edge in close to his door, which is open revealing rows of praying heads, he eases over by me, puts a giant hand on my shoulder and whispers, "We'll put you right in there in a minute. Plenty of good seats in front." Aqua Velva washes over me. Big Al wears a big purple and gold Masonic knucklebuster, and his hairy hand is as wide as a stirrup. He slips me a bulletin and I hear him breathe down deep in his troubled lungs. The other ushers are all praying, staring ferociously at their toes and the bright red carpet, their eyes resolutely open.

"I'll just stand a minute, if it's all right," I whisper. We are old friends after all, both lifelong Presbyterians.

"Sure-you-bet, Jim. Stay right there." Big Al nods in complete assurance, then eases back with the other ushers and bows his head dramatically. (It is not surprising that he thinks of me as someone else, since nothing here could matter less than my own identity.)

The sanctuary is swimming in permanent, churchy light and jam-packed with heads and flowered hats bowed in beseechment. The minister, who seems a half-mile away, is a hale and serious barrel-chested, rambling-Jack type with a bushy beard and an Episcopal bib—without any doubt a seminary prof. He gives in to the old bafflement in a loud actor's voice, his arms raised so his gown makes great black bat wings over the lilied altar. "And we take, Oh Lord, this day as a great, great gift. A promise that life begins again. Here we are on this earth . . . our day to day comings. . . ." Predictably on and on. I listen wide-eyed, as if hearing a great new secret revealed, a promised message I must deliver to a faraway city. And I feel . . . what, exactly?

A good ecumenist's question, for a well-grounded fellow like me. Though the answer is plain and simple, or I wouldn't be here at all.

I feel just as I wanted to feel, and knew I would when I made that hard left and came barreling back to the parking lot—a sweet and expanding hieratic ardor and free elevation above low spirits, a swoony, hot tingle right down to my toe tips, something akin to what sailors in the brig must feel when the president visits their ship. Suddenly I'm home, without fear, anxiety, or for that matter even any burdensome reverence. I'm not even in jeopardy of being bested at religion here—it's not that kind of place—and can feel damn pleased with both myself and my fellow man. A rare immanence is mine, things falling back and away in the promise that more's around here than meets the eye, even though it is of course a sham and will last only as far as my car. Better this than nothing, though. Or worse. To have hollow sorrow. Or regret. Or to be derailed by the spiky fact of being alone.

Then suddenly: "Rise my soul and stretch thy wings, thy better portion trace; Rise from transitory things toward heaven, thy destined place. . . ." My voice springs forth strong and unequivocal, with Big Al's baritone behind me in the chorus of confident, repentant suburbanites. (I can never think what the words mean or even imply.) The organ rattles the windows, raises the roof, tickles the ribs, sends a stirring through all our bellies—Jim's, the ushers', the preacher's.

And then I'm gone.

A secret high sign to big Al, who understands me and everything perfectly and clasps his big stirrupy hands in front of him in a Masonic one-man handshake. It is time for the "Race to the Tomb," and I am in no need of messages, having taken in all I want and can use, am "saved" in the only way I can be *(pro tempore)*, and am ready to march on toward dark temporality, my banners all aflutter.

IO

Under the visor I have a Johnny Horizon Let's-Clean-Up-America map, printed for the Bicentennial, and taped to the dash a page of directions in Vicki's own hand on the "smart way" to get to Barnegat Pines. 206-A to 530-E to 70-S and (swerving briefly north) to an unnumbered county road referred to only as Double Trouble Road, which supposedly delivers you neat as a whistle to where you're going.

Her directions route me past the most ordinary but satisfying New Jersey vistas, those parts that remind you of the other places you've been in your life, but in New Jersey are grouped like squares in a puzzle. It is a good time to put the top down and let in the winds.

Much of what I pass, of course, looks precisely like everyplace else *in* the state, and the dog-leg boundaries make it tricky to keep cardinal points aligned. The effect of driving south and east is to make you feel you're going south and west and that you're lost, or sometimes that you're headed nowhere. Clean industry abounds. Valve plants. A Congoleum factory. U-Haul sheds. A sand and gravel pit close by a glass works. An Airedale kennel. The Quaker Home for Confused Friends. A mall with a nautical theme. Several signs that say HERE! Suddenly it is a high pale sky and a feeling like Florida, but a mile farther on, it is the Mississippi Delta—civilized life flattened below high power lines, the earth laid out in great vegetative tracts where Negroes fish from low bridges, and Mount Holly lumps on the far horizon just before the Delaware. Beyond that lies Maine.

I stop in the town of Pemberton near Fort Dix, and put in another call to X to express Easter greetings. Her recording talks in the same brassy business voice, and this time I leave a number—the Arcenaults'—where she can reach me. I also put in a call to Walter. He is on my mind today, although no one answers at his house.

In Bamber—a town that is no more than a post office and small lake across Route 530—I stop for a drink in a cozy rough-pine roadhouse with yellow lowlights and log tables. Sweet Lou's Sportsman's B'ar, owned—the signs inside all say—by a famous ex-center on the '56 Giants, Sweet Lou Calcagno. Jack Dempsey, Spike Jones, Lou Costello, Ike and a host of others have all been close friends of Sweet Lou's and contributed pictures to the walls, showing themselves embracing a smiling, crewcut bruiser in an open collar shirt who looks like he could eat a football.

Sweet Lou isn't around at the moment, but when I sit down at the bar, a heavy pale-skinned woman in her fifties with beehive hair and elastic slacks comes out from a swinging door to the back and begins to clean an ashtray.

"Where's Lou today," I ask after I've ordered a whiskey. I would, in fact, like to meet him, maybe set up a *Where Are They Now* feature: "Former Giant lugnut Lou Calcagno once had a dream. Not to run a fumble in for a touchdown or to play in a league championship or to enter the Hall of Fame, but to own a little watering trough in his downstate Jersey home of Bamber, a quiet, traditional place where friends and fans could come and reminisce about the old glory days. . . ."

"Lou who?" the woman says, lighting a cigarette and blowing smoke away from me out the corner of her mouth.

I widen my grin. "*Sweet* Lou."

"He's where he is. How long since you been in?"

"A while, I guess it's been."

"I guess too." She narrows her eyes. "Maybe in your other life."

"I used to be a big fan of his," I say, though this isn't true. I'm not even sure I ever heard of him. To be honest, I feel like an idiot.

"He's dead. He's *been* dead maybe, thirty years? That's approximately where he is."

"I'm sorry to know that," I say.

"Right. Lou was a real nunce," the woman says, finishing wiping

out the ashtray. "And he was a big nunce. I was married to him."
She pours herself a cup of coffee and stares at me. "I don't wanna
ruin your dreams. But. You know?"

"What happened?"

"Well," she says, "some gangsters drove over here from Mount
Holly and walked him into the parking lot out there like it was
friends and shot him twenty or thirty times. That did it."

"What the hell had he done to *them?*"

She shakes her head. "No idea. I was right here where I am behind
this bar. They came in, three of them, all little rats. They said they
wanted Lou to come out and talk, and when he did, boom. Nobody
came back in to explain."

"Did they catch the people?"

"Nope. They did not. Not one was caught. Lou and I were getting
divorced anyway. But I was working for him afternoons."

I look around the dark bar where Sweet Lou stares down at me
from long ago and life, surrounded by his smiling friends and fans,
an athlete who left sports a success to achieve a prosperous life in
Bamber, which was no doubt his home, or near it, yet came to a
bad end. Not the way these things usually turn out and not exactly
what you'd want to read about before dinner behind a chilled martini.

Someone else, I see, is in the bar, an older gray-haired man in an
expensive-looking silverish suit sitting talking to a young woman in
red slacks. They are in the corner by the window. Above them is
a huge somber-looking bear's head.

I cluck my tongue and look at Lou's widow. "It's nice you keep
the place this way."

"He had it in his will that all these had to be left up, or I'd have
changed it, what, a hundred years ago? It has to stay a B'ar, too,
and buy from his distributorship. Otherwise I lose it to his guinea
cousins in Teaneck. So I ignore him. I forget whose picture it is,
really. He wanted to run everybody's life."

"Do you still own the distributorship?"

"My son by my second marriage. It fell in his lap." She sniffs, smokes, stares out the small front door glass which casts a pale inward light.

"That's not so bad."

"It was the best thing he ever did, I guess. After he was in the ground he did it. Which figures."

"My name's Frank Bascombe, by the way. I'm a sportswriter." I put my dollar on the bar and drink up my whiskey.

"Mrs. Phillips," she says and shakes my hand. "My other husband's dead, too." She stares at me without interest and opens a saltine packet from a basket of them on the bar. "I haven't seen one of you guys in years. They used to come all the time to interview Fatso. From Philly. He kept 'em in stitches. He knew jokes by the hundreds." She drops the little red saltine ribbon into the clean ashtray and breaks the cracker in two.

"I'm sorry I didn't know him." I'm on my feet now, smiling, sympathetic, but ready to go.

"Well, I'm sorry I did. So we're even." Mrs. Phillips stubs out her cigarette before biting the saltine. She looks at it curiously as if considering Lou Calcagno all over again. "No, I take it back," she says. "He wasn't so awful *all* the time." She gives me a sour smile. "Quote me. How's that. Not all the time." She turns and walks stoutly down the bar toward a TV that is dark. The other two patrons are getting up to go, and I am left with my own smile and nothing to say but, "Okay. Thanks. I'll do it."

Outside in the white-shell parking lot there is the promise of approaching new weather—Detroit weather—though the sun is shining. A wet wind has arrived over Bamber Lake, unsettling the dust, bending the pines along the row of empty lake cottages, sending the Sportsman's B'ar sign wagging. The older man and the young woman in slacks climb into a red Cadillac and drive away toward the west, where a bank of quilty clouds has lowered the sky. I stand beside my car and think first of Lou Calcagno coming to his sad end where I am parked, and that this is exactly the place for such things, a place that was something once. I think about the balloonists I saw this morning, and if they will get down and moored before the stiff blow comes. I am glad to be away from home today, to be off in the heart of a landscape that is unknown to me, glad to be bumping up against a world that is not mine or of my devising. There are times when life seems not so great but better than anything else, and when you're happy to be alive, though not exactly ecstatic.

I run the top up now against a chill. In a minute's time I'm fast down the road out of scrubby Bamber, headed for my own rendez-vous on Double Trouble Road.

Vicki's directions, it turns out, are perfect. Straight through the seaside townlet of Barnegat Pines, cross a drawbridge spanning a tarnished arm of a metallic-looking bay, loop through some beachy rental bungalows and turn right onto a man-made peninsula and a pleasant, meandering curbless street of new pastel split-levels with green lawns, underground utilities and attached garages. Sherri-Lyn Woods, the area is named, and there are streets like it along other parallel peninsulas nearby, though there are no woods in sight. Most of the houses have boat docks out back with a boat of some kind tied up—a boxy cabin-fisherman or a sleek-hulled outboard. All in all it is a vaguely nautical-feeling community, though all the houses down the street look Californiaish and casual.

The Arcenaults' house at 1411 Arctic Spruce is vaguely similar to the others, though hanging on its front at the place where the two levels join behind beige siding there is a near life-size figure of Jesus-crucified that makes it immediately distinctive. Jesus in his suburban agony. Bloody eyes. Flimsy body. Feet already beginning to sag and give up the ghost. A look of redoubtable woe and calm. He is painted a lighter shade of beige than the siding and looks distinctly Mediterranean.

The Arcenaults—the swaying plaque out front says—and I wheel in just ahead of unkind weather and come to rest beside Vicki's Dart.

"Lynette just had to have ole Jesus hung out there," Vicki whispers, when we're only half in the door, where she has met me looking put out. "I think he's the tackiest thing in the entire world and *I'm* a Catholic. You're thirty minutes late, anyway." She is a vision in a pink jersey dress, serious rose-colored heels, snapping stockings and crimson fingernails, her black hair uncurled and simplified for home.

Everybody, she says, is scattered through the house on all levels at once, and I am only able to meet Elvis Presley, a tiny white poodle wearing a diamond collar, and Lynette, Vicki's stepmother, who comes to the kitchen door in a chef's apron, holding a spoon and sings out "Hi, hi." She is a pert and pretty little second wife with bright red hair and bunchy hips descending to ankletted ankles. Vicki whispers that she hails from Lodi, West Virginia, and is a thick-as-rock hillbilly, though I have the feeling we could be friendly if Vicki'd allow it. She is cooking meat and the house airs smell warm and thick. "Hope you like your lamb well, well, *well* done, Franky," Lynette says, disappearing back into the kitchen. "That's the way Wade Arcenault likes his."

"Great. That's exactly how I like mine," I lie, and am suddenly aware that not only am I late but I haven't brought a gift for anybody, not a flower, a greeting card, or an Easter bonbon. I am certain Vicki has noticed.

"You better put plenty of mint jelly on my plate." Vicki rolls her eyes, then says to my ear, "You don't either like it well done."

Vicki and I sit on a big salmon-colored couch, with our backs to a picture window that faces Arctic Spruce Drive. The drapes are open and an amber storm light colors the room, which has old-master prints on the walls—a Van Gogh, a Constable seascape, and "The Blue Boy." A plush blue carpet (a hunch tells me Everett had a hand here) covers the floor wall to wall. The house has exactly the feel of Vicki's apartment, but its effect on me—in my youthful seersucker—is that I am the teacher who has given Vicki a bad mark at midterm and who has been invited to Sunday dinner to prove the family's a solid one before finals. It isn't a bad way to feel, and when dinner is over I'm sure I can leave in a hurry.

The television, a cabinet model the size of a large doghouse, is showing another NBA game without sound. I would be happy to watch it the rest of the afternoon, while Vicki reads *Love's Last Journey*, and forget all about dinner.

"I'm hot, aren't you hot?" Vicki says, and she suddenly jumps up, crosses the room and twists the thermostat drastically. Cooling, forced air hits me almost immediately from a high wall louver. She switches around, showing her nice fanny and gives me a witchy smile. This is a different girl at home, there's no doubting that. "No need us smotherin indoors, is it?"

We sit for a while and silently watch the Knicks beat hell out of the Cavaliers. Cleveland plays its regular leggy, agitating garage-ball game while the Knicks seem club-footed and awkward as giraffes but inexplicably score more points, which makes the Cleveland crowd good and mad. Two giant Negroes start to scuffle after a loose ball, and a vicious fight breaks out almost instantly. Players, black and white, fall all over the floor like trees, and the game quickly becomes a free-for-all the referees can't handle. Police come onto the floor and begin grabbing people, smiles on their big Slovak faces, and things seem likely to get worse. It is a usual Cleveland tactic.

Vicki clicks off the picture with a remote box hidden between the couch cushions, leaving me wide-eyed and silent. She jerks her dress down around her sleek knees and sits up high like a job applicant. I can see the broad, all-business outline of her brassiere (she needs a good-sized one) through the stretchy pink fabric. I would like to snake a hand round to one of those breasts and pull her back for an Easter kiss, which I still have not been given. Meat smell is everywhere.

"Did you read that *Parade* today," she asks, giving her jersey another tug and staring across the room at an electric organ sitting against the wall underneath the flat and florid Van Gogh.

"I guess not," I say, though I can't remember actually what I have been doing. Waiting to be here. My sole occupation for the day.

"Ole Walter Scott's said that a woman washed her hair with a honey shampoo and walked out in the backyard with a wet head and got stung to death by bees." She casts a fishy eye around at me. "Does that sound like the truth?"

"What happened to the woman who washed her hair with beer? Did she end up marrying a Polack?"

She tosses her head around. "You're a regular Red Skeleton, aren't you?"

Out in the kitchen Lynette drops a pan with a loud bangety bang. "Scuze me, kids," she calls out and laughs.

"You drop the set out of your ring?" Vicki says loudly.

"I coulda said something else," Lynette says, "but I won't on Easter."

"Small favors, please," Vicki says.

"I *had* a ring that big once," Lynette's friendly voice says.

"So where'd *he* go?" Vicki says and gives me a hot look. She and Lynette are not the best of friends. I wish, though, that they could pretend to be for the afternoon.

"That poor man died of cancer before you were in the picture," Lynette says light-heartedly.

"Was that about the time you converted over?"

Lynette's beaming face pops around the kitchen door molding, her eyes sharpened. "Shortly after, sweetheart, that's right."

"I guess you needed help and guidance."

"We all do, don't we, Vicki sweet? Even Franky, I bet."

"He's Presbyterian."

"Well-o-well." Lynette is gone from the door back to her stove. "Back in the hills we called them the country club, though I understand they've gotten pious since Vatican II. The Catholics got easier and the others had to get harder."

"I doubt the Catholics got any easier," I say, though for this Vicki fires me a savage look of warning.

Lynette suddenly reappears, nodding seriously at me and pulling a curl of damp orange hair off her temple. She still seems someone a person could like. "We ought none of us to get lax the way this world is headed," she says.

"Lynette works at the Catholic crisis center in Forked River," Vicki says in a tired singsong.

"That's mighty right, sweetheart." Lynette smiles, then is gone again and begins making thick stirring noises in a bowl. Vicki looks as disgusted with everything as it's possible to be.

"What it comes down to is she answers the phone," Vicki whispers, but loud enough. "And they call that a crisis-line." She flounces back on the couch and buries her chin over in her collarbone, staring at the wall. "I guess I've seen a crisis or two. Some guy came in one time down in Dallas with his entire *thing* sticking out of his friend's pocket, and we had to sew that gentleman right back on."

"Alienation didn't work out, you see." Lynette speaks energetically from the kitchen. "That's what we're finding out now from the colleges. A *lot* of people want to get back in the world now, so to speak. And I don't try to force my religion onto them. I'll stay on a line as much as eight straight hours with some individual and he won't be Catholic at all. Course, I have to stay in bed two days after that. We all wear headphones." Lynette walks into the doorway, cradling a big crockery bowl in her arms like a farm wife. Her smile is the most patient one in the world. But she has the look of a woman who wants to start something. "Some crises don't bleed out in the open, Vicky hon."

"Whoop-dee-do," Vicki says and rolls her eyes.

"Now you're a writer, right?" Lynette says.

"Yes, ma'am."

"Well, that's awfully nice too." Lynette gazes down lovingly into her bowl while she thinks this over. "Do you ever sometimes write religious tracts?"

"No ma'am, I never have. I'm a sportswriter."

Vicki signals the TV to start again, and sighs. On the screen a tiny dark-skinned man is diving off a high cliff into a narrow inlet of surging white water. "Acapulco," Vicki mutters.

Lynette is smiling at me now. My answer, whatever it was, has been enough for her, and she just wants to take this chance to look me over.

"Well, Lynette, why don't you stare at Frank an hour or two," Vicki nearly shouts and crosses her arms angrily.

"I just want to see him, hon. I like to have one time to see a whole person clearly. Then I know them. It doesn't hurt a thing. Frank can tell I mean only good, can't you, Frank?"

"Absolutely." I smile.

"I'm glad I ain't livin here," Vicki snaps.

"That's why you have a nice place all your own," Lynette says amiably. "Of course, I've never been invited there." She ambles into the steamy, meaty kitchen, leaving the two of us on the couch alone with the cliff-divers.

"You and me ought to have a talk," Vicki says sternly, her eyes suddenly red and full of tears. The forced air comes on again and drums us both with a cool mechanical influx. Elvis Presley trots to the door and looks at us. "Get outa here, Elvis Presley," Vicki says. Elvis Presley turns around and trots into the dining room.

"What about?" I smile hopefully.

"Just a bunch of things." She wipes her eyes with her fingertips, which requires her to duck her head.

"About you and me?"

"Yes." She makes her pouty lips go sour. And once again my poor heart drums fast. Who knows why? To save me? I don't have a liar's clue to what needs to be said between us, but her mood is a mood with unhappy finality in it.

Why, though, can't everything—just for today—wait? Wait a beat as the actor says. Just go on without change a bit longer? Why can't every sweet untranscendent thing we know or think we know go on along a little longer without closure having to rear its practical head? Walter *Luckless* Luckett could not have been more right about me. I don't like to think of this or that thing ending, or even changing. Death, the old streamliner, is not my friend, nor will he ever be.

Though I can't put off whatever this is, and maybe I don't even want to. She is a demon after changes today, her whole person exuding transition. Only there's no real need for it, is there? (*Thunk-a, thunk-a thunk*, my heart's pumping.) We haven't even had dinner yet, not tasted the lamb cooked hard as a coaster. I have yet to meet her father and her brother. I had sheltered hope that her dad and I could become bosom buddies even if Vicki and I didn't work things out. He and I could still be friends. If his tire went flat some rainy night in Haddam or Hightstown or anyplace within my area code, he could call me up, I'd drive out to get him, we'd have a drink while the tire was being fixed at Frenchy's and he would go off into the Jersey darkness certain he had a friend worthy of his trust and who looked down life's corridor more or less the way he did. Maybe we could take the brother fishing at Manasquan (no need to bring the women in on it). Vicki could be married to Sweet Lou Calcagno's stepson over in Bamber, have a wonderful life as a beer distributor's wife with all the hullygully of kids. And I could be the trusted family friend with a heart of gold. I'd renounce my failed suitor's glower for the demeanor of a wise old uncle. That would be enough for me, just the natural playing out of the pleasing present.

Vicki stares out the window at the houses along Arctic Spruce, her arm on the couch back. Sometimes it is possible to see in her face the lineaments of the older woman she will be, when her features will take on dimension, weight around the chin, a character more serious than now. She will undoubtedly be stout in later life, which is not always a hopeful sign.

Amber light has turned the lawns as green as England. In driveways all up the curving curbless street sit bright new cars—Chryslers, Olds, Buicks—each one with a hefty, moneyed look. In the middle distance a great white RV sits in a side yard. Smoke curls from almost every white brick chimney, though it is not cold enough by a long shot. Some doors have wreaths up since Christmas. My trailing wind has arrived.

Someone, I see, has set white croquet wickets around the Arcenaults' front lawn. Two striped stakes face each other at less than regulation distance. Games have been planned for the day, and here is how I will paint my trapdoor to escape the incoming empty moment I feel.

"Let's play," I say, giving Vicki's arm an uncle's squeeze. This is not a ruse I'm up to, only a break in the broody unfinished silence we've fallen victims to.

She looks amazed, though she isn't. Her eyes round out like dimes. "In all this wind and the rain comin?"

"It isn't raining yet."

"Man-o-man-o-man," Vicki says, and snaps her fingers in hot succession. "It's your funeral." But she is off the couch quick, and headed for some upstairs storage room for mallets.

On television, CBS is trying to get us settled back into basketball, now that things are under control again. However, each time they show what's happening on the court, a short, bulb-nosed, red-faced man wearing a loud, checked sport coat comes into the picture shouting "Aw, fuck you" soundlessly at someone on the New York team, waving a stubby arm in disgust. This checked coat guy is one of my favorites. Mutt Greene, the Clevelands' G.M. I interviewed him once just after I'd restarted life as a sportswriter. He was a coach in Chicago then, but by his own choice has since moved up to the front office in another city, where I'm sure life seems better. He said to me "People surprise you, Frank, with just how fuckin stupid they are." He was smoking a big expensive cigar in a cramped coach's office under the Chicago arena. "I mean, do you *actually* realize how much adult conversation is spent on this fuckin business? Facts treated like they were opinions just for the simple purpose of talking about it longer? Some people might think that's interesting, bub, but I'll tell you. It's romanticizing a goddamn rock by calling it a mountain range to me. People waste a helluva lot of time they could be putting to useful purposes. This is a game. See it and forget about it." Afterwards we got involved in a pretty lively conversation about grass seeds and the piss-poor choices you face when your trouble was a high water table and inadequate drainage, which was not my problem, but was the case at his home on Hilton Head.

The interview wasn't very productive on the subject of "seeing the keys" in classic big-man, small-man match-ups, which is what I was after. But I think of it as informative, though I don't agree with everything he said. Still, he was happy to sit down with a young sportswriter and teach a lesson in life. "Keep things in perspective and give an honest effort" is what I took back to the Sheraton Commander that night. And when you've done with that take an interest in a new grass seed or an old Count Basie record you've missed listening to lately, or a catalog or a cocktail waitress, which— the last of these—is precisely what I did and wasn't sorry about it.

On the court now the players are paying everyone murderous looks and pointing long bony fingers as threats. In particular the black players look fierce, and the white boys, pale and thin-armed, seem to want to be peacemakers, though they are actually just trying to stay out of trouble's way. The trainer, a squat, worried-looking man in white pants, is trying to pull Mutt Greene down a runway below the stands. But Mutt is fighting mad. To him, real life's going on here. Nothing's for show. He has lost all perspective and wants to raise a little hell about the Knicks' way of playing. He's come out of the stands to show what he's worth, and I admire him for it. I'm sure he misses the old life.

Suddenly the picture flicks and another cliff-diver stands staring down at his frothy fate. CBS has given up.

Elvis Presley trots into the kitchen door again, jingling his little diamond collar, and sniffs the air. He is uncertain about me, and who could blame him?

Lynette is right behind him, her eyes sparkly and furtive but full of good cheer. "Elvis Presley 'bout runs this whole family." She taps Elvis Presley lightly with her toe. "He's fixed, of course, so you don't have to worry about your leg. He idn't but half a man, but we do love him."

Elvis Presley sits in the doorway and stares at me.

"He's something," I say.

"Doesn't Vicki seem like she's worried to you?" Lynette's voice becomes cautionary. Her bright eyes are speculative and she crosses her arms in absolute slow motion.

"She seems just fine to me."

"Well, I thought maybe since you all went to De-troit, something unhappy'd happened."

So! Everybody including Elvis Presley knows everything, and wants to turn it to their own purposes, no matter how idle. A full-disclosure family. No secrets unless individuals make decisions for themselves, which runs the risk of general disapproval. Vicki has obviously told an aromatic little-but-not-enough, and Lynette wants filling in. She is not exactly as I want her to be, and as of this moment I transfer fully back to Vicki's alliance.

"Everything's great that I know of." I admit nothing with a smile.

"Well good-should, then." Lynette nods happily. "We all just love her and want the best for her. She's the bravest ole thing."

No answer. No "Why is she brave?" or "Tell me what you make of Everett?" or "In fact, she *is* seeming just the least little bit peculiar all of a sudden." Nothing from me, except "She's wonderful," and another grin.

"Yes she is now," Lynette beams, but full of warning. Then she is gone again, leaving Elvis Presley in the doorway, frozen in an empty stare.

In the time it takes Vicki to come back with the mallets, her brother Cade comes pushing through the front door. He has been out back tying down a tarp on his Boston Whaler, and when I shake his hand it is rock-fleshed and chilled. Cade is twenty-five, a boat mechanic in nearby Toms River, and a mauler of a fellow in a white T-shirt and jeans. He is, Vicki has told me, on the "wait list" for the State Police Academy and has already developed a flat-eyed, officer's uninterest for the peculiarities of his fellow man.

"Down from Haddam, huh?" Cade grunts, once we've let go of each other's hands and are standing hard-by with nothing to say. His speech does not betray one trace of Texas, where he grew up, and instead he has developed now into full-fledged Jersey young-manhood with an aura of no-place/no-time surrounding him like poison. He looms beside me like a mast and stares furiously out the front window. "I useta know a girl in South Brunswick. Useta take her skatin in a rink on 130. You might know where that is?" A snicker and a sneer appear on his lips at once.

"I know exactly," I say and sink my hands deep in my pockets.

Indeed I've watched my own two precious children (and once my third) skate there for hours on end while I hugged the rail in estranged admiration.

"There's a Mann's Tri-Plex in there now, I guess," Cade says, looking around the room as if perplexed by getting into this embarrassing conversation in the first place. He'd feel much better if he could put the cuffs on me and push me head-down into the back seat of a cruiser. On the ride downtown we could both relax, be ourselves, and he could share a cruel joke with me and his partner— amigos in our roles, as God intended. As it is I'm from an outside world, the type of helpless citizen who owns the expensive boats he repairs; the know-nothings with no mechanical skills he hates for the way we take care of property he himself can't afford. I am not who normally comes for dinner, and he's having a hard time being human about me.

My advice to him, though unspoken, is that he'd better get used to me and mine, since I am the people he'll be giving tickets to sooner or later, average solid citizens whose ways and mores he'll ridicule at the risk of getting into a peck of trouble. I can, in fact, be of use to him, could be instructive of the outside world if he would let me.

"Uhn, where's Vicki?" Cade looks suddenly caged, glancing around the room as if she might be hiding behind a chair. Simultaneously he opens his thick fist to display a piece of silvery, tooled metal.

"She's gone to get croquet mallets," I say. "What's that?"

Cade stares down at the two-inch piece of tubular metal and purses his lips. "Spacer," he says and then is silent a moment. "Germans make it. It's the best in the world. And it's a real piece of crap's what it is."

"What's it to?" My hands are firm and deep in my pockets. I'm willing to take an interest in "spacer" for the moment.

"Boat," Cade says darkly. "We should be making these things over here. That way they'd last."

"You're right about that," I say. "It's too bad."

"I mean, what're you gonna do if you're out on the ocean and this thing cracks? Like this." One greasy finger fine-points a hairline

fissure in the spacer's side, something I'd never have noticed. Cade's
dark eyes grow hooded with suppressed annoyance. "You gonna call
for a German? Is that it? I'll tell you what you'd do, mister." His
eyes find me gazing stupidly at the spacer, which seems obscure and
unimportant. "You kiss your ass goodbye if a storm comes up."
Cade nods grimly and pops his big hand shut like a clam. All his
feelings are pretty closely positioned into this conceit—the strongest
chain is no stronger than its weakest link, and he's resolved never
to be that link in his personal life, where *he's* in control. This is the
central fact of all tragedy, though to me it's not much to get excited
about. His is the policeman's outlook, mine the sportswriter's. To
me a weak link bears some watching, and you'd better have replace-
ments handy in case it goes. But in the meantime it could be interesting to see how it bears up and tries to do its job under some bad
conditions, all the while giving its best in the other areas where it's
strong. I've always thought of myself as a type of human weak link,
working against odds and fate, and I'm not about to give up on
myself. Cade, on the other hand, wants to lock up us offenders and
weak links so we'll never again see the light of day and worry anybody. We would have a hard time being good friends, this I can
see.

"You been to Atlantic City lately?" Cade says suspiciously.

"Not in a long time." X and I went on our honeymoon there,
stayed in the old Hadden Hall, walked on the boardwalk and had
the time of our lives. I haven't been back since, except once for a
karate match, when I flew in after dark and left two hours later. I
doubt Cade is interested in this.

"It's all ruined now," Cade says, shaking his head in dismay.
"Hookers and spic teenagers all over. It useta be good. And I'm not
even prejudiced."

"I'd heard it's changed."

"Changed?" Cade smirks, the first sign of a real smile I've seen
so far. "Nagasaki changed, right?" Cade suddenly flings his head
toward the kitchen. "I'm hungry enough eat a lug wrench." And a
strangely happy smile breaks over his tragic big bullard's face. "I've

got to go wash up or Lynette'll shoot me." He shakes his head, appreciative and grinning.

Suddenly all is good cheer. Whatever troubled him is gone now. Atlantic City. Weak links. Faulty spacers. Spics. Criminals he will someday arrest and later want to joke with on the long ride downtown. All gone. This is a feature of his outlook I have not expected. He can forget and be happy—a real strength. A good meal is waiting somewhere. A TV game. A beer. Clear sailing beyond the squall-line of life. It isn't so bad, when you don't think of it.

In the front yard Vicki displays for me the most excellent way to hit a croquet ball, the between-the-straddled-legs address, which lets her give her ball a good straight ride that makes her whoop with pleasure. I am a side-approacher by nature, having played some golf at Lonesome Pines and when I first married X. I also enjoy hitting the stupid striper with one hand, though I give up *touch* every time. Vicki gives me dark and disreputable looks when I hit, then even more aggressively straddles her green ball and hikes her skirt above her knees to get the straightest pendulum swing. She's half around the course before I'm through a wicket, though I'm a tinge dreamy now, my mind not truly on our game.

The Detroit weather has arrived finally, though it is not the same storm. All the anger has gone out of it, and it consents to being just a gusty, plucky breeze with a few sprinklings of icy rain—a mild suburban shower at best, though the light has passed from Sunday amber to late afternoon aquamarine. In fact it's wonderful to be out of doors and away from the house, even though we play under the eyes of crucified Jesus. I have no idea where Vicki's father is. Is this interpretable as a dark sign, a gesture of unwelcome? Should I be asking what I'm doing here? I was, after all, invited, though I feel in an unavoidable way as alone as a nomad.

"You havin fun?" Vicki says. She has managed to nest her green stripe close enough to my yellow ball to give it a good clacking whack under her stockinged foot, scooting it through the grass and into the flowerbed where it is lost among the snapdragons against the house.

"I *was* doing pretty good."

"Gogetchanotherball. Get a red one—they're lucky." She stands like a woodsman, with her mallet on her shoulder. She has but two wickets remaining, and pretends to want me to catch up.

"I resign," I say and smile.

"Say what?"

"That's what you say in chess. I'm not a match for you, not even a patch on your jeans."

"Chest nothin, you're the one wanted to play, and now you're the one quittin. Go on and get a ball."

"No I won't. I'm no good at games, not since I was little."

"People bet on this game in Texas. It's taken very serious."

"That's why I'm no good at it."

I take a seat on the damp porch step beside her red shoes and admire the green-tinted light and the lovely curving street. This snaky peninsula is the work of some enterprising developer who's carted it in with trucks and reclaimed it from a swamp. And it has not been a bad idea. You could just as easily be in Hyannis Port if you closed your eyes, which for a moment I do.

Vicki goes back to hitting her green stripe, but carelessly now, using my method to show she isn't serious. "When I was a lil girl I saw *Alice in Wonderland*, Cade and me. You know?" She looks up to see if I'm listening. "In the part where they played croquet with ostriches' heads, or whatever those pink birds are, I cried bloody murder, 'cause I thought it killed 'em. I hated to see anything get hurt even then. That's why I'm a nurse."

"Flamingos," I say and smile down at her.

"Is that what they were? Well, I know I cried about 'em." Whack-crack. Her green makes a hard driving run toward the striped stake, then twirls by on the left. "There you go, that's your fault. Shoot-a-mile." She stands thrown-hipped in the breeze. I watch her with terrible desire. "You don't play games, but you write about 'em all the time. That's backwards."

"I like it that way."

"How'd you like ole Cade. Idn't he great?"

"He's a good fellow."

"If he'd let me dress him he'd be a whole lot better, I'll tell you that. Cade needs him a little girlfriend. He's got being a policeman on the brain." She comes over and sits on the step below mine, hugs her knees and tucks her skirt up under her. Her hair is sweet-smelling. While she was gone she has put on a good deal of Chanel No. 5.

I wish we could not talk about Cade now, but I have nothing much to substitute for him. Vicki has no interest in the upcoming NFL draft, or the early lead the Tigers have opened up in the East, or who might be ahead in the Knicks game, so I'm content to sit on the porch like a lazy freeholder, breathe in the salt air and look upwards at the daylight moon. In its own way this is quite inspiring.

"So how do you like it out here?" Vicki looks at me up over her shoulder, then back at the house across the street—another split-level, but with an oriental façade, its cornices tweaked, and painted China red.

"It's great."

"You don't fit in at all, you know that."

"I'm here to see you. I'm not trying to fit in."

"I guess," she says, and hugs her knees hard.

"Where's your dad? I sort of have the feeling he's ducking me."

"No way for that, José."

"I could get lost in a hurry, you know, if being here is one bit of trouble."

"Right, you're a heap of trouble. Breakin things and spillin food and roughin up poor ole Cade. Maybe you *had* better leave."

She turns and gives me a different look, a look you'd give a man trying to recite the Lord's Prayer in pig Latin. "Just don't be dumb," she says. "That man dudn't duck nobody. He's in the basement with his hobby. He probably dudn't even know you're here." She glares into the moiling sky. "If anybody's trouble it's ole you-know-who in there. But I can't talk about that. It's his poison, let him drink it."

"Just like you're mine." I scoot down a step so I can hug her shoulders around tight. No one up or down Arctic Spruce could care less, a far different place from prudent Michigan. The feeling out here is we can hug and smooch on the steps till our arms fall off and it'll be just fine with folks.

Her shoulders rise and settle inside my bear's hug. "I'm not so sweet," she says.

"Don't tell me any bad news now."

She furrows her brow. "Well, look."

"It's okay. I give you my word; whatever it is, later's good enough." I breathe in washed sweetness from her warm hair.

"Well, I do have something to tell you."

"I just don't want to spoil this afternoon."

"Maybe it won't."

"Do I really have to hear it?"

"I think you should, yes." She sighs. "You know that clam-handed old sawbones you were talkin' to at the airport the other day? The one I came up and killed with a look?"

"I don't want to know about you and Fincher," I say. "It would count as a terrible part of my day. I command you never to tell me." I stare at the swarming green sky. A small Cessna mutters across our airspace, seeking, I'm sure, a safe landing in Manahawkin or Ship Bottom, ahead of the storm. It does not seem a bit like Easter now, only another day without safeguards. Though the more normal the April day the better for me. Holidays can hold too many disappointments that I then have to accommodate.

"Look. I hadn't been with that ole character."

"Okay. That's good to hear."

"It's *your ex*. She's slippin' off with him. The only reason I know is that I've seen her pick him up at the ER entrance three or four times. She's got the light brown Citation, right?"

"What?"

"Well," Vicki says. "If it hadn't been he kissed her, I would've thought it was just innocent. But it idn't innocent. That's why I acted so peculiar at the airport. I figured ya'll was about to fight."

"Maybe it was somebody else," I say. "There's a lot of brown cars. G.M. made millions of them. They're wonderful cars."

"G.M." She shakes her head in a teacherly way. "Not with your wife in 'em, they don't."

And for a sudden moment my mind simply ceases—which isn't even so unusual, and there are times when nothing else will help. Sitting next to Ralph's bed at the instant the nurse came in and said, "I'm sorry, Ralph has expired" (he was actually cold as an oyster when I touched his small clenched fist, and had been dead probably for an hour), at that moment when I knew he was dead, I remember my mind stopping. No other thought occurred to me immediately. No association or memory latched on to the event, or to the next one, for that matter, whatever it might've been. I don't remember. No lines of poetry. No epiphanies. The room became like a picture of a room, though more greenish and murky for that time of the morning, and then it sank away and became tiny—as though I was having a look at it through the wrong end of a telescope. I have since heard this explained as a protective mechanism of the mind, and that I should be grateful for it. Though I'm certain it was brought on as much by fatigue as the shock of grief.

Nothing now grows smaller because of this unexpected news, though the air around me is tinged a stormy bottle green. The Chinese split-level maintains its ground in full view. Nothing has been thrown for a loop. I simply find myself staring across Arctic Spruce Drive at a chimney painted white, from which a gusty wind is drawing smoke at an angle perfectly perpendicular to the flue. All the draperies are closed. The grass out front is unspeakably green. You could putt on it and expect a good true roll to the cup.

I admit I am surprised; that the picture Vicki would like to paint of X *kissing* Fincher Barksdale in the front seat of her Citation outside the emergency room—when he is just off the cancer ward, smelling of disease and bodies—is as revulsive as any I could think of on my own. That the next scene, the one she hasn't painted yet, of wherever the two of them are slying off to for whatever itchy plans they have, clouds up pretty fast—aided by the revulsion. At the same time it's true I have to fight back a black hole of betrayal—for me and for Fincher's wife, Dusty, which is totally unwarranted since she might not even care and I hardly know her anymore. This in turn makes me feel a sense of Fincher's lizard's depravity, which brings about more disgust.

But a *thought* I do not think. Nor contrive a mean and explicatory synthesis to formulate my position regarding what I've heard.

In other words, I do not exactly respond; except to remember: *people will surprise you.*

"I guess not," I say agreeably, and stare off.

Vicki has twisted around to face me, her face above the split horizon of my two knees. She looks concerned, but willing to swap this look for a happy one. "So what're you thinkin?"

"Nothing." I smile, revulsion faded in me, leaving me only a little weak. I am glad I don't have to stand up. The simple words "You cannot" come to mind, but I don't have a finish for the phrase. "You cannot . . . what?" Dance? Fly? Sing an aria? Control the lives of others? Be happy all the time? "Why is it so important to tell me that just now?" I ask in a sudden but friendly way.

"Well, I just hate secrets. And I had this one with me a while. And if I waited any longer you might get to feeling so good that maybe I couldn't tell you at all or it'd ruin your whole day. I coulda told you in De-troit, but that would've been awful." She nods at me soberly, chin out, as if she couldn't agree more with what she's just heard herself say. "This way, you got time to get over it."

"I appreciate your thinking about me," I say, though I'm sorry she is such a spendthrift of secrets.

"You're my ole pardner, aren't you?" She gives me a pat on my knees and the grin she's wanted to give me all along. It's nice to see, in spite of everything.

"What am I again?"

"My ole pardner. That's what I use to call Daddy when I was a little bitty thing." She bats her eyes at me.

"I'm more than that, at least I *used* to be. I still want to be, anyway." And I have to staunch a terrible tear that fills my eye like a freshet.

In some of the heart's business there is really no net gain. Let someone who knows tell you.

"Why, you bet," Vicki says. "But cain't we be friends, too? I'm gon always want to be your pardner." She plants a big fishy kiss upon my cold cheek. And up above me the sky swirls and tears apart, and on my face I feel the first serious drop of storm that's all along been waiting for its time.

W ade Arcenault is a cheery, round-eyed, crewcut fellow with a plainsman's square face and hearty laugh. I instantly recognize him from Exit 9, where he has taken my money hundreds of times but doesn't recognize me now. He is not a large man, hardly taller than Lynette, though his forearms, exposed and khaki sleeves up for washing at the sink, are ropy and tanned. He gives my hand a good wet shake right where he's washing. With a sly-secret smile he tells me he's been "down in his devil's dungeon" rewiring a Sunbeam fry-pan for Lynette to use to make Dutch Babies—her favorite Easter dessert. The pan sits splendidly fixed now on the counter top.

He is not at all what I expected. I had envisioned a wiry, squint-eyed little pissant—a gun store owner type, with fading flagrant tattoos of women on emaciated biceps, a man with a cruel streak for Negroes. But that is the man of bad stereotype, the kind my writing career foundered over and probably should have. The world is a more engaging and less dramatic place than writers ever give it credit for being. And for a moment Wade and I do nothing more than stand and stare at the fry-pan's drastic utilitarian lines like deaf-mutes, unable to get a better subject out in the open.

"So now how was the trip down, Frank?" Wade says with brusque heartiness. There is a frontier tautness in his character that makes him instantly trustworthy and appealing, a man with his priorities straight and a permanent twinkle in his eye that says he expects someone—me, maybe—to tell him something that will make him extremely happy. Nothing, in fact, would please me more.

"I came down through Pemberton and Bamber, Wade. It's one of my favorite drives. I'd like to take a canoe in the Rancocas one of these days. Parts of Africa must be a lot like that."

"Isn't it something, Frank?" Wade Arcenault's eyes ramble around in their sockets, seeking what, I don't know. Strange to say, Wade has no more of a Texas accent than Cade. "This is our little Garden of Eden down here, and we want to keep it so the outsiders don't ruin it for us, which is why I don't mind driving fifty miles to work. Though I guess I shouldn't be closing the drawbridge." His clear eyes sparkle with admission. "We're all from someplace else these days, Frank. People who were born right here don't even recognize it anymore. I've talked to them."

"But I bet they like it. This peninsula is a good idea."

"There's just the *ti*-niest little erosion problem out back," Wade says, finishing drying his hands with a dish towel. "But we've got our builder, this smart young Rutger's grad, Pete Calcagno." (A name I know!) "He's done his share with his backhoe and sandbags, and he'll get her licked, is what I think." Wade beams at me. "Most people want to do right, is my concept."

"I agree." And I most surely do! It is certainly true of me, and unquestionably true of Wade Arcenault. He, after all, bought his divorced daughter a house full of new furniture, and stood by and let her pick out every stick, then stepped up and wrote a whopper check so she could get a good start in a new northern environment. A lot of people would like to do that, but not many would follow through all the way.

Wade's blue eyes cut mischievously toward the basement door. Something I've done or said seems to have made him take to me, at least in a preliminary way. "Lynette," he says loudly, putting his eyes on the ceiling. "Have I got time to take this boy down to my devil's dungeon?" He gives me a wide wink and looks upwards again. (Maybe we'll be able to get a fishing trip planned, no matter how things go with Vicki.)

"I doubt if Grant's army could be expected to stop you, could it?" Lynette smiles in at us through the serving bay to the dining room, shakes her pretty red head, and waves us on.

In through the living room door I spy Vicki and Cade sitting on the salmon couch having what looks like an intimate talk. Cade's wardrobe and stultifying social life are no doubt under reappraisal.

Wade goes tromping off down the dark basement steps with me right behind. And immediately the heavy kitchen air is exchanged for the cool, chemically pungent odors indigenous to suburban basements where the owner is nobody's fool and has his termite contract up-to-date. I am one of their number.

"All right now, stay there, Frank," Wade says, lost in darkness ahead of me, his steps crossing concrete. Behind me Lynette's plump arm closes the kitchen door.

"Hold your horses, now." Wherever he is, Wade is enthusiastic.

I hold on to a wood 2x6 bannister, not certain of even one more step. Something, I sense, is large and in front of me.

Wade is fiddling with metal objects, possibly the shade of a utility lamp, a fuse-box door, possibly a box of keys. "Ahh, the Christ," he mutters.

Suddenly a light flutters on, not a utility lamp but a shimmering white fluorescence in the raftered ceiling. What I see first in the light is not, I think, what I'm supposed to see. I see a big picture of the world photographed from outer space, fastened to the cinderblock wall above Wade's workbench. In it, all of space is blue and empty, and North America clear as in a dream, from miles away, in perfect outline white against a dark surrounding sea.

"What d'you think, Frank?" Wade says with pride.

My eyes try to find him, but instead find, directly in front of me where I could touch it, a big black car—so close I can't make out what it is, though it certainly is a car, with plenty of chrome and a glassy black finish. CHRYSLER is lettered above big wide louvered grillwork.

"By God, Wade," I say and find him down the long-fendered side, his hand on the tip of a high rear fin above the red taillight.

He's grinning like a TV salesman who this time has put together something really special, something the little woman will *have* to like, something anyone in his nut would be proud to own as an investment, since its value can only increase.

It is a big box-safe of a car with fat whitewalls, ballistic bumpers, and an air of postwar styling-with-substance that makes my Malibu only a sad reminder.

"They don't make these anymore, Frank." Wade pauses to let these words hold sway. "I restored it myself. Cade helped me some, but he got bored soon as the motor work was over. Bought this off a soapstone Greek in Little Egg, and you should've seen it. Brown. Full of holes. Chrome half gone. Just a Swiss cheese, is what it was." Wade looks at the finish as if it might have murmured. It's chilly in the basement, and the Chrysler seems as cold and hard as a black diamond. "The roll-pleat inside still needs work," Wade admits.

"How'd you get it in here?"

Wade grins. He's been waiting for this one. "One Bilco door, back around there where you can't see it. The tow truck just slid it down. Cade and I had a ramp rigged out of channel irons. I had to relearn welding. You know anything about arc welding, Frank?"

"Not a damn thing," I say. "I should, though." I look at the photo of the earth again. It is a good thing to have, I think, for maintaining a sense of perspective, though in its homely surroundings the globe seems as exotic as a tapestry.

"Not necessary," Wade says soberly. "The principles are all pretty straightforward. Resistance is the whole thing. You'd pick it up in a minute." Wade smiles at the thought that I might someday own a marketable skill.

"What're you going to do with it, Wade?" I say, a question that just came to me.

"I haven't thought about that," Wade says.

"Do you ever drive it?"

"Oh, I do. Yes. I start it up and drive it a foot one way and a foot or two back. There isn't much room down here." He stuffs his hands in his pockets and leans sideways on the fender, looking up and around at the low rafters into the dark cinderblock crawl space. Above us I hear muffled voices, the sound of footsteps squeezing from kitchen to dining room. I hear Cade's clomping off in another direction, no doubt upstairs to change clothes. I hear Elvis Presley's paws tick the kitchen floor. Then nothing. Wade and I are silent in the presence of his Chrysler and each other.

This situation could, of course, result in disaster, as many such situations do. A fear of what he may innocently ask me now, or a greater fear that I may have nothing special to say in answer and be left standing here as mute as a rocker panel—these make me wish I were back upstairs seeing the Knicks whip tar out of the Cavaliers, cheek-by-jowl with my old friend Cade. Sports is a first-rate safety valve when you and your whole value system are brought under friendly but unexpected scrutiny.

"Just what kind of fellow are you?" would be a perfectly natural curiosity. "What are your intentions regarding my daughter?" ("I'm not at all sure" would not be much of an answer.) "Who in the world do you think you are?" (I'd be stumped.) Suddenly I feel cold, though Wade doesn't seem to have any tricks up his sleeve. He is someone with codes I respect and that I would like to like me. All the best signs, in other words, are not so different from all the worst. Wade puts his fingertips to the porcelain-black fender and stares at them. I'm sure if I were closer every feature of me would be spelled out clear as a mirror.

"Frank," Wade says, "do you like fish?" He looks up at me almost imploringly.

"You bet I do."

"You do, huh?"

"I sure do."

Wade peers down at the shiny black surface again. "I was just thinking maybe you and me could go eat at the Red Lobster some night, get away from these women. Really have us a talk. You ever been there?"

"I sure have. Plenty of times." In fact, when X and I were first divorced, I went practically no place else. All the waitresses got to know me, knew I liked the broiled bluefish not overcooked and went out of their way to cheer me up, which is exactly what they're paid to do but usually don't.

"I go just for the haddock," Wade says. "It's a meal in itself. I call it the poor man's lobster."

"We ought to go. It'd be great." I slip my cold hands in my jacket pockets. All in all I would still jump at the chance to get back upstairs.

"Frank, where're your parents?" Wade looks gravely at me.

"They're both dead, Wade," I say. "A long time now."

"Mine, too." He nods. "Both of 'em gone. We all come from nowhere in the end, right?"

"I guess I don't really mind that part," I say.

"Right, right, right, right." Wade has crossed his arms and backed up against the Chrysler fender. He gives me a right-angles glance, then stares off into the crawl space again. "What brought you to New Jersey? You're a writer, is that right?"

"It's a pretty long story, Wade. I was married before. I've got two kids up in Haddam. It would take some time to explain all that." I smile in a way I hope will head him off, though I know Wade probably doesn't give a damn about it. He's just trying to be friendly.

"Frank, I like women. How about you?" Wade swivels his crewcut head toward me and grins, a straightforward grin of amusement, founded on the old anticipation of pleasure, the source of eighty percent of all happiness. It is the same to him as liking haddock, though more interesting because it might turn out to be a little dirty.

"I guess I do too, Wade." And I smile broadly back.

Wade raises his chin in an "I-knew-it" way, and puts his tongue against his cheek. "I've never wanted a night out with the boys in my life, Frank. What fun that is, I don't know."

"Not much," I say. And I think of my doleful nights in the "Back in Action" course, and with the Divorced Men, floating higgledy-piggledy on the chilly waters off Mantoloking like an army planning its renewed attack upon the beaches of lived life. I silently pledge never again to be in their number. I am finished with that and them. Life's ashore, after all (though God love them).

"Now don't get me wrong, Frank," Wade says warily, still staring off, as if I was standing somewhere else. "I'm not into your and Vicki's business. You two'll just have to fight that out."

"It gets complicated."

"You bet it does. It's hard to know what to want at your age. How old are you, anyway, Frank?"

"Thirty-eight," I say. "How old are you?"

"Fifty-six. I was forty-nine when my wife died of cancer."

"That's young, Wade."

"We were living in Irving, Texas, then. I was a petroleum engineer for Beutler Oil, worked a mile from a house I owned outright. I had a daughter married. I took my son to Cowboys' games. We lived what we thought was a good life. And then, bang, we suffered a heckuva terrible loss. Just overnight, it seemed like. Vicki and Cade just were wrecked by it. So you bet I know what complicated is." He nods toward his own private miseries.

"I know it was a hard time," I say.

"Divorce must be something like that, Frank. Lynette's divorced from a pretty decent guy, you know. Her second husband—her first died, too—I've met him. He's a decent guy, though we're not friends. But they couldn't make it together. It's no reflection. She's had a son killed in Oklahoma, herself."

Vicki has apparently mentioned Ralph, which is all right with me. He is, after all, part of my permanent public record. His lost life serves to further explain and punctuate mine. Wade, I'm happy to say, is doing his best here to "take me on as an individual," to speak in his own voice, and let me speak in mine, to be as within himself as it's possible to be with someone he doesn't know and could just as easily hate on sight. He could be giving me the third-degree down here, and I'd like to let him know I appreciate it that he isn't— though I'm not sure how to. By being direct and unambiguous and nothing like what I expected, he has left me nothing to say.

"Wade, what part of Texas did you grow up in?" I say, and grin hopefully.

"I'm from northeast Nebraska, Frank. Oakland, Nebraska." He scratches the back of his hand, perhaps thinking of wheat fields. "I went to *school* in Texas, now. Started in 1953 at A&M. Already married. Vicki was on the way, I think. It took me forever to graduate, and I worked in the oil fields all that time. But what I was saying about women, though, was that when my first wife, Esther, died, I was afraid I wouldn't be interested in women anymore. You know? You can just lose interest in women, Frank. I don't mean in a lead-in-your-pencil sense. But up here." Wade looks at me and points a finger right at the middle of his forehead. "You lose touch with *you*," he says. "With your own needs. And I did that. Vicki can tell you about it, 'cause she took care of me." Wade rolls his eyes in a way that is ridiculously outside his character, though I've seen Vicki do it plenty of times, and it is entirely possible that he learned it from her. It is a woman's gesture and makes Wade seem womanly, as if life had taught him some harder lessons than he was man enough to suffer. "I did some crazy, crazy things along in there, Frank," Wade says and smiles in a self-forgiving way (he is no New-Ager, I can tell you that). "I kidnaped a baby out of a shopping mall. Now is that crazy?" Wade looks at me in amazement. "A little colored baby girl. I can't even tell you why now. At the time I would've said it was reaching out for commitment, I guess. Crying in the wilderness. I'd have been doing my crying on death row if they'd caught me, I can tell you that. And I damn well would've deserved it." Wade nods solemnly into the shadows as if all his darkest motives were imprisoned there now and could not reach him anymore.

"That's a helluva thing to do, Wade. What'd you do about it?"

"It was one *hell* of a pickle, Frank. Fortunately I returned that little baby to its stroller. But I'd already had it in the car with me. God knows what I would've done with it. That's when you hit the twilight zone."

"Maybe you didn't want to do it. That you didn't follow up on that is a pretty good argument, if you ask me."

"I know that theory all right, Frank. But I'll tell you what happened. I bumped into this Aggie classmate, Buck Larsen. It was at a reunion in College Station. We hadn't seen each other in probably twenty-six years. And it so happens he was with the Turnpike Authority. And we just started jabbering like you do. I told him that Esther had died, on and on, kids, women, tears, and that I had to get out of Dallas. I didn't even know it myself, you understand? You know how that is. You're the writer."

"Pretty well, I guess." (At least he and Buck didn't go to a motel.)

"It's pretty hard to tell where your intentions lie exactly, isn't it?" Wade offers me a pitiful smile.

"It's a lot easier in books. I know that."

"Damn right it is. We read some books at A&M. Not *that* many, I guess." Now we can both grin together. "Where'd you attend, Frank?"

"Michigan."

"East Lansing, right?"

"Ann Arbor."

"Well. You read more books there than I did at College Station, I know that."

"Just looking at everything around here now, it looks like you made the right choices, Wade."

"Frank, I guess so." With his toe Wade pokes at a scuff of dry concrete on the floor. He pressures it until it's clear it won't budge, then he shakes his head. "Your life can change a hundred ways, I'll tell you that."

"I know it, Wade."

"I took a job with the Turnpike Authority. I left Cade with Esther's folks in Irving and came up and lived a bachelor's life for a year. As far away from my other life as I could get. I went from being an engineer in Texas to being a toll-taker in New Jersey in a week's time. With help of course. It was a step down. With a big

cut in pay. But I didn't care because I was a total wreck, Frank.
You don't think you're a total wreck, but you are, and I had to start
over again, get taken up by a new place, as crazy a place as this is,
it didn't matter. I'm a problem-solver by nature, Frank. Engineers
always are. And this was my problem. If you ask me, Americans
are too sensitive to moving down in rank. It isn't so bad."

"It doesn't sound easy though. It makes my problems seem pretty
small in comparison."

"I can't tell you if it was easy or not." His forehead ravels as if
he wished he could, would like to be able to talk about that too,
only it is lost to him now—a mercy. "You know, son. There's a
fellow works for us up at Exit 9. I won't say his name. Except in
1959, he was living out west near Yellowstone. Had a wife and three
children, a house and a mortgage. A job, a life. One night he'd been
to a bar and was on his way home. And just after he left, a whole
side of a mountain collapsed down on the bar. He stopped in the
middle of the highway, he told me, and he could see back in the
moonlight to where a lot of lights had been that were all gone because
this huge landslide had taken place. Killed everybody but him. And
do you know what he did?" Wade raises his eyebrows and squints,
both at the same time.

"I've got a pretty good idea." (Who in a modern world wouldn't?)

"Well, and you'd be right. He got in his car and drove east. He
said he felt like somebody'd just said, 'Here, Nick, here's your whole
life being handed to you again. See if you can't do better this time.'
And he's reported dead right now out in Idaho or Wyoming, or one
of those states. Insurance paid. Who knows where his family is? His
kids? And he works right beside me on the Turnpike, happy as a
man can be. I'd never tell it, of course. And I'm a lot luckier than
he is. We both just had new lives served to us, and a conviction to
do something with them." Wade looks at me seriously, rubs his
palms delicately on the chrome door handle beside him. He wants
me to know that he's discovered something important late in life,
something worth knowing when very few people ever discover any-

thing by just living. He'd like to pass some wisdom along from the for-what-it's-worth department, though I can't help wondering what his friend's wife would think if she ever came through Exit 9 at just the right moment. It could happen. "Do you want to get married again, Frank?"

"I don't know."

"That's a good answer," Wade says. "I didn't think I did. Living alone didn't seem so bad after being married for twenty-nine years. What do you think?"

"It has its plusses, Wade. Did you meet Lynette up here?"

"I met her at a rock concert, and don't ask me what I was doing there because I couldn't tell you. This was in Atlantic City, three years ago. I'm not a joiner, and if you're not a joiner you can end up in some pretty strange places proving to yourself how independent you are."

"I usually end up staying home reading. Though I get in my car sometimes and drive all day, too. It sounds like what you're talking about."

"That's not so good, doesn't sound to me like."

"It isn't always, no."

"Well, anyway. Here was ole Lynette. She's about your age, Frank. Been widowed, divorced, and came to this concert with a Spanish guy who was about twenty-five. And he had just up and disappeared on her. I won't tell you all the gory details. But we ended up out at the Howard Johnson's on the freeway drinking coffee and talking the truth to each other till four in the morning. It turns out we both had a yearning to do something useful and positive with what time we had left to us, and neither one of us was much of a perfectionist, by which I mean we both knew we weren't exactly perfect for each other." Wade folds his arms and looks stern.

"How long before you got married, Wade? Not that long, I'll bet." I direct a sly grin at Wade because a big sly grin needs to come on his face at the thought of that starry night on the smoggy Atlantic City Expressway, and I'm glad to help him out. It must've seemed to them that they had beached together on a blasted, deserted shingle, and were damned lucky to be there. It is not a bad story, and worth a hundred grins.

"Not *that* long, Frank," Wade says proudly, cracking the very grin needed to get into the spirit of that old charmed time again. "Her divorce was settled, and we didn't see any use waiting. She's a Catholic, after all. A divorce was bad enough. And she didn't want us to be living together, which would've been fine with me. Only in a month I was married, and had this house! Boy!" Wade smiles and shakes his head at the remarkable singularity of unplanned life.

"You struck it rich, I'd say."

"Well, Lynette and I are opposites of a sort. She's pretty definite about things. And I'm a lot less definite, nowadays anyway. She takes being a Catholic pretty seriously—more so since her son got killed. And I kinda let her have her way there. I joined just for her sake, but we don't hold mass here, Frank. I'd say we were just alike in the one thing that counts—we're not rich people, and I'm not sure we really love each other or need to, but we want to be a good force in a small world and give a good accounting in the time that's left." Wade looks at me on the steps as if I were going to judge him, and he was hoping I'd come down and give him a big crack on the shoulders like a linebacker. I'm sure he has told me all this—a subject we might've gotten into in greater depth at the Red Lobster, and where I might've done more of the talking—because he wants to give me a fair sense of what the family is here, just in case I was weighing joining up. And it's true that the Arcenaults are a world apart from what I expected. Only better. Wade couldn't recommend himself or his tidy life to me in sweeter, more agreeable terms. What better prospects than to hitch up here. Forge a commitment in Sherri-Lyn Woods (odd weekends and holidays). I might eventually make friends with Cade, write him a subtle letter of recommendation to a good junior college; get him interested in marketing techniques instead of police work and guns. I might buy my own Whaler and dock it behind the house. It could be a damn good ordinary life, that's for sure.

Though for some reason I am nervous and embarrassed. My hands are still cold and stiff, and I stuff them inside my pants pockets and stare at Wade blank as a tomb door. That I withhold at just this moment is a major failing in my character.

"Frank," Wade says, sharp-eyed and studious now. "I want to hear from you on this. Do you think it's too little to do with your life? Just collect tolls, raise a family, work on an old car like this, go out on the ocean with your son and fish for fluke? Maybe love your wife?"

I cannot answer fast enough, all reluctance aside. "No," I almost shout. "Not a bit. I think it's goddamn great, Wade, and you're a damn lucky son of a bitch to get it." (I'm shocked to hear myself call Wade a son of a bitch.)

"There's more romance, I'd guess, in what you do, though, Frank. I don't see a lot of the world where I stand, though I've already seen plenty of it."

"Our lives are probably a lot more alike than you'd think, Wade. If you don't mind my saying so, yours might even be better."

"There are a lot of things went into an old car like this, if you get my meaning." Wade smiles proudly now, happy for my vote of approval. "Little touches I can't put into words. I'll come down here at four in the morning sometimes and tinker till daylight. And I have it to look forward to when I drive home. And I'll tell you this, son. Any day I come up upstairs, I'm happy as a lark, and my devils are in their dungeon."

"That's great, Wade."

"And it's every bit of it completely knowable, son. Wires and bolts. I could show you everything, though I can't tell you. You could sure do it yourself." He looks at me and shakes his head in amazement. Wade is not a full-disclosure kind of man, no matter how it might seem. And in this case, I know exactly what he's discovered, know the worth and pleasure it can be to anyone. Though for some strange reason, as I look down at Wade looking up at me, what I think of is Wade alone, walking down a long empty hospital corridor, holding a single suitcase, stopping at a numberless door and peeking in on a neat, empty room where the bed is turned down and harsh sunlight comes through a window, and things inside are clean as they can be. *Tests* are what he's here for. Many, many of them. And once he's walked in the room he will never be the same. This is the beginning of the end, and frankly it scares me witless and gives me a terrible shudder. I would like to hug him now, tell him to stay out of hospitals, meet the reaper at home. But I can't. He would get the wrong idea and everything between us would be ruined just when it's started so well.

Above us, in the fitful activity of the house, someone has begun to play the bass intro to "What'd I Say" on the electric organ, the four low minor-note sex-and-anticipation vamp before ole Ray starts his moan. The hum sinks through the rafters and fills the basement with an unavoidable new atmosphere. Despair.

Wade glances at the ceiling, happy as a man could have any right to be. It is as if he knew this very thing would happen and hears it as a signal that his house is in superb working order and ready for him to find his place in it once again. He is a man completely without a subtext, a literalist of the first order.

"I feel, Frank, like I've seen your face before. It's familiar to me. Isn't that strange?"

"You must see a lot of faces, Wade, wouldn't you guess?"

"Everybody in New Jersey's at least once." Wade flashes the patented toll-taker's grin. "But I don't remember many. Yours is just a face I remember. I thought it the moment I saw you."

I can't bear to tell Wade that he has taken my $1.05 four hundred times, smiled and told me to have myself "a super day," as I whirled off into the rough scrimmage of Route 1-South. That would be too ordinary an answer for his special kind of question, and for this charged moment. Wade is after mystery here, and I am not about to deny him. It would be as if Mr. Smallwood from Detroit had turned out to be a former grease jockey at Frenchy Montreux's Gulf, who had changed my oil and given me lubes, only I hadn't noticed, but suddenly did and pointed it out: mystery, first winded, then ruined by fact. I would rather stay on the side of good omens, be part of the inexplicable, an unexpected bellwether for whatever is ahead. Discretion, oddly enough, is the best response for a man of stalled responses.

Behind me the kitchen door opens, and I turn to see Lynette's cute cheerleader's face peering down at both of us, looking amused— a palpable relief, though I read in her look that this whole man-talk-below-decks business has been scheduled in advance and that she's been minding the kitchen clock for a prearranged moment to call us topside. I'm the lucky subject (but not the victim) of other people's scheming, and that is never bad. It is, in fact, a cozy feeling, even if it can be put to no good use.

The brooding, churchy Ray Charles chords come down louder now. This is Vicki's work. "You men can talk old cars all day if you want to, but there's folks ready to sit down." Lynette's eyes twinkle with impatient good humor. She can tell everything's A-Okay down here. And she's right. If we are not great friends, we soon will be.

"How 'bout let's eat a piece of dead sheep, Frank?" Wade laughs, giving his belly a rub. "Agnus dei," he chortles up toward Lynette.

"That is *not* what it is," Lynette says, and rolls her eyes in the (I see now) Arcenault manner. "What'll he say next, Frank? Agnus Dei is what *you* are, Wade, not what we're eatin. Heavens."

"I'm sure too tough to chew, Frank, I'll tell you that right now. Haw." And up out of the shadowy basement we come—all hands on deck—into the warm and sunlit kitchen, the whole Arcenault crew arrived and ready for ritual Sunday grub.

*D*inner is a more ceremonial business than I would've guessed. Lynette has transformed her dining room into a hot little jewel box, crystal-candle chandelier, best silver and linens laid. The instant we're seated she has us all join hands around the obloid so that I end up uneasily grabbing both Wade's and Cade's (no resistance from Cade) while Vicki holds Wade's and Lynette's. And I can't help thinking—eyes stitched shut, peering soundlessly down into the familiar death-ball of liquid crimson flame behind which waits an infinity of black soul's abyss from which nothing but Wade and Cade's cumbersome hands can keep me from tumbling—what strange, good luck to be reckoned among these people like a relative welcome from Peoria. Though I can't keep from wondering where my own children are at this moment, and where X is—my hope being that they are not sharing a fatherless, prix fixe Easter brunch at some deserted seaside Ramada in Asbury Park with Barksdale, back on the sneak from Memphis, taking my place. That news I could've passed a happy day without, though we can never stop what comes to us by right. I am overdue, in fact, for a comeuppance, and lucky not to be spending the day cruising some mall for an Easter take-out—the way poor Walter Luckett no doubt is, lost in the savage wilderness of civil life.

Lynette's blessing is amiably brief and upbeat-ecumenical in its particulars—I assume for my benefit—taking into account the day and the troubled world we live in but leaving out Vatican II and any saintly references unquestionably on her mind—where they count—and winding up with a mention of her son, Beany, in a soldier's grave at Fort Dix but present in everyone's mind, including mine. (Molten flames, in fact, give way at the end to reveal Beany's knifey mug leering at me out from oblivion's sanctum.)

Wade and Cade have both put on garish flower ties and sports jackets, and look like vaudevillians. Vicki gives double cross-eyes at me when I smile at her and attempt to act comfortable among the family. Talk is of the weather as we dig into the lamb, then a brief pass into state politics; then Cade's chances of an early call-up at the police academy and speculation about whether uniforms will be assigned the first morning, or if more tests will need to be passed, which Cade seems to view as a grim possibility. He leads a discussion on the effect of driving fifty-five, noting that it's all right for every-body else but not him. Then Lynette's work on the Catholic crisis-line, then Vicki's work at the hospital, which everyone agrees is both as difficult and rewarding a service to mankind as can be—more, by implication, than Lynette's. No one mentions our weekend in the faraway Motor City, though I have the feeling Lynette is trying to find a place for the word Detroit in practically every sentence, to let us all know she wasn't born yesterday and isn't making a stink since Vicki, like all other divorced gals, can take care of her own beeswax.

Cade cracks a baiting smile and asks me who I like in the AL East, to which I answer Boston (my least favorite team). I, of course, am behind Detroit all the way, and know in fact that certain crucial trades and a new pitching coach will make them virtually unstoppable come September.

"Boston. Hnuhn." Cade leers into his plate. "Never see it."

"Wait and see," I say with absolute assurcdness. "There're a hundred and sixty-two games. They could make one smart trade by the deadline and pretty much have it their way."

"It'd have to be for Ty Cobb." Cade guffaws and eyes his father slavishly, his mouth full of a dinner roll.

I laugh the loudest while Vicki crosses her eyes again, since she knows I've led Cade to the joke like a trained donkey.

Lynette smiles attcntively and maneuvers her lamb hunk, English peas and mint jelly all nearer one another on her plate. She is an understanding listener, but she is a straightforward questioner too, someone who wouldn't let you off easy if you called up the crisis-line with a silly crisis. It seems she has me fixed in her mind. "Now were you in the service, Frank?" she says pleasantly.

"The Marines, but I got sick and was discharged."

Lynette's face portrays real concern. "What happened?"

"I had a blood syndrome that made a doctor think I was dying of cancer. I wasn't, but nobody figured it out for a while."

"You were lucky, then, weren't you?" Lynette is thinking of poor dead Beany again, cold in the Catholic section of the Fort Dix cemetery. Life is never fair.

"I was headed over in six more months, so I guess so. Yes ma'am."

"You don't have to ma'am me, Frank," Lynette says and bats her eyes all around. She smiles dreamily down the table at Wade, who smiles back at her in his best old southern gent manner. "My former husband was in Vietnam in the Coast Guard," Lynette says. "Not many knew the Guard was even there. But I have letters postmarked the Mekong Delta and Saigon."

"Where've you got 'em hid?" Vicki smirks at everyone.

"Past is past, sweetheart. I threw them out when I met that man right there." Lynette nods and smiles at Wade. "We don't need to pretend, do we. Everybody's been married here except Cade."

Cade blinks his dark eyes like a puzzled bull.

"Those guys saw some real tough action," Wade says. "Stan told me, Lynette's ex-husband, that he probably killed two hundred people he never saw, just riding along shooting the jungle day after day, night after night." Wade shakes his head.

"That's really something," I say.

"Right," Cade grunts sarcastically.

"Are you sorry not to have seen real action," Lynette says, turning to me.

"He sees enough," Vicki says and smirks again. "That's my department."

Lynette smiles dimly at her. "Be nice, sweetheart. Try to be, anyway."

"I'm perfect," Vicki says. "Don't I *look* perfect?"

"I'd have some more of that lamb," I say. "Cade, can I pass some your way?" Cade gives me a devious look as I catch a slab of gray lamb and pass him the platter. For some reason, my mind cannot come up with a good sports topic, though it's trying like a computer. All I can think is facts. Batting averages. Dates. Seating capacities. Third-down ratios of last year's Super Bowl opponents (though I can't remember which teams actually played). Sometimes sports are no help.

"Frank, I'd be interested to hear you out on this one," Wade says, swallowing a big wedge of lamb. "Just in your journalist's opinion, are we, would you say, in a prewar or a postwar situation in this country right now?" Wade shakes his head in earnest dismay. "I guess I get sour about things sometimes. I wish I didn't."

"I haven't paid much attention to politics the last few years, to tell the truth, Wade. My opinion never seemed worth much."

"I hope there's a world war before I'm too old to be in it. That's all I know," Cade says.

"That's what Beany thought, Cade." Lynette frowns at Cade.

"Well," he says to his plate after a moment's numbed silence.

"Now seriously, Frank," Wade says. "How can you stay isolated from events on a grand scale, is my question." Wade isn't badgering me. It is just the earnest way of his mind.

"I write sports, Wade. If I can write a piece for the magazine on, say, what's happening to the team concept here in America, and do a good job there, I feel pretty good about things. Pretty patriotic, like I'm not isolating myself."

"That makes sense." Wade nods at me thoughtfully. He is leaning on his elbows, over his plate, hands clasped. "I can buy that."

"What *has* happened to the team concept," Lynette asks, and looks at everyone by turns. "I'm not sure I know even what that is."

"That's pretty complicated," Wade says, "wouldn't you say so, Frank?"

"If you talk to athletes and coaches the way I do, that's all you hear, from the pros especially. Baseball, football. The line is, everybody has a role to play, and if anybody isn't willing to play his role, then he doesn't fit into the team's plans."

"It sounds all right to me, Frank," Lynette says.

"It's all a crocka shit's what it is." Cade scowls miserably at his own two hands, which are on the table. "They're just all assholes. They wouldn't know a team if it bit 'em on the ass. They're all prima donnas. Half of 'em are queers, too."

"That's certainly intelligent, Cade," Vicki says. "Thanks very much for your brilliant comment. Why don't you tell us some more of your philosophies."

"That wasn't too nice, Cade," Lynette says. "Frank had the floor then."

"Ppptttt," Cade gives a Bronx cheer and rolls his eyes.

"Is that some new language you learned working on boats?" Vicki says.

"Okay, seriously, Frank." Wade is still leaning up on his elbows like a jurist. He's hit a subject with some meat on its bones, and he's ready to saw right in. "I think Lynette's got a pretty valid point in what she says here." (Forgetting for the moment Cade's opinion.) "I mean, what's the matter with following your assignment on the team? When I was working oil rigs, that's exactly how we did it. And I'll tell you, too, it worked."

"Well, maybe it's too small a point. Only the way these guys use team concept is too much like a machine to me, Wade. Too much like one of those oil wells. It leaves out the player's part—to play or not play; to play well or not so well. To give his all. What all these guys mean by team concept is just cogs in the machine. It forgets a guy has to decide to do it again every day, and that men don't work like machines. I don't think that's a crazy point, Wade. It's just the nineteenth-century idea—dynamos and all that baloney—and I don't much like it."

"But in the end, the result's the same, isn't it?" Wade says seriously. "Our team wins." He blinks hard at me.

"If everybody decides that's what they want, it is. If they can perform well enough and long enough. It's just the *if* I'm concerned about, Wade. I worry about the *decide* part, too, I guess. We take too much for granted. What if I just don't want to win that bad, or can't?"

"Then you shouldn't be on the team." Wade seems utterly puzzled (and I can't blame him). "Maybe we agree and I don't know it, Frank?"

"It's all niggers with big salaries shootin dope, if you ask me," Cade says. "I think if everybody carried a gun, everything'd work a lot better."

"Oh, Christ." Vicki throws down her napkin and stares away into the living room.

"Who's he?" Cade gapes.

"You can just be excused, Cade Arcenault," Lynette says crisply, with utter certainty. "You can leave and live with the other cavemen. Tell Cade, Wade. He can leave the table."

"Cade." Wade beams an unmistakable look of unmentionable violence Cade's way. "Put the lock on that, mister." But Cade cannot stop smirking and lurks back in his chair like a criminal, folding his big arms and balling his fists in hatred. Wade balls his own fists and butts them together softly in front of him, while his eyes return to a point two inches out onto the white field of linen tablecloth. He is cogitating about teams still, about what makes one and what doesn't. I could jawbone about this till it's time to start home again, though I admit the whole subject has begun to make me vaguely uneasy.

"What you're telling me then, Frank, and I may have this all bum-fuzzled up. But it seems to me you're saying this idea—" Wade arches his eyebrows and smiles up at me in a beatific way "—leaves out our human element. Am I right?"

"That says it well, Wade." I nod in complete agreement. Wade has got this in terms he likes now (and a pretty versatile sports cliché at that). And I am pleased as a good son to go along with him. "A team is really intriguing to me, Wade. It's an event, not a thing. It's time but not a watch. You can't reduce it to mechanics and roles."

Wade nods, holding his chin between his thumbs and index fingers. "All right, all right, I guess I understand."

"The way the guys are talking about it now, Wade, leaves out the whole idea of the hero, something I'm personally not willing to give up on yet. Ty Cobb wouldn't have been a role-player." I give Cade a hopeful look, but his eyes are drowsy and suffused with loathing. My knee begins to twitch under the table.

"I'm not either," Lynette says, her eyes alarmed.

"It also leaves out why the greatest players, Ty Cobb or Babe Ruth, sometimes don't perform as greatly as they should. And why the best teams lose, and teams that shouldn't win, do. That's team play of another kind, I think, Wade. It's not role-playing and machines like a lot of these guys'll tell you."

"I think I understand, Wade," Lynette says, nodding. "He's saying athletes and all these sports people are just not too smart."

"I guess it's giving a good accounting, sweetheart, is what it comes down to," Wade says somberly. "Sometimes it'll be enough. Sometimes it isn't going to be." He purses his lips and stares at my idea like a crystal vase suspended in his mind's rare ether.

I stare at my own plateful of second helping I haven't touched and won't, the pallid lamb congealed and hard as a wood chip, and the untouched peas and brocoli flower alongside it cold as Christmas. "When I can make that point in one of our 'Our Editors Think' columns, Wade, that half a million people'll read, then I figure I've addressed the big picture. What you said: events on a grand scale. I don't know what else I really can do after that."

"That's everything in life right there, is my belief," Lynette says, though she's thinking of another subject, and her bright green eyes scout the table for anyone who hasn't finished his or hers yet.

In the kitchen an electric coffeemaker clicks, then spurts, then sighs like an iron lung, and I get an unexpected whiff of Cade who smells of lube jobs and postadolescent fury. He cannot help himself here. His short life—Dallas to Barnegat Pines—has not been especially wonderful up to now, and he knows it. Though to my small regret, there's nothing on God's green earth I can do to make it better for him. My future letter-of-recommendation and fishing excursions with just the three men cut no ice with him. Perhaps one day he will stop me for speeding, and we can have the talk we can't have now, see eye-to-eye on crucial issues—patriotism and the final rankings in the American League East, subjects that would bring us to blows in a second this afternoon. Life will work out better for Cade once he buttons on a uniform and gets comfortable in his black-and-white machine. He is an enforcer, natural born, and it's possible he has a good heart. If there are better things in the world to be, there are worse, too. Far worse.

Vicki is staring down at her full plate, but glances up once out the tops of her eyes and gives me a disheartened sour-mouth of disgust. There is trouble, as I've suspected, on the horizon. I have talked too much to suit her and, worse, said the wrong things. And worse yet, jabbered on like a drunk old uncle in a voice she's never heard, a secular Norman Vincent Pealeish tone I use for the speaker's bureau and that even makes *me* squeamish sometimes when I hear it on tape. This may have amounted to a betrayal, a devalued intimacy, an illusion torn, causing doubt to bloom into dislike. Our own talk is always of the jokey-quippy-irony style and lets us leap happily over "certain things" to other "certain things"—cozy intimacy, sex and rapture, ours in a heartbeat. But now I may have stepped out of what she thinks she knows and feels safe about, and become some Gildersleeve she doesn't know, yet instinctively distrusts. There is no betrayal like voice betrayal, I can tell you that. Women hate it. Sometimes X would hear me say something—something as innocent as saying "Wis-sconsin" when I usually said "Wisconsin"—and turn hawk-eyed with suspicion, wander around the house for twenty minutes in a brown brood. "Something you said didn't sound like you," she'd say after a while. "I can't remember what it was, but it wasn't the way you talk." I, of course, would be stumped for what to answer, other than to say that if I said it, it must be me.

Though I should know it's a bad idea to accompany anyone but yourself home for the holidays. Holidays with strangers never turn out right, except in remote train stations, Vermont ski lodges or the Bahamas.

"Who'll have coffee?" Lynette says brightly. "I've got decaf." She is clearing dishes smartly.

"Knicks," Cade mutters, pounding to his feet and slumping off.

"Nix to you too, Cade," Lynette says, pushing through the kitchen door, arms laden. She turns to frown, then cuts her eyes at Wade who is sitting with a pleasant, distracted look on his square face, palms flat on the tablecloth thinking about team concept and the grand scale of things. She widely mouths words to the effect of getting a point across to this Cade Arcenault outfit, or there'll be hell to pay, then vanishes out the door, letting back in a new scent of strong coffee.

Wade is galvanized, and gives Vicki and me a put-on smile, rising from the head of the table, looking small and uncomfortable in the loose-fitting sports jacket and ugly tie—unquestionably a joke present from the family or the men at the toll plaza. He has worn it as a token of good spirits, but they have temporarily abandoned him. "I guess I've got a couple things to do," he says miserably.

"Don't you rough up on that boy now," Vicki threatens in a whisper. Her eyes are savage slits. "Life ain't peaches-and-milk for him either."

Wade looks at me and smiles helplessly, and once again I imagine him peeping into an empty hospital room from which he'll never return.

"Cade's fine, sister," he says with a smile, then wanders off to find Cade, already deep in some squarish room of his down a hallway on another level.

"It'll be all right," I say, soft and sober-voiced now, meant to start me back on the road to intimacy. "There's just too many new people in Cade's life. I wouldn't be any good at it either." I smile and nod in one fell motion.

Vicki raises an eyebrow—I am a strange man with inexpert opinions concerning her family life, something she needs like a new navel. She turns a dinner spoon over and over in her fingers like a rosary. The boat collar of her pink jersey has slid a fraction off-center exposing a patch of starkly white brassiere strap. It is inspiring, and I wish this were the important business we were up to instead of old dismal-serious—though I have only myself to blame. *Sic transit gloria mundi.* When is that ever not true?

"Your father's a great guy," I say, my voice becoming softer with each word. I should be silent, portray a different fellow entirely, affect some hidden antagonism of my own to balance hers. Only I'm simply not able to. "He reminds me of a great athlete. I'm sure he'll never have a nervous breakdown."

Lynette clatters dessert plates and coffee cups in the kitchen. She's listening to us, and Vicki knows it. Anything said now will be for a wider consumption.

"Daddy and Cade oughta be living here by theirselves," Vicki says scornfully. "He oughtn't to be hooked up with this ole gal. They oughta be both big bachelors havin the time of their lives."

"He seems pretty happy to me."

"Don't start on me 'bout my own daddy, if you please. I know *you* well enough, don't I? I ought to know *him!*" Her eyes grow sparkly with dislike. "What's all that guff you were spewin about. Patriotism. Team con-cept. You sounded like a preacher. I just about mortified."

"They're things I believe in. More people could stand to think that way, if you ask me."

"Well, you oughta believe them to yourself quietly then. I can't take this."

At this moment, Elvis Presley comes to the living room door and stares up at me. He's heard something he doesn't like and intends to find out if I'm responsible. "I don't even like men," Vicki says, staring belligerently at her spoon. "Ya'll don't make yourselves happy ten minutes at a time. You and Everett both. Y'act like tormented dogs. Plus, you bring it all on yourselves."

"I think it's you that's unhappy."

"Yeah? But it's really you, though, idn't it? You hate everything."

"I'm pretty happy." I put on a big smile, though it's true I am heartsick. "You make me happy. I know that. You can count on that."

"Oh boy. Here we go. I shouldn't of told you about your ex and whatever his name is. You been Serious Sam ever since."

"I'm not Serious Sam. I don't even care about that."

"Shoot. You should've seen your face when I told you."

"Look at it now, though." My grin is ear-to-ear, though it is impossible to argue in behalf of your own good spirits without defeating them completely and getting mad as hell. Elvis Presley has seen enough and goes back behind the couch. "Why don't we just get married?" I say. "Isn't that a good idea?"

"Because I don't love you enough, that's why." She looks away. More dishes clatter in the kitchen. Cups settle noisily into saucers. Far away, in a room I know nothing of, a phone rings softly.

"Now that's the phone," I hear Lynette say to no one in particular, and the ringing stops.

"Yes you do," I say brightly. "That's just a bunch of hooey. I'll get right down on my knees right now." I get onto my knees and walk on them all the way around the table to where she sits, thighs crossed regally and entombed in taut panty hose. "A man's on his knees to plead and beg with you to marry him. He'd be faithful, and take out the garbage and do dishes and cook, or at least pay someone to do it. How can you say no?"

"It ain't gon be hard," she says giggling, embarrassed at me for yet another reason.

"Frank?"

My name. Unexpected. Called from somewhere in the unexplored cave of the house. Wade's voice. Probably he and Cade want me up there to watch the end of the Knicks game—once again everything decided in the last twenty seconds. But wild horses couldn't pull me away from here. This is serious.

"Ho, Wade," I call out, still on my knees in my pleader's pose in front of his regal daughter. One more bout of ardent pleading-tickling and we'll both be laughing, and she'll be mine. And why shouldn't she? My *always* needn't be forever. I'm ready for the plunge, nervy as a cliff-diver. Though if down the line things go rotten we can both climb the cliffs again. Life is long.

"Phone's for you," Wade calls. "You can take it up here in Lynette's and my room." Wade sounds sobered and bedeviled, a pitiable presence from the top of the stairs. A door clicks softly shut.

"Who's that?" Vicki says scratchily, tugging on her pink skirt as if we'd been caught in heavy petting. Her brassiere strap is now exposed completely.

"I don't know." Though I have a terrible bone-aching crisis fear that I have forgotten something important and am about to stare disaster in the face. A special assignment I was supposed to write but have somehow completely neglected, everyone up in New York rushing round in emergency moods trying to find me. Or possibly an Easter date I made months ago and have overlooked, though there's no one I know well enough to ask me. I cannot guess who it is. I plant a quick kiss of promised return on Vicki's stockinged knee, get to my feet and head off to investigate. "Don't move," I say. The kitchen door is just opening as I leave.

Above floors, a dark and short carpeted hall leads to a bathroom at the end where a light is on. Two doors are shut on one side, but on the other, one stands open, a bluish light shining through. Ahead of me I hear a thermostat click and the sound of whooshing air.

I step into Wade and Lynette's nuptial sanctum where the blue light radiates from a bed lamp. The bed is also blue, a skirted-and-flounced four-poster canopy, king-sized and wide as a peaceful lake. Nothing is an inch out of place. Rugs raked. Vanity sparkling. No underwear or socks piled on the blue Ultrasuede loveseat beside the window overlooking the windy boat channel. The door to the bathroom is discreetly closed. A smell of face powder lingers. The room is perfect as a place where strangers can accept personal phone calls.

The phone is on the bed table, its conscientious little night light glowing dimly.

"Hello," I say, with no idea what I will hear, and sink expectant into the soft flounced silence.

"Frank?" X's voice, solemn, reliable, sociable. I am instantly exhilarated to hear her. But there is an undertone I do not comprehend. Something beyond speech, which is why she is the only one who can call me.

I feel a freeze going right to the bottom of my feet. "What's the matter?"

"It's all right," she says. "Everyone's all right. Everyone's fine here. Well, everyone's not, actually. Someone named, let's see, Walter Luckett is dead, apparently. I guess I don't know him. He sounds familiar, but I don't know why. Who is he?"

"What do you mean, he's dead?" Consolation spurts right back up through me. "I was with him last night. At home. He isn't dead."

She sighs into the receiver, and a dumb silence opens on the line. I hear Wade Arcenault's voice, soft and evocative, speaking to his son across the hall behind a closed door. A television mumbles in the background, a low crowd noise and a ref's distant whistle. "Now in the best of all possible worlds. . . ." Wade can be heard to say.

"Well," X says quietly, "the police called here about thirty minutes ago. They think he's dead. There's a letter. He left it for you."

"What do you mean?" I say, and am bewildered. "You sound like he killed himself."

"He shot himself, the policeman said, with a duck gun."

"Oh no."

"His wife's out of town, evidently."

"She's in Bimini with Eddie Pitcock."

"Hmm," X says. "Well."

"Well what?"

"Nothing. I'm sorry to call you. I just listened to your message."

"Where're the children?"

"They're here. They're worried, but it isn't your fault. Clary answered the phone when the police called. Are you with what's-her-face?" (A first-rate Michigan expression of practiced indifference.)

"Vicki." Vicki Whatsherface.

"Just wondering."

"Walter came to the house last night and stayed late."

"Well," X says, "I'm sorry. Was he a friend of yours, then?"

"I guess so." Somebody in Cade's room claps his hands loudly three times in succession, then whistles.

"Are you all right, Frank?"

"I'm shocked." In fact, I can feel my fingertips turning cold. I lie down backwards on the silky bedspread.

"The police want you to call them."

"Where was he?"

"Two blocks from here. At 118 Coolidge. I may have even heard the shot. It isn't that far."

I stare up through the open canopy into an absolutely blue ceiling. "What am I supposed to do? Did you already say that?"

"Call a Sergeant Benivalle. Are you all right? Would you like me to come meet you someplace?"

Cade lets out a loud, raucous laugh across the hall.

"Isn't that the goddamn truth!" Wade says in high spirits. "It is the god-*damndest* thing, I swear."

"I'd like you to meet me someplace," I say in a whisper. "I'll have to call you, though."

"Where in the world are you?" (This, in her old scolding lover's style of talk: 'Where *will* you turn up next?' 'Where in the *world* have you been?')

"Barnegat Pines," I say softly.

"Wherever that is."

"Can I call you?"

"You can come over here if you want to. Of course."

"I'll call soon as I know what to do." I have no idea why I should be whispering.

"Call the police, all right?"

"All right."

"I know it's not a happy call."

"It's hard to think about right now. Poor Walter." In the pale blue ceiling I wish I could see something I recognized. Almost anything would do.

"Call me when you get here, Frank."

Though of course there is nothing to see above me. "I will," I say. X hangs up without saying anything, as if "Frank" were the same as saying "Goodbye. I love you."

I call information for the Haddam police and dial it immediately. As I wait I try to remember if I've ever laid eyes on Sergeant Benivalle, though there's no doubt I have. I've seen the whole guinea lot of them at Village Hall. In the normal carryings-on of life they are unavoidable and familiar as luggage.

"Mr. Bascombe," a voice says carefully. "Is that right?"

"Yes."

I recognize him straight off—a big chesty, small-eyed detective with terrible acne scars and a flat-top. He is a man with soft thick hands he used, in fact, to take my fingerprints when our house was broken into. I remember their softness from years ago. He is a good guy by my memory, though I know he'd never remember me.

And in fact Sergeant Benivalle might as well be talking to a recording. Death and survivorship have become the equivalents of pianos to a house-mover—big items, but a day's work that will end.

He explains in a voice void of interest that he would like me to offer positive identification of "the deceased." No one nearby will, and I reluctantly agree to. Yolanda is unreachable in Bimini, though he seems not to be bothered by it. He says he will have to give me a Thermofax of Walter's letter, since he needs it to keep "for evidence." Since Walter left another note for the police, there is no suspicion of foul play. Walter killed himself, he says, by blowing his brains out with a duck gun, and the time of death was about one P.M. (I was playing croquet on the lawn.) He bolted the shotgun, Sergeant Benivalle says, to the top of the television set and rigged a remote control to release the trigger. The TV was on when people arrived—the Knicks and Cavaliers from Richfield.

"Now, Mr. Bascombe," the Sergeant says, using his private, off-duty voice. I hear him riffling through papers, blowing smoke into the receiver. He is sitting, I know, at a metal desk, his mind wandering past other crimes, other events of more concern. It is Easter there, too, after all. "Can I ask you something personal?"

"What?"

"Well." Papers riffle, a metal drawer closes. "Were you and this Mr. Luckett, uh, sorta into it?"

"Do you mean did we have an argument, no."

"I don't, uhm, mean an argument. I mean, were you romantically linked. It would help to know that."

"Why would it help you to know that?"

Sergeant Benivalle sighs, his chair squeaks. He blows smoke into the receiver again. "Just to account for the, uh, event in question here. No big deal. You of course don't have to answer."

"No," I say. "We were just friends. We belonged to a divorced men's club together. This seems like an intrusion to me."

"I'm sort of in the intrusion business down here, Mr. Bascombe." Drawers open and close.

"All right. I just don't exactly see why that has to be an issue."

"It's okay, thanks," Sergeant Benivalle says wearily (I'm not sure what he means by this either). "If I'm not here, ask for the copy with the watch officer. Tell 'em who you are so you can, ah, identify the deceased. All right?" His voice has suddenly brightened for no reason.

"I'll do that," I say irritably.

"Thanks," Sergeant Benivalle says. "Have a good day."

I hang up the phone.

Though it is *not* a good day, nor is it going to be. Easter has turned to rain and bickering and death. There's no saving it now.

"Whaaaat?" Vicki shouts, all shock and surprise at the death of someone she has never met, her face creased into a look of pain and uninterested disbelief.

"Why, oouu noouu," Lynette exclaims, making the sign of the cross twice and in a devil's own hurry, without leaving the kitchen door. "Poor man. Poor man."

I've told them only that a friend of mine is dead and I have to go back right away. Dutch Babies and piping hot coffee sit all around, though Wade and Cade are still upstairs ironing things out.

"Well course you do," Lynette says sympathetically. "You better go on right now."

"Dyouwanme to go with you?" For some reason Vicki grins at this idea.

Why do I have the feeling she and Lynette have struck some sympathetic pact while I was on the phone? An understanding that puts a ceiling and a floor to old grievances and excludes me—the family closing ranks suddenly and officially, leaving me in the cold. This is the grim side of the non-nuclear family—its capacity to pile disaster on disaster. (Son of a bitch!) After I leave they'll stoke the fire, haul out the sheet music and sing favorite oldies—together alone. I am called away at the very worst time, before they realize how much they all really like me and want someone just like me around forever. Preemptive, ill-meant death has intruded. Its gluey odors are spread over me. I can smell them myself.

"No," I say. "There wouldn't be anything for you to do anyway. You go on and stay here."

"Well it's the God's truth, idn't it?" Vicki gets up and comes to stand beside me in the dining room archway, looping her arm encouragingly through mine. "I'll walk with you out, though."

"Lynette. . . ." I start to say, but Lynette is already waving a spoon at me from the end of the table.

"Now don't say a word, Franky Bascombe. Just go see 'bout your friend who needs you."

"Tell Wade and Cade I'm sorry." I want more than anything not to leave, to be around another hour to sing "Edelweiss" and doze off in my chair while Vicki files her nails and daydreams.

"About what? What is it's going on?" Wade has heard commotion and come right down to see what all the trouble is about. He's at the top of the stairs, half a level above us, leaning over as if he were about to fly.

"Let me explain it all to you later, Dad," Lynette says, and raises her fingers to her lips.

"You two haven't had a fuss, have you?" Wade's look is pure bafflement. "I hope nobody's mad. Why are you leaving, Frank?"

"His best friend's dead, that's all," Vicki says. "That's what the phone call was about." It's clear she wants me out of here and in a hurry, and intends to be on the phone to the dagger-head in Texas before my key is in the ignition.

Though what have I done that's so wrong? Can a longed-for life sink below the waves because a tone in my voice wasn't exactly appreciated? Can affections be frail as that? Mine are heartier.

"Wade, I'm just as sorry as hell about this." I reach up the short carpeted stairway to shake his hard hand. Bafflement has not altogether left him nor me.

"Me too, son. I hope you'll come on back here. We're not going anyplace."

"He'll come back," Lynette chirps. "Vicki'll see to that." (Vicki is silent on this subject.)

"Tell Cade goodbye," I say.

"Will do." Wade comes down and squares me up with a small earnest hand on my shoulder—half a manly hug. "Come back and we'll go out fishing." Wade makes a squeaky, embarrassed laugh, and in fact looks slightly dizzy.

"I'll do it, Wade." And God knows I would. Though that will never happen in a hundred moons, and I will never see his face again outside a toll plaza. We will never stalk, hungry as bears, into a Red Lobster, never be friends in the ways I had hoped—ways to last a lifetime.

I wave them all goodbye.

On the front lawn everything including our empty croquet wickets is lost and gray and gone straight to hell. I stand in the fluttering wind and sight down the unpeopled curve of Arctic Spruce to the point where it sweeps from sight, all its plantings fresh and immature, its houses split-level and perfectly isosceles. Wade Arcenault is a lucky man to live here, and I am, at heart, cast down to loss in its presence.

Vicki knows I'm stalling and tampers with the door latch of my Malibu until, as if by magic, it swings open.

She is bemused, in no mind for words. I, of course, would talk till midnight if I thought it could improve my chances.

"Why don't we just go get a motel room right now?" I paint a grin on my face. "You haven't been to Cape May. We could have a big time."

"What about your ole dead guy? Herb?" Vicki sets her chin up haughtily. "What about him?"

"Walter." She's made me feel slightly embarrassed. "He's not going anywhere. But I'm still alive. Frank's still among the living."

"I'd be ashamed," Vicki says, shoving the door wide open between us. The wind now has a wintry grit in it. The front has passed quickly and left us in a gray spring chill. In half a minute, she is going. This is the last chance to love her.

"Well, I'm not," I say loudly into the wind. "I didn't kill *my* self. I want you to go off and let me love you. And tomorrow we'll get married."

"Not hardly." She looks glumly at the dry black weather stripping on my poor car's poor window frame. She picks off a piece with a crimson fingernail.

"Why not?" I say. "*I* want to. This time yesterday we were in bed like newlyweds. I was one of the only six people in the world then. What the hell happened? Did you just go crazy? Twenty minutes ago you were happy as a monkey."

"No way *I* went crazy, José," she says coarsely.

"My name's not José, goddamn it." I cast a wintry eye at Lynette's spurious beigey Jesus nailed to the siding. He makes life a perfect misery for as many as he can, then never takes the heat. He should try resurrection in today's complex world. He'd fall right off His cross on His ass. He couldn't sell newspapers.

"We don't have none of the same interests, doesn't look like," Vicki says nearly inaudibly, fumbling a finger at her blue Navajo earring. "I just figured that out sitting at the table."

"But *I'm* interested in *you!*" I shout. "Isn't that enough?" The wind is kicking up. From around the house Wade's Boston Whaler blunks against the dock. My own words are broken and carried off like chaff.

"Not to be married, it isn't," she says, her jaw set in certainty. "Just foolin like what we been doin is one thing. But that won't get you all the way to death."

"What will? Just tell me and I'll do it. I want to go all the way to death with you." Words, my best refuge and oldest allies, are suddenly acting to no avail, and I am helpless. In the wind, in fact, words hardly seem to clear my mouth. It is like a dream in which my friends turn against me and then disappear—a poor man's Caesar dream, a nightmare in itself. "Look here. I'll get interested in nursing. I'll read some books and we can talk about nursing all the goddamn time."

Vicki tries to smile but looks dumbfounded. "I don't know what to say, really."

"Say yes! Or at least something intelligent. I might just kidnap you."

"Right you won't." She curls her lip and narrows her eyes, a look I've never seen and that scares me. She is without fear if fearlessness is what's asked for. But just so long as she is fearlessly mine.

"I'm not going to be fooled with," I say, and move toward her.

"I just don't love you enough to marry you." She throws down her hands in exasperation. "I don't love you in the right way. So just go on. You're liable to say anything, and I don't like that." Her hair has become whipped and tangled.

"There isn't any right way," I say. "There's just love and not love. You're crazy."

"You'll see," she says.

"Get in this car." I pull back the door. (She has decided not to love me because I might change her, but she couldn't be more wrong. It is I who'll happily bend.) "You just think you want some little life like Lynette's to complain about, but I'm going to give you the best of all worlds. You don't know how happy you're going to be." I give her a big signpost grin and step forward to put my arms around her, but she busts me full in the mouth with a mean little itchy fist that catches me midstride and sends me to the turf. I manage to grab onto the car door to ease my fall, but the punch is a looping girl's left hook straight from the shoulder, and I actually walked directly into it, eyes wide open.

"I'll 'bout knock you silly," she says furiously, both fists balled like little grapeshoots, thumbs inward. "Last guy took holt of me went to eye surgery."

And I can't help smiling. It is the end to all things, of course. But a proper end. I taste thick, squeamish blood in my mouth. (My hope is that no one inside has seen this and feels the need to help me.) When I look up, she has backed off a half step, and to the right of dolorous Jesus I see Cade's big head peering down at me, impassive as Buddha. Though in all ways Cade does not matter in this, and I don't mind his seeing me in defeat. It is an experience he already knows, and would sympathize with if he could.

"Get on up and go see your dead guy," Vicki says in a quavery, cautionary voice.

"Okay." I'm still smiling my dopey Joe Palooka smile. Possibly there are even stars and whirligigs shooting above my head. I might not be in complete control, but I'm certain I can drive.

"You awright, aren't you?" She will not come a step closer, but squints an assessing eye at me long-distance. I'm sure I am pale as potatoes, though I'm not ashamed to be decked by a strong girl who can turn grown men over in their beds and get them in and out of distant bathrooms single-handed. In fact, it confirms everything I have always believed of her. There may be hope yet for us. This may be the very love she's been seeking but hasn't trusted, and needed only to whop me good to make us both realize it.

"Why don't you call me tomorrow?" I say, sprawled on my elbows, my head starting to ache, though I'm still smiling a good loser's smile.

"I doubt that." She crosses her arms like Maggie in the funnies. Who is a better Jiggs than I am? Who is worse at learning from his experience?

"You better go inside," I say. "It's an indignity for you to see me get on my feet."

"I didn't mean to hit you," she says in a bossy way.

"Like hell. You'd've knocked me out if you knew how to make a fist. You make a girl's fist.

"I don't hit too many."

"Go on," I say.

"You sure you're awright?"

"Would you call me tomorrow?"

"Maybe, maybe not." I can actually hear her stockings scrape as she turns and starts back across the lawn in the wind, her arms swinging, each foot planted toe-down to keep from sinking in the sod. She does not look back—as she shouldn't—and quickly disappears into the house. Cade has likewise left the window. And for a time then I sit where I've fallen beside my car and stare up at the rending clouds, trying to make the world around me stop its terrifying spin. Everything has seemed beckoning and ahead, though I am unsure now if life has not suddenly passed me like a big rumbling semi and left me flattened here by the road.

11

Winds buffet me on my way home and impede my progress. It has, in fact, been a terrible weekend weatherwise, though who could've predicted it on Friday morning at my son's grave.

My choice of routes home is not a wise one—the Parkway—where there is no consoling landscape, only pines and sad sedgy hummocks and distant power right-of-ways trailing skyward toward Lakehurst and soulful Fort Dix. An occasional Pontiac dealer's sign or a tennis bubble peeps above the conifers, but these are far too meager and abstracted. I'm on the old knife-edge of dread, without constructive distance from what's to come, and I see only the long, empty horizon that X told me about but that I was too idiotic to fear.

All the traffic is coming up from Atlantic City and the beaches in a hurry, and at Route 98 I consult the map and turn out hoping to square off to Route 9 and then, by driving the farmy section lines toward Freehold, get home. The foul weather has moved on past, and on the radio unexpected stations turn up with unexpected news— what's for lunch tomorrow at the Senior Citizens' Center in South Amboy (city chicken and Texas Toast); the weather in Kalispell and Coeur d'Alene (much summerier than here). On the feminist station from New Brunswick, a woman with a sexy voice reads dirty passages from *Tropic of Cancer*—Van Norden's soliloquy on love, where he compares orgasm to holy communion, then prays for a woman who's better than he is. "Find me a cunt like that, will you?" Van Norden pleads. "If you could do that I'd give you my job." Afterwards the female DJ gives poor Miller a good whipping for his attitudes, followed immediately by a "get acquainted" offer for a sex club not far from my office. I stay tuned until winds carry the words away and I'm left with the pleasant if brief idea of a hundred dollar whore waiting for me somewhere if I only had the gumption to find her and didn't have other duties. Unhappy ones. The worst kind.

Suddenly, in two dreadful minutes, I make an inventory of *everything* that could possibly turn out better in the next twenty-four to thirty-six hours, and come up with nothing except a wavering mirage memory of Selma Jassim from years ago and our late-night hours, half-asleep and half-drunk and in a high state of excitement, with her moaning in unintelligible Arabic and me in animal anticipation (all this when I should've been reading student essays). Of course I can't remember one thing we could've said, or how we kept each other interested very long with the little we had to offer from the fringes of our upturned lives. Though anything is possible, any amount of rapturous transport, when you're lonely enough and at the nubbins end of your rope. Mutinous freedom awaits there for those who can bear it.

What I actually remember are long sinuous sighs in the night and the intermittent tinkle of ice cubes from glasses, her cigarette smoke in the dark of the dance-lady's house and the still October air turned electric with longing. And then, the next day, the long fog of having been up and awake all night, and a sense of accomplishment for having gotten through the night at all.

I don't regret a moment of it, the way you wouldn't regret wolfing down the last crumbly morsel of, say, the blackberry cobbler you had when you were snowbound in December on a rural highway in Wyoming and no one knew you were there, and the sun setting on you for the last time. Regret is not part of that, I'll tell you (even though knowing her absolutely lengthened the distance between X and me at the time, and made me dreamy and untalkative at the wrong crucial moment).

But I am no martyr to a past. And halfway through the town of Adelphia, New Jersey, on Business 524, I pull into an empty Acme lot and put in a call to Providence, where I think she might be. A voice could help. Better than four hundred-dollar prostitutes and a free trip to Coeur d'Alene.

In the phone booth I lean heavily on the cool plexiglass, staring at a wire shopping cart stranded in the empty parking lot, while the operator in faraway 401 runs through her listings. At a distance across the blacktop, a burger joint is open on Easter. Ground Zero Burg—a relic of the old low-slung Forties places with sliding screens, windows all around and striped awnings. A lone black car sits nosed under the awning, a carhop leaned in talking to the driver. The sky is white and skating toward the ocean at top speed. Things can happen to you. I know that. Evil lurks most everywhere, and death is too severe for most ordinary remedies. I have dealt with them before.

A ring and then an answer straightaway.

"Halloo."

"Selma?" An inexplicable name, I know, but it's pronounced differently in Arabic.

"Yes?"

"Hi Selma, it's Frank. Frank Bascombe."

Silence. Puzzlement. "Oh. Yes. Of course. And how are you?" Cigarette smoke in the receiver. Nothing surprising here.

"Fine. I'm fine." I couldn't be worse, though I won't admit it. And what next? I have nothing else to say. What do we expect other people can do for us? One of my problems is that I am *not* a problem-solver. I rely on others, even though I like to think I don't.

"So. How long has it been?" It's damn good of her to try and make conversation with me, since I seem incapable of it.

"Three years, Selma. Seems like a long time."

"Ah, yes. And you still write . . . what was it you wrote that I thought so amusing?"

"Sports."

"Sports. Yes indeed. I remember now." She laughs. "Not novels."

"No."

"Good. It made you so happy."

I watch the stoplight on Route 524 as it changes from yellow to red, and try to picture the room where she is sitting. A Queen Anne–style house, white or blue, on College Hill. Angell Street or Brown Street. The view from the window: a nice prospect of elms and streets running down to the old factory piles with the big bay far in the hazy afterground. If only I could be there instead of a parking lot in Adelphia. I would be miles happier. New prospects. Real possibilities rising like new mountains. I could be convinced in no time flat that things weren't so bad. "Frank?" Selma says into the musing silence at my end. I am putting a sail in on the bay, calculating winds and seas. Populating a different world.

"What."

"Are you sure you're feeling well? You sound quite strange. I'm always very happy to hear from you. But you don't sound particularly as if you're all right. Exactly where are you now?"

"In New Jersey. In a phone booth in a town called Adelphia. I'm not as good as I could be. But that's all right. I just wanted to hear your voice and think about you."

"Well, that's very nice. Why don't you tell me what's wrong." The familiar tinkle of a single ice cube (some things remain the same). I wonder if she is wearing her Al Fatah burnoose right now, which drove our Jewish colleagues crazy. (In private, of course, they loved it.)

"What are you doing right now," I say, staring across the Acme lot. The name "Shelby" has been scratched on the glass in front of my eyes. A cool urine scent hangs around me. At Ground Zero Burg the carhop suddenly stands back from the lone car, hands on her hips in what looks like disgust. Trouble may be brewing there. They don't know how good they have it.

"Oh. Well. I'm reading today," Selma says and sighs. "What else do I do?"

"Tell me what. I haven't read a book in I don't know when. I wish I had. The last one I read wasn't very good."

"Robert Frost. I'm meant to teach him in a week's time."

"That sounds great. I like Frost."

"Great? I don't know about that." Tinkle, tinkle.

"It sounds great to me. I'll tell you that. You're going to take all the I's out of it, aren't you?"

"Yes, of course." A laugh. "What silliness that was. He's a bore, though, really. Just a mean child who wrote. Occasionally he's amusing, I suppose. He's short, leastways. I've read Jane Austen now."

"She's great, too."

Angry blue-white smoke spews suddenly from underneath the tires of the black car, though there's no sound. The carhop turns and steps languidly up onto the curb, unimpressed. The car bolts back, halts, then squeals forward directly at her, but she doesn't even bother to move as the bumper bulls her way, stopping short and diving. She raises her arm and gives the driver the finger, and the car spurts back again with more white smoke, all the way into the Acme lot, and makes a one-eighty right out of TV. Whoever's driving knows his business. Adelphia may be where race drivers live, for all I know.

"So, well. Are you married now, Frank?"

"No. Are you? Have you found an industrialist yet?"

"No." Silence, followed by a cruel laugh. "People ask me to marry them . . . quite a number, in fact. But. They're all idiots and very poor."

"What about me?" I take another mental glimpse out her window into the atmospheric Narragansett town and bay. Plenty of sails. It's all wonderful.

"What about you?" She laughs again and sips her drink. "Are you rich?"

"I'm still interested."

"*Are* you?"

"You're damn right I am."

"Well, that's good." She is amused—why shouldn't she be? General amusement was always her position vis-à-vis the western world. There is no harm meant, really. Frost and I are just a couple of cutups. I don't even mind admitting I feel a tiny bit better. And what has it cost anyone? Two minutes of palaver charged to my home phone.

For some reason the car in the Acme lot has stopped. It is a long Trans-Am, one of the sharky-looking GMs with a wind fin like a road racer. A small head rides low behind the wheel. Suddenly more white smoke blurts from underneath the raised tires, though the car doesn't exactly move but seems to want to move—the driver is standing on the brake, is my guess. Then the car positively leaps forward ahead of all its tire-smoke and fishtails across the Acme lot (I'm sure the driver is having a devil of a time holding it straight), barely misses one of the light stanchions, achieves traction, flashes by a second stanchion, and whonks right into the empty grocery cart, sending it flying, end-over-end, casters rocketing, plastic handles splintered, red "Property of Acme" sign sailing up into the white sky, and the bulk of the basket atumble-and-whirligig right at the phone booth where I'm talking to Selma in Rhode Island, the Ocean State.

The shattered cart hits—BANG—into the phone booth, busts out a low pane of plexiglas and rocks the whole frame. "Christ," I shout.

"What was that," Selma says from Providence. "What's happened, Frank? Has something gone wrong?"

"No it's fine."

"It sounded like an explosion in a war."

Dust has been shaken all over me, and the Trans-Am has stopped just beyond where it hit the shopping cart, its motor throbbing, *ga-lug, ga-lug*.

"A kid hit a shopping cart in his car and it flew over here and crashed into this phone booth. A pane of glass came out and broke. It's strange." The glass pane is now leaned against my knee.

"Well. I suppose I don't understand."

"It's hard to understand, really."

The driver's door on the Trans-Am opens and a Negro boy in sunglasses gets out and stares at me, his head barely clearing the top of the window. He seems to be considering the distance between us. I don't know if he's thinking of going ahead and ramming the phone booth or not.

"Wait a minute." I step out to where he can see me. I wave and he waves back, and then he gets back in his car and slowly backs up twenty yards—for no reason at all, since he's in the middle of an empty lot—and drives slowly around toward the exit by Ground Zero. As he turns out into the street, he honks at the carhop, and once again she gives him the finger. She, of course, is white.

"What's actually happening," Selma asks. "Is someone hurting you?"

"No. They missed me." With my foot I shove the corner of the shopping cart back out the broken window. A breeze flows in at knee level. Across the lot the carhop is talking to someone about what's just happened. This would make a good Candid Camera segment, though it isn't clear who the joke would be on. "I'm sorry to call you up and then have all this go crash." The cart falls free out the window.

"It doesn't matter," Selma says, and laughs.

"It must seem like I live a life of chaos and confusion," I say, thinking about Walter's face for the first time all afternoon. I see it alive, then stone dead, and I can't help thinking he has made a terrible mistake, something I might've warned him about, except I didn't think of it in time.

"Well, yes. I suppose it does seem that way." Selma sounds amused again. "But it doesn't matter, either. It doesn't seem to bother you."

"Listen. How about if I took the train up to see you tonight? Or I could drive. How about it?"

"No. That wouldn't work out too well."

"Okay." I am feeling light-headed now. "How about later in the week? I'm not very busy these days."

"Maybe so. Yes." (Scant enthusiasm for this plan, though who would want me as an after-midnight guest?) "It might not be that good an idea to come, really." Her voice implies several things, a plethora of better choices.

"Okay," I say, and find it possible to cheer up a little. "I'm glad to get to talk to you."

"Yes, it's very very nice. It's always *very* nice to hear from you."

What I'd like to say is: *Go to hell, there aren't that many better choices in the world than me. Look around. Do yourself a favor.* But what kind of man would say that? "I should probably go. I have to drive home."

"Yes. All right," Selma says. "You should be careful."

"Go to hell," I say.

"Yes, goodbye," Selma says—Queen Anne house, bright prospects, tidy faculty life, sailboats, leafy streets all spinning around every which way, and all suddenly gone.

I step out of the shambles into the breezy parking lot, my heart thumping like an outboard. A few slow cars cruise Route 524, though the town, here on its outer edge, lies sunk in the secular aimlessness of Sunday that Easter only worsens for the lonely of the world. And for some reason I feel stupid. The colored boy in the Trans-Am slides by, looks at me and registers no recognition, then heads on out to the nappy countryside, running the yellow light toward Point Pleasant and the beaches, more white girls on his mind. His dashboard, I can see, is covered with white fur.

How exactly did I get to here, is what I would like to know, since my usual need, when I find myself in unaccustomed environs, is to add things up, consider what forces have led me here, and to wonder if this course is typical of what I would call my life, or if it is only extraordinary and nothing to worry about.

Quo vadis, in other words. No easy question. And at the moment I have no answers.

"Ahnnn, you aren't dead, are ya?" A voice speaks to me.

I turn and am facing a thin, sallow-faced girl with vaguely spavinous hips. Her sleeveless T-shirt has a rock group's name, THE BLOOD COUNTS, stenciled on its flat front, her pink jeans pronounce all out of happy proportion the bone-spread of her hips. She is the carhop from Ground Zero Burg, the girl who gives men the finger. She has come to get a first-hand look at me.

"I don't think so," I say.

"You oughta call the cops on that little boogie," she says in a nasty voice meant to portray hatred, but failing. "I seen what he didja. I use to live with his brother, Floyd Emerson. He isn't that way."

"Maybe he didn't mean to do it."

"Uh-huh," she says, blinking over at the shattered telephone booth and the crumpled cart, then back at me. "You don't already look too sharp. Your knee's bleedin. I think you banged your mouth. I'd call the cops."

"I hurt my mouth before," I say, looking at my knee, where the seersucker has been razored and blood has soaked through the blue stripes. "I didn't think I got hurt."

"You better siddown before you fall down then," she says. "You look like you're gonna die."

I squint at the orange awnings of the Ground Zero, fluttering like pennants in the breeze, and feel weak. The girl, the broken phone booth, the bent shopping cart suddenly seem a far distance from where I am. Inexplicably far. A gull shouts in the high white sky, and I have to stand against my car fender for balance. "I don't see why that should be true," I say with a smile, though I'm not quite sure I know what I mean. And for a little while then, I do not remember anything.

The girl has gone and come back. She stands by the door of my car, holding out a tall brown and white Humdinger cup. I am in the driver's seat, but with my feet sticking out on the pavement like a dazed accident victim.

I try to smile. She's smoking a cigarette, the hard pack stuck in her jeans pocket so the outline shows. A thick diesely smell is in the air. "What's that," I ask.

"A float. Wayne made it for you. Drink it."

"Okay." I take the foamy cup and drink. The root beer is sweet and creamy and hurts my teeth with goodness. "Wonderful," I say, and reach in my pocket for money.

"Naa, ya can't, it's free," she says, and looks away. "Where're you going?"

I drink some more of my float. "Haddam."

"Where's that at?"

"West of here, over by the river."

"Ahnnnn, the river," she says and glances skeptically out at the wide street. She is maybe sixteen, but you can't really tell. I would hate to have Clary looking like her, though now that is pretty much out of my hands. I wouldn't mind, however, if Clary were as kind as she seems to be.

"What's your name?"

"Debra. Spanelis. Your knee's quit." She looks at my torn knee with revulsion. "A good cleaner'd fix that."

"Thanks. Spanelis is a Greek name, isn't it?"

"Yeah. So how'd you know?" She looks away and draws on her cigarette.

"I met some Greek people the other night on a boat. They were named Spanelis. They were wonderful people."

"It's, like a common, a real common Greek name." She depresses the door lock button then pulls it back up, taking a flickering look at me as if I were the rarest of exotic bird. "I tried to get you a band-aid, but Wayne doesn't keep 'em anymore." I say nothing as she stares at me. "So, like. Whaddaya do?" She has adopted a new sleepy way of talking, as if nothing could bore her more than I do. Again I hear a gull cry. My lip, where Vicki socked me, throbs like a goddamn boil.

"I'm a sportswriter."

"Uh-huh." She parks one hip against the door molding and leans into it. "Whaddaya write about?"

"Well. I write about football and baseball, and players." I take a sip of my sweet, cold float. I actually feel better. Who would've thought a root-beer float could restore both faith and health, or that I would find it in as half-caste a town as this, a place wizened to a few car lots, an adult book store, a shut-down drive-in movie up the road—remnants of a boom that never boomed. From this emerges a Samaritan. A Debra.

"So," she says, scanning the highway again, her little gray eyes squinting as if she expects to see someone she doesn't know drive by. "Do you have a favorite team and all?" She smirks as if the whole idea embarrassed her.

"I like the Detroit Tigers for baseball. Some sports I don't like at all."

"Like what?"

"Hockey."

"Right. Forget it. They had a fight and a game broke out."

"That's my feeling."

"So, were you, like, a pretty great jock sometime when you were young?"

"I liked baseball then, too, except I couldn't hit or run."

"Uh-huh. Same here." She takes a preposterous puff on her cigarette and exhales all the smoke out her mouth and into the shopping center air. "So. How'd you get interested in it? Did you read about it someplace?"

"I went to college. Then when I got older, I failed at everything else, and that's all I could do."

Debra looks down at me, worry hooding her eyes. Her idea of a big success has a different story line, one that doesn't confess any start-up problems. I can teach her a damned useful lesson in life about that. "That doesn't sound so great," she says.

"It *is* pretty great, though. Successful life doesn't always follow a straight course to the top. Sometimes things don't work out and you have to change the way you look at things. But you don't want to stop and get discouraged when the chips are all down. That'd be the worst time. If I'd stopped when things went the wrong way, I'd be a goner."

Debra sighs. Her eyes fall from my face to my torn and bloody knee, to my scuffed wingtips and back up to the damp, soft Humdinger I'm holding in both hands. I'm not what she had in mind for a great success, but I hope she won't ignore what I've said. A little of the real truth can make a big impression.

"Have you got any plans," I ask.

Debra takes a cigarette drag that requires her to lift her chin in the air. "Whadda ya mean?"

"College. Not that that's necessary. It's just an idea of what to do next."

"I'd like to go out and work in Yellowstone Park," she says. "I heard about that." She looks down at her BLOOD COUNTS T-shirt.

But I'm immediately enthusiastic. "That's a great idea. I wanted to do that myself once." In fact, I actually considered it while I was poring over life choices after my divorce. A blue plastic name tag that said: FRANK: NEW JERSEY seemed good at the time. I thought I could manage the gift shop in the Old Faithful Inn. "About how old are you, Debra?"

"Eighteen." She stares studiously at the barrel of her cigarette as if she'd noticed some defect in it. "Like in July."

"Well, that's the perfect age for Yellowstone. You're probably graduating this spring, right?"

"I quit." She drops the cigarette on the blacktop and mashes out the hot end with her sneaker.

"Well, that probably doesn't even matter to the people out there. They're interested in everybody."

"Yeah. . . ."

"Listen, I think it's a good idea. It'll sure widen some horizons for you." I'd be happy to write a recommendation for her on magazine letterhead: *Debra Spanelis is not at all the kind of girl you meet every day.* They would take her in a heartbeat.

"I've got a baby," Debra says and sighs. "I doubt if the Yellowstone people would let him come." She looks at me, flat-eyed, her mouth hard and womanish, then glances away at the Ground Zero, carless, awning flaps aflutter.

She has lost all interest in me, and I can't blame her. I might as well have been speaking French from the planet Pluto. I am not an answer man of any kind.

"I guess not," I say dimly.

Debra's eyes come back round to me, and she is unexpectedly loose-limbed. My Humdinger is soft and waxy, and there's no longer much for us to say. Some meetings don't lead anyone anywhere better—an unassailable fact of life. Some small empty moments cannot be avoided, no matter how hard good will and expectations for the best try to make it so.

"So how do you feel now?" Like a lawyer, she touches her chin with her index finger.

"Better. A lot better. This made a lot of difference." I smile hopefully at my Humdinger.

"It used to be medicine, I guess." She throws her hip to one side and holds onto the window glass with her fingertips. "Do you think it's bad if I don't have any of my plans set yet?" She squints at me, trying to guess my real answer in case I decide to lie.

"Not one bit," I say. "You'll have plans. And they won't be long in coming, either. You'll see." I blink at her uncertainly. "Your life'll change fifty ways before you're twenty-five."

"Cause I'm gettin older, okay? I don't wanna piss away my whole life." She drums her fingernails on the window glass, then leaves off. I can't help thinking of Herb Wallagher's dream of death and hatred. Everybody has the most perfect right to be happy, but sometimes there's nothing you can do to help yourself.

"You won't," I say. "It's all ahead of you." I give her a big encouraging grin, though I don't think it can do the trick for either of us.

"Yeah, okay." She smiles for the first time, a shy-girl's smile of politeness and misgiving. "I gotta go." She glances over at the Ground Zero, where a yellow Corvette has slid in under the awning, its red blinker blinking.

"Can I give you a ride?"

"Naa, I can walk."

"Thanks a million." She looks at the phone booth where the shopping cart is resting against the frame, and the receiver has fallen off its hook. It's a bleak-looking place. I would hate to make a phone call from it now.

"Did you ever like write about skiing?" she says, and shakes her head at me as if she knows my answer before I say it. The breeze blows up dust and sprinkles our faces with it.

"No. I don't even know how to ski."

"Me neither," she says and smiles again, then sighs. "So. Okay. Have a nice day. What's your name, what'd you say it was?" She is already leaving.

"Frank." For some reason I do not say my last name.

"Frank," she says.

As I watch her walk out into the lot toward the Ground Zero, her hands fishing in her pocket for a new cigarette, shoulders hunched against a cold breeze that isn't blowing, her hopes for a nice day, I could guess, are as good as mine, both of us out in the wind, expectant, available for an improvement. And my hopes are that a little luck will come both our ways. Life is not always ascendant.

12

It is the bottom of the day, the deep well of shadows and springy half-light when late afternoon becomes early evening and we all want to sit down in a leather chair by an open window, have a drink near someone we love or like, read the sports and possibly doze for a while, then wake before the day is gone all the way, walk our cool yards and hear the birds chirp in the trees their sweet eventide songs. It is for such dewy interludes that our suburbs were built. And entered cautiously, they can serve us well no matter what our stations in life, no matter we have the aforementioned liberty or don't. At times I can long so for that simple measure of day and place—when, say, I'm alone in misty Spokane or chilly Boston—that an unreasonable tear nearly comes to my eye. It is a pastoral kind of longing, of course, but we can all have it.

Things seem to move faster now.

I buzz through Freehold, turn east at the trotter track, then wrangle toward Route 1, past Pheasant Run & Meadow. A Good Life Is Affordable Here, reads the other side of the sign.

On the Trenton station the announcer has a sports quiz going to which I do not know one answer, though I take educated guesses. Whose record did Babe Ruth break when he hit sixty in 1921? Harry Heilmann is my guess, though the answer was, "His own." Who was the MVP in the Junior Circuit in '41? George Kell, the Newport Flash, is my choice. Phil Rizutto, the Glendale Spaghetti, is the answer. In most ways I am content not to know such information, and to think of sportswriting not as a real profession but more as an agreeable frame of mind, a *way* of going about things rather than things you exactly do or know. A reasonable guess is a source of pleasure, since it makes me feel like one of the crowd rather than a human FORTRAN spitting our stats and reducing sports to unsavory accountancy. When sports stops being a matter for speculation, even idle, aimless, misinformed speculation, something's gone haywire—no matter what Mutt Greene thinks—and it'll be time to get out of the business and for the cliometricians and computer whizzes from Price Waterhouse to take over the show.

At the intersection of Routes 1 and 533, I head south toward Mrs. Miller's. I would like the consultation I missed on Thursday, possibly even a full reading. If, for instance, Mrs. Miller were to tell me I was risking a severe emotional breakdown if I identified Walter in the morgue and would possibly never see my children as long as I lived, I'd start thinking about Alaska king crab and a night of HBO in a Philadelphia-area Travel-Lodge, and a new look at things in the morning. Why sneer in the face of unhappy prophecy?

Unfortunately, however, Mrs. Miller's little brick-and-asphalt ranchette looks locked up tighter than Dick's hatband. No dusty Buicks sit in the drive. No sign of the usual snarling Doberman in the fenced-in back. The Millers (what could their name really be?) are gone for the holiday, and I have now missed consultations two times running—not a good sign in itself.

I pull into the drive and sit as I did three nights ago, staring at an opening in the heavy drawdrapes as if I could will someone to be there. I give my horn an "accidental" toot. I'd be happy to see the opening widen, a door inched back behind the dusty metal screen, as it did the last time. A nice niece would do. I'd pay ten bucks to make small talk with a dark-skinned female in-law. She wouldn't need divining powers. I'd still come away better.

But that is not to be. Cars beat the highway behind me, and no niece comes to signal. No door cracks. The future, at least my part in it, remains unassured, and I will need to take extra care of myself. I pull back out onto Route 1 toward home, just missing a big honking tractor-trailer headed south, and my jaw still throbbing from Vicki's knuckle sandwich, now two hours old.

I take the front way into Haddam, curling up King George Road and Bank Street, along the north lawns of the Institute and through the Square. Though once in the village limits I am at a loss for what to do first, and am struck by an unfriendliness of the town, the smallish way it offers no clue for how to go about things—no priority established, no monumental structures to determine a true middle, no Main Street to organize things. And I see again it can be a sad town, a silent, nothing-happening, keep-to-yourself Sunday town—the library closed and green-shaded. Frenchy's abandoned. The Coffee Spot empty (Sunday *Times* scattered from the breakfast crowd). The Institute lies remote and tree-shadowed, a remaining family from the morning services, standing on the Square with their son. It is unexpectedly a foreign place, as strange as Moline or Oslo, its usual informal welcomeness reefed in as if some terror was about, a crusty death's smell, a different bouquet from the swimming pool odor I trust.

I park in my drive and go in to put on new clothes. Hoving Road is somnolent, as blue-shaded and leaden as a Bonnard. The Deffeyes' sprinkler hisses, and up a few houses the Justice has set a badminton net onto his long lawn. An old Ford Woody sits in his drive. Somewhere near abouts I hear the sounds of light chatter-talk and glasses clinking in our cozy local backyard fashion—an Easter Egg hunt finished, the children asleep, the sound of a single swimmer diving in. But this is the day's extent. A private stay-home with the family till past dark. Wreaths are off all doors. The world once more a place we know well.

Inside, my house has a strange public smell to it, a smell I would like on any other day but that today seems unwholesome. Upstairs, I put Merthiolate and a big band-aid on my knee, and change to chinos and a faded red madras shirt I bought at Brooks Brothers the year my book was published. A casual look can sometimes keep you remote from events.

I haven't thought much about Walter. Occasionally his face has plunged into my thinking, an expectant sad-eyed face, the sober, impractical fellow I stood railside with on the *Mantoloking Belle* speculating about the lives ashore we were both embedded in, how we tended to see the world from two pretty distinct angles, but that on balance it didn't matter much.

Which was all *I* needed! I didn't need to know about Yolanda and Eddie Pitcock. Certainly not about his monkeyshines at the Americana. We didn't need to become *established*. That is not my long suit.

No one answers when I call up to Bosobolo. He and his Miss Right, D.D., are no doubt being entertained "in the home" by some old chicken-necked Christology professor, and at this very moment he is probably backed into a bookshelved corner, clutching his ebony elbow and a glass of chablis, while Dr. So-and-so prattles about the hermeneutics of getting the goods on that old radical Paul the Apostle. Bosobolo, I'm sure, has other goods on his mind but is learning to be a first-class American. Though he could have it worse. He could still be running around in the jungle, dressed in a palm tutu. Or he could be me, morgue-bound and fighting a willowy despair.

My plan, which I've come to momentarily, is to call X, go do what I have to at the police, possibly see X—at her house (a remote chance to see my children)—then do *what* I haven't a clue. The plan doesn't reach far, though the literal possibilities might be just a source of worry.

A silent red "3" blinks on the answering machine, when I go to call X. "1" is in all likelihood Vicki wondering if I made it home safely and wanting to set up a powwow somewhere in the public domain where we can end love like grownups—less stridency and fewer lefts to the chin—a final half-turn of the old gem.

And she is right, of course, and smart to be. We don't really share enough of the "big" interests. I am merely mad for her. And at best she is unclear about me, which leaves us where in six months time? I would never be enough for a Texas girl, anyway. Fascination has its virtuous limits. She needs attention to more than I could give mine to: to Walter Scott's column, to being a New-Ager, to setting up a love nest, to a hundred things I really don't care that much about but that grip her imagination. Consequently I'll cut loose without complaining (though I'd be willing to spend one more happy night in Pheasant Meadow and then call it quits).

I punch the message button.

Beep. Frank, it's Carter Knott.
I'm sneaking off to the Vet
tomorrow for the Cardinals
game. I guess I can't get
enough of you guys. I'm
calling Walter too. It's
Sunday morning. Call me at
home. *Click.*

Beep. Hey you ole rascal-thing.
I thought you were comin at
eleven-thirty. We're all mad
at you down here so you better
not show your face. You know
who this is, dontcha? *Click.*

Beep. Frank, this is Walter
Luckett, Jr., speaking. It's twelve
o'clock sharp here, Frank. I
was just throwing away some
old *Newsweeks,* and I found
this photograph of that DC-10
that went down a year or so
ago out in Chicago. O'Hare.
You might remember that.
Frank, you can see all those
people's heads in the windows
looking out. It's really
something. And I just can't
help wondering what they

must've been thinking about,
since they *are* riding a bomb.
A big, silver bomb. That's
about all I had in mind now.
Uhhmm. So long. *Click*.

Is this what he'd have told me if I'd been here to answer? What
an Easter greeting! A chummy slice o' life to pass along while you're
rigging your own blast-off into the next world. A *while you were out*
from the grave! What else can happen?

I still cannot think a long thought about Walter. Though what I
do think about is poor Ralph Bascombe, in *his* last hours on earth,
only four blocks from here in Doctors Hospital and a lifetime away
now. In his last days Ralph changed. Even in his features, he looked
to me like a bird, a strangely straining gooney bird, and not like a
nine-year-old boy sick to death and weary of unfinished life. Once
he barked out loud at me like a dog, sharp and distinct, then he
flopped up and down in his bed and laughed. Then his eyes shot
open and burned at me, as if he knew me better than I knew myself
and could see all my faults. I was in my chair beside his bed, holding
his water cup and his terrible bendable straw. X was at the window,
musing out at a sunny parking lot (and probably the cemetery).
Ralph said loudly at me, "Oh, you son of a bitch, what are you
doing holding that stupid glass? I could kill you for that." And then
he fell asleep again. And X and I just stared at each other and
laughed. It's true, we laughed and laughed until we cried with laughter. Not with fear or pain. What else was there to do, we must've
said silently, and agreed that a good laugh was all right this time.
No one would mind. It was at no one's expense, and no one but the
two of us would hear it—not even Ralph. It may seem callous, but
we had that between ourselves, and who's to be the judge when
intimacy's at work? It was one of our last moments of unalloyed
tenderness in the world.

Though I suppose that in this memory of bereavement there is some for poor Walter, as wrongly and surely dead as my son, and just as absurd. I have tried not to be part of it. But why shouldn't I? We all deserve mankind's pity, his grief. And maybe never more than when we go outside its usual reaches and can't get back.

No one answers at X's house. She may be taking the children to a friend's. Are we going to have to have another heart-to-heart, I wonder. Am I going to be the recipient of other unhappy news? Is Fincher Barksdale leaving Dusty and getting X knee-deep in mink-ranching in Memphis? On what thin strand does all equilibrium dangle?

I leave a message saying I'll be by soon, then I'm off to the police, to have a look at Walter, though I have hope that a responsible citizen—possibly one of the Divorced Men with a police scanner—will already have come forward and performed this service for me.

The police station occupies part of the new brick-and-glass car-dealerish Village Hall where I rode out the heart-sore days of my divorce. The Hall is located near some of our nicer, more established residences, and it is closed now except for the brightly lighted cubicles in the back where the police hang out. From the outside where you drive around the circular entry, the last drowsy hours of Easter have softened its staunch Republican look. But it remains a house of hazards to me, a place where I'm uneasy each time I set my foot indoors.

Sergeant Benivalle, it turns out, is still on duty when I give my name to the watch officer, a young Italian-looking brushcut fellow wearing an enormous pistol and a gold name plate that says, PA-TRIARCA. He is in wry spirits, I can tell, and smiles a secret smile that implies some pretty good off-color jokes have been going the rounds all day, and were we a jot better friends he'd let me in on the whole hilarious business. My own smile, though, is not in tune for jokes, and after writing down my name he wanders off to find the sergeant.

I sit down on the public bench beside a big framed town map, breathing in the floor-mop smell of waiting rooms, leaning on my knees and peering out the glass doors through the lobby and across the lawn of elms and ginkgoes and spring maples. Outside is all almond light now, and in an hour a dreamy celestial darkness will return and one more day find its end. And what a day! Not a typical one at all. And yet it ends as softly, in as velvet a hush and airish a calm as any. Death is not a compatible presence hereabouts, and everything is in connivance—forces municipal and private—to say it isn't so; it's only a misreading, a wrong rumor to be forgotten. No harm done. This is not the place to die and be noticed, though it isn't a bad place to live, all things considered.

Two cyclists glide across my view. A man ahead, a woman behind; a child in a child's secure-seat strapped snug to Papa. All three are white-helmeted. Red pennants wag on spars in the dusk. All three are on their way home from an informal prayer get-together somewhere down some street, at some Danish-modern Unitarian hug-a-friend church where cider's on tap and *damn* and *hell* are permissible—life on the continual upswing week after week. (It is the effect of a seminary in your town.) Now they're headed homeward, fresh and nuclear, their frail magneto lights whispering a gangway to old darkness. Here come the Jamiesons. Mark, Pat and baby Jeff. Here comes life. All clear. Nothing can stop us now.

But they are wrong, wrong these Jamiesons. I should tell them. Life-forever is a lie of the suburbs—its worst lie—and a fact worth knowing before you get caught in its fragrant silly dream. Just ask Walter Luckett. He'd tell you, if he could.

Sergeant Benivalle appears through a back office door, and he's exactly the fellow I expected, the chesty, flat-top, sad-eyed man with bad acne scars and mitts the size of work gloves. His mother must not have been a spaghetti-bender, since his eyes are pale and his square head stolid and Nordic. (His stomach, though, is firmly Italian and envelopes his belt buckle, squeezing the little silver snub-nose strapped above his wallet.) He is not a man to shake hands, but looks at the red EXIT sign above our heads when we meet. "We can just sit here, Mr. Bascombe," he says. His voice is hoarse, wearier than earlier in the day.

We sit on the shiny bench while he fingers through a manila file.

Officer Patriarca takes his seat behind the watch desk window, props up his feet and begins glancing through a *Road & Track* with a black drag-strip hero-turned-TV-personality smiling on the front.

Sergeant Benivalle sighs deeply and shuffles sheets of paper. Silent as a prisoner, I await him.

"Ahhh. Okay now. We've been in touch with family . . . a sister . . . in . . . Ohio, I guess. So . . ." He lifts a stapled page briefly to reveal a bright photograph of a man's feet clad in a pair of rope sandals, toes pointed upward. Absolutely these are Walter's feet, which I hope will be identification enough. *Bascombe identifies deceased from picture of feet.* "So that," Sergeant Benivalle says slowly, "should eliminate your need to identify the, uh, deceased."

"I didn't really feel that need, anyway," I say.

Sergeant Benivalle glances at me dismissively. "We have fingerprints coming, of course. But it's just easier to get a positive this way."

"I understand."

"Now," he says, flipping more pages. It's surprising how much paper work has already been compiled. (Was Walter in some other kind of trouble?) "Now," he says again and looks at me. "You're the sportswriter, aren't you?"

"Right." I smile weakly.

Sergeant Benivalle glances back into his papers. "Who's taking the AL East this year?"

"Detroit. They're pretty good."

He sighs. "Yep. Prolly so. I wish I had time to see a game. But I'm busy." He protrudes his bottom lip, looking down. "I play a little golf, once in a blue moon."

"My wife's the teaching pro over at Cranbury Hills," I say, though I add quickly, "my ex-wife, I mean."

"That right?" Benivalle says, forgetting golf entirely. "I've got grass asthma," he says, and since I can add nothing to that, I say nothing. "Do you," he pauses, "have any idea why this Mr., uh, Luckett would take his own life, Mr. Bascombe, just off the top of your head?"

"No. I guess he gave up hope. That's all."

"Um-huh, um-huh." Sergeant Benivalle reads down his folder. Inside, a form has been typed: HOMICIDE REPORT. "That usually happens at Christmas a lot more. Not that many people do it on Easter."

"I never thought much about it."

Sergeant Benivalle wheezes when he breathes, a small peeping noise down inside his chest. He fingers toward the back of the file. "I could never write," he says thoughtfully. "I wouldn't know what to say. That must be hard."

"It's really not too hard."

"Um-huh. Well. I've got this, uh, copy of this letter for you." He slides a slick Thermofax sheet out the back of his sheaf, holding it out daintily by a corner. "We keep the original, which you can claim in three months if the estate agrees to release it to you." He looks at me.

"Okay." I take the page by another of its greasy corners. It is badly copied in gray with a nasty embalming-fluid odor all over it. I see the script is a neat, very small longhand, with a signature near the bottom.

"Be careful with that stuff, it gets in your clothes. Cops smell like it all the time, it's how you know we're in the neighborhood." He closes his folder, reaches in his pocket and takes out a pack of Kools.

"I'll read it later," I say and fold the letter in thirds, then sit holding it, waiting for whatever is supposed to happen next to happen. We are both of us immobilized by how simple all this has been.

Sergeant Benivalle lights his cigarette and inserts the burnt match into the book behind the others. The two of us sit then and stare at the yellow street map of the town we live in—each probably looking at the street where his own house sits. They couldn't be far apart. Prolly he lives in The Presidents.

"Where'd you say this guy's wife was again?" Benivalle says, breathing smoke hugely into his lungs. Though he looks at least fifty, he is no older than I am. His life cannot have been an easy one so far.

"She went to Bimini with another man."

He blows smoke, then sniffs loudly two times. "That's the shits."
He braces against the curved back of the bench, clenching his cigarette in his teeth, thinking about Bimini. "There's gotta be better
things to do about it than kill yourself, though. It isn't that bad.
Wouldn't you think?" He turns his big head and fixes me with eyes
blue as fjords. He hasn't liked this business with Walter one bit
better than I have, and he'd like somebody to say a word to help
him out of worrying about it.

"I sure would think so," I say and nod.

"Boy-o-boy. Mmmmph. What a mess." He extends both his legs
and crosses them at the ankles. It is his way of inviting conversation
between menfolk, though I'm stumped for what to say. It's possible
he would understand if I said nothing.

"Do you think it would be all right if I went over to Walter's
house?" I actually surprise myself by saying this.

Sergeant Benivalle looks at me strangely. "What do you want to
do that for?"

"Just to have a look. I wouldn't stay long. It's just probably the
only way I'm going to get grips on this whole business. He gave me
a key."

Sergeant Benivalle grunts, thinking about this request. He smokes
his cigarette and stares at the smoke he exhales. "Sure," he says
almost indifferently. "Just don't take anything out. The family has
claims on everything. Okay?"

"I won't." Everyone trusts everyone here. And why not? No one's
ever up to anything that could cause harm to anyone but themselves.
"Are you married, Sergeant," I ask.

"Divorced." He throws a narrow, flinty look my way, his eyes
piggy with suspicion. "Why?"

"Well. Some of us, we're all of us divorced men—there's a lot of
us in town these days—we get together now and then. It's nothing
serious. We just gang up for a beer at the August once a month. Go
to a ball game or two. We went fishing last week, in fact. I thought

if you'd like to, I'd give you a call. It's a pretty good group. Everything's informal."

Sergeant Benivalle holds his Kool between his big thumb and his crooked forefinger, like a movie Frenchman, and flicks off an ash toward the polished floor. "Busy," he says and sniffs. "Police work. . . ." He starts to say more, then stops. "I forget what I was going to say." He stares at the marble floor.

I have embarrassed him without meaning to, and I'd just as soon leave now. It's possible Sergeant Benivalle is nothing but Cade Arcenault years later, and I should leave him to his police work. Though it never hurts to show someone that their own monumental concerns and peculiar problems are really just like everybody else's. We all have our own police work to do.

"I'll still call you, okay?" I grin like a salesman.

"I doubt I'll make it," he says, suddenly distracted.

"Well. We're pretty flexible. I don't come myself, sometimes. But I like the idea of going."

"Yeah," Sergeant Benivalle says, and once again fattens his heavy lower lip.

"I guess I'll take off," I say.

He blinks at me as if waked up from a dream. "How come you have a key to that place?" He cannot not be a policeman, a fact I find satisfying. He is hard to imagine as anything else.

"Walter just gave it to me. I don't know why. I don't know if he had many friends."

"People don't usually give their keys to people." He shakes his head and clicks back in his mouth.

"People do weird things, I guess."

"All the time" he says and sniffs again. "Here," he says. He reaches in his pocket behind his pack of Kools and pulls out a little blue plastic card case. "Keep this if you go over there." He hands me a printed card with his name and title and the Haddam town seal printed on it. "Gene Benivalle. Sergeant of Detectives." His no doubt unlisted home number is printed at the bottom. I could call him about the Divorced Men's Club at this very number, as I'm sure he knows.

"Okay." I stand up.

"Just don't take anything, right?" he says hoarsely, sitting on the bench with his sheaf of papers in front of his stomach. "That'd be wrong."

I stuff his card in my shirt pocket. "Maybe we'll see you some night."

"Nah," he says, pushing his foot down hard on his cigarette and blowing smoke across his big knees.

"I'll probably call you anyway."

"Whatever," he says, wearily. "I'm always here."

"So long," I say.

But he doesn't like goodbyes. He's not the type any more than he's the handshake type. I leave him where he sits, under the red EXIT sign in the lobby, staring out the glass door at me as I go.

X's car sits alongside mine in the deepening dusk in front of Village Hall. She herself sits on the front fender carrying on a coaxing conversation with our two children, who are performing cartwheels on the public lawn and giggling. Paul is unwilling to fling his legs high enough in the air to achieve perfect balance, but Clarissa is expert from hours of practice, and even in her gingham granny dress, which I gave her, she can "walk the clouds," her cotton panties astonishing in the failed daylight. On the front bumper of X's car is a sticker that says "I'd Rather Be Golfing."

"I bought these two some ice cream, and this is the result," X says, when I sit up on the warm fender beside her. She has not looked at me, merely taken my existence for granted from the evidence of my car. "It seems to have brought out the kid in them."

"Dad," Paul shouts from the grass. "Clary's going in the circus."

"*Please* scratch glass," Clary says and immediately gets onto her hands again. They aren't surprised to see me, though I notice they've passed a secret look between themselves. Their usual days are alive with secrets, and toward me they feel both secret humor and secret sympathy. They'd be happy for us to start a roughhouse on the lawn the way we do at home, but now we can't. Paul probably has a new joke by now, better than the one from Thursday night.

"She's pretty good, isn't she?" I call out.

"I meant it as a compliment, all right?" Paul stands, hands on his hips in a girlish way. He and I suffer misunderstanding poorly. Clary lets herself fall on her bottom and laughs. She looks like her grandfather and has his almost silvery hair.

"I think it's odd that a town like this could have a morgue, don't you?" X says, musing. She's wearing a bright green-and-red sailcloth wraparound and a mint-colored knitted Brooks' shirt like the ones I wear, and looks coolly clubby. She smoothes the material over her knees and lets her heels kick against the tire wall. She is in a generous mood.

"I never thought about it," I say, watching my children with admiration. "But I guess it's surprising."

"One of Paul's friends is a pathologist's son, and he says there's a very modern facility in the basement in there." She gazes at the brick-and-glass façade with placid interest. "No coroner, though. He drives down from New Brunswick on a circuit of some kind." For the first time she looks at me eye to eye. "How are *you*?"

I am happy to hear this confiding voice again. "I'm all right. This day'll be over with."

"Sorry I had to call you at wherever that was."

"It's fine. Walter died. We can't help that."

"Did you have to *view* him?"

"No. His relatives are coming from Ohio."

"Suicide is very Ohio, you know."

"I guess." Hers, as always, is a perfect Michigan attitude. No one there has any patience for Ohio.

"What about his wife?"

"They're divorced."

"Well. You poor old guy," she says and pats me on my knee and gives me a quick and unexpected smile. "Want me to buy you a drink? The August is open. I'll run these two Indians home." She glances into the near dark, where our children are sitting in a private powwow on the grass. They are each other's confidants in all crucial matters.

"I'm okay. Are you going to marry Fincher?"

She glances at me impassively then looks away. "I certainly am not. He's married unless something's changed in three days."

"Vicki says you two are the hot topic in the Emergency Room."

"Vicki-schmicky," she says and sighs audibly through her nostrils. "Surely she's mistaken. Surely you can't be interested."

"He's an asshole and a change-jingler, that's all. He's down in Memphis starting an air-conditioned mink ranch at this very moment. That's the kind of guy he is."

"I'm aware."

"It's true."

"True?" X looks at me heartlessly. I am the asshole here, of course, but I don't care. Something seems at stake. The stability and sanctity of my divorce.

"I thought you were interested in software salesmen."

"I'll marry *and fuck*," she whispers terribly, "whoever I choose."

"Sorry," I say, but I'm not. Out on Seminary Street I see the lights go on weakly, blink once, then stay on.

"Men *always* think other men are assholes," X says, coldly. "It's surprising how often they're right."

"Does Fincher think I'm an asshole?"

"He's intimidated by you. And anyway, he isn't so bad. He's pretty certain about some things in his life. He just doesn't show it."

"How about Dusty?"

"Frank, I will take your children to Michigan and you'll never see them again, except for two weeks every summer in the Huron Mountain Club with my father to chaperone. This if you don't lay off me at this moment. How would you like that?" She isn't serious about this, and it's possible, I think now, that Vicki has made this whole business up for reasons of her own, though I would rather believe it was a mistake. X sighs again wearily. "I gave Fincher putting lessons, because he's playing in a college reunion tournament in Memphis. He was embarrassed about it, so we went over to Bucks County to Idlegreen and putted for a few days. He needed to improve his confidence."

"Did you put some iron in his putter?" I would like to ask about the putative kiss, but the moment's passed.

It is full dark now, and we are silent and alone in it. Cars murmur along Cromwell Lane, their headlights sweeping in the direction of the Institute, where an "Easter sing" is no doubt on for tonight. St. Leo the Great chimes out a last chance, admonitory call. Three uniformed policemen stroll outside laughing, heading off for a supper at home. I recognize officers Carnevale and Patriarca, whom I imagine, for some reason, to be distant cousins. They walk in lock step toward their personal cars and pay no attention to us. It is a dreamy, average, vertiginous evening in the suburbs—not too much on excitement, only the lives of isolated individuals in the harmonious secrecy of a somber age.

I can't deny I'm relieved about Fincher Barksdale, though—a misunderstanding, that is what I'm ready to believe. "Your father sent a message," I say.

"Oh?" Her face grows instantly skeptical.

"He told me to tell your mother he has bladder cancer."

"She told him the same thing once when I was a little girl, and he forgot to ask her about it the next day and went away on business. Only now it's different. It's a way to make them feel passionate. She'll think that's hilarious."

"He said I could marry you again if I wanted to."

X sniffs, then looks into her hands as if one might contain something she's forgotten. "He can't stop giving me away."

"He's a nice guy, isn't he?"

"No, he's not." She casts a secret glance at me. "I'm sorry about your friend. Was he a nice, good friend?" The footlights that illumine the shubbery around Village Hall all go on at once. A Negro janitor steps to the glass door and peers out between his palms, then wanders back with a long dust mop in tow. It is cool now out of doors. A car horn blows briefly. The policemen's taillights disappear down the dark streets.

"No. I didn't know him very well."

"What could've happened?" I hear my children giggle in the damp grass, sweet music of not-to-worry-in-this-world.

"He quit being interested in what's next, I guess. I don't know. I tend not to be much of an alarmist."

"You don't worry that it was your fault, do you?"

"I hadn't thought about that. I don't see how."

"You have awfully odd relationships. I don't know how you stand it."

"I don't have any relationships at all."

"I know that. But it's the way you like it."

Clarissa calls out from the darkness haltingly, wanting to know the exact time. It is 7:36. She is beginning to feel a strangeness out of doors, as though she might suddenly be cut loose and abandoned. "It's early," Paul whispers.

"I'm going over to Walter's house tonight. Would you like to come with me?"

X turns to me with a look of outlandish surprise. "What on earth? Did he have something of yours?"

"No. I just want to go by there. He gave me a key, and I want to use it. The police don't mind if I don't take anything."

"It's ghoulish."

I sit in silence, then, and listen for meaningful sounds in the darkness—a train whistle far out on the main line, a long-haul trucker drumming up Route 1 from as far away as Arkansas, a small plane humming through the angelic night sky—anything to console us two in these last thin moments. Genuinely good conversations with your ex-wife are limited by the widening territories of intimacy from which you're restricted. It is finally okay, I guess. "That's fine," I say.

"But you're probably going anyway, aren't you?" X looks at me, then stares out at the lighted foyer of Village Hall, through which is the tax assessor's glassed-in office. We can both see the janitor with his dust mop moving in slow motion.

"I guess so," I say. "It's really all right."

"Why?" She looks at me with narrow eyes, her look of skepticism at earthly uncertainties, entities she has never much liked.

"I don't need to say. Men feel things women don't. You don't have to disapprove of it."

"You do such odd things." She smiles sympathetically, though magisterially also. "You're so vague sometimes. Are you *really* all right? You looked pale when I could see you."

"I'm not completely all right. But I will be." I could tell her about Vicki knocking my block off, and being hit by a shopping cart. But what the hell good would it do? It would be in the way of full disclosure, and neither of us wants that again, now or ever. We have probably been here too long.

"We just see each other about deaths now," X says, somberly. "Isn't that sad?"

"Most divorced people don't see each other at all. Walter's wife went to Bimini, and he never saw her again. So I think we do pretty well. We have wonderful children. We don't live very far apart."

"Do you love me," X says.

"Yes."

"I was wondering about it. I haven't asked you in a long time."

"I'm always glad to tell you, though."

"I haven't really heard it in a long time, except from the children. I'm sure you've heard it several times."

"No." (Though it would be a lie to say I haven't heard it at all.)

"Sometimes I think about you being involved with all different kinds of people I don't know anything about, and it seems so odd. I don't like the feeling."

"I'm involved with fewer people all the time."

"Does that make you lonely?"

"No. Not a bit."

The fender of her Citation has grown cold in the darkness. Our two children—weary at last of each other's secrets—have climbed to their feet and are standing out in the dark like shy ghosts of themselves, wanting to be pleased and made over. It is like old times in a way. They stand not far from us and stare, wondering what's going on, saying nothing, exactly like their very ghosts might.

"Do you really want me to go over there with you?" X says, blinking but ready to give in.

"You don't have to."

"Yes. Well," she says and sniffs a little chuckle laugh. "I can drop these two at the Armentis' for half a hour. They like it over there, anyway. I don't know what might happen to you alone."

"I'll pay if it costs anything."

X shakes her head and slides off the fender. "You'll pay, huh?" The moon has appeared suddenly over the stalky elms—a bright, wide and ethereal world above us, illuminating trees and patches of empty street and the older white residences beyond. She glances at me in amusement. "Who did you think was going to pay?" She laughs.

"I just wanted to be a good sport."

"What do you really care most about in the world? That's the question of the hour, I think."

"You. That's all."

X laughs again and opens the door wide. "You're a sport, all right. You're the original sport."

I smile at her in the public darkness. My children pile past me inside. The car door closes. And once again we are off.

Walter's place at 118 Coolidge is a two-story cinderblock apartment row between two nicer older colonials whose young-couple-owners have sunk reasonable money into them, and are home tonight. I've never noticed the place, though there is a streetlight out front and it is only two streets over from X's house, and a block exactly like hers in every way but for this very building. The windowless front has been decorated with aluminum strips made like Venetian blinds, with "The Catalina" painted in script across it and backed by a wan light. Exterior lights along the side-facing doors burn visibly to the street. It is a place for abject senior seminarians, confirmed bachelors and divorcées—people in transition—and it is not, I think, such a bad place. I wouldn't have minded it in Ann Arbor in the middle sixties, say, or even today if I was fresh out of law school, trying to get my legs under me before starting life in earnest and annexing a little wife. Though it is not a place I'd be happy to end up, or even pass through as a way-station toward somewhere else in adult life. The Catalina would be too unpromising for those conditions. And it would certainly not be a place I'd choose to die. Seeing it makes me wonder exactly what kind of lovers' nest Yolanda and Eddie Pitcock share in Bimini. I'm sure it's nothing like this. I'm sure a blue ocean is nearby, and cooling breezes rattling banana palms, and wind chimes punctuating languorous afternoons. Better on all accounts.

X parks behind Walter's MG, and we walk up the concrete to the mailboxes where a single buggy globe shines dimly. Walter's business card has been pruned to fit the space marked 6-D, and we start down the lower row of doors where I hear the mutter of televisions.

"It's *dank* here," X says. "I've never been anyplace I could actually say was dank. Have you?"

"Locker rooms," I say, "in some of the older stadiums."

"I suppose that shouldn't surprise me, should it?"

"I doubt if Walter liked it much either."

"Well, he's fixed that."

6-D's outside light is off, and a bright orange sticker masks the door saying POLICE INVESTIGATION. AUTHORIZED ENTRY ONLY. I turn the key and open the door into darkness.

A small green light and the tiny numerals 7:53 shine from the black. I own the very same clock at home.

"This *is* very, *very* unpleasant," X says. "I think this man would hate my coming in here."

"You can go back," I say.

A smell is in the room and seems not to belong there, a medical smell from a doctor's office closed for vacation.

"Can't we turn on a light?"

Though for a moment I can't find a wall switch, and when I do it is out of service. "This doesn't work."

"Well, for God's sake find a lamp. I don't like his clock."

I bump across the dark floor, the furniture around me thick as elephants. I brush what feels like a leather couch, scrape a leg on an end table, pat across the back of a chair, then somewhere in the middle of the room touch the neck of a hanging lamp and pull the chain.

X appears alone in the doorway, her face fixed in a frown. "Well, for God's sake," she says again.

"I just want to see it," I say, standing in the middle of Walter's living room, seeing spots.

The hanging lamp casts dishy yellow light everywhere, though it is, in truth, a perfectly nice room. There are varnished paneled walls and a doorway leading to a dark bedroom. A pullman kitchen is behind a counter-thru, everything there put away and straight. There is plenty of big comfortable, new-looking furniture—a red leather couch across from a big RCA 24 with bolt holes on top where Walter has attached his duck gun. A set of barbells leans in a corner, several tables hold lamps with interesting oriental shades. A small mahogany secretary sits against a wall with blank paper and pencils laid out neatly as though Walter had intended to do some serious writing.

On the wall outside the bedroom door is a gallery of framed photographs I am eager to see. Pictured is the '66 Grinnell wrestling team in black and white with Walter, a rangy 145-er, kneeling in an old wire-window gym, arms folded thick, sober as an Indian. Under that is a pretty blond girl with a slightly heavy upper lip and wide-spaced eyes—no doubt Yolanda—taken in a row boat with the wind blowing. Here is the Delta Chi fraternity on risers; here is a picture of two stern-looking senior citizens, a man in a stiff wool suit, a woman in a flowered dress—Ma and Pa Luckettt in Coshocton, without doubt. Here is Walter in a full-traction leg-cast on a hospital bed beside a pretty nurse, both giving a big thumbs-up; and Walter in a convict's suit and cap beside Yolanda in a dancehall getup, each sneering. Walter has framed his Harvard Business School acceptance letter, and to the side there is a picture of a younger Walter seated at a desk with a stack of businessy-looking papers, smoking a Meerschaum pipe. At the bottom, and to my surprise, is a photo of the Divorced Men's Club ganged around our big circular table in the August. It is during one of our Thursday night sessions. I'm holding a huge beer mug and wearing an idiot grin, listening animatedly to something Knot-head Knott is spieling about and am undoubtedly bored blind. Knot-head is holding back a big guffaw, but I have no recollection of what we might've been talking about. I do not even remember the time's happening, and seeing it makes me feel it all must've been in Walter's imagination.

I poke my head back into the bedroom and snap on the ceiling light. Here it is sparer than out front, but still satisfactory in its own way. An aquarium sits on the dresser, its lurid light exposing floating, tiny black mollies. Walter's bed has a geometric-design cover with three oversized pillows, and on the night table there is a copy of my book, *Blue Autumn*, with my author's picture face-up, and myself looking remarkably lean and ironic. I am drinking a beer, elbowed-in to an open air bar in San Miguel Tehuantepec. I have a crewcut and am smoking a cigarette, and couldn't look more ridiculous. "Mr. Bascombe," my biography says, "is a young American living in Mexico. He was born at the end of World War II, served in the Marines, and has attended the University of Michigan." I pick it up and see it is the Haddam Public Library copy, with the plastic cover taken off. (Walter has boosted it! He told me in the Manasquan that he had a library copy, but I didn't believe him.) He has jotted small plusses and zeros by certain titles on the contents page. I'd like to see more about that, possibly take the book with me, though I know there's an inventory inside Sergeant Benivalle's folder. I set the book back, take a quick look around—shoes, shoetrees, a skinny closet of suits and shirts, a silent butler, a computer terminal on the floor in the corner, an air-conditioner built through from the outside, a Grinnell pennant—the unextraordinary remains of a life at loose ends.

X is seated on the edge of the leather couch, her wrists on her

knees, looking at a red ceramic lobster peeking out over the rim of
a large green "dip bowl" on the coffee table. "You know?" She stares
closely at the lobster's eyes. Her voice makes a hollow, echoey sound.

"What?"

"It reminds me of a frat house in here, a Phi Delt's room I used
to go into. Ron something. Ron Kirk. It was fixed up exactly this
way, like a dentist's office somebody'd lived in. Just horrible boy's
stuff. I bet there's a set of *Playboys* in here somewhere. I looked
around for it a little." She shakes her head in wonder. On the floor
in front of the coffee table is more orange tape the police have laid
around the chair Walter was sitting in, a chair that is missing. Two
large dark brown stains have dried on one of the hooked rugs, and
these have been covered with clear plastic, then taped. An area on
the wall has also been covered and sealed. X has made no reference
to either of them. "You're just so strange, Frank, my God. I don't
see how any of you get along alone." She blinks up at me, smiling,
curious at who would kill himself, wishing for a common-sensical
explanation for such a strange event. "You know?"

"I was just wondering how Walter rigged up the switch. He was
probably an expert."

"Do you think you understand all this?"

"I think so."

"Then tell me, would you?"

"Walter gave himself up to the here and now, but got stranded.
Then I think he got excited, and all he knew how to do was senti-
mentalize his life, which made him regret everything. If he'd made
it past today he'd have been fine, I think." I pick up an Americana
matchbook off the kitchen counter, and read the address and phone
number to myself. Below it is a copy of *Bimini Today* with a photograph on the cover of a long silver beach. I put the matchbook
down.

"Do you think you were supposed to help him?" X says, still
smiling. "He seems so conventional. Just seeing in here."

"He should've helped himself" is my answer, and in fact it is what

I believe. "You can't be too conventional. That's what'll save you." And for a moment a sudden unwanted grief sweeps up in me; a grief, I suppose, for possibilities misconstrued, for consolation not taken (which is what grief is all about). I share, I know, and only for a moment, the grief poor Walter must've felt alone here but shouldn't have. This is not a perfectly good room. There's little here for small mystery and hope and anticipation to flicker on—yet there's nothing so corrupting or so lonely here as to be unworkable. I could hang in here until I got myself headed right, though I'd see that I did it in a hurry.

"You look like your best friend died, sweetheart," X says.

I smile at her and she stands up in the shadowy, death-smelling room, taller than I usually think of her, her shadow rising to the nubbly ceiling.

"Let's leave," she says and smiles back in a friendly way.

I think a moment about the drinking glasses Walter probably owned, that I'm sure I was right about them, though I won't bother looking. "You know," I say, "I suddenly had this feeling we should make love. Let's close the door there and get in bed."

X stares at me in sudden and fierce disbelief. (I can see she is horrified by this idea, and I wish I could take the words back right away, since it was a preposterous thing to say, and I didn't mean a word of it.) "That's something we don't do anymore. Don't you remember?" X says, bitterly. "That's what divorce means. You're really a terrible man."

"I'm sorry," I say. Sergeant Benivalle would understand this and have a strategy for getting it straightened out. It has not been the best day of either of our lives, after all.

"I remember why I divorced you now." X turns away, reaching the door in three unexpectedly long steps, "You've really *become* awful. You weren't always awful. But now you are. I don't like you very much at all."

"I guess I am," I say and try to smile. "But you don't have to be afraid."

"I'm not afraid," she says, and laughs a hard little laugh, turning through the doorway just as a small man in a white shirt arrives into it. It stops her cold to see him.

The man's eyes look wide behind thick glasses, and he blocks X's way without intending to. He leans around her to look at me. "Are you the sister and brother?" he says.

I lean exactly as he does, trying to see him and look pleasant. "No," I say. "I'm a friend of Walter's." This is the only explanation I have, and I can see from his expression that it isn't enough. He is a youngish Frank Sinatra type with pale, knobby cheeks and curly hair (possibly he's not as young as he looks, since he has a dry librarian's air about him). He suspects something's up, though, and means to get to the bottom of it pronto using this very air. His presence makes me realize how little I have to do with anything here, and that X was right. It's just lucky we were not getting into bed.

"You don't belong here," the young man says. He is for some reason flustered and trying to decide whether to get damn good and mad about everything. Conceivably I could show him Sergeant Benivalle's card.

"Are you the manager?"

"Yes. What are you stealing? You can't take anything."

"We're not taking anything."

"Excuse me," X says, and shoulders past the man into the dark. She has nothing more to say to me. I listen to her footsteps down the sidewalk and feel awful.

The man blinks at me in the living room's light. "What the hell *are* you doing here? I'm going to call the police about it. We'll get—"

"They know about it already," I say wearily. Here without a doubt is where I should present Sergeant Benivalle's card, but I do not have the heart.

"What do you want here?" the man says painfully, stranded in the doorway.

"I don't know. I forgot."

"Are you some kind of newspaperman?"

"No. I was just Walter's friend."

"No one's allowed in here but the family. So just get out."

"Are you a friend of Walter's, too?"

He blinks several times at this particular question. "I was," the man says. "I certainly was."

"Then why didn't you go down and identify him?"

"Just get out," the man says, and looks dazed.

"Okay." I start to turn off the light, and remember my book in the dark bedroom. I would like to take it with me to return to the library. "I'm sorry," I say.

"I'll turn that off," the man says abruptly. "You just leave."

"Thanks." I walk past the man, brushing his sleeve, then out where the air awaits me, sweet and thick and running full of fears.

X sits in her Citation beneath the streetlight, motor idling, the dashboard lights green in her face. She has waited here for me.

I lean in the passenger window, where the air is warm and smells like X's perfume. "I don't see why we had to go in there," she says stonily.

"I'm sorry about it. It's my fault. I didn't mean that in there."

"You are *such* a cliché. God." X shakes her head, though she is still angry.

This is perfectly true, of course. It is also true that I have tried for a kind of sneaky full disclosure, been caught at it, and am about to be left empty-handed.

"I don't really see why I have to distinguish myself, though I'm a grown man. I don't have to impress anybody now."

"You just embarrass me. But that's right." She nods, staring unhappily straight into the night. "I was going to ask you to come home with me. Isn't that funny? I left the kids at the Armentis'."

"I'd go. That's a great idea."

"Well, no." X reaches round and buckles her seat belt over her wonderfully skirted thighs, sets both hands on the steering wheel.

"That little man in there just seemed so strange to me. Was he a friend of your friend's?"

"I don't know. He never mentioned him." She is probably worrying that Walter and I were "romantically linked."

"Maybe your friend was just meant to kill himself." She smiles at me with too much irony, too much, anyway, for people who have known each other as long as we have, and slept together, had children, loved each other and been divorced. Irony ought to be outlawed from this kind of situation. It is a pain in the ass and doesn't help anybody. Hers, regrettably, is a typical midwestern response to the complicated human dilemma.

"Walter didn't understand his own resources. He didn't have to do this. It seems to me you could stand to be more adaptable yourself. We could just go home right now. No one's there."

"I don't think so." She smiles still.

"I still want to," I say. I grin through the window. I smell the exhaust flooding underneath me, feel the car shuddering behind its safe headlights. The change scoop between the bucket seats, I see, is filled with orange golf tees.

"You're not a real bad man. I'm sorry. I don't think divorce has worked wonders for you." She puts the car into gear so that it lurches, yet doesn't quite leave. "It was just a bad idea I had."

"Your loved ones are the ones you're supposed to trust," I say. "Who's after that?"

She smiles at me a sad, lonely smile out of the instrument panel twilight. "I don't know." I can see her eyes dancing in tears.

"I don't know either. It's getting to be a problem."

X lets off on her brake and I step back in the grass. Her Citation hesitates, then hisses off from me up Coolidge and into the night. And I am left alone in the cool silence of dead Walter's yard and MG, an unknown apartment house behind me, a neighborhood where I am not known, a man with no place to go in particular—out, for the moment, of any good ideas, at the sad end of a sad day that in a better world would never have occurred at all.

Where, in fact, do you go if you're me?

Where do sportswriters go when the day is, in every way, done, and the possibilities so limited that neither good nor bad seems a threat? (I'd be happy to go to sleep, but that doesn't seem available.)

It is not, though, a genuine empty moment, and as such, war needn't be waged against it. It need not even be avoided or faced up to with particular daring. It is not the prologue to terrible regret. An empty moment requires both real expectation and its eventual defeat by the forces of fate. And I have no such hopes to dash. For the moment, I'm beyond all hopes, much as I was on the night X burned her hope chest while I watched the stars.

Walter would say that I have become neither the seer nor the thing seen—as invisible as Claude Rains in the movie, though I have no enemies to get back at, no debts to pay off. Invisibility, in truth, is not so bad. We should all try to know it better, use it to our advantage the way Claude Rains didn't, since at one time or other— like it or not—we all become invisible, loosed from body and duty, left to drift on the night breeze, to do as we will, to cast about for what we would like to be when we next occur. That, let me promise you, is not an empty moment. And further yet from real regret. (Maybe Walter *was* interested in me, but who knows? Or cares?) Just to slide away like a whisper down the wind is no small freedom, and if we're lucky enough to win such a setting-free, even if it's bad events that cause it, we should use it, for it is the only naturally occurring consolation that comes to us, sole and sovereign, without props or the forbearance of others—among whom I mean to include God himself, who does not let us stay invisible long, since that is a state he reserves for himself.

God does not help those who are invisible too.

I drive, an invisible man, through the slumberous, hilled, post-Easter streets of Haddam. And as I have already sensed, it is not a good place for death. Death's a preposterous intruder. A breach. A building that won't fit with the others. An enigma as complete as

Sanskrit. Full-blown cities are much better at putting up with it. So much else finds a place there, a death as small as Walter's would fit in cozy, receive its full sympathies and be forgotten.

Haddam is, however, a first-class place for invisibility—it is practically made for it. I cruise down Hoving Road past my own dark house set back in its beeches. Bosobolo has not returned (still away in the bramble bush with plain Jane). I could talk to him about invisibility, though it's possible a true African would know less than one of our local Negroes, and I would end up explaining a lot to start with, though eventually he would catch on—committed as he is to the unseen.

I cruise through the dark cemetery where my son is put to rest, and where the invisible virtually screams at you, cries out for quiet, quiet and more quiet. I could go sit on Craig's stone and be silent and invisible with Ralph in our old musing way. But I would soon be up against my own heavy factuality, and consolation would come to a standstill.

I drive by X's house, where there is bright light from every window, and a feeling of bustle and things-on-tap behind closed doors, as if everyone were leaving. There's nothing for me here. My only hope would be to make trouble, extenuate circumstances for everybody, do some shouting and break a lamp. And I—it should come as no surprise—lack the heart for that too. It's nine P.M., and I know where my children are.

Where is there to go that's fun, I wonder?

I drive past the August, where a red glow warms the side bar window, and where I'm sure a life-long resident or a divorced man sits wanting company—a commodity I'm low on.

Down Cromwell Lane at Village Hall a light still burns in the glass lobby—in the tax office the janitor stands at the front door staring out, his mop at order arms. Somewhere far off a train whistles, then a siren sings through the heavy elms of the Institute grounds. I catch the wink of lights, hear the soft spring monotone of all hometown suburbs. Someone might say there's nothing quite so lonely as a suburban street at night when you are all alone. But he

would be dead wrong. For my money, there're a lot of things worse.
A seat on the New York Stock Exchange, for instance. A silent death
at sea with no one to notice your going under. Herb Wallagher's
life. These would be worse. In fact, I could make a list as long as
your arm.

I drive down the cobblestone hill to the depot, where, if I'm right,
a train will soon be arriving. It is not bad to sit in some placeless
dark and watch commuters step off into splashy car lights, striding
toward the promise of bounteous hugs, cool wall-papered rooms,
drinks mixed, ice in the bucket, a newspaper, a long undisturbed
evening of national news and sleep. I began coming here soon after
my divorce to watch people I knew come home from Gotham, watch
them be met, hugged, kissed, patted, assisted with luggage, then
driven away in cars. And you might believe I was envious, or heartsick, or angling some way to feel wronged. But I found it one of
the most hopeful and worthwhile things, and after a time, when the
train had gone and the station was empty again and the taxis had
drifted back up to the center of town, I went home to bed almost
always in rising spirits. To take pleasure in the consolations of others,
even the small ones, is possible. And more than that: it sometimes
becomes damned necessary when enough of the chips are down. It
takes a depth of character as noble and enduring as willingness to
come off the bench to play a great game knowing full well that you'll
never be a regular; or as one who chooses not to hop into bed with
your best friend's beautiful wife. Walter Luckett could be alive today
if he'd known that.

But I am right.

Out of the burly-bushy steel darkness down the line comes the
clatter of the night's last arrival from Philadelphia, on its way back
to New York. Trainmen lean out the silver vestibules, eyeing the
passing station, taking notice of the two waiting cars with workmanlike uninterest. Theirs is another life I wouldn't like, though
I'm ready to believe it has moments of real satisfaction. I'm sure I
would pay undue attention to my passengers, would stand around
hearing what they had on their minds, learning where they were off

to, conversing with them on train travel in general, picking up a phone number here and there, and never get my tickets clipped on time and end up being let go—no better at that than I'd be at arc welding.

The local squeezes to a halt beside the station. The trainmen are down on the concrete, swinging their tiny flashes like police even before the last cars are bucked stopped. The lone taxi switches on its orange dome light and the two waiter cars rev engines in unison.

Within the yellow-lit coaches, pale dreamy faces stare out into the Easter night. *Where are we now*, they seem to ask. *Who lives here? Is this a safe place? Or what?* Their features are glassy and smooth with drowse.

I stroll to the platform and up under the awning, hands in pockets, stepping lively on my toes as if I'm expecting—a loved one, a girl-friend, a best friend from college long out of touch. The two trainmen give me the mackerel eye and begin some exclusive talk they've been putting off. But I don't feel the least excluded, since I enjoy this closeness to trains and the great moment they exude, their implacable hissing noise and purpose. I read somewhere it is psychologically beneficial to stand near things greater and more powerful than you yourself, so as to dwarf yourself (and your piddlyass bothers) by comparison. To do so, the writer said, released the spirit from its everyday moorings, and accounted for why Montanans and Sherpas, who live near daunting mountains, aren't much at complaining or nettlesome introspection. He was writing about better "uses" to be made of skyscrapers, and if you ask me the guy was right on the money. All alone now beside the humming train cars, I actually do feel my moorings slacken, and I will say it again, perhaps for the last time: there is mystery everywhere, even in a vulgar, urine-scented, suburban depot such as this. You have only to let yourself in for it. You can never know what's coming next. Always there is the chance it will be—miraculous to say—something you want.

Off the train steps a buxom young nun, in the blackest, most orthodox habit, carrying a slick attaché case and a storky umbrella. She is bright-eyed, round-faced, smiling, and passes a teasing "thanks, goodbye" to the trainmen, who touch their hats and smile, but also give her a swarthy look the instant her back is turned. She is met by no one, and trudges past me cheerfully, heading, I'm sure, up to the seminary on some ecclesiastical business with the Presbyterians. As she passes me by I give her a smile, for she will encounter no dangers on our streets, I can assure her. No would-be rapists or scroungy types. Though she seems like someone to look danger in the eye and call its bluff.

Next, two business types with loose ties, single-suiters and expensive briefcases—lawyers, without doubt, up from Philadelphia or the nation's capital, come to do business with one or another of the world headquarters that dot the lócal landscape. Both are Jews, and both look dog-tired, ready for a martini, a bath, a set of clean sheets and a made-for-TV movie. They crawl into the taxi. I hear one say "The August," and in no time they go murmuring up the hill, the taxi's taillights red as smudged roses.

Two blond women scurry out, give each other big phony hugs, then jump in the two waiting cars—each driven by a man—and disappear. For an instant, I thought one of them was familiar, someone I might've met at a cocktail party in the old days. A spiky married Laura or Suzannah with boyish hips, red silk pants and leathery skin: someone of my own rough age, whom I more than likely bored the nose off of but was too bored back by to stop. Possibly a friend of X's, who knows the truth about me. One blonde indeed did give me a lashing, feral half-glance before stepping into her waiting Grand Prix and delivering Mr. Inside a big well-rehearsed kiss, but she seemed not to recognize me. A big problem of being divorced in a town this size is that all the women immediately become your wife's friends whether they know her or not. And that's not just paranoia. Being a man gets harder all the time.

The trainmen part company and sidle back toward their vestibules. The wig-wag headlight careers over the open rails. The inside passengers have all gone back to sleep. It is time, almost, to turn to home. And do what?

Out of the far silver car comes a last departer. A small fawn-haired woman of the frail but vaguely pretty category, not of this town. That much is clear the moment her shoes—the kind with heels lower than the toes—touch ground. She is wearing a tent dress, though she is wire-thin, with a pleasant, scrubbed look on her wren's features, and a self-orienting way of looking round about, which makes her turn her nose up testingly to the air. In one hand she is carrying some kind of deep Brazilian wicker basket as luggage, on top of which she's strapped a bulky knitted sweater. And in the other there's a fat copy of what I can make out as *The Life of Teddy Roosevelt*, with plenty of paper bookmarks sprouting from the pages.

She sniffs the air as if she's just detrained in the Punjab, and turning her head with a scent, moves to say a word to the older of the two trainmen, who points her in the direction the nun has taken, up the hill into town and directly by me, leaned against a girder beside the phalanx of newspaper boxes, growing sleepy in the springtime evening.

The word "taxi" is spoken, and both of them look toward the empty parking spaces and shake heads. My Malibu sits alone across the street, angled into the murky Rose of Sharon hedge behind the regional playhouse—a dark and barely detectable blob. I see the two of them look toward me again, and I sense a connection being made. "Maybe that gentleman right there will give you a lift into town," one of them is saying. "This is a town of gentle folk. Not one in ten thousand will murder you."

I am unexpectedly visible!

The woman turns with her orienteering wren's look. She and I are the same vintage. We have learned to trust strange people in the sixties, and it hasn't yet dawned on us that it might've been a mistake (though one clue should've been our own perfidies).

Hands thrust in back pockets, though, I am ready to be used; to lend a hand, prove myself guileless as old Huck. There might, in fact, be a late-night cocktail invitation in the works as a "thankee," an *intime* in the dark taproom of the August, alongside the bushed lawyers. After that, who knows? More? Less?

Deep in my pocket my fingers touch an inconclusive paper. Walter's poor letter, folded in thirds and tucked behind my wallet, forgotten to this moment. And a sudden cheerless warmth rises out under my chin and stings my ears and scalp.

This is Walter's sister, this woman! Wicker basket. Healthy shoes. Roosevelt bio. She has already arrived for her doleful duties, and with enough dry, grief-dispelling practicality to send a drowning man clambering for the bottom. She is some miserable Montessori teacher from Coshocton. A woman with a reading list and an agenda, friends in the Peace Corps, an NPR program log deep in her Brazil bag. A tidy, chestless Pat or Fran from Oberlin or Reed, with high board scores. My heart pounds a tomtom for the now disappeared blondie, whirling away in her Grand Prix to some out-of-the-way Italian snuggery with the nerve to stay open Easters. I ache to be along. Dinner could be on me. Drinks. The tip. Don't leave me to sensible grief and a night of plain-talk. (Of course I'm not sure it's her, but neither am I sure it isn't.) This woman has the look to me of trouble's sister, and I'd rather put my trust in my heart and my money where my mouth isn't.

"Excuse me, please," scratchy Fran/Pat says in her bony, businesslike voice as she comes toward me. She has an iron handshake, I'm sure, and knows death to be just one of life's slow curves you have to stand in on, brother or no brother. I would hate to see what else she has in that basket. "I wonder if you'd mind terribly. . . ." She speaks in a phony boarding school accent, nose up, seeing me— if at all—out the bottom third of her eyes.

The train discharges a loud hiss. A bell rings a last shrilling peel. "Boooard," the trainman shouts from his dark vestibule. The train lurches, and in that sudden instant I am aboard, hurt knee and all, unexpectedly a passenger, and away. "I'm sorry," I say, as my face slides past, "I've got to catch a train."

The woman stands blinking as I recede, her mouth open for the next words I will not have to hear, words for which even a roll in the hay would not be antidote.

She grows small—gnawingly small and dim—in the powdery depot light, poised in a moment when certainty became confusion;

confused among other things, that people do things so differently out here, that people are more abrupt, less willing to commit themselves, less schooled in old-fashioned manners; confused why the least of God's children would do anyone a bad turn by not helping. Maybe Pat/Fran is right. It *is* confusing, though sometimes—let me say—it's better not to take a chance. You can take too many chances and end up with nothing but regret to keep you company through a night that simply—for the life of you—won't end.

13

Clatter-de-clack, we swagger and sway up through the bleak-lit corridor of evening Jersey. Mine is one of the old coaches with woven brown plastic seats and bilgy window glass. A cooked metal odor fills the aisles and clings to the luggage racks, as the old lights flicker and dim. It is another side to the public accommodation coin.

Still, it's not bad to be moving. With the traveling seat turned toward me, it's easy to make myself comfortable, feet up, and watch float past the sidereal townlets of Edison, Metuchen, Metropark, Rahway, and Elizabeth.

Of course, I have no earthly idea where I'm bound or what to do once I get there. Fast getaways from sinister forces are sometimes essential, though what follows can mean puzzlement. I haven't ridden the night train *to* New York, I'm sure, since X and I rode up to see *Porgy and Bess* one winter night when it snowed. How long ago—five years? Eight? The specific past has a way of blending, an occurrence I don't particularly mind. And tonight the prospect of detraining in Gotham seems less spooky than usual. It seems a more local-feeling place with a sweet air of the illicit, like a woman you barely know and barely want, but who lets you anyway. Things change. We have that to look forward to. In fact, climbing down tonight onto the streets of any of these little crypto-homey Jersey burgs could heave me into a panic worse than New York ever has.

Only a few solitary passengers share my coach. Most are sleeping, and I don't recognize any as faces I saw from the platform. I wouldn't even mind seeing someone I knew. Bert Brisker would be a welcome companion, full of some long, newsy ramble about the book he's reviewing or some interview he's conducted with a famous author. I'd be interested to hear his opinion about the future of the modern novel. (I miss this clubby in-crowd talk, the chance to make good on the conviction that your formal education hasn't left you completely shipwrecked.) Usually Bert is deep in his own work, and I'm in mine. And once we leave the platform, where we chuckle and grouse in special code talk, we rarely utter another word. But I'd be glad now for some friendly jawboning. I haven't done enough of that; it is a bad part of being in the company of athletes and people I don't know well and will never know, people who have damned little of general interest to talk about. To be a sportswriter, sad to say it, is to live your life mostly with your thoughts, and only the edge of others'. That's exactly why Bert got out of the business, and why he's at home tonight with Penny and his girls and his sheepdogs, watching Shakespeare on HBO, or dozing off with a good book. And why I'm alone on an empty, bad-smelling milk train, headed into a dark kingdom I have always feared.

The young mackerel-eye trainman sways into my car and gives me a look of distrust as he processes my ticket money and dedicates a stub on my seatback. He does not like it that I have to buy my passage en route, or that I wouldn't give a lift to Walter's sister back up the line, or that I'm wearing a madras shirt and seem happy and so much his opposite when the rest of the world known to him— in his sheeny black conductor's suit—is strictly where it belongs. He is not yet thirty, by my guess, and I give him a good customer's no-sweat smile to let him know it's really all right. I'm no threat to any of his beliefs. In fact, I probably share most of them. I can tell, though, by his fisheye that he doesn't like the night and what it holds—inconstant, marauding, sinister, peaceless thing to be steered clear of here inside the thrumming tube of his professional obligation. And since I've come out of it, unexpectedly, I am suspect too. Quick as he can, he pockets his punch, scans the other passengers' stubs down the aisle and abandons me for the bar car, where I see him begin talking to the Negro waiter.

When I paid for my ticket, I've once again fingered Walter's letter, and under the circumstances there's nothing to do but read it, which I do, starting in Rahway, with the aid of the pained little overhead light.

Dear Franko,

I woke up today with the clearest idea of what I need to do. I'm absolutely certain about it. Write a novel! I don't know what the hell it will be for or who'll read it or any of that, but I've got the writer's itch now and whoever wants to read it can or they can forget about it. I've gotten beyond everything, and that feels good!

What I wrote was:"Eddie Grimes waked up on Easter morning and heard the train whistle far away in a forgotten suburban station. His very first thought of the day was, 'You lose control by degrees.' " That seemed like a hell of a good first line. Eddie Grimes is me. It's a novel about me, with my own ideas and personal concepts and beliefs built into it. It's hard to think of your own life's themes. You'd think anyone could do it. But I'm finding it very, very hard. Pretty close to impossible. I can think of yours a lot better, Frank. I'm conservative, passionate, inventive, and fair—as an investment banker, which works great! But it's hard to get that down and translated into the novel form, I see. I've gotten side-tracked in this.

Maybe a good way to start a novel is with a suicide note. That'd be a built-in narrative hook. I know it's been done before. But what hasn't? It was new to me, right? I'm not worried about that.

I've gone away and come back. The suicide note idea doesn't really lead anywhere interesting novel-wise, Frank. I'm not sure which fickle master I'm trying to serve here (ha-ha). I apologize for the message about the airplane, by the way. I was just trying to manipulate my feelings, get the right mood going for writing. I hope you're not pissed off. I admire you all the more now for the work you've done. I still consider you my best friend, even though we don't really know each other that well.

I tried to call Yolanda earlier. No answer, then busy. Then no answer. I also got things straightened out with Warren. That was a fine thing I did there. I admit I should've just been friends with him. But I didn't. So what, right? Sue me. Take care of yourself, Frank.

I would like this to be an interesting letter anyway if it can't be a best-selling novel. I feel I know exactly what I'm doing now. This is not phony baloney. You're supposed to be crazy when you kill yourself? Well forget that. You'll never be saner. That's for sure.

Frank, here's the kicker now, alright? I have a daughter! And I know all about what you're thinking. But, I do. She's nineteen. One of those ill-begotten teenage liaisons back in Ohio early in the summer, sophomore year, when I was nineteen myself! Her name is Susan—Suzie Smith. She lives in Sarasota, Fla, with her mother, Janet, who lives with some sailor or highway patrolman. I don't know which. I send them checks still. I'd like to go down there and shed some light on all this for her. And me, too. I've never actually seen her. There was a lot of trouble at the time. Of course it wouldn't happen today. But I feel very close to her. And you're the only person who'll be able to make sense out of this, Franko. I hope you don't mind my asking you to go down there and have a talk with her. Thanks in advance. You needed the vacation, right?

I really haven't felt this clear-headed about things since I was out at Grinnell and had to make the decison to move up to 152, and give up at 145 where I was successful, because there was someone there all of a sudden who was better—a freshman, no less. I had to give up or make a big decision. I finally won matches at the higher weight, but I was never as good. I never was prideful again either. I'm not prideful now, but I think I have a right to be.

All best,

Wally

All *best*? Talk about losing your authority! All best, then go boom-blow-your-brains-out? How do we get bound up with people we don't even know, is my question for the answer man. I'd give anything in the world at this moment never to have known Walter Luckett, Jr., or that he could be alive so I could drop him like a hot potato, and he could have no one to address his dumb-ass letter to and have to figure out the big questions all by himself. Maybe he could've finished his novel then. In a way, if it weren't for me being his friend, he'd be alive.

Whose life ever has permanent mystery built into it anyway? An astronaut? The heavyweight champ? A Ubangi tribesman? Even old Bosobolo has to pursue an advanced degree, and then it's not a sure thing, which accounts for his love interest on the side. If Walter were here I'd shake the bejesus out of him.

He could've found Mrs. Miller (if he knew about her); or read catalogs into the night; or turned on Johnny; or called up a hundred dollar whore for a house call. He could've hunted up a reason to keep breathing. What else is the ordinary world good for except to supply reasons not to check out early?

Walter's circumstances would be a good argument for a trip to Bimini to settle his debts, or a camping trip to Yellowstone in a land yacht. Only now I don't even have *those* luxuries. What I have is awful, mealy factual death, which once you start to think of it, won't go away and inhabits your life like a dead skunk under the porch.

And a daughter? No way. I have my own daughter. One day soon enough she'll want to hear some explaining, too. And that, frankly, is all I care about: the answers I come up with then. What happened to Walter on this earth is Walter's own lookout. I'm sorry as hell, but he had his chance like the rest of us.

Suddenly we are through the rank, larky meadowlands and entered in the long tunnel to Gotham, where the lights go out and you can't see beyond your reflected self in gritty window glass, and I have the sudden feeling of falling out of space and into a perilous dream—a dream, in fact, I used to suffer after my divorce (though I am sure it's primed this time by Walter) in which I am in bed with someone I don't know and cannot—must not—touch (a woman, thank God), but whom I must lie beside for hours and hours on end in a state of fear and excitation and scalding guilt. It is a terrible dream, but it wouldn't surprise me if all men didn't have it at one time or other. Or many times. And in truth, after I had had it for six months I got used to it and could go back to sleep within five minutes. Though if I wasn't already on the floor, I was at least on the edge of the bed when I woke up, cramped and achy as though clinging at the edge of a lifeboat on a vast and moody sea. Like all things bad and good, we get used to them, and they pass us by with age.

In ten minutes we have docked in the vault of Penn Station, and I am up and out of its hot tunnel, across the bright upper lobby, my dream faded in the crowd of derelicts and Easter returnees, then out onto breezy Seventh Avenue and the wide prospects of Gotham on a warm Easter night. It is now ten-fifteen. I have no idea what I'm supposed to do.

Though I am not sorry to be here. The usual demoralizing firestorm of speeding cabs, banging lights and owl-voiced urban-ness has yet to send me careening into the toe-squeezing funk of complication and obscurity, in which everything becomes too important and too dangerous to be tolerable. Here, out on Seventh and 34th, I feel an unaccustomed lankness, a post-coital midwestern caress to things—the always dusky air still high and hollowish, streets alive with the girdering wheels of hungry traffic that pours past me and quickly vanishes.

And I sense, standing in the exit crowds from a Shaggy Chrysanthemum show at the Garden, gazing across at the marquee and night lights of the old Statler Hotel, that a person could have a few laughs here, might even find the exhilaration of a woman tolerable excitement, given the right quarters and timing. A person might even have his actions speak (if briefly) for themselves—something that never seemed possible here before—and actually put up with the old ethicless illicit for a while before escape became essential. This must be how all suburbanites feel when the suburbs suddenly go queer and queasy on them; that things cannot continue to fall away forever, and it's high time for a new, quick age to dawn. It's embarrassing to be so unworldly and timid at my age.

But still. What am I to do in this fragile truce? If I'm not simply ready to sprint back downstairs, buy my return and sleep all the way home, what am I *supposed* to do?

My answer, even with the city tamed and seemingly willing to meet my needs halfway, just proves my lack of expertise with the complicated life of real city-dwellers. I jump in the first cruising cab and beat it uptown to 56th and Park, where I practice my sportswriter's trade. There's nothing I'd rather do than try out some fresh strategies on Herb and turn that emblem of desolation into something better, even if it means putting a wrench to a fact or two.

The twenty-second floor is abuzz with fluorescent light down the rows of cubicles. When I leave the elevator, I hear loud, contentious voices wrangling in the back offices. "Aw-right . . . Aw-*right!*" Then: "Naaa-na,na,na,na. He's glue. Pure donkey." Then: "*I don't* believe this. This guy'll be alive in your nightmares, believe me. Be-*leeve* me!" It's the Pigskin Preview. The NFL draft is in ten days, and they are in extraordinary session.

I head toward my own cubicle, but stop and stick my head in the crowded conference room. Inside, sits a long Formica table littered with yellow hamburger bags and ashtrays and paper coffee cups, thick green ring-bound notebooks, a green computer screen showing a list of names drawn up. A white grease-pencil board is leaned against the wall. The entire football staff with a few of the younger boys on the low end of the masthead are staring in eagle-eyed attention through a layer of smoke at a big video machine showing a football play on a wide imitation-grass field. This is the skull session where our experts decide the first forty college players to be picked by the pros and in what order. After the World Series Roundup it is the most important issue of the year. As a young staffer, I sat in on these very sessions, chewed a cold cigar, shouted my favorites the way these boys are going at it (there's one female at the back I'm vaguely familiar with) and it became a damned valuable experience. Younger writers, researchers and interns out of Yale and Bowdoin get to see how these old heads do their stuff, how things really go on. The older writers would normally just settle this kind of thing over drinks at a sushi place around the corner. But for the Preview—and to their credit—they bring all the machinery out in the open and run the show as though it were really democratic. Later they'll all wind up strolling into the early morning streets, feeling good about themselves and football and the world in general, laughing and swearing, and having a round or two at some spudbuster bar over on Third Avenue. Sometimes they'll all stay out till dawn, and by nine can be seen around the coffee machine, or floating back to their desks with bushed-but-satisfied looks, ready to put the whole business into print.

Plenty of times I've seen writers, famous novelists and essayists, even poets, with names you'd recognize and whose work I admire, drift through these offices on one high-priced assignment or other. I have seen the anxious, weaselly lonely looks in their eyes, seen them sit at the desk we give them in a far cubicle, put their feet up and start at once to talk in loud, jokey, bluff, inviting voices, trying like everything to feel like members of the staff, holding court, acting like good guys, ready to give advice or offer opinions on anything anybody wants to know. In other words, having the time of their lives.

And who could blame them? Writers—all writers—need to belong. Only for real writers, unfortunately, their club is a club with just one member.

The Pigskin Preview boys are at odds over the talents of a big Polack from Iowa State who has speed and heart, versus a venomous-looking black cornerback from a small Baptist college in Georgia, who's tiger quick and blessed with natural talent. Big cigars wag from clenched fingers. Piles of print-out rap sheets are scattered around. All eyes are on the screen as the black boy—referred to as Tyrone the Murderer—in a blue and orange #19 delivers a blow to a spindly white wide-out that would put most people right onto a respirator. Both players, however, bounce up like toys and Tyrone pats the white boy on the butt as they trot back to their huddles.

"Son of a bitch, The Murderer was on *that* play," a junior man from someplace like Williams shouts. "The bastard started late, missed his key, and still delivered like a fucking freight train." Eddie Frieder, the managing editor, teeth clenching a cigarette, and wearing a Red Sox cap, raises his brows and nods, then goes back to making computations. He's in charge here, but you'd never know. Agreement ripples among the other younger men, though it's clear there's still division. Two men express uneasiness with The Murderer's friendly pat on the backside. They suspect the pros might translate it into an impure competitive instinct, while others think it's a mark of good character on The Murderer's part. "This guy's no higher than eight in round two," they seem to agree.

"What do you think, Frank?" Eddie looks up at the door where I'm half-hidden, wanting not to be singled out.

All eyes see me—a smiling, slender, slightly flushed man in a madras shirt and chinos. A couple of young guys put down pencils and stare. I'm not a pigskin prognosticator; Eddie, in fact, knows I don't even like football, though I'll probably end up rewriting a lot of what gets done here and putting together a sidebar about The Murderer's life-long fear of inheriting his dad's fatal alcoholism (that can take a notch out of one's competitive instinct).

"I hear good things about this Hawaiian kid, from Arkansas A&M," I say. "He runs a four-five and likes contact."

"Gone already!" four people shout at once. Heads shake. Eyes blink. Everyone returns to his rap sheet. Someone rerolls The Murderer's murderous tackle, and people scribble, which reminds me again that I have found out nothing in Detroit for use here. "Denver's got him on a player-to-be-named with Miami. He can't miss," Eddie Frieder says officially, then looks at his notes.

"Here's our next millionaire, Mike," someone cracks.

"You're the experts," I say. "I just got in from Altoona." I wave to Eddie, then slip away down the row of cubicles to my own.

My desk. My typewriter. My video console. My rolodex. My extra shirt hung on the modular wall. My phone with three lines. My tight window-view into the city's darkness. My pictures: Paul and Clary under an umbrella and smiling during a Mets' rain delay. X and Clary wearing Six Flags T-shirts, taken on our front steps six months before our divorce (X looks happy, progressive in spirit). Ralph on a birthday pony in our backyard looking bored. A taped-up glossy of Herb Wallagher in his Detroit helmet, beside another of Herb in a suit of clothes, in his wheelchair on the lawn in Walled Lake. He is smiling in the second, glasses cleaned, hair combed—beatific. In the first he is simply an athlete.

My plan of attack is to write on a legal pad the very first things that come into my head—sentences, phrases, a concept, a balancing word or detail. When I was writing seriously I used to sit for hours over a sentence—usually one I hadn't written yet, and usually without the first idea of what I was trying to say. (That should've been a clue to me.) But the moment I started writing sports, I found out it really didn't matter that much what the sentence looked like, or even if it made sense, since somebody else—Rhonda Matuzak, for instance—was going to have it the way she liked it before it went into print. I got into the habit of putting down whatever occurred to me, and before long the truth of most things turned out to be waiting just over the edge of worried thought, and eventually I could write with practically no editing at all. If I ever write another short story I'm going to use the same technique; the way I would if I were writing about an American hockey player who becomes a skid-row drunk, rehabilitates himself at AA, scores forty goals and wins the Stanley Cup as the captain and conscience of the Quebec Nordiques.

In the case of Herb Wallagher I write: *Possibilities Limited.*

I think for a moment, then, about the first trip I ever made to New York. It was 1967. The fall. Mindy Levinson and I drove all night from Ann Arbor in one of my fraternity brother's cars so I could attend a law school interview at NYU. (There was a brief period when I got out of the Marines, when I wanted more than anything to be a lawyer and work for the FBI.) Mindy and I stayed— as man and wife—in the old Albert Pick on Lexington Avenue, rode the IRT to Greenwich Village, bought a brass wedding ring to make things look legal and spent the rest of our time in bed woogling around in each other's businesses and watching sports on TV. Early the very next morning I took a taxi to Washington Square and attended my interview. I sat and talked amiably with a studious-looking fellow I'm now sure was only a senior work-study student, but who impressed me as a young and eccentric Constitutional genius. I didn't know the answers to any of the questions he asked me, nor, in fact, had I ever even thought of anything like the questions he had in mind. Later that day Mindy and I checked out of the hotel, drove across the George Washington Bridge, down the Turnpike and back to Ann Arbor, with me feeling I'd done a better than fair job answering the questions that *should've* been important but weren't even asked, and that I would end up editing the law review.

Naturally I wasn't even admitted to NYU, nor to any other of the law schools I applied to. And today I can't walk through Washington Square without thinking of that time with minor regret and longing. What might've happened, is what I usually think. How would life be different? And my feeling is, given the swarming, unforeseeable nature of the world, things could've turned out exactly as they have, give or take a couple of small matters: Divorce. Children. Changes in careers. Life in a town like Haddam. In this there is something consoling, though I don't mind saying there is also something eerie.

I go back again to Herb and write: *Herb Wallagher doesn't play ball anymore.*

I think, then, of the people I might possibly call at this hour. 10:45 P.M. I could call Providence again. Possibly X, though activities at her house made me think she is already on her way to the Poconos or elsewhere. I could call Mindy Levinson in New Hampshire. I could call Vicki at her parents'. I could call my mother-in-law in Mission Viejo, where it's only a quarter till eight, with the sun barely behind Catalina on an Easter ocean. I could call Clarice Wallagher, since it's possible she's up late most nights, wondering what's happened to her life. All of these people would talk to me, I know for a fact. But I am almost certain none of them would particularly want to.

I return to Herb once more; *The way Herb Wallagher sees it, real life's staring at you everyday. It's not something you need to go looking for.*

"Hi," a voice with an almost nautical lilt to it says behind me.

I swivel around, and framed there in the aluminum rectangle is a face to save a drowning man. A big self-assured smile. A swag of honey hair with two plaited strips pulled back on each side in a complex private-school style. Skin the clarity of a tulip. Long fingers. Pale blond skim of hair on her arm, which at the moment she is rubbing lightly with her palm. Khaki culottes. A white cotton blouse concealing a pair of considerable grapefruits.

"Hi." I smile back.

She rests a hip against the door frame. Below the culottes' hems her legs are taut and shiny as a cavalry saddle. I don't exactly know where to look, though the big smile says: *Look square at what you like, Jack. That's what God made it for.* "You're Frank Bascombe, aren't you?" She's still smiling as if she knows something. A secret.

"Yes. I am." My face grows pleasantly warm.

Eyes twinkle and brows arch. A look of admiration with nothing shady necessarily implied—a punctilio taught in the best New England boarding schools and mastered in adulthood—the simple but provoking wish to make oneself completely understood. "I'm sorry to butt in. I've just wanted to meet you ever since I've been here."

"Do you work here," I ask disingenuously, since I know with absolute certainty that she works here. I saw her down a corridor a month ago—not to mention ten minutes ago at the Pigskin Preview—and have looked up her employment files to see if she had the right background for some research. She is an intern down from Dartmouth, a Melissa or a Kate. Though at the moment I can't remember, since her kind of beauty is usually zealously overseen by some thick-necked Dartmouth Dan, with whom she is sharing an efficiency on the Upper East Side, taking their "term off" together to decide if a marriage is the wise decision at this point in time. I remember, however, her family is from Milton, Mass., her father a small-scale politician with a name I vaguely recognize as lustrous in Harvard athletics (he is a chum of some higher-up at the magazine). I can even picture him—small, chunky, shoulder-swinging, a scrappy in-fighter who got in Harvard on grades then lettered in two sports though no one in his family had ever made it out of the potato patch. A fellow I would usually like. And here is his sunny-faced daughter down to season her résumé with interesting extras for med school, or for when she enters local politics in Vermont/New Hampshire midway through her divorce from Dartmouth Dan. None of it is a bad idea.

But the sight of her in my doorway, healthy as a kayaker, Boston brogue, "experienced" already in ways you can only dream about, is a sight for mean eyes. Maybe Dartmouth Dan is off crewing dad's 12-metre, or still up in Hanover cramming for the business boards. Maybe he doesn't even find this big suavely beautiful girl "interesting" anymore (a decision he'll regret), or finds her wrong for his career (which demands someone shorter or a little less bossy), or needing better family ties or French. These mistakes still happen. If they didn't, how could any of us face a new day?

"I was just sitting in on the football meeting," Melissa/Kate says. She leans back to glance down the corridor. Voices trail away toward elevators. Forecasting work is over. Her hair is cut bluntly toward her sweet little helical ears so she can flick it as she just did. "My name's Catherine Flaherty," she says. "I'm interning here this spring. From Dartmouth. I don't want to intrude. You're probably real busy." A shy, secretive smile and another hair flick.

"I wasn't having much luck staying busy, to tell you the truth." I push back in my swivel chair and lace my hands behind my skull. "I don't mind a little company."

Another smile, the slightest bit permissive. *There's something kinda neat about you*, it says, *but don't get me wrong.* I give her my own firm, promise-not-to grin.

"I really just wanted to tell you I've read your stories in the magazine and really admire them a lot."

"That's kind of you, thanks." I nod as harmless as old Uncle Gus. "I try to take the job here pretty seriously."

"I'm *not* being kind." Her eyes flash. She is a woman who can be both chatty and challenging. I'm sure she can turn on the irony, too, when the situation asks for it.

"No. I don't believe you'd be kind for a minute. It's just nice of you to say so, even if you're not being nice." I rest my jaw, right where Vicki has slugged it, in the soft palm of my hand.

"Fair 'nuff." Her smile says I'm a pretty good guy after all. All is computed in smiles.

"How's the old Pigskin going?" I say, with forced jauntiness.

"Well, it's pretty exciting, I guess," she says. "They finally just throw out their graphs and ratings and play their hunches. Then the yelling really starts. I liked it."

"Well, we do try to factor in all the intangibles," I say. "When I started here, I had a heck of a time figuring out why anybody was right, ever, or even how they knew anything." I nod, pleased at what is, of course, a major truth of a lived life, though there's no reason to think that this Catherine Flaherty hasn't known it longer than I have. She is all of twenty, but has the sharp-eyed look of knowing more than I do about the very things I care most about— which is the fruit of a privileged life. "You thinking of taking a crack at this when school's over?" I say, hoping to hear *Yep, you bet I am*. But she looks instantly pensive, as though she doesn't want to disappoint me.

"Well, I took the Med-Cats already, and I spent all this time applying. I oughta hear any day now. But I wanted to try this, too. I always thought it'd be neat." She starts another wide smile, but her eyes suddenly go serious as if I might take offense at the least glimmer of what's fun. What she really wants is a piece of good strong advice, a vote in one direction or the other. "My brother played hockey at Bowdoin," she says for no reason I can think of.

"Well," I say happily and without one grain of sincerity, "you can't go wrong with the medical profession." I swivel back in mock spiritedness and tap my fingertips on the armrest. "Medicine's a pretty damn good choice. You participate in people's lives in a pretty useful way, which is important to me. Though my belief is you can do that as a sportswriter—pretty well, in fact." My hurt knee gives off a bony throb, a throb almost surely engineered by my heart.

"What made you want to be a sportswriter?" Catherine Flaherty says. She's not a girl to fritter. Her father has taught her a thing or two.

"Well. Somebody asked me at a time when I really didn't have a single better idea, to tell you the truth. I'd just run out of goals. I was trying to write a novel at the time, and that wasn't going like I wanted it to. I was happy to drop that and come on board. And I haven't regretted it a minute."

"Did you ever finish your novel?"

"Nope. I guess I could if I wanted to. The trouble seemed to me that unless I was Cheever or O'Hara, nobody was going to read what I wrote, even if I finished it, which I couldn't guarantee. This way, though, I have a lot of readers and can still turn my attention to things that matter to me. This is, after I'd earned some respect."

"Well, everything you write seems to have a purpose to show something important. I'm not sure I could do that. I may be too cynical," Catherine says.

"If you're worried about it, you probably aren't. That's what I've found. I worry about it all the time myself. A lot of guys in this business never think about it. And some of those are the mathematical guys. But my thinking is, you can learn how not to be cynical—if you're interested enough. Somebody could teach you what the warning signs are. I could probably teach you myself in no time." Knee throbbing, heart a-pounding: Let me be your teacher.

"What's a typical warning sign?" She grins and flicks her honey hair in a this-oughta-be-good way.

"Well, *not* worrying about it is one. And you already do that. Another is catching yourself feeling sorry for somebody you're writing about, since the next person you're liable to feel sorry for is you, and then you're in real trouble. If I ever find myself feeling like somebody's life's a tragedy, I'm pretty sure I'm making a big mistake, and I start over right away. And I don't really think I've ever felt stumped or alienated doing things that way. Real writers feel alienated all the time. I've read where they've admitted it."

"Do you think doctors feel alienated?" Catherine looks worried (as well she might). I can't help thinking about Fincher and the dismal, jackass life he must lead. Though it could be worse.

"I don't see how they can avoid some of it, really" is my answer. "They see an awful lot of misery and meanness. You could give medical school an honest try, and then if that doesn't work out you can be pretty sure of a job writing sports. You could probably come right back here, in fact."

She gives me her best eye-twinkling smile, long Beantown teeth catching the light like opals. We're all alone here now. Empty cubicles stretch in empty rows all the way to the empty reception area and the empty elevator banks—a perfect place for love to blossom. We've got things in hand and plenty to share—her admiration for me, my advice about her future, my admiration for her, her respect for my opinion (which may rival even her old man). Forget that I'm twice her age, possibly older. Too much gets made of age in this country. Europeans smirk behind our backs, while looking forward to what good might be between now and death. Catherine Flaherty and I are just two people here, with plenty in common, plenty on our minds and a yen for a real give-and-take.

"You're really *great*," she volunteers. "You're just a real optimist. Like my father. All my worries just seem like little tiny things that'll work out." Her smile says she means every word of it, and I can't wait to start passing more wisdom her way.

"I like to think of myself as pretty much a literalist," I say. "Whatever happens to us is going to be literal when it happens. I just try to arrange things the best way I know how according to my abilities." I glance around behind at my desk as if I'd just remembered and wanted to refer to something important—a phantom copy of *Leaves of Grass* or a thumbed-up Ayn Rand hardback. But there's only my empty yellow legal pad with false starts jotted down like an old grocery list. "Unless you're a real Calvinist, of course, the possibilities really aren't limited one bit," I say, pursing my lips.

"My family's Presbyterian," Catherine Flaherty says, and perfectly mimics my own tight-lipped expression. (I'd have given racetrack odds she was on the Pope's team.)

"That's my bunch, too. But I've let my lines go a little slack. I think that's probably okay, though. My hands are pretty full these days."

"I've got a lot to learn, too. I guess."

And for a long moment sober silence reigns while the lights hum softly above us.

"What've they got you doing around here to soak up experience," I ask expansively. Whatever idea is dawning on me is still below the horizon, and I don't intend to seem calculating, which would send her out of here in a hurry. (I realize at this moment how much I would hate to meet her father, though I assume he's a great guy.)

"Well, I've just done some telephone interviewing, and that's sort of interesting. The retired crew coach at Princeton was a Russian defector in the fifties and smuggled out information about H-bombs during athletic meets. That was all hushed up, I guess, and the government had his job at Princeton all ready for him."

"Sounds good," I say. And it does. A low-grade intrigue, something to get your teeth in.

"But I have a hard time asking good questions." She wrinkles her brow to show genuine concern with her craft. "Mine are too complicated, and no one says much."

"That isn't surprising," I say. "You just have to keep questions simple and remember to ask the same ones over and over again, sometimes in different words. Most athletes are really dying to tell you the whole truth. You just need to get out of their way. That's exactly why a lot of sportswriters get cynical as hell. Their role's a lot smaller than they thought, and that turns them sour. All they've done, though, is learn how to be good at their business."

Catherine Flaherty leans against the aluminum door jamb, eyes gleaming, mouth uncertain, and says exactly nothing at this important moment, merely nods her pretty head. Yes. Yes.

It's all up to me.

The clear moon on this night has posted a smooth silver hump above my dark horizon, and I have only to stand up, put my hands firmly on my chest like St. Stephen and suggest we stroll out into the cool air of Park Avenue, maybe veer over to Second for a sandwich and a beer at someplace I will have to know about (but don't yet), then let the dreamy night take care of itself and us from there on. A couple. Regulation city-dwellers, arm-in-arm under that dog moon, familiars strolling the easy streets, old hands at the new business of romance.

I take a peek at the clock above Eddie Frieder's cubicle, see through his office window, in fact, and out through the bright night at the building across the street. The windows there are yellow with old-fashioned light. A heavy man in a vest stands looking down toward the avenue. Toward what? What is on his mind, I cannot help wondering. A set of alternatives that don't appeal to him? A dilemma that could consume his night in calculating? A future blacker than the night itself? Behind him, someone I cannot see speaks to him or calls his name, and he turns away, raises his hands in a gesture of acceptance and steps from view.

By Eddie Frieder's clock it is the eleventh hour exactly. Easter night. The office is silent and still, but for a far-away computer's hum and for the clock itself, which snakes to its next minute station. There is a sweet smell on the odorless air—the smell of Catherine Flaherty, a smell of full closets, of secret private-school shenanigans, of dark (but not too dark) rendezvous. And for a moment I am stopped from speech and motion, and imagine precisely how she will take on the duty of loving me. It is, of course, a way I know already, cannot help but know, all things considered (that's one subject that does not surprise you once you're an adult). It will be the most semi-serious of ways. Not the way she would love Dartmouth Dan, nor the way she will love the lucky man she is likely to marry—some wide-eyed Columbia grad with a family law practice all in place. But something in the middle of those, a way that means to say: This is pretty serious, though only for experience sake; I'd be the most surprised little girl in Boston if this turns out to be important at all; it'll be interesting, you bet, and I'll look back on it someday and feel sure I did the right thing and all, but not be sure exactly why I think so; full steam ahead.

And what's my attitude? At some point nothing else really matters *but* your attitude—your hopes, your risks, your sacrifices, your potential islands of regret and reward—as you enter what is no more than rote experience upon the earth.

Mine, I'm happy to say, is the best possible.

"Well, hey," I say in a stirring voice, hands upon my breast. "What say we get out of here and take a walk? I haven't eaten since lunch, and I could pretty much eat a lug wrench right now. I'll buy you a sandwich."

Catherine Flaherty bites a piece of her lip as she smiles a smile even bigger than mine and colors flower in her tulip cheeks. This is a pretty good idea, she means to say, full of sentiment. (Though she is already nodding a business woman's agreement before she speaks.) "Sounds really *great*." She flips her hair in a definitive way. "I guess I'm pretty hungry too. Just let me get my coat, and we'll go for it."

"It's a deal," I say.

I hear her feet slip-skip down the carpeted corridor, hear the door to the ladies' sigh open, sigh back, bump shut (always the practical girl). And there is no nicer time on earth than now—everything in the offing, nothing gone wrong, all potential—the very polar opposite of how I felt driving home the other night, when everything was on the skids and nothing within a thousand kilometers worth anticipating. This is really all life is worth, when you come down to it.

The light across the street is off now. Though as I stand watching (my bum knee good as new), waiting for this irresistible, sentimental girl's return, I can't be certain that the man I saw there—the heavy man in his vest and tie, surprised by the sudden sound of a voice and his own name, a sound he didn't expect—I can't be certain he's not there still, looking out over the night streets of a friendly town, alone. And I step closer to the glass and try to find him through the dark, stare hard, hoping for even an illusion of a face, of someone there watching me here. Far below I can sense the sound of cars and life in motion. Behind me I hear the door sigh closed again and footsteps coming. And I sense that it's not possible to see there anymore, though my guess is no one's watching me. No one's noticed me standing here at all.

THE END

Life will always be without a natural, convincing closure. Except one.

Walter was buried in Coshocton, Ohio, on the very day I sounded the horns of my thirty-ninth birthday. I didn't go to his funeral, though I almost did. (Carter Knott went.) In spite of everything, I could not feel that I had a place there. For a day or two he was kept over in Mangum & Gayden's on Winthrop Street, where Ralph was four years ago, and then was driven back to the midwest by long-haul truck. It turns out it wasn't his sister I saw on the train platform in Haddam that night, but some other woman. Walter's sister, Joyce Ellen, is a heavy-set, bespectacled, YWCA-type who has never married and wears mannish suits and ties, is as nice a person as you will ever meet, and has never read Teddy Roosevelt's *Life*. She and I had a long, friendly visit at a coffee shop in New York, where we talked about the letter Walter had left and about Walter in general. Joyce said he was a kind of enigma to her and her entire family, and that he hadn't been in close touch with them for some time. Only in the last week of his life, she said, Walter had called up several times to talk about hunting and the possibility of moving back there and setting up a business and even about me, whom he described as his best friend. Joyce said she thought there was something very strange about her brother, and she wasn't all that surprised when the call came in. "You can feel these things coming," she said (though I do not agree). She said she hoped Yolanda wouldn't come to the funeral, and I have a suspicion she got her wish.

Walter's death, I suppose you could say, has had the effect on me that death means to have; of reminding me of my responsibility to a somewhat larger world. Though it came at a time when I didn't much want to think about that, and I still don't find it easy to accommodate and am not completely sure what I can do differently.

Walter's story about a daughter born out of wedlock and grown up now in Florida was, it turns out, not true, but simply a gentle joke. He knew, I think, that I would never run the risk of letting him down, and he was right. I flew to Sarasota, did a good bit of sleuthing, including some calls about birth records in Coshocton. I called Joyce Ellen, even hired a detective who cost me a good bit of money but turned up nothing and no one. And I've decided that the whole goose chase was just his one last attempt at withholding full disclosure. A novelistic red herring. And I admire Walter for it, since for me such a gesture has the feel of secrecies, a quality Walter's own life lacked, though he tried for it. I think that Walter might've even figured out something important before he turned the television on for the last time, though I wouldn't want to try to speak for him. But you can easily believe that some private questions get answered—just in the nature of things—as you anticipate the hammer falling.

Coming to Florida has had a good effect on me, and I have stayed on these few months—it is now September—though I don't think I will stay forever. Coming to the bottom of the country provokes a nice sensation, a tropical certainty that something will happen to you here. The whole place seems alive with modest hopes. People in Florida, I've discovered, are here to get away from things, to seek no end of life, and there is a crispness and a rightness to most everyone I meet that I find likable. No one is trying to rook anybody else, as my mother used to say, and contrary to all reports. Many people are here from Michigan, the blue plates on their cars and pickups much in evidence. It is not like New Jersey, but it is not bad.

The time since last April has gone by fast, in an almost technicolor-telescopic way—much faster than I'm used to having it go—which may be Florida's great virtue, instead of the warm weather: time goes by fast in a perfectly timeless way. Not a bit like Gotham, where you seem to feel every second you are alive, but somehow miss everything else.

With my bank savings, I have leased a sporty, sea-green Datsun on a closed-end basis and left my car and my house in Bosobolo's care. This has allowed him—as he explained in a letter—to bring his wife over from Gabon and to live a real married life in America. I don't know the fate of the dumpy white girl. Possibly he has put her aside, though possibly not. And neither do I know what my neighbors think of this new arrangement—seeing Bosobolo out in the yard, surveying the spirea and the hemlocks, stretching his long arms and yawning like a lord.

I have a furnished adults-only condo out on a pleasant enough beachy place called Longboat Key, and have taken a leave of indefinite absence from the magazine. And for these few months I've lived a life of agreeable miscellany. At night someone will often put on some Big Band or reggae records, and men and women will gather around the pool and mix up some drinks and dance and chitter-chat. There are, naturally, plenty of girls in bathing suits and sundresses, and once in a while one of them consents to spend a night with me, then drifts away the next day back to whatever interested her before: a job, another man, travel. A few agreeable homosexuals live here, as well as an abundance of retired Navy men—midwestern guys in most cases, some of them my age—with a lot of time and energy on their hands and not enough to do. The Navy men have stories about Vietnam and Korea that all together would make a good book. And one or two have asked me about writing their life stories once they learned I write for a living. Though when all that begins to bore me, or when I don't feel up to it, I take a walk out to the water which is just beyond the retaining wall and hike a while in the late daylight, when the sky is truly high and white, and watch the horizon go dark toward Cuba, and the last tourist plane of the day angle up toward who knows where. I like the flat plexus of the Gulf, and the sensation that there is a vast, troubling landscape underwater all lost, with only the definite land remaining, a sad and flat and melancholy prairie that can be lonely but in an appealing way. I've even driven up to the Sunshine Skyway, where I have thought of Ida Simms, and of the night Walter and I talked about her and of how much she meant to him. I have wondered if she ever woke up there or in the Seychelles or some such place and went home to her family. Probably not.

I realize I have told all this because unbeknownst to me, on that Thursday those months ago, I awoke with a feeling, a stirring, that any number of things were going to change and be settled and come to an end soon, and I might have something to tell that would be important and even interesting. And now I am at the point of not knowing the outcome of things once again, a frame of mind that pleases me. I sense that I have faced up to a great empty moment in life but without suffering the usual terrible regret—which is, after all, the way I began to describe this.

Some days I drive over in my Datsun and roam around the Grapefruit League parks, where not a lot is going on now. The Tigers have clinched at least a magic number, and seem to me unstoppable. Around the player complex there is a strange, anxious merriment. A few prospects are beginning in the fall instructional leagues, Latin boys plus a few older players on their way down the ladder, some of whom I even know from years ago. Hanging around on their own, they're hoping to motivate some kid to hit or shake a bad attitude and to impress someone as being a good coach or a scout, maybe with a farm club out in Iowa, and in that way live a life of their choosing. It is a poignant life here, and play is haphazard at best, listless in its pleasures, and everyone waits for victory. A good human-interest article could be worked up from this small world. An old catcher actually came up to me and confessed he had diabetes and was going blind, and thought it might make a good story for younger readers. But I'll never write it, just as I never properly wrote about Herb Wallagher and had to accept defeat there. Some life is only life, and unconjugatable, just as to some questions there are no answers. Just nothing to say. I have passed the catcher's story and my thoughts on to Catherine Flaherty, in the event her current plans do not work out.

Things occur to me differently now, just as they might to a character at the end of a good short story. I have different words for what I see and anticipate, even different sorts of thoughts and reactions; more mature ones, ones that seem to really count. If I could write a short story, I would. But I don't believe I could, and do not plan to try, which doesn't worry me. It seems enough to go out to the park like a good Michigander, get the sun on my face while somewhere nearby I hear the hiss and pop of ball on glove leather. That may be a sportwriter's dreamlife. Sometimes I even feel like the man Wade told me about whose life disappeared in the landslide.

Though it's not true that my old life has been swept away entirely. Since coming here the surprise is that I have had the chance to touch base with honest-to-goodness relatives, some cousins of my father's who wrote me in Gotham through Irv Ornstein (my mother's stepson) to say that a Great-Uncle Eulice had died in California, and that they would like to see me if I was ever in Florida. Of course, I didn't know them and doubt I had ever heard their names. But I'm glad that I have now, as they are genuine salt of the earth, and I am better that they wrote, and that I have taken the time to get to know them.

Buster Bascombe is a retired railroad brakeman with a serious heart problem that could take him any hour of the day or night. And Empress, his wife, is a pixyish little right-winger who reads books like *Masters of Deceit* and believes we need to re-establish the gold standard, quit paying our taxes, abandon Yalta and the UN, and who smokes Camels a mile a minute and sells a little real estate on the side (though she is not as bad as those people often seem). Both of them are ex-alcoholics, and still manage to believe in most of the principles I do. Their house is a big yellow stucco bungalow outside Nokomis, on the Tamiami Trail, and I've driven down at least four times and had steak dinners with them and their grown children—Eddie, Claire Boothe, and (to my surprise) Ralph.

These Florida Bascombes are, to my mind, a grand family of a modern sort who trust that the world has some important things still in it, and who believe life has given them more than they ever expected or deserved of it, not excepting that young Eddie at the present time is out of work. I'm proud to be the novelty member of their family.

Buster is a big humid-eyed, pale-skinned jolly man who sees a palmist about his heart trouble and enjoys taking strangers like me into his confidence. "Your daddy was a clever man, now don't you think he wasn't," he has told me on his screened back porch after dinner, in the sweet aroma of grapefruit groves and azaleas. I hardly remember my father, and so it is all news to me, news even that *anyone* knew him. "He had a way of seeing the future like no one else," Buster says and grins. He'd never met my mother. And my admission that I hardly remember anyone from back then doesn't faze him. It is merely a regrettable mistake of fate he is willing to try to correct for me, even though I have no interesting confidences to return. And truthfully, when I drive back up Highway 24 just as the light is falling beyond my condo, behind its wide avenue of date palms and lampposts, I am usually (if only momentarily) glad to have a past, even an imputed and remote one. There is something to that. It is not a burden, though I've always thought of it as one. I cannot say that we all need a past in full literary fashion, or that one is much useful in the end. But a small one doesn't hurt, especially if you're already in a life of your own choosing. "You choose your friends," Empress said to me when I first arrived, "but where your family is concerned you don't choose."

*F*inally, what is left to say? It is not a very complicated business, I don't think.

My heart still beats, though not, in truth, exactly as it did before.

My voice is as strong and plausible as I can ever remember it, and has not gone soft on me since that Easter day in Barnegat Pines.

I have stayed in close touch with Catherine Flaherty, and after the two days we spent together in her untidy little flat on East 5th Street, we saw a good deal of one another until I picked up and came down here. She is a wonderful, curious-minded, tendentious girl, ironic in the precise ways I half-suspected, and serious things continue to be mentioned between us. She has started med school at Dartmouth, and plans to fly here for Thanksgiving if I'm still here, though there's no reason to think I will be. It turns out there is no Dartmouth Dan, which should be a lesson to all of us: the best girls oftentimes go unchosen, probably precisely because they are the best. It is enough for me to realize this, and for us to act like two college kids, talking on the phone until late at night, planning holiday visits, secretly hoping never to see each other again. I doubt ours is a true romance. I am too old for her; she is too smart for me. (I would never have the nerve to meet her father, whose name is "Punch" Flaherty, and who is planning a run for Congress.) Though as a postscript, I'll admit I have been wrong altogether about her attitudes toward love and lovemaking, and have also been pleased to find out she is a modern enough girl not to think that I can make things better for her one way or another, even though I wish I could.

From Vicki Arcenault I have not heard so much as a word, and I wouldn't be surprised to learn that she has moved to Alaska and reconciled with her first husband and new love, skin-head Everett, and that they have become New-Agers together, sitting in hot tubs discussing their goals and diets, taking on a cold world with *Consumer Reports*, assured of who they are and what they want. The world will be hers, not mine. I could've postponed her development, but only for a while, and we'd surely have ended in bitter divorce. My guess is, and it's not a happy one, that she will one day discover she doesn't like men and never did (just as she said), her father included, and will carry a banner in public with those very words written on it. That is the way with things: expectations reversed in matters of the heart; love, a victim of chance and fate; the thing we say we'll never do is the very thing, after all, we want to do most.

I believe now she told me a lie about Fincher Barksdale and my former wife, though it was finally not a hurtful lie. Maybe she's embarrassed about it all. But she had purposes of her own to serve, and if I was not going to confide in her (and I wasn't) there was no reason for her to confide in me. I wasn't harmed more than a sore jaw can harm you, and I hold no bad feelings. Sailor-Vee, as she herself often said.

I have finally resigned from the Divorced Men's Club. Though after Walter's death it really seemed to me there was not much enthusiasm left. It did not seem to serve its purpose very well, and the other men, I think, will eventually just go back to being friends in the old-fashioned ways.

Regarding my children, they are planning a visit, though they have planned to come all summer long, and it could be their mother suspects I'm leading an unsavory bachelor's life here and will not send them. Somehow something always seems to come up. They were disappointed not to take our trip around Lake Erie, but there will be other times while they are still young.

X's mother, Irma, has moved back to Michigan with Henry. Together again after twenty years. They are afraid, I'm sure, of dying alone. Unlike me, they can feel time flying. In her last letter Irma said, "I read in the *Free Press*, Franky, *many* prominent people—except for one woman broadcaster—read the sports sometime early each day. I think that's encouraging. Don't you?" (I do.) "I think you should pay closer attention."

Regarding X herself, I can only say, who knows? She does not think I'm a terrible man, which is more than most marriages have to go on into the future. She has lately begun competing on the mideast club pro tour, challenging other groups of women in Pennsylvania and Delaware. She told me on the phone that lately she's played the best golf of her life, putts with supreme confidence, and has a deft command over her long irons —skills she isn't even sure she would have if she'd played competitively all these years. She also said there are parts of her life she would take back, though she wasn't specific about which ones. I am afraid she has become more introspective now, which is not always a hopeful sign. She talked about moving, but did not say where. She said she would not get married. She said she might take flying lessons. Nothing would surprise me. Just before she hung up the last time she asked me why I hadn't consoled her on the night our house was broken into, those

years ago, and I told her that it all seemed at once so idiotic and yet
so inexplicable that I simply had not known what I could say, but
that I was sorry, and that it was a failure on my part. (I didn't have
a heart to say I'd spoken, but she hadn't heard me.)

As I've said, life has only one certain closure. It is possible to love
someone, and no one else, and still not live with that one person or
even see her. Anything or anyone who says different is a liar or a
sentimentalist or worse. It is possible to be married, to divorce, then
to come back together with a whole new set of understandings that
you'd never have liked or even understood before in your earlier life,
but that to your surprise now seems absolutely perfect. The only
truth that can never be a lie, let me tell you, is life itself—the thing
that happens.

Will I ever live in Haddam, New Jersey, again? I haven't the
slightest idea.

Will I be a sportswriter again and do those things I did and loved
doing when I did them? Ditto.

I read in the *St. Petersburg Times* a week ago that a boy had died
in De Tocqueville Academy, the son of a famous astronaut, which
is why it made the news, though he died quietly. Of course it made
me think of Ralph, my son, who did not die quietly at all, but
howling mad, with a voice all his own, full of crazy curses and
outrage and even jokes. And I realized that my own mourning for
him is finally over—even as the astronaut's is just beginning. Grief,
real grief, is relatively short, though mourning can be long.

I walked out of the condos onto the flat lithesome beach this
morning, and took a walk in my swimming trunks and no shirt on.
And I thought that one natural effect of life is to cover you in a thin
layer of . . . what? A film? A residue or skin of all the things you've
done and been and said and erred at? I'm not sure. But you *are*
under it, and for a long time, and only rarely do you know it, except
that for some unexpected reason or opportunity you come out—for
an hour or even for a moment—and you suddenly feel pretty good.
And in that magical instant you realize how long it's been since you
felt just that way. Have you been ill, you ask. Is life itself an illness

or a syndrome? Who knows? We've all felt that way, I'm confident, since there's no way that I could feel what hundreds of millions of other citizens haven't.

Only suddenly, then, you are out of it—that film, that skin of life—as when you were a kid. And you think: this must've been the way it was *once in my life*, though you didn't know it then, and don't really even remember it—a feeling of wind on your cheeks and your arms, of being released, let loose, of being the light-floater. And since that is not how it has been for a long time, you want, this time, to make it last, this glistening one moment, this cool air, this new living, so that you can preserve a feeling of it, inasmuch as when it comes again it may just be too late. You may just be too old. And in truth, of course, this may be the last time that you will ever feel this way again.

BOOKS BY RICHARD FORD

"One of the most compelling and eloquent
storytellers of his generation."
—Michiko Kakutani,
The New York Times

INDEPENDENCE DAY

In this moving, peerlessly funny odyssey through America,
Ford follows Frank Bascombe, who in the aftermath of his
divorce and the ruin of his career, has entered an "Existence
Period," selling real estate in Haddam, New Jersey, and
mastering the high-wire act of normalcy. But over one
Fourth of July weekend, Frank is called into sudden, bewil-
dering engagement with life.

Winner of the PEN/Faulkner Award for Fiction
Winner of the Pulitzer Prize
Fiction/Literature/0-679-73518-6

A PIECE OF MY HEART

Richard Ford's mesmerizing first novel is the story of two
godless pilgrims. Robert Hewes has driven across the country in the service of a destructive passion. Sam Newel is
seeking the missing piece of himself. When these men con-
verge on an uncharted island in Mississippi, each discovers
the one thing he's looking for.

Fiction/Literature/0-394-72914-5

ROCK SPRINGS

In these ten exquisite stories, Richard Ford mines literary
gold from the wind-scrubbed landscape of the American
West—and from the guarded hopes and gnawing loneliness
of the people who live there. A refugee from justice driving
across Wyoming with his daughter, an unhappy girlfriend,
and a stolen car; a boy watching his family dissolve in a
night of tragicomic violence; two men and a woman swapping hard-luck stories. *Rock Springs* is a masterpiece of taut
narration and empathy so generous that it feels like a kind
of grace.

Fiction/Literature/0-394-75700-9

THE SPORTSWRITER

As a sportswriter, Frank Bascombe makes his living studying people—men, mostly—who live entirely within
themselves. This is a condition Frank himself aspires to. But
at thirty-eight, he suffers from incurable dreaminess, occasional pounding of the heart, and the not-too-distant losses
of a career, a son, and a marriage. And in the course of the
Easter week in which Richard Ford's wonderfully eloquent
novel transpires, Bascombe will end up losing the remnants
of his familiar life, though with spirits soaring.

Fiction/Literature/0-679-76210-8

THE ULTIMATE GOOD LUCK

In this masterful novel of menace and eroticism, psychological revelation and shimmering atmosphere, Ford updates
the tradition of Conrad for the age of cocaine smuggling.
The setting is Oaxaca, Mexico, where Henry Quinn has
come to free his girlfriend's brother, Sonny, from jail and,
ideally, to get him away from the suavely sadistic drug dealer who suspects Sonny of having cheated him.

Fiction/Literature/0-394-75089-6

WILDLIFE

The setting of this luminous novel is Great Falls, Montana,
where the Rockies end and where, in 1969, the promise of
good times seems as limitless as the sweep of prairies
beyond. Great Falls is where the Brinson family hopes to
find a better life. Instead, sixteen-year-old Joe Brinson
watches his parents discover the limits of their marriage
and, at the same time, unexpected depths of dignity and
courage remain even when love dies.

Fiction/Literature/0-679-73447-3
